Quickly, I scout the long promenade below. There are masses of humanity down there, and too many wear brown. Yet instantly I spot him, brown hair and blazer, pulling away from me. Perhaps it is the fact that he moves purposefully, while the others linger. My heart is squeezed by the idea that I will lose him. He is already near the exit, his steady stride stretching the distance between us like a rubber band about to snap. Damn his speed. Must he be that anxious to leave, knowing he's left me behind? My foolish expectations winter with the chill at his back, and I start to wilt. There, he's gone. My grip on the rail slackens, and I go limp.

"Promise me you will not jump."

The shock of him, standing at my elbow and wearing a crooked smile. I immediately start to hiccup.

"Your jacket"—*hic*—"is gray."

"Your eyes are blue."

The French, of course, are famous for their seductive powers. One should really keep her guard up around them. He didn't, after all, admit that my eyes are a pretty shade of blue, or some variation on the theme. It doesn't matter. He could have said my eyes were the color of dried cement, and the same giddy glee would have throbbed through my bones. It is the look, not so much the words. And that look is international.

"I am Mathieu," he says, extending his hand. He moves toward me but stops. I can tell he's not sure about the cheek kissing—that I, as an American, might think it too forward. This consideration touches me, even as I lament the absence of those lips upon my ready cheek.

"Daisy," I say, looking down.

I take his hand, waiting for a muffled guffaw, an ironical smile. But his hand is warm, and he presses mine lightly, letting it linger.

"Daisy, would you like to share a cup of coffee with me?"

Surprised, I look up. Our hands are still clasped, each reluctant to let go. He gestures toward the café behind us.

And that is when I start loving Paris.

Plum Blossoms in Paris

Sarah Hina

Plum Blossoms in Paris

Sarah Hina

MEDALLION
P R E S S

Medallion Press, Inc.
Printed in USA

Plum Blossoms in Paris

Sarah Hina

DEDICATION

For Paul

Published 2010 by Medallion Press, Inc.

The MEDALLION PRESS LOGO
is a registered trademark of Medallion Press, Inc.

Copyright © 2010 by Sarah Hina
Cover design by Arturo Delgado
Edited by Helen A Rosburg

Typeset in Adobe Garamond Pro
Printed in the United States of America

ISBN: 978-160542126-1

10 9 8 7 6 5 4 3 2 1
First Edition

ACKNOWLEDGMENTS

I am deeply indebted to my agent, Jeffery McGraw, of The August Agency, for his tenacity, his handholding, and his knowledge and passion for good and smart books. His colleague, Cricket Freeman, also provided excellent support and guidance. I am very grateful to the editorial team at Medallion Press, including Helen A Rosburg, Emily Steele, and Lorie Popp, as well as Ramona Tucker, for their friendly professionalism and tireless efforts to make the novel shine. I also want to thank Christy Phillippe, who acquired the book for Medallion, Arturo Delgado, for his lovely cover art, and James Tampa, Medallion's director of art and production.

My friendship with Jason and Aine Evans was invaluable during the rewriting process, and I will always be grateful for their help and enthusiasm. I'd also like to express my appreciation for Courtney and Tony Xenos, two friends who have shared in the joys of this journey and made my life fuller. All of my blogging buddies (you know who you are) deserve big hugs and smiley-faced emoticons.

I am happy to thank my mom, Judy Harmon, for giving me her unconditional love and support, and my dad, Bill, who provided me with an early love of literature and the discipline to follow through on my dreams. My siblings, Katherine and John, are equally important in my path, and I thank them for their great examples and cheerleading. My wonderful children, Caroline and Alex, have been very patient with Mom's computer addiction, and I love them for that, and much more.

Lastly, I would like to single out my husband, Paul, without whom this book would not have been written. You've given me Paris, and so much more. From my heart, I thank you.

Plum Blossoms in Paris

Sarah Hina

In Paris, everybody is an actor; nobody is content to be a spectator.
—Jean Cocteau

Nowhere is one more alone than in Paris . . . and yet surrounded by crowds. Nowhere is one more likely to incur greater ridicule. And no visit is more essential.
—Marguerite Duras

You know what they call a Quarter Pounder with cheese in Paris? They got the metric system. They wouldn't know what the fuck a Quarter Pounder is. They call it "royale with cheese."
—Jules to Vincent in *Pulp Fiction*

ChApter 1

When he told me he no longer loved me, I fell to my knees. I know. Even I was conscious of caving to melodrama as I collapsed toward the pea-puke, paisley carpet.

I offered my forehead like a fallen prayer to the floor, and when my new roommate, smiley Selena, came in, that's where she found me—nose to spit, prostrate with misery. She took the scene in, and since we never had much to say to one another (her bumper sticker cheeps, *Abstinence Rocks!*), she just as efficiently turned to leave. I never appreciated anyone's callousness so much in all my life.

Where was the mysterious lover, the dumper, in all of this? Five hundred miles away, numbing his nerves with alcohol—or so I want to believe. He could have been taking a nap, jacking off, or studying for a test. It was not within my power to know. I should have mentioned, from the start, that he was a slippery, sucker-punching coward. He broke up with me, in spite of a six-year relationship, by e-mail. A nice, clean channel of cyberspace, where messy conflict does not compute. He apologized for this, of course.

I know I should tell you this myself, but I'm afraid the sound of your voice might prevent me from speaking the absolute truth. I know you would only want me to be honest; I respect you too much for anything less.

I felt very respected by that chummy, conjugal semicolon. So *respected,* I nearly vomited on Selena's pile of *Cosmopolitans* stacked neatly against the couch.

After a moment, or a lifetime, I looked up. My laptop blinked sanguinely at me from the coffee table. The mouse was grimed up with powdered cheese from the chips I still tasted. There were other artifacts of a familiar life—my favorite coffee mug (*Naturally Selected to be* Awesome!), a worn *Neuroscience* textbook, a framed picture of Irene and me swooning for Bono, and the latest untouched offering from my father—W. Somerset Maugham's *A Razor's Edge*. But I mostly just saw Andy's words. In brutal black and white.

I felt assaulted. But, if I'm honest, also the faintest exultation. My body, unaccustomed to anything but the paperwork of living, flickered to life. My stomach bubbled. Senses sharpened. I was conscious of the smallness of my hands braced, like bird's feet, across the carpet, as my lungs tugged for more oxygen. The room's molecules swirled in a chaotic dance while the faint scent of chemicals floated off my lab jacket and scratched at my nose.

None of it could save me. Destruction can be the spark for a rebirth by fire, but I knew that all my body's heightened defenses couldn't keep me from just feeling burned. Not reborn.

Yet something *was* different. Andy didn't love me anymore.

He was my high school sweetheart, even if the preciousness of that term seemed all wrong for us. We were brainy, self-absorbed, and, okay, innocent of the world's demands when we started dating at sixteen. He read all of my haikus in *The Spartan Pen* and never quite laughed. I went to all of his basketball games and never quite slept. We were nearly as ambitious for our relationship as we were for THE FUTURE. We both enrolled at Ohio State because he couldn't afford Princeton, and we shook our heads over lesser high school couples who splintered within one year of college. After he was bounced into Harvard Medical School from the waiting list, I settled for Case Western Reserve University's Neuroscience Program and shot him off to Cambridge with a smile and all the goodwill I could afford. I swallowed my pride, though it choked a little. We suffered through one year apart, and though we were too busy to spend any substantial part of the summer together, I was confident we were happy and satisfied. I felt settled. Thoughts of a ring had drifted through my head lately—a sweet tonic to the institutional boredom of lab work. But I didn't allow myself to linger over those daydreams. I wasn't going to be a girl about it.

Okay, I lingered on it long enough to decide on a PhD at Harvard after a summer wedding and a honeymoon in Europe.

Just. That. Long.

We were a match, a team, a mission. Andy and Daisy. Daisyandandy.

I don't know how to be alone, I confided to the carpet, where I saw myself scattering into a thousand paisley pieces. Like a tree robbed of all its leaves, I was all nerves and no color.

Outside, the October air whispered, then shouted. I shivered. It was the season of my discontent.

Chapter 2

I'm not terribly comfortable on my knees.

And so I struggled to my feet, brushed myself off, and fled back to the lab. My second home. The microscopes and slides, my extended family.

By the time I got there, the building was abandoned. Even Dr. Choi—a man so enraptured with work that he has been known to whistle "The Surrey With the Fringe On Top" while euthanizing turtles—appeared to have retired to his wife and five kids. I sequestered myself in the small fluorescent microscopy room and trolled through images that have soothed me before. But this night was different. In lieu of a beautiful, mysterious order, total anarchy flapped through my brain. I couldn't decipher designs. I couldn't see the familiar patterns connecting the inner ear hair cells, those precise instruments of spatial orientation we research. My mind kicked with too much stimuli, and my eyes unfocused in surrender. Eventually, I shut down the computer, throwing the room into darkness, except for the red lights blinking on the microscope's instrument panel.

Which, because our minds claw meaning from sense, led me to sex.

Since Andy was my high school boyfriend, as well as my lone college and postgraduate lover, my sexual history is, well, limited. There's a benefit to monogamy, of course: even if you suck, your partner, equally clueless of anything outside your distorted fishbowl, isn't likely to complain. I've often thought it similar to my short stint as a pianist, where my indulgent mother smiled at every missed cue, all along believing me to be the next Art Tatum. Once I played at my school recital and suffered the tight smiles and forced applause, I realized how sweetly delusional she was. And I understood that experience was essential to discovering the truth. That's why I repeat experiments several times, always hoping to arrive at the same conclusion. Dr. Choi calls me The Machine. I try to take it as a compliment.

However, since Andy was even jealous of my perfectly healthy obsession with Daniel Day-Lewis (I begged Andy for months to don the *Last of the Mohicans* loincloth—big mistake to sacrifice one's fantasy for parody), wider sexual experience was not an option. And that was all right with me. Andy was a considerate, if inarticulate, lover, and the two of us had come a long way from the first furious rubbings in the backseat of his Toyota Corolla.

Sitting in the blackness at the lab, pierced only by the red alarm of those buttons, I once again ached for those inexperienced hands on my body. His naiveté made me feel like a goddess, and as a seventeen-year-old male, he was obliged to worship at my altar.

"What *is* that crease right there?" he asked once, his adoring eyes fixed somewhere below my Wonderbra.

I peered down doubtfully. "What?"

"That crease, between your belly button and hip." He ran his hand across the skin and marveled at the hollow.

It was rather remarkable. "You mean above the iliac crest?" I winced. Nothing dilutes the poetry of a thing more than naming it.

But Andy took no notice. He only had eyes for that moon-struck flesh. "Yeah. It's like the one spot in the world where I could lay all my dreams."

Okay, he didn't say that. Andy wasn't one for purple prose. But his eyes told me. I'd never felt lovelier in all my life, or more desired. We hadn't even had sex yet, but it didn't matter. He loved my body, and I loved him loving it.

Why did he stop? What led him astray?

I kneeled my head on the microscope panel and cried steel tears. Free-falling, I looked for answers in a lab that had always provided them. For the first time in a too lucky life, I came up with nothing but myself. The only thing I knew for certain was that I needed a soft place to land. A new place to look.

Down the long hall a door creaked open, then closed with a bang.

My neck lifted and tensed.

Footsteps followed. Then, whistling. George Gershwin, as interpreted by Dr. Choi. The notes soared and sank. Like a careless breeze.

"An American in Paris."

Almost unconsciously, I started humming along. And then stopped.

Paris . . .

Paris.

A word that could split the night. Even *this* night.

"Paris."

It felt good on my lips, too. In fact, they very nearly stretched into a smile.

I stood and started to pace my cage. My thoughts couldn't pull me hard enough now.

I would take my honeymoon. I would wrench myself from the soggy ashes of this despair. After all, what remained for me here?

I scanned the tight room, its silent weight of expectation anchoring a suddenly windy spirit. All this cold equipment was hatched from a desire to penetrate the truth—objective truths. Those tiny, impersonal mysteries supporting and binding us all. It's noble work, and I've been proud to be part of it. But am I to spend my entire life, lids pressed against the microscope, never turning those powerful lenses around on myself?

No.

I braced myself on the desk and sucked a deep breath. Pouring clean air into my lungs.

Andy was the catalyst. But I would be the experiment. And what better laboratory for a girl in darkness than the shimmering City of Light?

"Daisy? What are you doing here so late?"

Dr. Choi sounded eager, in spite of the hour. Clearly, I wasn't the only weirdo.

"Have you been examining those slides again?" he asked, unruffled by the fact that he was talking to my back.

I turned to face him, trying to offer a very human smile . . . of apology.

The slides would have to wait. This Machine had sprouted wings.

So, eighteen hours and one reprieve later, here I am. Sitting with my feet firmly planted on the floor of an Air France plane, nervously awaiting Toronto's signal for liftoff.

It must be Paris. Daisy Miller, my namesake, went to Rome, but that was her fatal mistake. Rome is dead. It's a city for archaeologists, for looking back. I'm looking forward. And though Paris, as Gertrude Stein eloquently put it, "was where the twentieth century was," I hope it will suffer this belated member of the Lost Generation. I already see myself sliding, like a seraph (for I am not quite real), into the Panthéon, bypassing the tombs of Hugo, Voltaire, and Rousseau, seeking the resting place of my own torchbearer: the indelible Marie Curie. I do not consider much beyond this, having only a rudimentary idea of the city cobbled from *The Hunchback of Notre Dame*, a Rick Steves travel show, and *Moulin Rouge*. I'm sure there's more, but if so, it must be buried under the sad refrain of an Edith Piaf *chanson*. All I know is that Rick Steves can run circles around a city in the time it takes my mother to torch her *crème brûlée*.

But don't we all know Paris? Skimming away the shell of that rich *brûlée*, hasn't something more substantial lodged itself within our imaginations, like the germ of an idea waiting to take root? I'd wager that if you were to ask two people—one from blue New York, another from red Arkansas—where they'd most like to arrive in Europe, the answer would be Paris. And they might not have the foggiest idea why; the word will stumble to their lips like a forgotten reflex, emboldening a dreamy smile and a nagging nostalgia. For older folks, the melancholia of Bogart's "We'll always have Paris" might be enough, while for kids my age, it's the iconic bohemian chase. The lament and the promise. Paris is the nutty center. Our journey. Picasso, who was not really Picasso until he arrived, may have been a Spaniard by birth, and Hemingway American, but they were Parisians by choice. Runaways welcomed.

Not that I'm comparing myself.

I have neither great art nor the scars from a war burdening me. I'm just trying to outrun a broken heart, which is nothing to sneeze at, for a broken heart breaks a person. Paris is my promise of rehabilitation. I vaguely hope, as the engines roar and I dig in my heels, that it will become my lament. There is an infinite number of paths, confluences of latitudes and longitudes, that might take me there. But this one is marked for me.

I place my palm on the cool Plexiglas of the window, leaving behind a sweaty imprint. I have passed the authority of my life into other hands. I hope these Icarus wings won't melt.

"Are you going to Paris, then?"

It's my jittery seatmate, who has been white-knuckling the armrests almost as tenaciously as I. He offers a guilty smile. He must be emerging from the fog of his own fear, ready to apologize for it by striking up a conversation that I know I will hate but can't seem to avoid.

Should I be rude? I could really use the rest.

"Yep."

Well, no use starting a trip feeling guilty.

He nods and snaps his gum, happy to have this in common with me, along with the other two hundred eighty people. "Me too, as well, I mean."

"Yes, well," I offer, pointedly looking down at Rick Steves' smiling face on the back cover of my book, bought at the airport. He beams, trusting me to conquer Paris's tourist attractions while ingratiating myself with the locals and ubiquitous "culture." I have my concerns.

"I'm Cliff, by the way." He sticks out his hand.

"Daisy," I say and try not to redden. You'd think twenty-three years of a name would get you used to it. But I'm not quite there.

"Daisy" was my dad's idea. He teaches American literature at a liberal arts college in Ohio and was emboldened enough by his love for Henry James to anoint me the spiritual descendant of this gauche, mindless flirt ridiculed by European society and, in her outcast status, stricken by "Roman fever"—malaria to us—dying without redemption at a tender and nubile age. My younger brother, lucky in his maleness, got by with "Henry," which, while old-fashioned, has an urbane charm. If only my dad had been more taken with Emily Dickinson, queer old bat that she was, I wouldn't detect that glint in a stranger's eye whenever I'm introduced, as he tries to reconcile my dark, humorless looks with a name that conjures artless grace and a sunny disposition. As a child, I nearly got away with it. Now it's a juicy offering for those who get off on irony. And don't ask why my mom didn't put up more of a fight. It's still a sore point.

To be fair, Cliff doesn't seem overly amused. In fact, I'm not sure he even heard what I said.

"I'm going to meet my girlfriend. She's studying abroad and has no idea I'm coming. It should be a big surprise," he continues, cheerfully ignoring my very faint interest. "I'm going to take her up the Eiffel Tower and ask her to marry me." Busting to tell someone, especially an admiring female, of this ingenuous plan, he now looks at me for approbation.

"How romantic!" I assent.

"I'm glad you think so. The idea came to me all at once, while I was watching *National Lampoon's European Vacation*. You know, when the Griswolds go to the Eiffel Tower?"

"Sure, sure."

Smile, Daisy. *Smile.*

"Well, that scene, and the one where they're sitting at their hotel and they see those newlyweds making out like, well, newlyweds, got me thinking. I kind of put the two together. After all, Paris *is* the city for romance, right?"

"Yes, that's what they say . . . and sing."

He looks at me sharply, and I show him my teeth. He nods, mollified.

"So where are you from?" he asks, after requesting a ginger ale from the flight attendant. I don't drink, but order a vodka tonic. Since this is Air France, no one asks for my ID. Even though I'm twenty-three, I feel like I've gotten away with something.

Sarah Hina

I take a sip, wincing a little. "Cleveland."

"Ah, American," he pronounces, somewhat cuttingly. My curiosity is piqued by this sudden boon of superiority from a man inspired toward romance on the confused logic torn from a *National Lampoon* movie (a profoundly American piece of cinematic magic, by the way). I'm grateful for a distraction, so I start to dig.

"You're not American?" I ask, smiling sweetly.

"No, no." He coughs, looking forward. "Canadian. I live twenty minutes outside Toronto." His goatee sticks out like an Egyptian pharaoh's as his posture improves.

I know a little something about Canadians. I went on a two-week Contiki trip through Italy and Greece three summers ago (I recall little about the Medicis and their passion for the arts, or whether the Parthenon's columns were Doric or Ionic, but that Aussies are the friendliest and most dedicated drinking mates on this planet is a comfortable stereotype I will take to the grave), and there was a tight clique of my northern neighbors on that trip. If they hadn't repeatedly emphasized they were not American, we would never have noticed . . . well, except for the iconic maple leaf adorning their backpacks, jackets, and probably their underwear, if anyone had cared to look. I've never seen a group of people so terrified of mistaken identity or so proud of their murky heritage. Nor had I ever been bullied to listen to the Barenaked Ladies so repeatedly.

I examine my drink, while the Canuck sips from his. The silence is oppressive. Somehow I want this inconsequential person, this peacock, to inquire about me, to find me worth the mild strain of his attention. When he won't, I force myself on him.

"I'm actually going to Paris to get over a broken heart," I say, reddening. It sounds like I'm bragging.

"Oh?"

"Yes, my boyfriend, my high school sweetheart too"—I take a sip of my drink—"dumped me yesterday, so I'm going to lose myself in Paris.

Or find myself. Whichever." I gulp some more liquid courage. "Quit grad school for the semester and everything. Totally freaking crazy, eh?"

Eh?!

"Could be."

I bob my head and grin like a salesman. He thinks Americans are impulsive, shoot-from-the-hip types. I'm doing him a great favor by satisfying his preconceptions.

Clearing his throat, he asks more graciously, "What are you studying?"

"Neuroscience." I start lecturing him on my ear cells, to illuminate my intelligence (not all Americans are ignorant, apathetic asses, though I cannot, for the life of me, remember the name of Canada's prime minister, or is it president?), but notice his attention wandering. "I know, it's not AIDS." I laugh.

His face hardens. Too bad for the string of cheese or nicotine gum suspended from the tip of his goatee because he'd like to wear contempt well. "That's not something to joke about."

Cliff has AIDS. Or his girlfriend does. Or someone close, like Uncle Mountie, or maybe a hockey buddy.

"I-I'm sorry."

He nods curtly and turns toward his book. My eyes flash to the cover: *The Da Vinci Code.* Of course. What else could it be, on the way to Paris? I see him darting through the Louvre, sniffing for Mary Magdalene's remains, ignoring the great art in favor of a good conspiracy. He wants to close the book on our conversation, but something's caught, like a hook in his lip. Finally, he turns and says, "I can't bear for an American to say anything about AIDS. Not with the way your government is forcing it upon the people of Africa and Southeast Asia."

This is surprising. "Do you mean how we haven't backed up our promise of more money?" I ask, perfectly willing to admit some stinginess.

"No, I mean how you're purposefully injecting people with the AIDS virus to kill off poor people."

Okay, so he's a nut, certifiable. I shouldn't take the bait. I really shouldn't.

"Are you implying that the United States government is bent on a plan of wiping out poverty, and our tiny commitment to international aid, by murdering millions of people around the globe?"

"No."

Relieved, I laugh.

"I'm not implying. It's a fact."

I cough out my drink, not sure whether to laugh, cry, or hastily change seats.

"It's not just about your aid obligations. It's all about the supposed War on Terror. Poverty breeds terrorism. So if you kill the poor people, you kill future terrorists." Nostrils flaring, he backs into his seat.

The lady across the aisle raises her head at the word *terrorists* and stares.

"And there are so many anti-American terrorists coming out of sub-Saharan Africa these days?" I snort.

Wait . . . are there? Before he can answer, I roll on, my voice climbing with our elevation. "And anyway, the terrorists on September 11 weren't poor for the most part. In fact, many were highly educated. So I don't think your plan, without entering into the nightmare logistics of it, would even work." I shake my head. "Not to mention the level of evil intent it would require."

He looks at me pityingly, like I'm some naïve stump. "And your government is so concerned about workable solutions to actual problems and doing good? Tell that to the children of Baghdad you've bombed in your search for weapons of mass destruction. The prisoners at Abu Ghraib tortured by your army."

Okay. I do not appreciate being lumped in with Lynndie

England or George Bush. It's funny how as soon as you're out of America, you become the Face of America. Especially in October of 2004, with the world snapping its jaws for a little American red meat. I am responsible for Everything . . . and Nothing. Whereas, in Cleveland, my complicity was dulled by the sincerity with which I shook my head over the stinking, faraway mess of it.

I can no longer abide Mr. You-Are-Your-Country's-Actions. I don't hold him accountable for . . . well, geez, anything Canada might do that could actually be bothersome to an American. Even if I thought their pair skaters were a little annoying last Olympics, I didn't object to their belated gold medal. I even sang the first bars of "O Canada" during the second ceremony and hummed the rest. It's a lovely little song.

I stand, sandwiched between two rows of seats and a low ceiling. "Excuse me."

He reels in his legs, and I find freedom in the aisle. There are no empty seats, but I will hide in the bathroom for a while.

"Hey!" he calls after me.

I flip my black ponytail over my shoulder and glance back, careful to maintain my scornful smile.

"Don't take it so personally," he says, shrugging. "My girl-friend is American, too."

I spin back around, advancing toward the front of the plane. As the turbulence jolts us and I pinball across strangers' knotty shoulders, purled together by destination, I hear him say, "I try not to hold it against her."

ChApter 3

Nothing makes you feel so completely American as faking French to that first native speaker. The way those round vowels flatten on my Ohio tongue shrivels me before this customs agent, who regards me with a mix of native hostility and bureaucratic boredom. I quickly abandon the hope of securing his, or anyone's, real respect in this country, whose mean, clenched *r*s serve as a verbal green card I have no hope of securing. The French language is like a headmistress at a Catholic boarding school for atheists: fearsome, controlling, a real bitch. She won't get you to accept that there is a God exactly, but she'll damn well make you believe in divine judgment.

Why, *por qué,* did I take Spanish in high school?

"Excusez-moi. Parlez-vous anglais?" I smile hopefully at the young guy whose badge reads, *Marcel Duchamp.* I blink. His photo smiles, but the real Marcel doesn't bother with trifles.

"Yes."

"Is there a problem?"

He ignores me.

Eventually, Marcel motions me to the side. My bag is to be searched. I endure the small humiliation of having a male handle my tampons, my ratty underwear, my A cup bras. People filing by glance at us, curious to witness someone's privacy pillaged. Marcel lingers over this stuff, like it's some kind of feminine contraband. I feel like an anthropological subject without the benefit of being dead.

Finally, Marcel pulls up sharply. His eyes target mine, and the satisfaction boned within recalls a dog worrying his chewy hide. There is something in his hand. For a minute, I panic. Did I smuggle some pot from Toronto? A handgun from Cleveland? I squint, prepared for tears, resigning myself to Javert in a French interrogation room, when I finally recognize what Marcel is examining with the vigilance of a bloodhound on the trail.

It's my box—ample enough, to be sure—of Celestial Seasonings' organic, chamomile tea.

Really, Daisy.

It turns out, Marcel humorlessly explains (after filling out the very necessary paperwork) that there is a weight limit on imported tea. Mine is ten grams over, and they can't have that. Tea has proven a potent brew of revolutionary fervor in my country, yet I find myself surrendering easily enough. I'm more concerned with being tagged an Ugly American than with justice right now. The older American couple next to me, however, valiantly waves the flag as they go down with the ship.

The man, jiggering with his hearing aid, asks, "What's that, now?" to Marcel's glowering coworker. I briefly wonder who the "good cop" is.

The man's wife, hair curled into a brass claw, shouts, "HE NEEDS TO SEE YOUR PILLS, BUZZ. THE PILLS!"

"On whose authority? We licked the Gestapo once, young man, and I'm not afraid to do it again."

His grip on the walker does much to sell his point.

Marcel's lips curl with derision, and he waves me away. Sadly, I am tarred through association. I sigh, wondering if anyone will drink the tea, or for how long it will sit on some dusty shelf, next to a bottle of Jack Daniel's and a withering begonia.

Suddenly, Paris seems like the least impulsive place in the world.

I collect my miserable suitcase with as much dignity as I can muster and follow the signs to the RER. It is a torturous path, and I get lost, twice. I don't mind so much, content to melt into the slush of bodies. I've always liked shuffling through airports. They're all the same, which is reassuring. I appreciate the bustling, frantic anonymity of travelers corralled into an artificial pen, until they disperse, like atoms of a liquid dissolving into air. I am going here; you are going there. We shall never meet again.

Jesus, a McDonald's.

There it is, sandwiched between a *parfumerie* and a luxury luggage store. I'm not sure whether it's my exhaustion, crippled emotions, or the lingering effects of being treated like a criminal, but I almost collapse with gratitude. Familiarity may breed contempt in saner surroundings, but here, in the great unknown, it feels good. Never mind that, in Cleveland, I begrudgingly ate McDonald's only at Irene's insistence. I enter the restaurant and demand an Egg McMuffin, feeling like I can speak English, or more precisely American, without a trace of self-consciousness under the yawning sanctuary of the golden arches. The meat muffin, complete with fatty white globules, is greasy, disgusting, and totally delicious.

And I'm lovin' it.

Irene, devotee of Quarter Pounders with cheese, connoisseur of an

American specialty described, in our house, as ketchupfied meat loaves, is my closest friend at work, where I'm an adult service aide to the developmentally disabled. Before anyone pats me on the back, let me acknowledge that it is more of a gesture than anything; grad school costs $13,000 a year, and I make $9.25 an hour, twelve hours a week. My parents foot some of my bills, and I have the requisite loans that will haunt me for twenty years. But I had to do something, and there was this ad over the summer that filled me with noble thoughts for about five minutes. Long enough to employ me at a home with my new clients, Bill, Irene, and Lucy—all of whom I had just left behind without a backward glance. My Canadian friend's arguments aside, *I* am actually the personification of America's international aid policy: a spew of lofty rhetoric with a predisposition to exaggerate its compassion and, when push comes to shove, to skip out on its responsibilities.

It should be hard to forget about my clients, especially Irene. Every Saturday and Sunday, she comes up to me, that wretched pair of grandma glasses perched on the end of her nose, before taking my hand and tentatively asking, "Friend, Daisy?" It is the only question anyone has ever asked that makes me feel both hopeful and lousy. There's too much naked vulnerability there; I don't know where to park it. Usually, I just say, "Yes, friend, Irene," and direct her toward her "memorabilia," which is what we call the box full of other people's, mostly kids', crap she has picked up on her walks. She can tell me what she ate for dinner on each day that she acquired a new "artifact."

A rainbow pencil, personalized "Brittany": ham salad sandwich, pickle and coleslaw on the side.

A jolly snowman mitten: pork chop, green beans, au gratin potatoes.

A cheap watch stopped at 2:23 ("Day or night, Daisy?" "I don't know, Irene."): meat loaf, baked potato, more green beans.

For my clients, time is measured by meals, or game shows.

I considered bringing Irene with me. Simply having the thought grew me another inch, as I breathed the full-bodied air of the selfless and inspired. Just imagine the good stuff she could pick up in Paris! And the meals she could eat! It would put ketchup-ified meat loaves and prissy pencils to shame. I encouraged the daydream, wrapping my generosity around myself until it hugged me tight. Too tight.

For as much as it pains me to think of a stranger taking Irene to McDonald's, I couldn't have her with me now. There's to be no context for old Daisy here. Besides, Irene loves meat loaves, particularly the ketchup on top.

And she always asks for a slice of Wonder Bread on the side.

Rejuvenated, and more generous toward a country that isn't too proud to own its nook of global commerce, I easily find the train. It's about a thirty-minute trip into the heart of Paris, so once I exchange money and board, I lean back into my nubby seat contentedly. Not wanting to look like a tourist with Rick on my lap, I pretend to read *The Razor's Edge* (the back says something about Paris and, curiously, India), which I tossed into my carry-on at the last moment. It's about eight in the morning, three in the a.m. Cleveland time. I slept precious little on the flight, wasn't even tired until touchdown. Restless to be removed from The Great Accuser, I squeezed closer to the window, wearily trying to follow *The Apartment*, which, surprisingly, was the second selection in the double feature. Damn if Shirley MacLaine didn't once look kind of cute.

My reflection in the train window informs me that I am not so fortunate. I suppose a physical description is owed, though I squirm at the task. The vanishing night—that evaporated time, now swirling above the dark Atlantic waters—has wounded my face. It appears sunken, a little shadowy, with the deeply set, unspectacular blue eyes retreating under an awning of bangs and unruly eyebrows. The vertical thrust of my nose—which my father terms *aquiline*, but about which I have my doubts—and chin, admittedly saucy, strikes a jagged line in a more emphatic version of myself. All the softness is stripped away. A long glob of black hair hangs limply from the hallmark scrunchy, though wisps break free to tickle my neck.

It's not a pretty picture. In fact, I've rarely been described as such. Striking, yes. Arresting—gee, thanks. Someone, a colleague of my father's, once called me *handsome*—the horror. As a child, they told me I had a face full of potential: all it needed was time to blossom. I fervently pinned my girlish hopes on those celebrity anecdotes about how gawky and hideous they were once upon a time . . . back in the day . . . *like, really!* . . . envisioning when I, too, could screech and cringe when my mom slyly dragged out old class photos for my friends to laugh at. I am still waiting.

My face chugged along in much the same manner: with an excess of creativity, and not enough discretion to know when to stop. It is better when I smile. My mouth is my best feature—generous, with a fuller upper lip that arcs downward at the corners. Hence I have a tendency to look sulky, even peevish. But when I smile, the corners bow, and my teeth burst forth with radiant, bleached brilliance, to startle the person across from me. Accustomed to my moroseness, he will often look uncertain, like he's coaxed a smile from a sphinx.

Sometimes I think my appearance, coupled with the incongruity of my name, has afflicted my personality more than anything else. It's as if Goldie Hawn was born looking like Susan Sontag. Whichever direction you choose to go in, sparkly or painfully serious, you end up feeling ridiculous. Never underestimate the power of a name or a mouth that genes conspired to turn the wrong way. As Daisy Lockhart, I could never be considered quite brilliant; as the owner of a face sculpted by an anonymous, cubist hand (think Picasso's Dora Maar), I will never be the belle of the ball, even if it's Case Western's Annual Biology Boogie.

The train lurches forward, and I kick my carry-on bag, which holds a hodgepodge of items in disarray. Slumping forward, I see something cylindrical and urgently green roll down the long aisle. I gasp and make a grab for it, but it's too late. The thing lazily ricochets across the rubbery aisle, alerting everyone of my presence. Every French eye, snatched from perusing *Le Monde* or *Le Figaro*, watches its progress, as it pitches this way and that, according to the undulations of the train car. It hits an older lady on the back of her chunky heel before banking across the aisle and coming to rest against a leather bag whose owner I cannot fathom.

It's the portable oxygen mask sealed in a canister—"The Life Force 3000"—I take on every airplane flight, in case of emergency. My father bought my first one twelve years ago, before our family flight to England, and I have purchased this one, the third, from a catalogue that sells such things as radiation suits and water filtration devices and, well, lifesaving oxygen. The third, because they expire. Oxygen doesn't last forever, apparently.

I bolt from my seat, mortified to be an instigator. Each placid eye finds new focus, zeroing in as I stumble forward, fixing me with such a look of scientific detachment that I feel like a lab rat put through a maze for their study. At least the rat has some cheese to focus on. I compensate for my gaffe by mumbling, "Sorry, sorry," not even capable of locating "*Perdón*" in my small French repertoire during the low tide of this second, petty humiliation of the day. I am cognizant of how overly abused the word *surreal* is in our language, but I don't know how else to describe chasing down my emergency oxygen mask in a train barreling toward Paris on a foggy morning, with the imperious eyes of France judging me. I almost expect that lady, the one three rows up, with the fussy white dog whose eyes bulge and whose tongue pinkly protrudes, to drink her coffee from a cup wrapped in fur. I have never seen a dog like that, much less on a public train. It's wearing a pompadour and roosts like a hen on its silk, saffron pillow.

"Sorry. Sorry," I repeat as I inch forward, smiling nervously, hopeful that, at the very least, they find me colorful. But nobody, not even the dog, cracks a smile. A ticket agent approaches, and I perform a soft-shoe number with him, during which he has the nerve to frown disapprovingly. *"Pardonnez-moi, Monsieur!"*

Finally, I'm in range of the ridiculous object, which shrieks, *For Emergency Use Only!* I bend down to retrieve it. My out-stretched fingers brush against the leather of a black satchel. The bag is soft yet firm, like the skin of a man's shoulder. I lock onto the canister, relieved to be done with this genuflection, and start to rise.

"You bring your oxygen with you at all times, then?" a voice asks.

Half crouching, I confront a pair of almond-colored eyes, inches away. Startled, I retreat to a fully upright position. The stranger, the owner of the interested eyes, offers an amused half smile and continues, "Or is it only in France?"

Flustered, I laugh a little. I scramble to think how he knows I'm not French. There are three languages of cautionary warnings on the canister. Why couldn't I be French?

"I could use some right now. I think I just sucked all the air out of the car."

His face is long and intelligent, and when he looks at me, I feel like I might finally forget my name. "Do not let them fool you. Parisians are like a—how do you say?—a cult. They enjoy making outsiders, particularly Americans, feel like outsiders." His accent is thick, but his words aren't clunky, delivered with a natural rhythm that makes me believe he has spent a lot of time abroad, in England or the U.S.

"How did they know I'm American?" I can't help but ask, forgetting my little performance of thirty seconds ago.

"Well, are you not?"

"Yes, but I don't understand." I frown. "Are we that hopelessly out of place?"

"I heard your accent; the others likely did too. And the apologizing?" He nods and offers a wry smile. "For all their occasional bluster, I find Americans to be the most insecure nation of people."

Stung, I retort, "And I am finding the French to be the most judgmental."

He laughs. "You are probably right about this." His eyes flick to his book, about the size of his hand. Small, intense font. He seems finished with me.

His ready detachment curls my toes into their Keds.

The ticket agent returns to find me still making his life miserable. Turning to leave, I realize I have a book in my left hand, a finger marking some phantom place on page who-gives-a-crap. Before I can take a step, the stranger's eyes, alerted to the book by the flapping of its pages—a soft, airy *phfft*—as I allow the leaves to run over my thumb in dissatisfaction, catch the title. I don't know if it's my imagination, but his face illuminates, like a child's when entrusted with a delicious secret, and he exhales from a pocket of ecstasy I cannot fathom. Looking up at me, eyes burning, he remarks, "I apologize. I see the whole of your situation now."

"And what is that?" I ask, baffled. I'm not used to people talking like this. You know, with sincerity.

His eyes are like my father's at his best: clear and brilliant, believing the best in me. "You are no tourist."

He turns back to his little book without another word. I am

transported, without legs, back to my seat. I do not think I breathe until the train pulls into a station, and the doors part with a soft *swoosh*. He rises to exit the train, never looking back.

I watch him go.

Chapter 4

The stranger on the train derails me, and I am aimless. My mind slips around a circle's smooth edges. Forgetting the view outside my window, my first encounter with Paris is a blur, sliding past me like a silent, scratchy movie. I finally remember myself at Luxembourg station, which is on the Left Bank, adjacent to the famous Luxembourg Gardens. Catching the metro to Saint-Michel, I double back a bit. Muscles stitching from exhaustion, I lug my bags up the stairs, squinting into a patch of frail light. My eyes are not fixed for day yet. When I clear the station, I slow to look around and catch my breath, blinking like a nocturnal rodent faced with noon sun.

So this is Paris.

Adjusting the strap of my carry-on, I perform a shaky pirouette. Immediately, I hear the ruckus of automobiles, whirring like giant insects down a street that hugs the Seine. The cars are small, nothing like America's road beasts, and mopeds whip across the lanes, squeezing past cars stalled by traffic. Across the street lies a busy sidewalk, where fathoms of people tread at this early hour. I am acutely aware, already, of the chasm in sensibility between the tourists and natives. It is not hard to pick up on. The female tourists wear tennis shoes and dawdle; the Parisians wear heels and glide.

There are bookstalls, shaded by a generous stretch of trees, lining the river embankment. They are green, metal contraptions, modest in size, and sell a hodgepodge of items, including art prints, books, some touristy stuff. It is nine o'clock, and the one to my left is just opening for business. The small, beefy man with the cigarette clenched between his lips is lifting the roof with a practiced jerk. He stares off to the right, at some shapely legs carving a path through the crowd.

My eyes follow her, and there it is: Notre Dame. I inhale sharply, the inscrutable scent of tangerine finding my nose. The hulking grace of the ancient cathedral, fastened to the Île de la Cité, is smoky around its borders, but fresh, that sharp spire, with its plaintive cross, whistling heavenward, toward leavened clouds. It's almost enough to make you believe in fairy tales. The vision of each architect and laborer (coerced or not) who once laid a hand upon the cathedral's façade, its survival throughout the turbulent history of the city, and the modern mythology that has sprouted through its buttresses and bell tower make Notre Dame less a house of prayer than a national shrine. Gazing at the massive, but musical, structure, one does not expect Quasimodo, back hunched, to materialize atop its buttresses. More like Victor Hugo, wearing a stern look, flouting an awesome beard, parting the clouds like God Himself, and carrying the soul of a nation in his quill.

Mumbling something, a pinch-nosed woman bumps into my shoulder, breaking the spell. I smell car fumes. I am in the way. People have somewhere to be. I think I believed that humanity would be more retiring in Paris (something about a thirty-five hour workweek), but work is work, across the planet. The same sour expressions tarring my walk to school every day, making me feel guilty I don't share their dread, are superimposed on the faces here, like the traveling clothes of paper dolls, defying me to give a damn about a centuries-old building inspired by a religious fervor few now have the time or inclination to serve. Yet still I stare. Only I move to a more discrete location, next to an accommodating tree. After all, I grew up in a town where the oldest home was built in the nineteenth century. It's got an historic plaque next to it and everything.

As I turn to grab the obligatory camera from my bag, a modest, green sign on the building beside me catches my eye: *Shakespeare & Co.*

The Little America of Parisian bookstores. Former home to Sylvia Beach and her den of expatriate writers and wannabes. I smile reflexively, already succumbing to the shop's timeless draw. It must be genetic. My parents felt it, too.

I slip the camera's strap around my neck, shifting back and forth between Notre Dame and Shakespeare's façade, skirted by bins of bargain books. Honoring the tug of duty, I settle on the bookstore, and prepare to snap the picture.

Just like my dad told me to.

I hadn't phoned my parents to let them know about Paris until I was already packed. It seemed more convenient that way.

"Dad?"

"Daisy!" he barked. "I've forgotten the sound of your voice. It's been weeks, you know, since you've deigned to call your mother and me." I could hear him taking a sip of something, probably coffee, with a teaspoon of honey. "So how are you enjoying the bitter North?"

My dad has a habit of talking like books. And yes, I will say it: like overly ripe, second-rate novels that haven't aged well. It's a bit jarring to people who have never met him, but they soon settle into the mild drama of it. I live two hours north of him, on a slow day. "Fine, Dad. How are you?"

"Struggling to put the finishing touches on my latest study: James' iconic New York."

"Ah." Christ. I'd caught him postcoitus, upon finishing a paper that three dozen people may read.

"Yes. It's fascinating how a city develops its own skin when drawn by such a writer. You can almost hear its pulse on the page, shadowing the other characters," my dad purred, his voice warm and expansive, preparing for full lecture catharsis. Normally, I'd have relented. But time was of the essence, and damn it if my father, and Henry James, aren't too wordy by half.

"Yeah, Dad, that's great and all. The thing is, I'm going to Paris."

Pause.

"Dad?"

"I don't understand."

I knew it wouldn't be easy. So I tried for vague. "I've had a, um, personal experience lately that has, uh, caused me to reflect, yanno." I swallowed, then rammed ahead. "And I really feel like the realm of possibilities might be opening for me in some other orbit which, until now, has not been available in this rather, well, limited scope of experience I've had . . . thus far. You see?"

Capisce?

My dad did not mince words. "Daisy, English please?"

I don't handle anger, or parental disapproval, all that well. Dispirited, I squeaked, "Andy dumped me, Dad. I want to go to Paris to lick my wounds."

He offered a noise somewhere between a rumble and sigh. "I'm sorry, honey. That is an unfortunate decision on his behalf."

I grunted my agreement. Sometimes I'd like a show of righteous indignation from my father, some reaction beyond the sobriety of well-measured words. Like challenging Andy to a duel. Or at least calling him a "dumb-ass." Something stupid—and macho.

"How would a trip to Paris, and the responsibilities you're neglecting, make Andy disappear? You can't outrun your problems, Daisy. They'll just be waiting for you when you come back."

All of this was very sensible, and I wavered, glancing at my navy suitcase. It looked like an expectant child to me, leaning on a crutch of heavy hope. "I know it doesn't make sense. I just want to, is all." I sniffed.

"And your studies? You're simply going to unburden yourself of them?"

"It's been taken care of, Dad. They'll let me back in next semester."

"Daisy, I'm not sure what you hope to accomplish." His voice keened higher. If I weren't so constricted in the chest, I might have smiled at the boyish plaintiveness. "Hold on a second."

I could hear him mutter, "I don't know, Patty. Talk some sense into her."

"Daisy?" my mom's voice, sunny and resilient, chirped in.

"Hi, Mom."

"Hi, dear. Long time no talk."

Still a little dig about not calling. "Yeah, sorry."

"So what's this I hear about Andy and Paris?"

"Andy broke up with me. I'm going to Paris."

"I see."

My mom is a dazzling woman. No one is untouched by her charms. My dad certainly wasn't when he met her twenty-five years ago: he a grad student in Oxford, Ohio; she a piano major four years younger. She had ambitions for a jazz band and was considering dropping out of school for New York or New Orleans—someplace where she needn't be bothered by Chopin, or any other dead, white genius who couldn't titillate the way Thelonious Monk or Bud Powell could. Then she met Stephen Lockhart, a bookish introvert who revered Bach nearly as much as his beloved James.

I often wonder what made her fall for him. It's not an obvious case of opposites attracting. They make a certain kind of sense, with their love of the arts, their easy acceptance of the good life, but it's an uneasy math. Culture will only get you so far in a relationship of years, where disposition survives conversation. She's outgoing, earthy, spontaneous. He is not. I've been pulled by the two extremes of their personalities, forcing myself to be an extrovert but resenting the hollowness of it. Over the years, I have felt their disappointment, one in the other, as they became stranded on opposite poles of a social divide, and understand that my brother and I are the pawns in their game of parental hegemony. I have complied by distancing myself from the board.

There is some guilt in being the catalyst for the mild suburban melancholy affecting them. After all, it was my cellular reality that settled the matter of their marriage, that unhappy accident replacing my mother's jazz ambitions with serial maternal monotony. I know it was an unsatisfying improvisation for Patricia Lyons to go from jazz pianist to sometime piano teacher/child entertainer. She can make balloon animals while playing "The Itsy Bitsy Spider." Kids love it. They ask for The Balloon Lady at all their parties. She handles it with aplomb. Yet there is something violent about the way she twists and grinds the latex to form cute little giraffes, elephants, whatnot.

I groaned, tired of my mother's delaying tactic. "Mom, just say it already."

"Go."

The word landed soft, like a benediction.

"What?" my father, undoubtedly pacing, and I both said.

"I think you should go."

I smiled, feeling the first hint of happiness since Andy's e-mail, because deciding on Paris hadn't made me any less miserable than anyone who goes to the doctor, set on medicine, therapy, something palliative. You're still sick, naked, and chafing under a piece of plastic. Only now there is a process in place for restoration. This surprise reaction from my mom, though, was different, like a tiny salve on the bigness of my hurt. I heard my dad bellow, "Are you out of your mind, Patty?" and smiled further. It was an extra gift to hear my father so confounded. He of the iron will, the steady disposition, the unbearable self-righteousness. I love him, but he's a bit of a prick.

Her voice scooped up momentum. "Go, Daisy. You've been too tightly wrapped all your life. Find some freedom in Paris."

I couldn't help rolling my eyes a little. "Okay, Mom. Thanks," I interjected, hoping to ward off a recitation of "I Know Why the Caged Bird Sings."

A second phone picked up. "Daisy, your father here."

"Oh, for Pete's sake, Stephen, let the girl be. She's twenty-three years old."

"Now, Patty, you've had your say. And I couldn't disagree more ardently, by the way—"

"Big surprise there," my mom squeezed in.

I sighed, deflating.

"Daisy, I would like to remind you that it is unwise to believe that one's environment can cure unhappiness. The distance between the physical and emotional states won't be bridged by a mere change of scenery." He floundered a bit, coughing, and fell back on, "The grass is no greener in Paris, my dear."

"No, Dad, it isn't," I said quietly, but with urgency. "But maybe it doesn't have to be. Maybe I just want to escape, and Paris sounds nice, like a destination I can believe in right now. Why does it have to be more complicated than that?"

He pulled out the last stop. "But *why* Paris? Why not someplace American at least, like, I don't know . . . Boston. You know, Daisy, James warned a century ago that Americans are too apt to think of Paris as the celestial city. It will only disappoint."

I was ready for this. I must always consider this dead man's likely opinion when debating my father about my twenty-first century life. He is like the evil stepparent who will never earn a place in my heart, but whose wisdom must be consulted, if only for show. "Dad, I'm surprised you'd say that. What about *The Ambassadors*?"

"W-well . . ." he sputtered.

Triumph. "I have it right in front of me."

Actually, I'd googled "Paris Henry James" earlier. I got, on the thirty-second hit, a Miss Barrace saying, in *The Ambassadors*, "We're all looking at each other—and in the light of Paris one sees what things resemble. That's what the light of Paris seems always to show. It's the fault of the light of Paris—dear old light!" Someone named little Bilham echoed, "Dear Old Paris!" I didn't know these people, but anyone with "little" or "tiny" in front of his name must have the author's true feelings at heart. My dad knows little Bilham well; *The Ambassadors* is his, and James', favorite novel.

My mom snorted while my dad grumbled, "You will not find the Paris from *The Ambassadors* in the Paris of today, I assure you. Instead, you'll find a segment of people so self-satisfied and insulated from the world around them that they'll scorn your existence and your country."

"Oh, honey, your dad's just mad at Jacques Chirac for trying to spoil George W's warmongering efforts. Pay no attention."

My parents are Democrats, by the way. I am too, though my voting record, like many of my generation, is spotty at best. Usually, my mom and dad agree on politics, the few times it jags through the surface of their self-absorption. But my dad has a militaristic streak in him that defies easy categorization. I think it has something to do with a nostalgia for grand, just causes, like World War II. He bought those Tom Brokaw books before I could cough, "sucker." Dad's blustery idealism is stranger still since he grew up in the age of Vietnam. Yet, whenever anyone brings up 9/11 his eyes grow watery, and he has to turn away, chin weakening. When he thought Dean would win the nomination, he became so incensed by the "snot-nosed, yuppie pacifist" that he threatened to vote for Bush after all, despite their divergence on 90 percent of the issues. Now that Kerry is the man, my dad seems nervous about the fellow, like he can't quite trust someone so like himself. Anyway, the war is still a source of tension for my parents. I try to remain informed, if detached.

"Dad, I promise not to cavort with Chirac or any elder Frenchman who wants to lecture me on American imperialism. Frankly, the subject isn't uppermost in my mind."

Eventually, my dad gave in. What else could he do? I suppose he could revoke his financial support and refuse to see me, but for all of my father's drama, he's not operatic.

This is all he could muster. "Daisy, do me a favor. Go to Shakespeare & Co. It's a bookstore near the Seine, on the Left Bank."

My mom inhaled deeply in consent. The waves over the telephone aligned and vibrated.

"Take your time. Look around, and buy some books by authors you've never heard of. Take a picture while you're at it, and show it to me when you get back, so I can imagine I was there," he added ruefully.

My eyes welled. My parents, on the whole, are lovable creatures. "Sure, Dad. No problem," I said.

He sighed one last time and hung up the phone, dewy in defeat.

I was about ready to hang up too, when I heard my mom venture, "Daisy?"

"Yeah?"

"Make sure you take some condoms. French men are not always so conscientious about these things."

"Mom!"

Really, parents are insufferable.

"And honey?"

"What?"

"Your father isn't always wrong."

Click.

There is a bleating of horns, and the moment discharges with the camera.

Shakespeare & Co. will have to wait. I require a hotel. Retrieving my map, I unfold the awkward sections, scanning its iconography until my arms ache. I am somewhere on the Left Bank. The city expands outward, its own universe, with me as an infant planet, choking on its stardust.

This camera suddenly feels like an albatross about the neck.

Rick likes the Latin Quarter. I like it because it's near. I start the journey.

The sky is clearing, and though chilly, Paris feels warmer than Cleveland. The sunlight, bounced from the husks of pearly buildings, has found the darker people, including me, bundled in a black cardigan. I shuttle into the heart of the Latin Quarter through a network of arteries that seem familiar, culled from snapshot memories of the handful of films I've seen shot in this famous *quartier*. Every corner comes with a café. Most customers huddle inside, but a few hardy souls stake out positions on the sidewalk, eyeing passersby while they raise *café au lait* to thinly pressed lips. Croissants sit at their elbows, half neglected. A few have dogs with them, but most are alone. Contrary to the solitary diners in America, they do not strike me as lonely.

There are also bookshops, scores of them, boutiques, and small markets hustled like afterthoughts in between, the latter advertising their bins of fruit as appealingly as Cezanne's still lives, luring me to stop and squeeze a few. Some of it I don't recognize, but all of it looks fresh and honest; there is none of that waxen appearance some produce has back home. Red, enticing strawberries bleached out on the inside, little teases. Apples that turn to mush in the mouth. I take a paper bag and fill it with small apples that have a red, angry skin. The shopkeeper, an older lady wearing a fringed shawl, smiles and nods as I bumble with the euros. I am so touched by the smile, by the fringe, that tears spring to my eyes. She clucks and calls me *chérie*. I could kiss her. I hum as I walk down the road, crossing the notorious Boulevard St. Germain refreshed and ready to embrace humanity. I bet these apples really crunch.

I turn left, down the wide, commercial Rue des Écoles, and start looking for a hotel in earnest. I want to feel settled in, take a nap. When I pass some potted evergreen plants, I pause and peer in the large glass window, where bland, unlived-in lobby furniture awaits. I step back to catch sight of what's written on the red awning. When I spy the elegant, unlikely name in gold cursive, my jaw slackens.

Hotel California.

I laugh, feeling like Holly Golightly, and bounce slightly on my heels. Closing my eyes, I hope for a sign. None comes. Yanking the double doors open, I push my way through. We'll see. It could be heaven or it could be hell.

"May I help you, *mademoiselle*?" the concierge inquires from behind the C-shaped desk. He has obviously been waiting all morning for me to enter his life.

I smile brilliantly at him. "I hope so. A room for one, please."

"*Oui, mademoiselle.*" He starts punching keys on the computer. "How many nights will you be staying?"

Until I run dry. Patting the four thousand dollars' worth of traveler's checks in my bag, I sigh. Thank you, dear, dead Grandmother Lyons.

"Indefinitely."

ChApter 5

I "did" the Eiffel Tower and the Louvre in the following days. And arrived at the bleak realization that I would trade both of Venus de Milo's missing arms for a single squeeze of my hand in smog-choked Cleveland.

But it is not my intention to push postcards.

So, lifting a lens from *cinéma vérité*: imagine a movie montage, running over the accordion's wistful vibrato, tracking our heroine while she takes in the sights (do not fail to notice how achingly lonely, when lingering on charming bridges, one looks in Paris, all alone), and then imagine a slow fade to a more weary figure—let's call her "Seasoned Daisy," looking more languid than that fresh girl who gawked at Notre Dame, if also disappointed. For what is Paris but old, grave buildings, heavy with a history she cannot own, peopled by strangers she cannot talk sensibly with, and bittersweet with apples no more succulent than the fruit back home. And notice that this Daisy has bowing pouches under her eyes from crying herself to sleep, missing her boyfriend more than she might have in America because when you are in a new place, you want old, dear people to make it feel like home, especially in new places where romance is like a disease you cannot catch. And finally, envision the caption under this more melancholy manifestation hailing *Four days later* in rain-streaked letters. Good enough.

Besides, there is the stranger on the train. And I'm not a tease. Wednesday then. The thirteenth of October. Lucky thirteen.

I linger over my croissant and *café au lait* in the hotel restaurant. There are other travelers there, married couples efficiently downing the typical French breakfast, bread and coffee, the warm-up (*un petit déjeuner*) for the serious business of lunch, ginning up their enthusiasm so they can attack their itineraries with gusto. One fellow, an American (I just know), has it spelled out for him on his Palm Pilot. His wife, a wan forty-something with pink lipstick slashed across her lips, flakes the crust off her croissant with a fingernail and looks coolly into her steaming coffee rather than at her husband, who is likely determined to get his money's worth for this second honeymoon that has cleaved him from his TiVo and favored Adirondack chair.

It looks like I'm not the only one struggling to match the ideal of Paris with the reality. If I had to guess (and I will), they're both thinking that it was easier to ignore one another in a 3,000-square-foot house than locked side by side on their way to the Pompidou Centre. But the BlackBerry won't be denied. And so they march on.

While the wife buries her nose in a copy of *Elle*, I rise to leave. The husband looks at my ass and wipes his mouth with the back of his hand.

My outlook is on the grimmer side of gray today. Maybe I just sat in something gross.

I take the metro to the Musée d'Orsay. I visited last Saturday and fell in love with the third floor of the museum, which was transformed from an abandoned railroad station in the late seventies. Most of the pieces on the first floor pay homage to the academic painters, and while I dutifully scoot through the rooms, thick with Ingres and Delacroix, the idealized paintings and sculptures leave me a little flat, like a string of catwalk models too perfect to invest yourself in. Take *The Birth of Venus*, by Cabanel. What you have here is the soft-core porn of the age, made palatable for the masses by tapping a mythological figure, instead of a modern, breathing woman whose skin failed to achieve the same creamy luster, but in whose blemishes we might recognize ourselves.

Venus, exposed, is sprawled on the waves, affixed there by some force that has also rendered her unconscious, but oh-so fetchingly, that sinewy form and cascade of hair showing off every advantage of the female form. Lovely. I can appreciate the passive beauty there, but the appeal is corrupted by the most overused, nauseating figures in the history of painting: cherubs. A sexy woman is lying there, and it's disturbing to see little babies with wings flying rapaciously over her, like they're either going to pee on her or suckle her to death. It's cowardice to paint sex like that, and then couch it in cutesy, Rococo crap. This is a painting destined for wall calendars. Put it somewhere between Anne Geddes and *Maxim*. And yet this was *the* painting in the 1863 Salon. It's obvious men were the judges. Sexually repressed men, boasting boners beneath their breeches.

I advance further, past the academics and realists. Here's a real painting: *Olympia*, by the revolutionary artist Édouard Manet. She is also unclothed. But this woman is a prostitute. Her tight, compact form, propped up on pillows, is angular where Venus is curved, and she looks out evenly, not a little bored, scorning us a trifle for our churlish voyeurism. The brushwork, anticipating impressionism, is crude in places, but expertly employed to secure a sense of immediacy *and* permanence, like an entire lifetime can be held within a moment. The easy sentimentality of Cabanel, and of many of the Romantics, has been sloughed off, as Manet stakes his claim—on the tip of Olympia's kittenish heel—as the father of modern art. Olympia finishes this floor off (she has no use for its fawning slightness), for it is she, more than any goddess or virgin, who is ascending toward impressionism, and the future we still seek.

Dodging students on a school field trip, I ride on the escalator to the third floor, where Manet's second masterpiece, *Le Déjeuner sur L'Herbe* (*Lunch on the Grass*) takes center stage. Another naked woman (not a nude, which is classical) confronts us, sitting next to two clothed beatniks, deep in discussion. If Olympia's nakedness shocked, this woman, inserted without context next to disinterested men, scandalized.

A voice crawls over my shoulder, and I prickle with some misplaced sense of intrusion at my private devotion. The voice explains that the painting required two armed guards due to the outraged reception it received at The Salon. The idea of someone attacking the priceless piece of art rouses my interest, and I turn.

There is a middle-aged couple, complete with leather fanny packs, facing me. The man has a comb-over and looks as bored as some of the schoolchildren. His eyes rove like a blind man's, sweeping for a landing strip that doesn't require too much from him. He settles on a pretty blonde looking at a Pissarro. The wife fans herself with the museum pamphlet, while staring at the tour guide, who has his back to me. She asks him an insensible question about water lilies, and the tour guide explains that Éduoard *Manet* is not the same person as Claude *Monet*. "Common misconception, *madame*, for people unacquainted with the French language." His tone is cordial, if pointed.

I hide a smile.

The woman looks disappointed. "Because I've always loved them so. My daughter, Penelope, got me an umbrella with those lilies on them. She picked it up somewhere in Chicago, I think, on a business trip. She works for Ernst & Young, you know." Flip to the hair. "Anyway, it was darling. Phil had one of his lapses and forgot it in our rental car once, on a trip to Ocracoke, and *poof*—" here she unleashes a hand gesture meant to express contempt and remorse—"it was gone. Such a shame. I loved that little umbrella. *Adored* it."

Phil is nonplussed. The blonde has a friend.

"Anyway, do you think they might sell it in the gift store here?" she asks the guide, putting a hand on her fanny pack and stroking the money inside. *All in good time, my pretties . . . .*

"I'm sorry, *madame*," the guide replies. "One what?"

Something about that voice . . . low and clear, like a cello shadowing Bach.

The woman starts her obsessive fanning again, in spite of the cool temperature. "Why, the umbrella of course. With the lilies. Or maybe those sunflowers of Van Gogh's. You know"—she looks at him expectantly—"something pretty."

At this, the tour guide, just a man with brown hair and a smooth voice until now, turns toward me, mumbling, "I can inquire for you, *madame*. I am sure they have all sorts of pretty trivial things for you to choose from."

It should come as no surprise that it is my stranger from the train.

I draw back while he takes me in, almost knocking into the priceless treasure on the wall and inflicting more injury on it than my fellow Americans' indifference toward anything not made famous by its perversion. He smiles uncertainly, probably trying to place me, while I study him. He is older than I, likely dreaming of nailing Charlotte, or some French equivalent of the hot cheerleader, when I was still worried about losing my retainer on field trips. He is tallish, but not overbearing, and thinner than good health allows for, the hollow pockets under the high cheekbones designating him as the distractible type who neglects to eat because there are other, less ridiculous, matters at hand. I imagine him with coffee for breakfast, wine for dinner. With more potent hungers in between.

A pre-Raphaelite nose dominates his slim, oval face, but the effect is softened by wide, deeply held eyes whose outer corners drag slightly, their accompanying air of concern reinforced by that furrow between the brows. He has the most beautiful lips I have seen on a man, and it is impossible to look and not desire them to brush my more meager canvas. Not gratuitous, but still sensual, they hold soft indentations where the lips meet to suggest a phantom kiss. Never mind the rather crooked teeth they conceal. He is not ashamed of them, and smiles at will. He has a high, erudite brow and cropped brown hair. A layer of beard fuzz marks him as a casual shaver. His eyes, again? Like amber. And like any foolish creature silly enough to venture closer, I am caught.

Senses in overload, I scramble for sensibility. "Hey."

Hey? My right knee quivers, seemingly with laughter, or sobs.

"Hello again," he replies, and with a slight bow (yeah, that's right, a bow), escorts the two troglodytes away, toward the pretty, safe rooms of Renoir and Monet.

Again! I am reeling.

Love at first sight is pure foolishness, of course. It's probably the art. My loneliness. Paris.

If someone would only inform my knee. It continues to shiver from some internal hysteria I am at a loss to control. Like suffering the giggles in someplace sacred. Like an earthquake has just shuddered through my fault-ridden body, eviscerating everything. Like my nerves are pure, radiant electricity, feeling for a place to ground. It's not love, I tell myself. Just neurological mutiny.

Of course, it's not love at first sight at all. This man, and those eyes, have been with me all week. If I have been mourning my past with Andy, it was to prepare myself for this future. Rarely have

I been so conscious of the power of the present. I am here, now, perched on the pivot of time, leg shakily extended.

There is a choice to be made. Things don't just happen. Either I follow him, or I don't. There is risk, of course. My mind leapfrogs like a choose-your-own-adventure, foreseeing every denouement before we have a story. Being rebuffed seems the mildest possibility, and one I can handle. There is a permissive element to being in a foreign land, with only the judgment of strangers to reckon with, and I can bear, after pocketing a handful of disgraces in the past week, the humiliation of his laughing in my face. Swinging to the other, more dizzying side of the spectrum, there is the sad inevitability of our parting, perhaps a month away, after my money has run out, each of us unwilling to abandon our country of origin. I could never be French. I haven't the stomach for it. And I already see that he has a healthy disdain for Americans. Our affair will end, not like some inscrutable French film, but with a purer, American sense of tragedy. Like *Casablanca*, without the noble sacrifice. I'm already starting to miss him—us—and I don't even know his name.

Ridiculous to presume this on the piffling authority of a few careless looks and words? Perhaps. But entirely human.

So then, the question is one of longevity. What is a month worth? To entertain the old cliché about it being better to have loved and lost than never loved at all? I'm not sure. My tolerance for pain has been squeezed, my ego pinned by Andy's slippery half nelson. Uncertain, I look up at the naked woman in Manet's masterpiece, for I am still rooted, dumb, to this spot while a stream of tourists files past. Her gaze strikes me anew, in that sandpapery white noise. Now her stare is faintly conspiratorial, daring me. With a shudder, I remember that the woman is dead, that this museum is a morgue of sorts, and that the artists and their muses bewitch us into believing that they are immortal. That painful, naked flesh is no more except for this strange, beautiful painting and its bastard offspring, cloned onto coffee cups, tote bags, and umbrellas.

Her face is my springboard. I will throw myself at mortality, and take a leap of faith.

Primed, I dash into the adjacent gallery, stuffed with Monet's paintings of the Rouen cathedral. I look for my stranger's brown blazer among the shock of color, but this isn't his room. I cross into the next theater, where the swirling genius of Van Gogh rocks me violently. I am reminded of my hair cells back in Choi's lab, the way they startle upon stimulation. This is how I feel. Distorted. Dizzy. Charged with potential. Van Gogh's self-portrait pulses with a radiant turmoil. He was descending into insanity at the time. I am ascending into euphoric madness. Different thing, altogether. Him, estranged from his world; me, running to engage it. But the intensity of feeling is something we share. Falling and Rising. Passions of movement.

There they are—the American couple, the Fannies. They have seized one of the benches for their cage match, the woman gesticulating wildly. I look frantically for my brown blazer, but his is not among the palette of colors. Bullying my way through the crowd, I arrive at the couple's side, desperate enough to interrupt the woman's tirade. Their pettiness almost destroys my momentum. Almost. She looks at me crossly, and a bubble of my laughter escapes into the air.

"I'm sorry, but where is the tour guide who was with you just now?"

"Excuse me?" she asks, so archly I'm surprised her eyebrows don't leap off her face. She means to make this difficult.

I take a deep breath. "I'm sorry to be a nuisance. But I need to talk to him about something."

Her husband pipes up. "Lilla dismissed the poor fellow. Wasn't as impressed with her insights as she needed him to be."

He ignores Lilla's glare. "He headed that-a-way," the man says, pointing toward an exit.

"Thanks," I shout back, forgetting them and their old, tired ways. I am so young. My youth pounds like horses' hooves in my ears, urging me on. A frowning guard shushes me, but I turn and smile at him, jerking my shoulders up in that goofy confessional way people inflict on others when they don't feel responsible for their actions. Poor fellow thinks I'm taunting him. He's got lovely English ears that will turn red in a few seconds.

The exit dumps me into a no-man's-land, a cross section of confusion, and I hesitate. Stymied, the horses halt. There is a spacious café to be considered on my left, more rooms across the way for the post-impressionists to display their increasingly abstract works, and an escalator rolling to my right. I'm not sure. With sweaty palms, I grip the railing of a landing that grants a sweeping view of the museum's lower floor. It is a grand space, washed by light. Reminiscent of a Roman cathedral, the soaring, coffered ribs of the old train station alternate with arches of tinted glass, slants of sunlight spilling across a share of the marble sculptures below, which burst into reverent detail. This one humbles herself before God, while that one stretches toward ecstasy, the distance between them heightening the drama of their appeals, and inventing new relationships. The clean, art-deco lines, and terraced space, recall a gutted archaeological dig, where priceless treasures have been unearthed by raw, determined hands. But it is still dead air they breathe. My breaths are shallow but warm.

Quickly, I scout the long promenade below. There are masses of humanity down there, and too many wear brown. Yet instantly I spot him, brown hair and blazer, pulling away from me. Perhaps it is the fact that he moves purposefully, while the others linger. My heart is squeezed by the idea that I will lose him. He is already near the exit, his steady stride stretching the distance between us like a rubber band about to snap. Damn his speed. Must he be that anxious to leave, knowing he's left me behind? My foolish expectations winter with the chill at his back, and I start to wilt. There, he's gone. My grip on the rail slackens, and I go limp.

"Promise me you will not jump."

The shock of him, standing at my elbow and wearing a crooked smile. I immediately start to hiccup.

"Your jacket"—*hic*—"is gray!"

"Your eyes are blue."

The French, of course, are famous for their seductive powers. One should really keep her guard up around them. He didn't, after all, admit that my eyes are a *pretty* shade of blue, or some variation on the theme. It doesn't matter. He could have said my eyes were the color of dried cement, and the same giddy glee would have throbbed through my bones. It is the look, not so much the words. And that look is international.

"I am Mathieu," he says, extending his hand. He moves toward me but stops. I can tell he's not sure about the cheek kissing—that I, as an American, might think it too forward. This consideration touches me, even as I lament the absence of those lips upon my ready cheek.

"Daisy," I say, looking down.

I take his hand, waiting for a muffled guffaw, an ironical smile. But his hand is warm, and he presses mine lightly, letting it linger.

"Daisy, would you like to share a cup of coffee with me?"

Surprised, I look up. Our hands are still clasped, each reluctant to let go. He gestures toward the café behind us.

And that is when I start loving Paris.

Chapter 6

We went for coffee. We stayed for lunch.

I fell in love with him in fits and starts, like a woman laboring with birth. Big moves forward, small steps back. Doubt crept in, until he gave me reason to push it away. By the end, I had delivered myself to him.

The café at the Musée d'Orsay is extraordinary. An enormous, bifurcated room, it's welded together by the steel beams from the former rail station, its impregnability somewhat softened by the stucco walls, wicker chairs, and radiant, globed flowers. The most remarkable detail is the original rail clock, twenty feet in diameter and cobbled of steel and glass, which dominates the far wall, allowing the rooftops of Paris to filter through. From my seat, I see the white domes of the Sacré Coeur—The Sacred Heart— perched atop Montmarte.

We fumble for conversation, our bold heat blistering into a more temperate self-consciousness. But once committed to a roller coaster, it's impossible to get off. And so things progress. I fall in love with him three times over the next two hours, out of love twice. This math is child's play.

Cupid's first arrow, gold-tipped, finds its target: happens around fifteen minutes into our conversation. He tells me his mother recently died. Startled, I offer my condolences in that clumsy, lacking way people do when they don't know the deceased, and barely know the living. He shakes me off, smiling tightly. Says he never cared much for his mother. Calls her a phony. I'm uncertain how to respond to this. Intuiting my doubt, he explains: his mother never had time for him and his three older sisters, abandoned them all when Mathieu was six and sick with the (the English terminology stumps him, until he mimes frantic itching, and I, giggling, intervene) *chicken pox*, leaving for New York City, and later, to Los Angeles, to try her hand at acting. Someone once told her that she looked like a dark Catherine Deneuve, but could speak English as artfully as Sarah Bernhardt. Evidently, this was exaggerated. He saw her a handful of times after that, the visits separated by years, not months, until the sharp pain dulled into an ache and then exhausted into indifference, like she was just some woman whose face appeared a little altered each time he met her again. *Céline.*

At last she succumbed to lung cancer; he could not remember an occasion when she wasn't "sucking on a cigarette." She even smoked at the very end, while her lungs growled for oxygen. She was buried on a Thursday, and he did not cry. His sisters, his father, all cried. He wondered why they should. For Mathieu, she was an empty abstraction of maternity by this point, like those pastel moms of Mary Cassatt's down the hall—pretty, but illusory, for what could the childless Cassatt know about motherhood, really?

I do not fall in love with him as he talks about his mother's death, or the little boy he once was. These facts say something about a person's history, but they do not reveal the man.

Rather, I fall in love with him some minutes later, when he takes off his jacket and a pack of cigarettes spills from his breast pocket like an accidental confession. Women's cigarettes. The pink label, slims. He tries to convince me I didn't see them, with a sleight-of-hand trick that could fool no one. He continues to drink his coffee, his hand shaking slightly.

He kept her cigarettes.

The arrow pricks the skin: he has (gut-wrenching present tense) a girlfriend. He tells me this in the manner of someone relaying he owns a dog: incidental, as an aside, without consideration for the way my (startled blue) eyes are shining out at him, and ignoring the umbrage his right foot, shod in brown leather, is taking with my inner ankle, caressing it so gently that I am afraid to move, like it is a skittish cat I might frighten away. Suddenly he is a cad, and I am a foolish girl, too easily turned on by an accent and the mawkish hope of a foreign love. Cupid's just another cherub, after all. I yank my foot away and sit up smartly, attempting to reclaim the self-respect I, naked in relief, relinquished the second I hiccupped my delight at seeing him again.

"Your girlfriend."

He is surprised. "Pardon?" He has been recounting a rather charming story about a *boulangerie* near him, articulating, with great ardor, what constitutes a good baguette, emphasizing the caramelized exterior and the yeasty honeycomb within. I thrilled to myself, *How marvelous! The man is even passionate about bread!* But then he recounted how his *lady friend* worked there, concocting pastries, which she slipped to him for free.

I clap my hand over my mouth.

"Daisy? Are you well?"

I wave him off, nodding. "I didn't know."

"Did not know what?" he asks, confused.

"That you had a girlfriend." The tears do not fall but are poised for betrayal.

He starts to laugh. He rests his chin on his hand and laughs at me. My nerves, so splayed and painful of late, cannot withstand such open malice. I immediately hate him.

"I'm glad this is so amusing to you."

Mathieu sobers and takes my hand. "I said *lady* friend. Not girlfriend. I have a friend, and she is a lady who works at the *boulangerie*. She is also sixty-four and weighs one hundred kilos." He puffs out his cheeks. "She really loves her work."

I laugh with relief. I'm embarrassed because now he knows. I didn't fall out of love with him: I was just preparing myself for being in love with a cad.

Deeper it (and I) plunge: he wants to order my lunch for me. He looks serious, but uncertain, like all American females are uber-feminists who become offended at the slightest hint of male forwardness. In truth, back home, I might have hesitated, wondering if it was a power play. Here, I willingly give Mathieu lead. He pores intently over the menu before commiserating with the distracted waiter, ordering something I do not understand. It could be beef brains. I don't care. When he's nervous, he looks like a schoolboy, playing at grown-up things.

All bent askew: he wants to know everything about me, sitting back in his chair with the languorous expectation of a student at the start of class. His directness flusters me, since my first impressions of the French people have led me to conclude that personal forwardness is a little vulgar here. Yesterday, for example, I happily told the front desk guy, who was reviewing a pictography of the American West, about my trip to Yellowstone when I was twelve. I thought my personal recollection of Old Faithful might be illuminating for him. He regarded me skeptically for a moment before interrupting to ask if I "required more towels."

But then, Mathieu isn't France.

When I tell him that I'm studying to be a scientist, his face falls, just barely, but perceptibly. That little line between his eyes is worried. When he presses me for details, I give them, and the little line deepens, like a crevice in his understanding. How could the thoughtful woman reading *The Razor's Edge* on the train share an identity with the laboratory troll? We look so much alike, I understand his confusion. But he cannot know that I faked the book—that the nerd is nearer to reality.

"So you look at tiny projections in dead people's ears?" he asks, leaning back in his chair.

"Dead turtles."

"So you look at tiny projections in dead *turtles'* ears?"

"Well, that's a layman's explanation," I retort. "I would argue that we conduct experiments to further our knowledge and understanding of crucial biological processes."

He rubs his jaw. "And these experiments will better people's lives someday?"

"That's the idea."

Mathieu leans in. "In what way?"

Something shrinks inside me. It's not a question I've encountered before. The pursuit of something tangible, like a degree, and the comfortable future it promises, is enough for those nice, tactful souls who have bothered to ask about my studies. Most, in fact, are impressed, or bored, enough by the coupling of the words *neuroscience* and *graduate studies* to let it lie. Not Mathieu. He wants to know the *meaning* of my work. And I don't know what to tell him.

I smile. "It's complicated."

He returns the smile. "I have time."

Lunch comes. It's some kind of bisque, followed by *Tuna au Poivre*, but I barely taste it, too mired in explaining my work to Mathieu. I tell him about the luckless multitudes afflicted with Meniere's disease, that singular condition of the inner ear that causes vertigo, and make outrageous statements about the serendipity of scientific research. I point, with unearned self-importance, to Marie Curie as an example. She's French—through marriage, anyway. He should understand.

Mathieu swallows and lays down his fork. "This is all good to know. But tell me one more thing, and then I will leave it alone."

"What?"

His eyes are dark, almost threatening. "When you are secreted away in your lab, looking through your microscope, does your face illuminate the way it did when I saw you before the Manet, or are you doing someone else's work for him and pretending to yourself and others that it is enough?"

His presumption is intoxicating, galling. Like a stolen kiss deserving of a slap. You hate him for it, but then, what a kiss to land.

"You don't know me."

He raises his glass of wine and takes a leisurely sip. "Not yet," he murmurs.

What an ego. I should stand up, thank him for lunch, and leave. I really should.

But, pierced . . . I stay seated. I could argue that a strange force pins me to my chair, like Venus on the waves, smoking my blood, stealing my breath whenever he looks at me with that heady potion of playfulness and sincerity. That I remain, out of a sense of duty, to finish a shared lunch and the first conversation I've had in a week. That I want to watch, from my eyelet view, the sun pulling the gloss from the matte of pewter rooftops stacking the Paris skyline. The passing shadows through the old clock are the only indication that we have not managed an end to time, as the other diners in the café, our scenery, come and go, faceless, colorless next to our spectral display. They traverse the dead hallways of Degas' soulless ballerinas when they have this dynamic *pas de deux* before them! Silly people. Look at Mathieu's eyes crinkle like crescent moons when he laughs at my father's reaction to my coming here; how his jaw flexes with feeling when I recall my mother's words, urging me on; and finally, how he grips his fork at their shared insistence of a sojourn to Shakespeare & Co. What fool could stomach dead geniuses when this brilliant, living man sits before her!

I stay because I am starting to feel real again.

Mathieu informs me that he is a freelance tour guide. He wants to be my guide for the next—and here he breaks off, a cloud passing over the clock. The bubble of our delusion wavers. But we are not ready to invite endings.

He wants to be my tour guide. Mine.

"This is what I will do. You have, by now, transformed Paris into a long list of places and things to check off, have you not?" He eyes my bag under the table, suspicious of Rick's presence.

I nod sheepishly.

"You have been hiding out in McDonald's, tourist blights, avoiding places that might require a passing understanding of French." He says it like it's true, and I don't refute it. "This deadens the city. It puts you on the defensive, Daisy, like Paris is something to be overcome, not enjoyed." Even though he's lecturing, there is still profound joy at his saying my name—that horrid, hated name—like it's familiar living. "Paris is, above all, a sensual city. So this is what we will do." He sits up and looks deeper into my eyes. "We will drown ourselves in each sense and suck on its many pleasures until we are overcome and wasted on them. One day we will allow for the sound of Paris, another for the taste, still another for the vision of Paris . . . you understand." He smiles, a slow wonder. "By the end of each day, we will be so intoxicated that we will stumble to find our feet again. And then we will awaken and fill ourselves once more."

What do I do? What does any drunken person do when given a hand? Take it, and hold on for dear life.

We finally end our lunch because he has an engagement. An English couple. In town for two days, they have two things on their list: where Princess Di died and the Eiffel Tower. We laugh, a couple of contemptible bastards.

I have seen the Eiffel Tower. Yet at no time, while perched on its lofty lip, did I feel as elevated as I do now, darting down the littered stairs of the nearest metro station, birthing a hard seed of hope in my heart.

That moonless night, I lie atop a bed that is not my own, listening to the traffic whip down a street whose name I do not feel confident to pronounce, thinking not of Mathieu, born of a country that still feels strange, but of Andy. For when one, sober and alone, reflects on the drunkenness that comes before, there is doubt that any of it could have happened. Mathieu is still a dream. A lovely one, but hazy, and too wondrously fleeting. His eyes, so clear to me before, have faded to black. I cannot recall if he is right- or left-handed. I do not know his last name.

Andy Templeton I will not forget. Our sturdy seed laid roots and flowered perennially. If the blooms have withered and died with time—victims of too many fallow seasons—I can still press the dried petals to my heart and catch a last whiff of their fading scent. They smell like home.

After tossing and turning until even the traffic slumbers, I call his apartment. It is nine his time. He will be doing something predictable and Andy-like: studying, fixing a late dinner of jarred sauce and rotini after coming home from the library. I do not know what I will say to him, only that I must hear his voice across the ocean that divides us.

He does not answer.

I curl around my hurt and try not to think of what there is to do in Cambridge, on a starry night, for a newly single premed student sniffing for fresh memories.

Chapter 7

I am daunted the next morning. My eyes are wide, like a rabbit's, in the mirror. My hair empathizes by inventing a new part. Exasperated, I pull the shag back into my trained ponytail, impatient with the time and devotion it takes to look pretty. Oh, I want to look pretty for Mathieu. Not presentable or well kept, but undeniably pretty, wildly feminine—dazzling. I just don't know how to go about it. I flirt with the idea of makeup but abandon the notion when I check the time. It's 8:30, and I have no time to run out and purchase makeup. Contenting myself with lip gloss—*Strawberry Smack!*—I feel much like the Pentecostal teenager who begs her mother for this sad consolation. I shrug at my reflected image, and she shows a ready enough surrender. There is nothing we can do about the veiny saddlebags beneath my eyes or the suspicious white mass erupting on my chin. *C'est la vie.* It is the same strange face Mathieu stared into for two hours yesterday, without finding it entirely repulsive. I cannot help but think, through some oversight on his part, that he liked what he saw, whiteheads and all.

He is on his way, even now. Somewhere, in this sprawling city whose surface I have but scratched, a man makes his way toward this hotel, with plans for me, for a tentative hypothesis called "Mathieu and Daisy." The thought both tantalizes and distresses. My heart thuds like a warning in my chest, reminding me of its fresh injury. I cross the room to my window, throwing it open to lean across the wrought-iron bars, and scan the street below. I can barely make out the café on the corner to my left, where I dined alone last night, braving the French menu, and scarier still, the omnipotent French waiter, for the first time. I cautiously attempted a few words of French (which I have been studying diligently at night, because MTV Europe can only be tolerated, for its kitsch factor, on mute) and was rewarded with a look that, if not entirely equitable, could not be labeled contemptuous. I probably would have softened the stiff dignity of the fellow more if I had not asked for a Coke and pizza margherita. But baby steps were all I could contemplate. Today is the plunge.

The day is breezy and cool, the sun a cipher behind its shield of clouds. The bustle of the people, the start-and-stop crush of cars on the Rue des Écoles are oblivious to the sun's absence, or my plaintive form, clad in little-girl pajamas, spying on them. They simply scurry on. I am struck by how superfluous I am to the scene—at best, an extra in a long-running play—tucked away in this tiny hotel room, my money the umbilical of a slight attachment.

I have aborted all the others.

Before today, the condition of being alone bred loneliness. But now, there is a reckless freedom fluttering through me, around me, tickling the curtains, coaxing the hair on my flesh to stretch and stiffen like new grass. It's only just licking the surface, yes, but, given time, will spread with a wildfire's imprecision to consume that stagnant isolation, the great void I've carried (in the pit of my stomach, like an absent meal) since receiving Andy's e-mail a lifetime ago. Something happened in my sleep last night, and is now upon me, with the warmth and breath of another body. No longer witness to the outside view, I watch the film of my fear, like a cataract, being lifted from my eyes, the burdens of regret and sorrow lanced by a wayward breeze blowing through my window on a Paris morning.

Rebuffed by my backward appeal to Andy, and alert to the spectrum of possibilities shimmering ahead with Mathieu, some dormant antennae has curled around to take proper notice and recoiled at the state of dependency it found. To rely upon another person, no matter how dear, for my happiness will not work for me. I cannot live like half of a person. Yesterday served as an alarm, as I so eagerly strung myself between the two men. I have come too low. Like a snake chafing itself along a rock before shedding, I have rubbed up against my neediness, until it nicked and scorned me into action. This new skin—raw, but my own—feels like an old welcoming, a reassertion of some primal color. A thousand windows have opened, and a thousand winds may come. I have time to welcome them all.

Yet Mathieu comes now, like a tornado.

His eyes, clear to me in the unambiguous light of day, promised it at our departure, as he punctuated his intention with two kisses on my cheeks that, foolishly, made me not wash my face last night. And so I detach myself from the strange pull of the window and busy myself with the task of getting dressed, pulling a pair of dark jeans from the top of my suitcase, still unpacked, and sliding my newly shaved legs into them. I wrap my torso in a sweater the color of Cezanne's limes, and new grass, and consider myself absently in the oblong mirror. I have a long, lean look, my hips flaring slightly in the cinched jeans, my chest nearly unconscious. My eyes are not wounded, but defiant. I pull my black hair from its circular prison and shake it out. It is a little unruly, but I leave it.

Outside the window, the sun yawns itself awake and starts to burn.

I have to smile when I see him. He looks like an American caricature of a Frenchman, wearing dark slacks, a snug, horizontally striped shirt, the iconic black beret a jaunty saucer atop his head. Put some mime makeup on his face, and I'd throw some change at his feet, just to keep him away.

I had planted myself outside the Hotel California St. Germain to wait for him, hands clenched like clams inside my pockets. It occurred to me for the hundredth time that I know nothing about this person who's coming. Except that he is late. I was trying to decide if I felt disappointed, or relieved, when his figure caught my eye, striding across the Rue Montagne Ste-Geneviève. I am amused and mortified by his costume. If people should think he's serious—

"Bonjour, *Mademoiselle* Daisy," he greets me, seizing my shoulders and kissing me lightly on both cheeks. I am like a doll on delay, only coming to life in time to pucker at the air. He smells sharp and masculine, and for a moment, I have to fight the animal inclination to lean forward and breathe him in.

Laughing to cover for my embarrassment, I ask, "What's with the getup, Pierre?"

He steps back, looking down in confusion. "What do you mean?" Oh. Jesus.

"Do I not fit your ideal of the romantic French bohemian?"

I offer a small prayer of thanks. "I think you forgot the little moustache," I retort, "and the insufferable look of self-importance."

It is only the second time I make him laugh. I am determined to hold my own today. Yesterday I was a schoolgirl, his little Madeline, whom he led by the hand. I like his boldness. As long as it doesn't defeat my own.

He removes the beret, spinning it on his finger like an American teenager with a basketball, before stuffing it into his back pocket. He says, "You would be amazed at the additional gratuities I receive in this outfit." He grabs a sleek black sweater from a knapsack slung across his body and smiles wickedly. "Particularly from American professors on my famous 'Lost Generation' tour. I think I am fulfilling a sort of fantasy for them."

Mathieu sets his bag down and pulls the sweater over his torso. I am sorry for the lost definition of his arms, which have the pleasing utility of a musician or painter.

"Probably a little bit of a homoerotic one," I assent, admiringly. The fact is, though he had looked like a cartoon of a Frenchman, it was an appealing portrait. I can imagine men like my father getting a kick out of it, almost against their will. There is something in Americans that wants to stereotype the French, for good or ill. We are willing to acknowledge their superiority in cooking, matters of style and art (once upon a time, anyway), the staging of mass street protests, and staying thin, if we can publicly brutalize them for their snootiness, declining world influence, massive bureaucracy, the late Vichy government, and, well, their snootiness. It's similar to the strain of anti-elitism that has swept like a pandemic of polemical hand-wringing across America during the last decade, whenever anyone sprinkles talking-point words like *Ivy League* and *East Coast intellectualism* throughout a tiresome tirade. The French have a reputation for spawning philosophers with the startling frequency that we manufacture business moguls. Words, *French* words, and not the pan-Union euros, are the real currency of this country, maintaining her solvency, while in America, money serves that purpose more than satisfactorily, thank you very much and come again, sir.

I have watched the Sunday talk shows here in France, and while I cannot decipher what the panelists are saying, I know this: it's kind of like cable news, but without the bitch slapping. It makes me uncomfortable to witness such embarrassing displays of mutual respect. There is something preternaturally competitive in the American spirit that fashions discourse as blood sport. The French seem to regard the political and philosophical (which have a manner of colluding here more than anywhere else) the way some Americans practice religion: with strict devotion and spiritual reverence. We common-sense Yanks don't like to feel inferior to a group of people suspected to be smarter than us and, worse, uppity about it. Americans, in spite of Jesus' counsel, don't do modest, and we certainly aren't beholden to pipsqueak, past-their-prime countries whom we—and they really oughtn't forget this!—helped liberate and resurrect with the Marshall Plan.

So we come to France (after England, before Italy), expecting them to roll out the red carpet, receiving us in perfect English, and with the same frantic smiles on their faces that greet us at Red Lobster back home. If they don't, we revolt. And when we get back home, we grouse to sympathetic friends, "I don't know why they think they're so *above* everything . . . the food's not *that* great." And the legend of the Rude French as some monolithic whole (like the Hot-blooded Italian, the Pragmatic German) endures. I am not immune: see Chapter 3.

But Mathieu is looking at me, and it is plain that I am not paying him proper attention. Or he cannot decipher what *homoerotic* means, which is a shame because I was on a roll.

"Anyway." I smile apologetically. "Where are we going today?"

He leans in and kisses me. His lips are soft and gentle, yet could easily break me. I hesitate, then kiss him back. Our mouths are the only flesh of our bodies to touch, like leggy chromosomes meeting at their spindle. My eyes open, and he is looking at me. Into me. Flustered, I pull away. But my lips still tingle. He has revived them, and they're shuddering spectacularly, like two wings of a hummingbird.

He smiles and murmurs, "You were a million miles away. I wanted you to return to me."

I shuffle, looking down at my Keds. I didn't kiss Andy until our third date. By then, I knew his position on the junior varsity basketball team, that he almost died in a neighbor's swimming pool at the age of three, and that his favorite movie was *The Godfather*. Parts one and two, of course.

"What's your last name, Mathieu?" I ask.

He laughs harshly, twisting away to stare down the street. After a moment, he looks back at me. "Does it matter?"

I consider this. What do I know of Mathieu? That he likes his baguettes—a lot. That his mother just died. That he has a romantic streak in him as fiery and limbic as Andy's ambition. That he likes to surprise me.

That my mouth, awakened, is busy protesting the absence of his lips.

Bewildered, I take his hand in my own, looking down at the snarl of fingers inventing new, complex attachments. He has long, elegant hands, which an obtuse observer might call effeminate. They are simply well cared for. His nails almost look polished, half moons forming at the bases. Mine are jagged and irregular. He doesn't notice the nails, too occupied with caressing the shiver of skin over my pulse point with his thumb. The little vein is quickening.

I look at him and grin violently. "Do you promise never to tell me your last name?"

"What do we need of names? Besides," he says into my ear, "I would rather call you *mon petit chou*." He brings my wrist to his mouth and presses his lips to my blood.

It is hard to argue with the French. No matter what they say, it sounds inspired. I had no idea what he called me, except that it was "my little" something. Which, as I've put forth, has got to be a good thing. We start walking, arms twined like licorice, and feet floating. And so we pirouette and jeté, like the eponymous character in *An American in Paris* might, toward our unknown destination, the early morning's prescriptive caution outmatched by a lovely momentum.

That night, after consulting the French-English dictionary in my hotel room, I discovered that *chou* means "cabbage."

Mon dieu! I mean, really. Think of what he'd call me if he didn't like me.

Chapter 8

We start with the sights of Paris, because we are visual creatures, bamboozled by color and form, the rapturous anesthetics of the lesser senses. While we cannot escape biology, Mathieu argues, we are not hostage to its showier inclinations, which, I imagine, was the pointed joke of his earlier appearance. I also assume from his tone that we will not venture anywhere near the Moulin Rouge. He informs me, as we stroll down the Rue des Écoles toward Luxembourg Gardens, that he has not planned this day out, that he has no expectations for it. It is his intention to embrace a series of fortunate accidents and respond to them; this to that, to this again. We will walk with the wind at our backs.

I check his profile—the satisfied smile, the confident jut of his chin—and know that it's a crock. He has everything planned. For it is also human nature to want to impress someone you like, and especially in your hometown. As a tour guide, I have no doubt, Mathieu knows what the perfect Parisian day will entail. I frown, twisted by the wretchedly novel idea that I am not the first to experience it with him. I raise my chin and iron out my sweater to shake off the sooty shards of cynicism. I don't want to make a room in my heart for suspicion. Not this early. My heart is full.

We flounder, if not uncomfortably, for conversation, too occupied with glancing at one another from these come-to-me corners of our eyes. I make a happy cocktail of my self-restraint as I watch desire build in his eyes like a wave chasing the break. We are disgustingly pleased with ourselves. If we notice other people, it is only to feel sorry for them.

April in Paris has come late this year.

"So tell me why you are here."

"Right now? With you?"

"No, in Paris. What is it that you are running from?" It is asked lightly, but with a probing undercurrent.

I clear my throat. "You caught me. I'm running from the law."

Isn't that the standard movie-line answer?

Smiling, he accepts my hedge. "I see. What did you do back in Ohio?" He pronounces "Ohio" the way we sang it in a grade school song: with a raised emphasis on the "hi," like the state is peopled by Walmart greeters. "Theft? Murder? Campaigning for John Kerry?"

Funny. I cover my mouth and turn with confessional solemnity. "Worse. I slipped at a restaurant and called 'Freedom fries' French fries. Then I washed them down with a glass of merlot. All in front of my grandpa's buddies from the local chapter of the A.F.A.R.T.—you heard of them?" I think rapidly. "Americans For the Abstract Reinvention of Tyranny? Yeah, they're small now, but they're planning an Orwellian takeover as soon as one of them figures out how to work a computer."

Mathieu laughs, saying, "Yet it *was* an unforgivable offense, particularly toward the French."

"You're not a fan of French—oops, I mean 'Freedom'—fries?"

"Mmm. Nor merlot."

"And American jingoism?" I add lightly.

Mathieu doesn't answer right away, so I explain, "Jingoism—it's like patriotism run amok."

He nods absently. "Yes. An American specialty."

Sobered, I nod my assent. Strange how I should poke at my own country, but that I turn snippy and defensive when an outsider agrees with me. There's always a forked road to navigate, and pride is a less treacherous path than honesty. "We are loud with our patriotism, I admit. But we also have the eyes of the world watching us, so it is easy to trip and fall." I shrug and glance over at him. "Besides, France is easily as patriotic. It just manifests itself in different ways here."

Mathieu releases my hand and, mixing his stereotypes, starts gesturing like a Hot-Blooded Italian. "Yes, it does. Like not invading foreign countries that have done nothing to us. Like not isolating ourselves from the rest of the world by flaunting environmental treaties. Like not having a president too simple-minded to articulate a coherent thought without the help of tutors, yet who says, 'Bring it on,' like a cowboy drunk with power. Like not forgetting about the poor in our country, and making sure that everyone has health insurance. Like—"

"Touché." So much for the language barrier. I turn and grasp his hand with both of mine, pressing upon him my urgency. "Let's not—yet. Okay?"

He runs his free hand through his hair. "I apologize. It is difficult for me. As you said, the eyes of the world are on you, and everyone knows America's"—he smiles wryly—"indiscretions." He clasps my hand more tightly. "But they are not your indiscretions. I should not direct my frustrations toward you."

"But you will," I murmur, a little sadly. We carry the weight of our countries on our shoulders. And America is always the heavy.

Mathieu pulls eagerly on my hand as we enter a square whose

muted loveliness smooths our foray into raucous politics. In spite of the idea behind our walk today, I have only had eyes for Mathieu. But now I admire the exquisite lamppost at the center of the square, and the slender trees encircling it, which extend nerves of branches that must cast film noir shadows at night, when the bulbs incandesce into a tight galaxy of luminous moons. There are cars parked near small boutiques, but otherwise, the square is tranquil and nearly deserted. The white buildings framing the symmetrical sides are five stories high with white shutters—Parisians seem suspicious of height and color—and are just high enough to block out the sun. A small, nervous dog (there are no other kinds here) relieves itself on the far curb, in no hurry as its owner, a smartly dressed older woman (there are no other kinds here), removes a compact from her purse and dusts her nose.

"It's lovely," I sigh, content to stop and stare. But Mathieu and his plan pull me toward the far corner of the square and through a small Roman archway. An ancient doorway boasting the ubiquitous brass plaque confronts us. "What's this?" I ask.

"It's the *Musée Delacroix*," he announces, opening the door.

"Oh."

I must admit some disappointment. From what I remember of the Orsay and Louvre, I was not taken with Delacroix.

Mathieu laughs and, sensing my hesitation, waves me through. "Nobody can understand France, or Paris, without appreciating Delacroix. Baudelaire hailed him as the father of French modernity."

"Oh."

I will not let him know that the name *Baudelaire* means as little to me as *Proust*, or *Balzac*. They should mean something, but American education extends only so far, grazing the surface of world literature and history with the same level of introspection that a hand skimming the water outside its boat understands the ocean below. I was a biochem and evolutionary biology double-major in college, so there were whole buildings on campus never ventured into. Hey, I was busy. Liberal arts majors were the floating people who spent too much time in coffee shops. But I am beginning to realize that survival in France requires a balls-out, intellectual vigilance, a kind of Greek ambition for understanding everything. The French, you see, love their history, and their coffee shops . . . and their historical coffee shops.

Mathieu and I argue over the entrance fee to the museum. I insist, a little shrilly, on paying for my ticket, which he protests with a bereaved look and sigh, like we've segued into a comfortable middle age. I win, though I feel no satisfaction at his emasculation. I don't know why he shouldn't pay, but he shouldn't. Clutching my little prize, Mathieu leads us into the first gallery, which includes a biographical perspective on Delacroix's life.

We part ways and move silently around the exhibit—I, learning that Delacroix established himself in this modest home and workshop in order to be closer to the St. Sulpice church, where he was responsible for painting the acclaimed interior frescoes. It is noted that he died here too, a grim fact echoed by our funereal footsteps on the hardwood floor. I check Mathieu from the corner of my eye and discover that he is doing the same. I am the first to turn away, humming a little nothing song to myself, footsteps dissolving into notes. We are the only visitors inside the museum, which makes us pleasantly self-conscious, but which imbues the paintings with an abandoned, and lonely, affect. I feign interest in some sketches, and when I turn around again, Mathieu stands riveted before a small painting. He motions to me. I approach with a small, perplexed smile.

"Look at this," he whispers, clasping my arm above the elbow. "What do you think?"

What do I think? It is a study for a later painting. In it, a bare-chested man pinions a naked woman with his knee, his left hand shackling her elbow while his right angles a dagger across the white flute of her throat. Her breasts strain provocatively against his bind as her mouth assumes an expression of what may be (1) sexual ecstasy; (2) mortal anguish; or, in some perverse world, (3) both. Personally, I'm going with the second interpretation because she is clearly a lamb for his slaughter. Nice composition, though: beautiful use of color and dynamism, blah, blah, blah. But what do I think?

I wrinkle my nose. "Not my thing."

"But it is beautiful!"

I wiggle free from his grasp. "Beautiful? Sure, if rape and murder are beautiful, then Delacroix is the Picasso of the genre."

Mathieu frowns. "But you are viewing this with no filter. You must remove yourself from the subject matter to admire the skill and genius that brought it to life."

"Must I? Because what bothered me about Delacroix before," I argue, my voice quickening, "is that he takes too much pleasure in his brutality. So many of his works are gorgeously rendered, in that high romantic style, that they're morally ambiguous. He almost argues for these atrocities because he ravishes the viewer with color and vitality."

Mathieu shifts his weight. "But you cannot look at art from a moralist's perspective."

"I'm not a Puritan, in spite of what you think of America. This isn't about my personal squeamishness with violence or sexuality. I'm talking about an artist's motivation. Why did he paint it? What moved him? Was he after some kind of objective truth? These questions are important to me."

"But art *is* personal interpretation. Why should I care about the artist's motivation if I discover something different? I like the sharply executed angles of his composition and how the colors pulse with energy, foreshadowing the impressionists to come. The people in it are myths—they mean nothing to me." He smiles to blunt the sharpness of his words and falls back on his heels. "And Picasso would be flattered by your comparison. He was a great admirer of Delacroix."

I see his point of view. But . . . "Of *course* art is personal. I agree with that. And it's highly emotional. Which is why the artist must tread carefully. Which of our instincts does he want to inflame? What am I supposed to think about a guy who paints death with such sensuality?"

"But life is sensual. Death should be no different." He grins. "As for the dead artist? He means as little to me as the dead turtle does to you."

That sounds clever, but not right.

"But turtle tissue doesn't lie, Mathieu. You can call this a myth if that makes you feel better, probably because the victim has been pinned between a man's idea of climax and death. Because I wonder how you'd feel if it were a contemporary painting or photograph of a woman's murder, so artfully rendered. It might affect you differently."

Mathieu stares at me, but I cannot read him. Finally, he says, "But that is something, yes? To experience discomfort and revulsion and sympathy, to be reminded of all facets of our humanity, in reaction to a painting by a man who drew his last breaths before we drew our first. Delacroix has achieved the only immortality that is relevant. He has succeeded in—what is the expression—?" He tucks a lock of hair behind my ear. "Stirring you up."

"That he has," I say, shivering and brushing my ear against my shoulder. The tension broken, we both walk easily into the next room. "Maybe I just don't want to admit to myself that I can be captivated by such ugliness. It's like slowing to look at a car wreck, or those women who watch Lifetime movies back home."

Mathieu lifts an eyebrow.

I laugh and shake my head. "Sorry—Lifetime is a television station that plays movies with titles like"—I pounce upon the first drivel that comes to mind—"*The Black Widow Murders* . . . or . . . *A Wife's Charge to Keep*." He laughs incredulously, but little does he know about the dregs of American cable. "Basically, think of any heinous act someone might commit, and Lifetime will manipulate it into a two-hour melodrama where victimhood is equated with sainthood."

I halt in front of a charcoal drawing inspired by Delacroix's trip to Morocco. "Not that it's a fair comparison to your Delacroix," I admit. "It's just that his art reminds me of our baser instinct to turn tragedy into a gaudy entertainment." I turn my attention to the small portrait before me. "But not this. This is lovely."

"Yes, this is *Orphan Girl in a Cemetery*. The final painting hangs in the Louvre." Mathieu pauses for my reaction, his fingers hanging on his chin.

The girl, just shy of womanhood, is captured in profile as she looks across her bared shoulder, the strong, dark features of her face a study of tension and wonderment. Hair swept back into a loose chignon, her eyes latch on to something looming out of frame, the generous, downward curving mouth startled into parting. I misspoke earlier: she is not lovely, but aggressively striking, for there is a peasant's strength drawn in the shock of eyebrow, the tendons jutting from her neck thickly and unprettily, the sloping brow angled like a shield ready for battle. Her history is written on her face, and it has not been easy. She is exoticism. She is romanticism. She is mystery, my orphan girl.

I look sidelong at Mathieu. "What do you think she's looking at?"

"I have often wondered." He clasps his hands behind his back, almost like he is stopping himself from touching her. "This has always been my favorite work of Delacroix's. My mom brought me to the Louvre when I was a boy, whenever she felt guilty about something. Her restlessness inevitably got the better of her, and she would leave me in one of the big rooms, with instructions not to move, while she went for a smoke, or a fuck." He is silent for a beat, staring at the girl, while I swallow my shock.

He picks up the thread, his smile turning black. "But I always drifted toward Delacroix's *Orphan Girl*. I do not suppose I was aware of the symbolism. But I felt for her abandonment. And I always wanted to know what put that possessed look on her face. I tried to believe that it was something good—my childish form of denial, I imagine. But I could never quite convince myself of it." Mathieu turns to me. "Now I have you to satisfy my curiosity."

"Me?"

"Yes, you."

"Why me?" I ask, lost.

"She is you," he says, motioning to the portrait.

I look at the painting, baffled by his certainty. The orphan girl and I share a dark boldness and solemnity to our features, but there are countless points of departure. Our noses are nothing alike. She looks short and, to my one credit, has a neck like a tree trunk, whereas mine is slender and long. Her visible eye is enormous, like a Japanese anime figure. Her skin, though rendered in charcoal, achieves luminosity in the movie of my mind, and her expression is haunted. In short, she looks like a tragic heroine about to be swatted by the hand of fate. Whereas I am an American girl-woman who wears my aura of privilege as casually as my Gap jeans. There is really no comparison.

And while I hate to disappoint Mathieu's sense of destiny, this notion that I am the manifestation of his boyish desire for this girl's—and his mother's—understanding, I have no idea what she's looking at. I doubt Delacroix knew.

"I think you're mistaken," is all I say, a little embarrassed for him.

He chuckles to lighten the mood. "I did not mean to make

you uncomfortable. It was simply an observation. Perhaps it is the seriousness of your expression." He grabs my hand, and we walk away, orphaning her once more. "I think she may have traveled with supplemental oxygen too."

I stop and put my hands on my hips, while he keeps walking. "You're never going to let me forget that, are you?"

"No," he tosses back. "Some things are worth remembering."

"So why *were* you so eager to get away from me on the train?"

Having conquered Delacroix, we are walking at a good click. I feel reckless. The man is falling for me. He likes our little spats, the missteps, and the drawing together again, like any dance of seduction. He walks rapidly, challenging me to keep up with his longer strides. Romance is a game for him: not a brutish tug-of-war, but a grand chess match. He will not suffer boredom.

So I have set upon this strategy of saying whatever springs to mind, partly to engage him, and partly because it is my own game, and a novel one for someone conditioned to playing defense. My fledgling metamorphosis from this morning has not been forgotten; I'm merely stretching my wings, sharing some green space. After all, Paris has plenty to spare. Like her leaves thrilling to their autumn ballet, I, too, am spilling new colors.

"Eager to get away from you?"

"You bolted from that train, without ever looking back. I was so certain you'd at least look back." I don't try to suppress a reproach from dimpling my voice. It had hurt me that he hadn't looked back. I just didn't know it until now.

"I saw you looking. I knew you were there." Triumph is carved into his profile. He sensed his kingly power over my little pawn, even at that larval stage of our relationship.

"How did you know?"

Slowing, Mathieu turns toward me. We are walking toward the Luxembourg Gardens. I know because it has been my home this past week, and I can see the palace, stationed like a planet in the sky, off to the right. "Because there are mirrors at the front of the car. I saw your eyes watching me while I stepped off." He smiles with more alacrity than I'd like. "I saw your shoulders slump, and your mouth twist downward, like a disappointed child's." He mimes my woebegone look too skillfully.

Looking away, I remark, "And yet you left me there, disappointed."

Mathieu laughs, swinging my hand with careless bravado. "What was I to do? I had an appointment to attend to, and I knew you were on vacation." He shrugs. "I had just gotten out of a relationship. I was not eager to jump into something based solely on a pair of lapis blue eyes and an adorable insecurity."

I rip my hand from his. "There is nothing adorable about my insecurity." I try to sound haughty, but the spirit of the thing is diluted in equal parts by the description of my eyes as "lapis," and the fact that I am beyond besotted. "Besides, any insecurity I have only flares up in France. And I pin that directly on the Americans who came before me, for being so stupidly intimidated by the French, *and* on the people in that train, who proved them all right."

I point at him accusingly. "Especially you, with your superior look of detachment, and your talent for making cryptic pronouncements." It has not escaped my notice that he mentioned a prior relationship, but I don't know what to do with the information. "*You are no tourist*. What the hell does that mean? You made me ashamed to even take out my camera. I felt like everything I did after that would only be a disappointment."

"To me—or yourself?"

I hesitate. "Both, probably," I decide, and we laugh. I take his hand and wind my fingers through his. "I think that when you step into a foreign land, you no longer feel like yourself, so other people's interpretations of you end up filling in the gaps. I thought college was my shot at reinvention for the same reason."

All I wanted in college was for someone to tell me who I should be. But Andy was there to remind me of who I was. I tried to change my name to "Dana" my freshman year, but it's difficult to be credible when your boyfriend rolls his eyes behind your back.

"I felt like that after our conversation on the train. I thought I would find myself on the trail to enlightenment—that it was some kind of prophecy, and you were its messenger. Instead, I flailed around, hiding out in McDonald's to nod and smile at other guilty Americans, all of us checking the Rodin Museum off our list." I hesitate, wondering whether I can embrace that prickly path of honesty. "I hadn't even been reading *The Razor's Edge*, you know. I just grabbed it because I was embarrassed by my guidebook. So your interest in me is based on a lie, I guess."

I can't look at him, surprised by my level of shame. It's just a goddamn book.

Yet I had the gall to preach to him, and poor Delacroix, about authenticity.

"Do you think that is why I was interested in you?" he asks, stopping me abruptly. We are at the entrance to the Gardens. His eyes are intense, and I cannot look into them without my own wavering. His grip on me is firm, almost punishing.

"Wasn't it?" I ask. I remember the disinterest, the quiet amusement, until I pushed my book at him. Oh yes, it was deliberate. I knew what made Mathieu tick. Words, words, the splendor of words, written down and relayed to him through wormholes in time. Words that he can tongue, and swallow, and absorb, making them his own. I sized him up within a wink and judged him so presciently that I am not a little proud of myself.

"I was studying you, Daisy. I feigned indifference because your directness disoriented me. I sought my refuge in that calculated detachment. My ego demanded it." He smiles and touches my cheek. "You know nothing about men. We do not need literature to make us interested. Your manner, a little bewildered, and the angle at which your head tilted upon that graceful neck, was enough to make me think of you all the way home, while I slept, upon my awakening, and through the rest of my day. I wanted to know what put the wounded look in those eyes so that I could release you from it. The book was just kindling to the fire. You seeped into my dreams, Daisy, and when I wrote that night, something of your spirit danced on the page."

Checkmate.

Our eyes shine. His mouth is soft and pliant, his words warm and restorative. I knew it: he writes.

"You were a muse that day. My secret. When I saw you again, I had to stop myself from embracing you. I felt like we already owned each other. You had lingered in my imagination until your story grew and wrapped itself around me."

Am I happy being owned? Do I care?

He kisses me.

No, I don't care.

Our lips craft poems. My body curving around his arms. His hands tracing the small of my back, awakening the flesh on the right side of my body, like an avalanche released by a bird's tiptoe. Sinking, sinking. The light pressure of his mouth, so tender it's almost chaste, upon my parted lips. My fingers doing idle things with his hair. When will I land? If I land.

Our eyes are open, and I am struck by the fierceness of his gaze, the commitment of it, like he's willing himself to me. We

Sarah Hina

part reluctantly, but with the shivery knowledge that this is still prelude. We may take our time. Those arms of anticipation are the softest, and safest, refuge for two injured searchers.

And so we enter Luxembourg Gardens like it's our private Eden, for surely we are creatures newly born to the world. The rapid-fire creation of a divinity who whispers in our ears, and whom we exalt with our voices, celebrate with our bodies, and, lastly, sing his praises with secret, knowing smiles that nearly resemble that inward, ecstatic state of a Buddha's nirvana.

Chapter 9

We promenade. We amble. We stroll down wide paths hugged by two rows of chestnut trees, whose clinging leaves quiver with the breath of fall, delighting in the warm day, our melting hands, and the fanatical discipline of the Paris style, extended in every architectural line, from the dome of the grand palace to the manicured bushes circling the statuary. On other days, this obsessive quest for precision might be exasperating, but today it is merely as perfect as we feel. We barely notice the shadows of lesser mortals accompanying us, except for their momentary blocking of the sun lifted high upon our shoulders. The day is starting to sweat, and glow.

We talk about my family, and they feel far away. Not in a wistful, longing kind of way, but forgotten, like relatives long dead, whose links of attachment have been sawed through by the filing of time's dull, but steady, instrument. I tell Mathieu this, only slightly troubled about my descent into egoism. He smiles and points to my American guilt. I tell him, very earnestly, that I don't feel guilty about my estrangement, but that I am starting to feel guilty that I don't feel guilty about it. He explodes in laughter, and a poodlish woman passing by sniffs in disapproval. But I'm serious.

The Gardens are draped with people sucking the balm from the day. Small, wide-eyed *enfants* watch, with an attentiveness reserved for Barney back home, fantastical puppet theaters, while others leisurely push sailboats off the edge of the fountain, sending forth a tiny French armada. They seem merry, if a little sedate, compared to American beasties. I ask Mathieu about this. He explains that kids are not coddled here, that parents prioritize their own desires above their children's. This seems a severe assessment. I see plenty of mothers smiling indulgently at their kids' exploits, waving to them at every pass of the nearby carousel. But the children do seem a trifle self-contained, making me wonder if in America, the home of rugged individualism, we are ironically training our kids to be excessively dependent. I think back to my childhood and how judiciously my life was mapped out, from play dates to piano lessons, from soccer practice to space camp. I never questioned it; children don't. My life was as predictable as Irene's, the time measured in increments of "you have to" and "think about the future" rather than in slices of meat loaf or spins of *Wheel of Fortune*. Irene picks up other people's junk to throw a wrench in the routine. I picked up someone else's career.

My father wanted me to major in American literature, while my mother never abandoned her hopes for a musical prodigy. Parenthood seems like such a pathetic plea for second chances. But I spun off their axis and flew a different trajectory: into the cool world of clinical science, where detachment and patience are prized virtues and recklessness is a prescription for disaster. I convinced myself of my own rebellion. I wanted to believe that it was my choice. Yet I've been poisoning myself with more protocol, too preoccupied to notice that I was sick.

Until now. I finally have the proper perspective to observe

the delusion. Perhaps I needed to unhinge myself from the yoke of expectations—my family's, Andy's, and my own—to acquire true objectivity. Cleveland Daisy looks small from here, like an ant marching in a line that circles America. Mathieu has freed my passion, and I savor this new sensation of sailing it as breezily and buoyantly as the boys' and girls' boats along the rippling water, in a journey where the end always beckons beyond the flat horizon. I have found the freedom to live in this moment of time. I forget my guilt and usher my family back into the shadows, enjoying the sunlight on my freed hair and the haphazard way Mathieu kicks a pebble so that it is always just ahead.

He stops me to watch some older gentlemen play a popular game, with iron balls, called *pétanque*, under the trees. They are grave, and we mime their solemnity, standing at a respectful distance. One has a black sweep of mustache and a white mania of hair like the funny Einstein. A steel coat rack stands behind him, coatless today. Another nod toward order and propriety: I don't recall seeing coat racks in Central Park. Of course, they would be stolen. Monsieur Einstein rubs the ball with his sweater and predicts the physics of the situation, mumbling to himself. He crouches and wings the weight forward. It crashes into the crunchy pebbles before halting next to a small green ball, whose meaning is mysterious to me. Everyone bursts into exclamations, and Mathieu applauds. Monsieur Einstein used the right formula.

"My father loves this game," Mathieu says. "He used to play on Saturdays."

"But they're all so old," I whisper, not very tactfully. The youngest appears to be in his mid-sixties; the oldest, a man with a caved-in mouth and disappointed eyes, could be eighty, or a hundred.

Mathieu shrugs. "Yes, well, my father is eighty-six, so he fit in perfectly."

This startles me. My maternal grandfather is seventy-nine.

"So he must have been, what, sixty when you were born?"

Mathieu directs me away from the action and nods. "About."

Our steps are more measured now. "How old was your mom when she had your oldest sister?" I'm fishing, but this is curious.

"She must have been twenty-two," he answers, after a slight pause.

"My age," I muse. I try to imagine having a baby at my puppyish age, followed by three more in quick succession. All with a senior citizen. Bile surges to the back of my throat. I start to sympathize, a little, with Mathieu's mother. "How did they meet?"

Mathieu smiles wryly. "She was a performer in a revue. And he was her most dedicated admirer." He glances over at a couple necking on a bench and looks away. "My father never missed a show when she was in the city."

"What kind of performances?" It sounds like an improbable, dated existence. The real Moulin Rouge.

He releases my hand, the first indication that I have traversed too far. "She was a dancer. A Gypsy: La Esmeralda, for the modern age. But without the romance. Reckless, beautiful, a child in many ways. She performed as the mythic female: Delilah, Scheherazaude, Cleopatra. Any ploy to make her nudity more titillating for jaded men like my father, who were disappointed by earthly love but felt their age, positions, and money entitled them to impose on these young dancers. The girls' livelihoods depended on making the men feel appreciated, never pathetic, and even loved. Of course, it was all a lie." He pauses, and I am surprised by his vinegary contempt after all these years. In spite of everything, Mathieu is protective of his mother.

He shoots me a small smile to soften the vitriol, but continues. "She saw through him. He was enraptured, but not able to separate the lost girl from the disguises she assumed. So he pursued her. She resisted, unwilling to sell her youth for the cold comfort of a coin in her hand and an old man in her bed. But she weakened with time, with the bribes and promises." Mathieu's lip twitches. "The life of the vagabond is hard. And that bed, bought with my father's considerable government income, was so fucking soft."

He tames the lip, and the voice. "She chose the safe route. Most people would have. She bound herself to a husband and, eventually, to kids she never wanted."

He stops, spent.

"And resumed the life of the vagabond after all," I say.

He nods. Tentatively, I touch his hand. This is a man still in grief for his mother. A draft will keel him over.

We have arrived at the Medici Fountain, an idyllic spot on the outskirts of the Gardens that, in spite of its popularity, feels like a lovely secret. It is the only place in Paris permitted to run a little wild. The trees are many, their unpruned branches a leafy canopy. It's Love's cathedral—the gurgling water our organ music. Fashioned to resemble a grotto, the face of the fountain is punctuated by allegorical figures, the slow trickle of water cascading past the two lovers rendered in white marble—a man, not long past youth, tenderly cradling an exquisite, smiling girl—before flowing into a reflecting pool of black calm. Half-dead geraniums fill the magnificent urns spaced evenly around the rectangular perimeter. The sound of the water is soothing, if sad, like a sudden reminder of the hugeness of time, hurtling toward infinity . . . of my small place within its gathering body.

When I came here by myself, I only saw the lovers' rapturous embrace, their gorgeous white relief, and felt my loneliness keenly. Now, with Mathieu, lost in recollection by my side, I am struck by the grotesquely large Cyclops-like figure, in dark weathered bronze, suspended over the lovers. I sense the vulnerability in their fragile lovelock. The whispering water may echo their bliss but also warns of their destruction. For their love is as soft and supple as their glance, and like anything worth having, imminently destructible.

One cannot look at them without thinking of their end.

Mathieu looks into the fountain, his hand lifeless in my own. A sobering heaviness descends, and I feel the first dangerous pull of commitment to improving someone else's happiness. It has been too easy. We simply invented joy, like the stuff was as plentiful and cheap as oxygen, recycling it through a delicate membrane yet to be toughened by experience. My golden hour by the hotel window returns to me, that vivid dream I claimed as a new reality. I cannot say, with Mathieu here, which incarnation of myself— the love-struck romantic or the inviolate, autonomous force of nature—feels more like the truth. His hand, tucked like an obligation within my own, is too near, and already precious. There is no choice but to squeeze it harder . . . and try to bring a smile back to those lips, pebbled with bitterness.

"I have a joke."

I didn't say it would be subtle.

Mathieu glances over and raises an eyebrow, which I translate as mute permission.

"It's not very funny," I warn, my heart thudding queerly.

He sinks into an iron chair and spreads out his hands. "I am listening."

This is a bad idea. But . . . "How many Frenchmen does it take to screw in a lightbulb?"

"I could not say."

Ah, what is this? Success already! He smiles, a gorgeous lifting. A little thrill of victory courses through me, granting courage.

"One. He just stands there, and all of Europe revolves around him."

Mathieu chews on this, looking skeptically at an urn, before raising his eyes to my face. "That is awful, Daisy."

I laugh and fling myself into the chair next to his. "I know. I heard it on a late-night comedy show. This comic did an entire five minutes just on the French. That was the mildest joke of the bunch. And the funniest."

"Five minutes, you say? I should be honored, yes?" He clasps his hands together and slides into reflection. "I think that funny man needs new jokes."

"Okay, so how about this one? Irene told it to me one day at work." He has no idea who Irene is, or what I do at work, but you don't need a lot of backstory to do comedy. "Two muffins are in an oven. The first muffin says, 'Whew! It's really getting hot in here, don't you think?' And the second muffin jumps and screams, 'Aaauuugghhh! A talking muffin!'"

I throw myself into the part, channeling Stanislavski, and attracting the attention of the dozen people admiring the fountain. Mathieu merely looks startled and doesn't laugh. I conclude, a little sadly, that there is a cultural barrier in doing comedy. Except for Jerry Lewis and Woody Allen, who managed to break through in France (and what, besides their Jewishness, is the strange connector there?). I had a belly laugh when Irene told that joke to me. Of course, it could have been Irene telling it. I really believed she was a muffin.

"It makes no sense," Mathieu complains. "The second muffin is also conversing."

"But that's the joke!"

"Hmm . . . it is peculiar in its simplicity."

"Yes, well, Americans like simplicity." I throw my hands in the air and slump backward. "Farts and burps, and talking muffins: that's us."

Mathieu brightens, scooting his chair to where our knees touch. "Now I have a joke. It is an old one, but quite humorous."

Oh, goodie.

"Sartre sits in a café, frantically revising *Being and Nothingness*. He tells the waitress he wants coffee with sugar, but no cream."

Mathieu makes a slicing gesture with his hand, and I smile reflexively. "The waitress replies, 'I'm sorry, *monsieur*, but we are out of cream—how about with no milk?'"

Wait a beat . . . .

He looks expectant, a smile parading around the corners of his face. Oh, Lord, Sartre was an existentialist, right? And what is it that they *do*?

"Mathieu?" a voice chimes.

God is a devil, tempting us with promiscuous fruit. A gorgeous Mediterranean woman with breasts Delacroix would have immortalized stands before us, batting equally obscene eyelashes. I fold my arms over my pubescent nubs and fall back, bowing to the greater authority of her C cups. Mathieu looks flustered and glances over at me, then at the divine creature, whose chestnut tresses (she is the reason clichés exist) are backlit by a spear of sunlight the heavens have indulgently thrown down, then at me again. He must be thinking, as I am, that it is marvelous her skin should glow from within, like Vermeer's little milkmaids'. How fetchingly distracted she appears when her fingers trespass into the shadow above her cleavage, straining against a blouse that is one hardworking button away from inciting all assembled males to cast aside earthly things and bow down in worship. Yes, Mathieu's thinking this. The poor fool blushes and stammers like a schoolboy caught with his hand down his pants.

She talks to Mathieu in French and with that more intelligible body, ignoring me. Laughing throatily from time to time, her face erupts in dimples that seem charmingly at odds with her sophisticated appearance. Mathieu has risen and is all elbows as he runs a hand through his hair. The goddess licks her lips. Mathieu licks his. The goddess trails her fingers down the lily of her neck, arriving at the kissable hollow of her throat. Mathieu's eyes follow. The goddess smiles, revealing a gap between two front teeth, a requisite imperfection that makes her all the more beguiling. Mathieu shifts painfully from one foot to another. The goddess is breaking my heart.

Finally, my appearance is noted. Something should be done for the mouse worrying her whiskers at Mathieu's elbow. He motions toward me, and the goddess glances down, with mild curiosity. I scurry to my feet.

"Daisy, this is Camille Velay. We are old friends."

"*Enchantée*," she says, extending a hand while looking at my caterpillar eyebrows. Hers are like delicate parentheses. I limply shake her hand. *Enchanted*.

"You are American, no?"

"Yes," I answer, smiling humorlessly. If I hadn't told that stupid joke, I bet she never would have looked over. Thanks, Irene. I'll bring you home a souvenir of this humiliation.

"I love your country. Everyone is so pleasant to me. I am afraid to frown," she says, her giggles mixing musically with the gurgles of the water.

Crap, she's nice. I wanted an excuse to hate her. Something beside her looks, which might make me mean and small. I suppose I should say something equally *nice* now. Her inviting green eyes demand it. "Yes, most people are very nice in America." I should let it go, but, "Niceness is like a nervous condition there. It has a way of masking our other syndromes." Stop it, Daisy. "In fact, some of us can't help but smile, even through our tears."

Said grinning like a fool, of course.

Camille's expression stumbles as she looks to Mathieu for instruction. He laughs uncertainly and translates something for her. I don't know what I said. This is a situation for which I have no training. How might a mortal do battle with a goddess? Again, I'm sure the Greeks, and Mathieu, and Woody Allen would know.

Camille laughs politely and says, "I am sorry. My English

is not very good. I have a summer in Boston for cello internship many years ago, but I forget much."

She plays the cello. My favorite instrument. Probably studied at Juilliard. Surrendering Mathieu, I sigh, "Your English is very good. It is my French that is so very bad."

She laughs again, and demurs.

I think *I'm* beginning to fall in love with her. Clearly she, and not I, is the modern incarnation of the woman on the fountain, worthy of Mathieu's—I mean, our hero's—encircling arms. Which means that I'm the one-eyed monster hanging over them.

"I have to go. Julie waits." She slips into a few words of French and leans forward to kiss Mathieu on the cheeks. I squirm, despising this custom when it does not involve Mathieu's lips and my cheeks. She lingers on the last cheek, his right (my favorite too, as it holds a tiny scar on its outer rim whose origin I mean to plumb), and looks meaningfully into his eyes as they part. She tells me that it was "a pleasure" and brushes my cheeks with her lips. She smells like you'd expect a goddess to smell, the perfume succulent and mysterious, like a spicy ambrosia. She turns and departs, her ass really working in that slim ivory skirt. We watch her leave. She turns, smiles, and waves once.

And then she's gone.

I turn to Mathieu, who seems shaken. His hands are jawed into his pants pockets, affecting a casual interpretation of the event. He looks past me and says, "That was Camille." I am reminded of the guy on the plane. Master of the obvious.

"So I gathered."

"She is an old friend," he repeats, flatly. A boyish cowlick has been aroused on the crown of his head, which might be cute were it not for its resemblance to another manifestation of boyish excitement.

"I don't have friends who look like that," I mumble, slumping in my chair.

He takes his seat. "Few do."

I worry at my nails. The birds ply my ears with their final trills of the season, but their verdant slingshots bounce off my pea-green heart. Everything feels borrowed from someone else's dreams. Was it an hour ago that Mathieu kissed me, and I swooned? A half hour ago that we watched, like an old married couple, those sweet men play their game? Ten minutes ago that he laughed himself from the shadows? Now he is removed, traveling beyond the ghosts of the past, swinging in some plane of possibility, where the vision in white dances seductively, leaving me to this solitary shuffle by his side.

Of course Andy found someone else. Of course.

I feel myself slipping away.

"She is gay, you know."

Pause.

"What?"

Maybe he means *gay* like "happy."

"Camille is a lesbian," Mathieu says. He is serene, but very real.

"I don't believe you," I answer, equally calm. We are such adults.

"She is. It made us crazy back in school, but she knew then too."

"So she is a friend from school?" He hadn't mentioned this while she was here.

"Mmm. More of an acquaintance. She did not socialize much with the boys. We could not hold her interest," he says, flashing me an impish smile.

"Mathieu, that woman is not a lesbian. They don't make lesbians who look like that," I argue, throwing out my hands in disgust. Dumb logic, I know—egregious, backward thinking—but I saw how she looked at him. Why would he lie if he didn't have something to hide?

"Maybe not in America. They are—what is the expression?— a dime a dozen in France." His hand shields his eyes, for that sliver of sun has swung round to us, trolling for the departed angel, settling for Mathieu. "Many are bisexuals. But not Camille. She has the courage of her convictions."

I cross my legs impatiently. My reaction to her was almost sexual, though I am not gay, in either derivation of the word. Perhaps I did pick up on something from her. More likely, she is one of those rare individuals who transcends sexual boundaries, each gesture so sensual that she stirs and invents new, imaginative pots.

Camille is Venus on the waves. Without the bloody cherubs.

"But why were you so taken aback by her appearance? You looked stupefied."

Mathieu raises a hand from his eyes to squint over at me. "Is it not obvious?"

I shake my head.

He blindfolds himself again. "I was afraid she would hit on you."

I lean back my head and laugh liberally. "You are full of it, you know," I finally say, tears trickling down my cheeks.

He smiles. "Full of what?"

"*It.*"

Mathieu grabs my hand and pulls me on his lap. We are friends again. I don't know if I believe him, but the leap of faith is already taken. And faith is not reasonable.

It is only later, after recovering from kisses rained on earlobes and eyelids, while we flee our Garden in search of food, that I wonder how Mathieu adopts the American vernacular so well. Dime a dozen. Courage of her convictions. His English is almost better than mine. While Camille, who spent months in Boston, could not pin down a past tense verb if the smattering of adorable freckles under her eyes depended on it.

I'd like to think it's because Camille is dumb, and Mathieu brilliant. I'd like for things to be that simple, and to my benefit. But acquiring a new language is not rocket science. It just takes time and practice. Lots and lots of practice, around native speakers. Yet he has never mentioned spending time in America. Indeed, the image of Mathieu in America seems jammed, like trying to imagine George Bush reading Sartre.

When I look at Mathieu from the corner of my eye as we head down Rue de Écoles, I see someone I could walk with for all time. Nothing in his demeanor suggests otherwise from him. It is a heightened state we enjoy.

And yet, when I steal an uneasy glance back at our fair Eden, it already seems a bit spoiled, even—dare I say—fallen.

A little knowledge can be a dangerous thing.

Chapter 10

The roads and alleyways of Paris are designed for getting lost. Which is a fine thing if you don't have anywhere to be.

We retrace our steps to St. Sulpice, and, uncertain, linger in the cathedral's square. A gaggle of pigeons argue for food and wash their wings in the water of the square fountain, where four holy men are enthroned like grand inquisitors, before relieving themselves on the disciples' holy vestments. It is an unimpeachable fact of life that it is hard to maintain one's dignity, religious or otherwise, with bird shit on your head, and what I gather to be a petrified Sulpice looks understandably sullen. But this fountain of his is a great spot for people- and pigeon-watching, as tourists flock toward the church and natives grab a bite to eat on a park bench. Their unleashed kids chase the wary birds in games of chicken and hurl coins into the fountain with all the grace of miniature shot-putters.

Somehow I want people, and quarreling birds, around us right now. Mathieu scowls toward a corner café, murmuring darkly in French. It is nearly one o'clock, and the tables outside are stuffed with customers feasting on the mild weather.

"Do you want to try it?" I ask. I was too nervous to eat this morning and am hungrier than I'd care to admit (even the airy exercise of falling in love requires stamina and calories).

"It is not a place I care for," he hedges. "The tourists come to this place where Hemingway wrote, not knowing that five cafés in this *quartier* boast the same claim."

"Hemingway wrote there?" I ask, straining my neck toward the café. *A Farewell to Arms* is one of my favorite books.

Mathieu smiles. "See? It works every time."

"Well, so? I'd actually like to check out the Café Flore, or Les Deux Magots," I say, pronouncing *Magots* (rhymes with Margot) as Maggots (the larvae that gorge on dead flesh), while eyeing him for outward signs of disapproval. Not a wince in sight. Satisfied, I continue, "To sit and eat at the same spot where all those renowned writers worked—what's not to like about it?"

He scuffs his shoes on the cobblestone. "Yes, but Daisy, they are no longer there. Just little plaques that might say, 'Hemingway, probably drunk, spilled his café crème at this table,' or, 'This is the bathroom where Simone de Beauvoir took a really good crap.'" This is not the way to memorialize giants. It degrades them into tourist attractions, and only cheapens their legacies."

I plunk myself on the fountain's edge, cross my legs, and lean back on my palms, playfully pointing my foot at him. "I think you have a problem with famous places. It offends your idea of authenticity. You would have loved to be seen at the Café Flore at one time, but now that everyone else wants to go there, it's *très gauche*. You can't stand to be part of the herd, even if your instincts point you in that direction. Face it, Mathieu: you are a snob among snobs."

He furrows his brow in protest.

"Not a snob," he replies. Standing, he searches the stippled water behind me. "Perhaps suspicious of people's motivations. I have too much respect for the writers and thinkers who debated and wrote in those places, and for *what* was written, to let any fool come in and treat it like a photo opportunity. Those places were cathedrals devoted to the avant-garde, and there are many of us who still worship the ideas that flowed like honey through them."

I allow my foot to fall and sit at a more respectful attention. When he gets worked up, I experience a flurry in my chest, like something is singing.

"So many of the French surrealists and existentialists, as well as your American expatriates, invented modernity inside those modest cafés, where a struggling writer could drink beer and suck on inspiration, then write until his pen or endurance failed him. I think of your Hemingway scratching out *The Sun Also Rises,* that first lean novel, in six weeks at La Closerie des Lilas, poor as a mouse and happier than he will be again. I think of Sartre and Beauvoir living at the Flore, warming their toes near the mean heater, and jousting with the friends who called on them there, but, when the time was ripe, working like dogs in heat as they penned their manifestos, before stumbling home to fuck and write some more.

"Do you know," he exclaims, his face suffused with such admiration for people I know nothing about that I suffer pangs of exclusion and awe, "that Sartre called his Flore the 'Road to Freedom' during the Occupation, for it shone brightly as a beacon of enlightened thought during fascism's darkest hour, when this City of Light was as black as a starless sky?" He shakes his head, a little embarrassed by the openness of his ardor, and relaxes his hands out of fists, before sitting down.

I rest my leg against his.

"And so, for me, these places meant more than every grand building and monument in Paris, including this one," he says, waving a dismissive hand toward St. Sulpice. "But now those cafés are as contrived as neon churches, where the only ambition left is for the money to be milked from their reputations, so that you can pay three euros to take coffee and breathe the air of ghosts. The people who go there are looking for celebrities, Daisy. Me"—he breaks off to look over, with glittering eyes—"I would rather pay homage to those places by reading the books that were written there, and remember their authors that way."

He shrugs and rubs at the back of his neck in an effort to moderate himself. "So I guess I am a snob, yes. But a snob with good intentions."

We sit silently, though my ears roar with Mathieu's words. There is no greater aphrodisiac than loving someone in love with ideas. When Mathieu talks, I am transported into a world where thoughts matter as much as, if not more than, deeds. I have been starving on the easy, empty calories of perpetual action, which have left me, along with my countrymen, fat and sluggish in mind and spirit. When I'm with Mathieu, I don't eat; I savor.

But there is one matter at odds with his character, at least with my beginner's understanding of it, and the inconsistency sticks like a thorn in my mouth. I turn and ask him, "Is this why you're a tour guide? You cannot stand for anyone not to know what you know about these places?"

Mathieu sighs and looks away, deflated by my characterization. "I do not know why I am a tour guide. It was never something I planned. I fell into it while trying to make enough money to write. My mother sent an American friend to Paris with instructions that I show him around, and when he went home, he gave others my name. So *voilà*," he smacks his hands together, startling me, "I become a tour guide with a real distaste for the upper level of the Eiffel Tower and the tourists I must take there."

"Especially young American women who have never read Sartre?"

He rolls his eyes in mock dismay at my admission before throwing an arm about my shoulders to dip me toward the fountain.

Licking the beads of water off my laughing lips, my hair a wet fringe, I shriek at the upside-down saint, who juts his chin out in defense of his importance. "I will never take you to the Eiffel Tower," he promises, as my skin hangs past my cheeks.

I try to flex forward, but he has all the advantage, holding me prone like a rag doll. "But for not laughing at my Sartre joke, I condemn you to my recitation of his play, *No Exit*, in French, *mais oui*, some night soon, as you lie naked on my bed"—he raises an eyebrow to seductive heights and licks the spray from his lips, while a giggle gets caught in the tunnel of my throat—"looking precisely like Manet's little Olympia, as you contemplate Sartre's hypothesis of hell as other people."

Mathieu has me pinned. His eyes laugh into mine, and I squirm agreeably, content to be contained. Encouraged, he moves to kiss me. But as he relaxes his grip on the wrists behind my back, I spring nimbly from him, delighting in his clumsy fall toward the fountain. He barely catches hold of the edge before being pitched into the cold water. If I cannot surprise him in matters of the mind, where his experience is oceanic, I can still keep him off balance.

He curses in French (he falls back on his native dialect for effusions of love and vulgarity; perhaps when he's most authentic?) and glares at me, but I laugh at him and dance away. I run toward the cathedral, nailed into place by two bell towers, of which one is taller and showier than the other. I briefly wonder which one I am, and which one is Mathieu. But any whimsy is lashed away by Mathieu's footsteps and voice, imbuing my name with the French intonation, so that it sounds inquisitive and promising. *Day-Zee? Arrêt, Day-Zee!* I smile, trying to suppress a gurgle of laughter, and go faster, relishing the movement of my legs and the slapping of my feet on the old stone, affronting, in equal measure, spotty gatherings of pigeons and Japanese tourists, both of whom squawk at me in strange, otherworldly tongues. Gathering momentum, I fly toward the steps of the great cathedral, which I must reach before Mathieu, just beyond my shoulder, reaches out and snags me. Charging the steps, preserving myself as a blur in a couple's honeymoon photo, I take them three at a time before darting between the columns and launching myself through the heavy wooden doors that are, auspiciously, parted.

Breathlessly, I enter the cathedral and, slowing, turn right. I clamp a hand over my mouth in reaction to the looks lobbed my way but am unable to contain my giddiness, which, like anything under enormous pressure, explodes in inappropriate laughter as I slide swiftly along the back wall. Here is a small chapel swirling with Delacroix's murals, depicting a conclave of souls in a fury of tumult and torment. Losing my giggles, I linger over an effete angel wrestling, or doing a mean tango, with a muscle-bound man wearing leg warmers, when I feel a hand clamp down on my shoulder and wheel me around. Caught, I can only squeal out, "Sanctuary!" as I confront Mathieu's mouth, pressed fiercely against my laughing lips. I gasp into his kiss, slowly sinking into stone. But as his body relaxes, I hastily plant my lips over the scar on his cheek, ducking and dodging from those angel arms like a fleet flyweight, before dashing toward the side aisle.

I step urgently, him hissing my name in pursuit. I like the skeletal restraint imposed on us by the sacred stones. The chase is the thing, yet there should be consequences. The line is blurred. I want to see how far we can take it.

The heat of Mathieu's eyes on my neck enflames my madness. He reaches out and flips my wet hair. I flick it back. I can sense him recoil, and falter, before picking up the pursuit anew. He steps on the backs of my shoes, but little does he know (wearing those expensive-looking leather things) how one relies on Keds to slip on as readily as slippers. He tries feebly for my hand, but I shake him loose. I am young in flesh and blood, and I have a child's profane irreverence for the law of this house. Even Jesus up there, suffering for me on his eternal cross, cannot dam the wicked flow of mirth in my heart. I want Mathieu to hunt me until the end of time, so that we can, like the Hindus, create new cycles.

I run out of church. Confronting a barrier that points me to the pulpit, I move into that painful heart of a church and stop. Mathieu bumps into me in surprise. I look back at him and smile weakly. We stand in the middle of the transept, caught in the crucifix. Silently, we turn and regard the massive wooden organ at the rear of the church, with its tight fractals of pipes protected by dark angels. The organ is monumental, the biggest I've seen, so imposing that my ears instinctively cringe for the cacophony that must engulf this house of God during Sunday mass. How those unworldly notes ricocheting off the floating domes must storm the transept, before reverberating down, down into the smallest artery of the smallest worshipper's malleable tongue, commanding—like a father's grip—the rebellious blood flowing within to deliver the right words, with reverence. What a grand, and terrifying, magnification of a man's touch on a pedal, his pushing the right keys. I strain for the swell, knowing it won't come, but my ear, with its alerted machinery, cannot help but listen. It is deathly quiet. There is an uneasy dissonance: the expectation of sound slamming a hard silence. The flickering flame of my exuberance cannot survive this vacuum. A cold hole opens, and a memory surfaces.

There are wooden chairs, not pews, set up in rows throughout the nave, and I sit down, the chair rubbing harshly against the stone. Mathieu follows suit. There are half a dozen people scattered about, hands clasped in prayer, heads bowed, shaming my earlier exuberance. The remaining chairs are empty, some slightly askew, as if abandoned, en masse, by the secular citizens of this modern France. I finally turn toward Mathieu, who looks at me with some curiosity.

"You caught me," I whisper, trying to recapture our playfulness.

"Did I?" he asks, not fooled.

"Didn't you?"

"Something did."

"Yes, something." I place my chin in my hands' cradle. "Funny, huh?"

"What?"

"How churches make you feel like you're already dead."

He glances at the dogma of stonework and statuary. "I feel nothing."

"Really?" I ask, only a little surprised.

"No. But you do."

I nod. Who was that girl who wore laughter for wings? She has been clipped by the absent voices of a terrible superstition. "I just remembered something that I haven't thought of in years."

"Tell me."

I wave him off, embarrassed. "It's irrelevant . . . silly."

"I like silly irrelevance."

I smile, hesitating.

"Will it help if I promise to tell you something equally silly and irrelevant when you are finished?"

I laugh. "Okay." Taking a deep breath, I organize my thoughts. My eyes take solace in the half arches of natural light spilling from the generous windows that try mightily to brighten this darkened space. "When I was really little, I hated visiting airplane hangars." This is not an auspicious start. Compared to Mathieu's eloquence, the line is a letdown, my voice pinched and strange.

Daisy, just say what you want to say. Your essays always read like you're lifting a page from your father. Think for yourself, honey.

I clear my throat and try harder. "We lived near Dayton, a city famous for its Air Force base and not much else. But it had a great air and space museum, one of the best in the country.

Well, my dad loved to go, so we went often. My mom favored the astronaut displays, as most people did, because they were the more romantic—you know, man's heroic nature, the undiscovered country, all that *Star Trek* stuff. But not my dad. He went in for the old-timey displays: those rickety planes used in World War I with their funny nicknames and strange, savage caricatures. He'd stroke their frames, examine the slightest details, moving his hands over the rivets, like he had invented the damn things in some past life. I think he imagined himself as the Red Baron at times." Tears spring to my eyes. I shake my head, but Mathieu nods, and I gather myself.

"But me—I couldn't stand going. It undid me to be standing there, all of three feet tall, flanked by those enormous airplanes, hanging from ropes above me, spanning the length of football fields beside me. It was too overwhelming for a four-year-old pursued by this wild imagination. Put me in a real cemetery during daytime, and I would do fine. I knew what that was about. But I could not bear the emptiness of that huge space filled with dead machines." I shake my head at the absurdity of where I'm going, but soldier on, Mathieu's silence being of the encouraging sort. "I always had nightmares about walking through that place by myself at night, though I never told my parents. I suppose I was a little ashamed of myself. It seemed so silly, even then. Most kids dreamed about monsters. I was undone by an airplane graveyard." I breathe out. "But I couldn't escape the fact that the place provoked a kind of cold terror inside me."

"And this place? It gives you the same creeps."

I flash him a self-conscious look. "Crazy, I know."

"Not so crazy."

"The weird part is that I was never anything but a casual Christian. My mom is basically an agnostic, now, and my dad a lapsed Episcopalian. I went to church a few dozen times growing up, never really understanding what it was about, but still feeling the enormous power of these rituals and words. I mean—*the body and blood of Christ*—tell that to a kid once, and she will never look at her parents the same way again."

"Her parents?" he asks, frowning.

"For making her go up and be a party to that. Parents don't explain things—they just assume kids aren't paying attention. But I was. I thought I was literally eating the flesh of Jesus Christ, and drinking his blood . . . that the reverend up there had worked a magic trick with the little wafers that dissolved like cotton candy in my mouth. I mean, he even whispered it to me before putting the pretty silver cup to my lips. I was mortified by his words, but I always went through with it. Afterward, I couldn't get the taste out of my mouth. It tasted metallic to me, exactly like blood. I'd go home and brush my teeth to get rid of the taste. Even to this day, when I drink wine, I have this strange sacrilegious sensation of getting drunk on Jesus' blood. Andy bought me a nice bottle of red for my twenty-first birthday, and I couldn't drink the stuff."

Mathieu hides a smile with his finger, before saying, "It is a good thing you were not brought up Catholic. You would be a complete mess."

I lean my shoulder into him. "Easy for you to say. Does anyone in France believe in God anymore?"

"Nobody I know admits to it." He pauses. "Perhaps it is why we are so unhappy."

"Are you so unhappy?"

He tents his fingers and leans back. "We can be a little morose from time to time. It is the logical extension of not believing in an afterlife. You Americans can, as you say, 'smile through your tears' because you think your suffering is temporary: a kind of grand test from the Almighty. We French know it is cruel and random, that we are 'being-unto-death,' as Heidegger would say, before falling into oblivion."

I groan. "That sounds awful."

"Yes, it does. Why do you think Conrad called it *the horror*?" Mathieu shrugs and wipes at his thigh. "We are born clinging to life, and for most, that means ignoring death, or packaging death in such a way that we are lulled into complacency by myths and legends, like naïve children. But there is a third way, which sounds, to me, more like the truth you honor than any of this." He waves his hand contemptuously, before centering it on his breast and looking at me. "And that is to acknowledge that this life is all we have. *This* is my religion, and I am passionate about it."

I consider, chewing on the inside of my lip. "I know that what you say is entirely rational. It does sound like a fairy tale, and a rather vicious one at that." Eyeing the crucifix on the wall to my right, I sit a little straighter. Jesus' mournful, martyred expression is drilled across his strung flesh as a permanent reproach. "But it's a part of my DNA. Even if I don't believe it, I cannot entirely unbelieve it. Which doesn't make me a good Christian"—I sigh—"just a bad atheist."

Mathieu is not the sort to let someone off the hook easily. He licks his lips and charges. "But your little anecdote of two minutes ago demonstrates your true, authentic instinct for atheism."

I frown. "How so?"

"What were you scared of in that airplane graveyard? That the airplanes would come to life and run you down?"

"No, not exactly," I reply, worrying at my fingernails. I find myself hard to explain, the flood of today's emotions sweeping aside analysis. "I don't know what I was scared of," I admit. "That's why it was so scary."

"Exactly so. It was you confronting death for the first time, in a real, if limited, way. It was the awful stillness of those 'dead machines,' the great emptiness you felt by yourself in the darkness. You had the existentialist's perception of the void in front of you. As a four-year-old." Turning his chair sideways, he more aggressively confronts me. "So what happened in between now and then? What was lost along the way? Why did you wear a saint's medal, like a charm, around your neck the first time I saw you, on the train? And why is it that you cannot recognize that the shiver you felt in your spine five minutes ago was not the fear of divine judgment, but the fear of the absence of one?"

I flinch and retreat. He is too strident, too perceptive, too demanding of me. He's calling me out as a hypocrite, of keeping bad faith with myself, when I have tried to be honest. Again, tears reach my eyes, but they are symptoms of anger and pride, and do not fall. I do not look at him, and he makes no move to soften his indictment of me.

After a minute has passed, I observe, "Maybe it was the fear you describe. Very likely, in fact. For it's true: I have more doubt than faith."

I look up at the great domed ceiling, an architectural marvel, and my mind, streaming, turns toward the burning and brilliant minds that brought it to life over the decades. It is a noble, beautiful building they raised, in spite of my religious pathology. Centuries later, I sit inside their inspiration, and I fancy their attendance here, lording over the site of their creation, bound to it like a mother to her child. Would they trifle themselves with the purity of my presence within, or care that I doubt the divinity of their savior? Or would they simply hope that I was awed by their craftsmanship, by their scope? If their faith isn't enough to make me believe in Jesus Christ, their commitment to this *idea* makes me believe in their, and my, larger humanity.

This building is a monument to all creation, and my trepidation has no place within its walls. It is a fear born of a leaden myth that binds us down with burdens too great to cast off in a single life-time, and which tunnels our vision so that all we see in this world is what we *can't* see. But my wonder belongs up there, scaling these forgotten masters' buttresses and lofty domes, and is beholden to a very human act that leaped at transcendence. I smile. They must have felt such pride at its completion.

Mathieu was wrong about the Café Flore. Ghosts exist. Sometimes they even talk.

Stronger now, I say, "Or maybe things aren't so easily broken down into abstractions: faith versus reason, truth versus fiction. I think that we travel in muddier regions of the spectrum. And some of us need our myths to help us find the way."

Mathieu maintains his penetrating gaze. He's like one of the walls surrounding us, yielding nothing.

"I wore that medal because it was a gift from my grandmother, who died last year. She insisted I wear it on trips because St. Christopher is the patron saint of travelers. I wear it mostly for her memory, but yes, I have a silly superstitious belief in it too, and rub it like a rabbit's foot on takeoffs and landings. I'm not a very good traveler, Mathieu, so I can use all the help I can get.

"Sometimes people act upon a weak understanding of prob-ability. 'Okay, I don't have much faith in this, but if I don't do it, nothing will happen, whereas if I do it, something might happen.' It's a muddled way of proceeding, I grant you, but it works for a lot of people, including me, and if it doesn't sound enough like a personal philosophy to you, you can join Jesus up there on his cross," I suggest, jerking my chin toward the Son of God, "because you sound just as sanctimonious as he did, and I'll be pretty well sick of both of you in five minutes."

To my surprise, he laughs, grabbing my hand to kiss it before scooting back his chair. "You are charming like this, Daisy. I want to provoke you more often."

Enjoying my little moment, I pluck my hand away. "Please don't."

Now *he* looks uneasy. Oh, divine justice . . .

Mathieu's eyes flit about, like a moth searching for a flame. He lands upon something, and, stuffing his hands in his pockets, says, "Would you like for me to share my silly, irrelevant anecdote now?"

Hmph.

Mathieu sighs. I admit some interest through the tacit turn of my head. He licks his lips and murmurs, "Please, Daisy. You promised. This is difficult for me."

I allow a slim nod.

He takes a deep breath and declares, "I regret to say that I have never been traumatized by the ghosts of airplanes past—or present, though I cannot speak for the future—or by my parents forcing wine upon me during predictably pious and public brain-washing exercises."

My mouth falls open, but he checks my outrage by slipping to one knee and grasping my hand. "Sorry, Daisy. But I could not resist."

Actually making fun of me. The nerve! I glower at him, and he makes a poor show at staunching his laughter by biting on my knuckles. I withdraw my hands and look pointedly at the forbearing Virgin.

He looks too damn good on that knee.

"But more to the point," he says, struggling to his chair, "did you know, *mademoiselle*, that Victor Hugo was married here in 1862?" He adopts his best tour guide voice.

"Hmm." Though still playing at being miffed, I absorb this bit of trivia and look around the cathedral with increasing curiosity, trying to imagine what kind of bride Victor Hugo had. If she felt intimidated by the grand setting. And the grander man.

Mathieu nods. "Yes, beautiful ceremony," he adds, like he was there. But his voice is strangled, as if he's stifling more laughter. "Of course . . ."

"What?"

"The Marquis de Sade was baptized here too," he says, eyeing his fingernails.

I let this sink in. Victor Hugo and the Marquis de Sade. Like us in this church, it is the perfect mix of the sacred and the profane. The corners of my mouth start to wander.

Mathieu delicately clears his throat. "Do you think it helped the Marquis to wash away that original sin of his?"

"Mmm," I reply, not yet broken.

Suddenly, and with great authority, the bell of the cathedral sounds a single, solemn note. We jolt to attention, the vibrations pulsing through our bodies to their completion. It is gone as quickly as it came. We are quiet in its wake, though my heart echoes its thunder. Mathieu and I continue our forward meditation, but my mouth twitches.

"I don't know."

"You do not know . . . ?" he presses, spilling into a grin.

"Think how much worse things could have been if he *hadn't* been baptized." I shoot him an arch look, and he stares back for a beat.

We break into laughter, the healing kind. We lean in and rest our heads on one another's shoulders, bodies shuddering. I breathe the sharp scent of his shampoo in between convulsions. This is what I want to believe in. The smell of Mathieu's hair. It is enough, for now.

"Come on, let's get out of here," I say, and we jump to our feet, racing down the aisle like a couple of pagans dancing through fire, ignoring the pointed, righteous stares, eager to be on secular ground again.

Once outside, the wind whips up my wet hair, while godless pigeons coo at our feet. Mathieu turns to me and yells, "Admit it. You thought the bell was God."

"Of course not!"

I run down the stairs, leaping off the third from the last to land neatly on one foot. Smiling, I turn with a flourish. Separated by the steps—I looking up, he looking down—we square off.

"Well, maybe," I acknowledge, unembarrassed.

He shakes his head, but he's smiling too.

I jerk my shoulders up and explain, "Maybe God didn't have anywhere else to be just then. You might not know this about me, but I'm awfully important."

"And you are supposedly the scientist?"

I twist and bend to the breeze. "When I want to be."

"And it could not be that the clock was simply sounding one o'clock?"

"At the precise moment I needed a sign? Doubtful."

We crinkle our eyes and grin.

I conclude, "But if that were the case, then God must have known that I was hungry, and tired of all that pretentious conversation."

I bounce up the stairs to claim him. He descends at a leisurely rate, but I tug more insistently until he trips down, laughing in protest. My stomach is growling.

"I mean, Jesus. What does a girl have to do around here to get some lunch?"

Chapter 11

We have found a restaurant that gratifies Mathieu's sense of authenticity and my timid American palate. It is a teahouse called *L'Heure Gourmande* (the Greedy Hour, Mathieu informs me with a wink), tucked up a quiet alleyway. A hinged sign shaped like a teapot welcomes us, and a couple of tables lean drunkenly on the cobblestone. The tables are taken, so we enter and slide into an intimate corner booth backed by textured, gold-washed walls. Above us, in a charming manner that brings the outside indoors, is a recessed ceiling of puffy clouds billowing across the summer sky. I remove my sweater, settling in, and can sense Mathieu checking out my new reveal. Unaccustomed to men admiring me, I casually flaunt my assets, raising my arms to fuss with my damp hair, enjoying the way he ogles the swell of my breasts under my red V-neck while pretending to peer at the menu. I usually feel embarrassed by my limitations, but not today. Daisy Miller, that flirt, has got nothing on me.

I beam at the anonymous faces around me, wondering how their days led them here, bursting to tell them of ours. But there is no need. It should be obvious to anyone who looks that Mathieu and I are only touching down after a morning parade of cloud hopping.

"Are you going to pick out my lunch for me today?" I poke Mathieu, surveying the selections on the menu.

"That depends on what you want to order," he replies. He is all business with a menu before him. There are right foods and wrong foods to be tagged. His snobbishness should annoy me, but somehow it doesn't. It is not the superficial, self-satisfied vanity that I am accustomed to. He is so devoted to his struggle for superior living that I have to respect the quest, and find it endearing.

"What if I wanted this?" I ask, pointing to a quiche with ham and veggies.

"That is fine, if uninspired. I would recommend this entrée instead," he says, drawing my attention to the mezzaluna, a mushroom-stuffed ravioli with cream sauce. "It is appropriate for a beginner."

I am distrustful of any ravioli not stuffed with beef or cheese, and topped by Chef Boyardee's familiar marinara, but decide to humor him. Nodding my assent, I ask, "And wine, I suppose?"

He draws in his lower lip and looks at me. Redirecting his attention toward the menu, he observes, "I would not want you to suffer so."

I blush. "I think I can manage one glass."

Mathieu shakes his head and claps his menu shut. "No, we are at a teahouse. We shall have tea." He motions for the waitress, an efficient, older woman who looks like she may be the owner. She bustles over and raises an attentive eyebrow while Mathieu orders our food. Bestowing a gracious smile, she turns and is swallowed by the swinging doors to the kitchen. Perhaps she cooks the food as well. The restaurant has the feel of a one-woman show, like we've stumbled upon a great-aunt of Mathieu's who will herd us into her sheltering arms. I feel at ease for the first time in Paris.

This lasts twenty-eight seconds.

"So who is Andy?"

I cough.

"What?"

Mathieu plays with a pack of sugar. "You mentioned an Andy trying to get you drunk on your twenty-first birthday."

This elicits no reaction except for a swift succession of blinks on my part. Could I have been so stupid?

"The wine, the guilt . . . surely you remember this," he insists, throwing me a bemused smile.

"Oh, yes, *Andy*." I think rapidly. "I mentioned that I have a brother?"

"I believe you did." Mathieu taps the pack of sugar against the side of the table. "I believe he was a *younger* brother."

The implications of his logic are indisputable. But I swing wildly, anyway. "You're not so naïve as to think that teenagers can't get alcohol in America, are you?"

Mathieu laughs and tosses the sugar to the side. Grabbing hold of my slippery hands, he soothes, "It is all right, Daisy. We do not have to tell each other everything."

I feel foolish, and muddled. This is what happens when you play upon your past: wrinkles in time develop, and all this unconscious stuff is barfed into the present. Why can't I tell him about Andy? It's silly, but . . . "I'm sorry," I plead. "Maybe soon."

Mathieu squeezes my hands. Our hostess emerges with a green ceramic pitcher and a pair of teacups decorated in provincial toile, which she sets down noiselessly. Mathieu pours me a cup. I try to regain my composure while sipping the hot brew, but it burns my tongue, and I clumsily set the cup down, sloshing the contents about. My thumb and fingers are those of a giant. I smile feebly and play with my napkin, dabbing at the brown pool of liquid in the saucer. I usually love a good cup of tea.

But today, the leaves trace a long, bitter memory across the length of my tongue.

"Can I make you some tea?"

"What?" I looked up to see Rakesh, with his flip hairdo and hiker's backpack, braced in the doorway. "Oh, no. No thanks."

"Why are you still here, anyway?" he asked, after setting a kettle on the stove and lighting the gas burner. Rakesh wiped his hands on his pants, walked over, and sank down beside me, the secondhand couch squeaking like a rusty violin. The state government pays for our clients' general upkeep, but not for new furniture.

"Missy wanted me for the evening shift. Debbie called in."

"What was her excuse this time?" Rakesh rolled his eyes.

I smiled. We hadn't talked much before. As an undergrad, he always "worked" the night shift. It was a good trade: he got paid for studying and sleeping, and they got a warm body. "God knows. I think her kid lost his binky."

He laughed. "Sometimes I think she had kids just to get out of work."

I nodded, though my smile faltered. My chin ached.

"Hey, what's wrong?" he asked, placing a hand on my arm. He had brown eyes and very white teeth. They sliced through the darkness.

"My grandmother died last night."

His teeth slipped back under their covers. "Oh, man. That really . . . sucks."

"Yeah."

He kept his hand on my arm, rubbing the thumb back and forth, back and forth. "Were you guys close?"

I thought about this.

My grandmother (she wasn't the Grandma sort) was an elegant, austere woman who probably hated my name as much as

I did. A devotee of etiquette books, she had a library stocked with titles like *Thinking of You: The Art of the Hand-Written Note*, and *Setting a Gracious Table*, in addition to all of Emily Post's ruminations on wedding invitations, place settings, and displaying the flag (hoisted *briskly*, lowered *ceremoniously*—what ghostly italics to impress a young mind). Grandmother was a fundamentalist on these subjects, and like any extremist, did not tolerate dissenters. Propriety pleased her; it structured her life. Take her weekly bridge clubs. These luncheon soirees were an opportunity to shine, to bask in the adulation of her friends' lavish, insincere praise. When I turned twelve, I was allowed to help her serve the tea and tiny, insipid sandwiches. An Orange County Bat Mitzvah.

If Grandmother was a practiced socialite, I was a twelve-year-old debutante scuffing up against puberty, who did not so much transform from a caterpillar to a butterfly through that scripted rite of passage as curl into a mothy cocoon, refusing to show myself. Everything was on the move, but not enough had caught up. My legs were trestles; the train was a long time comin'.

I was a quarrel of emotions that summer and too dumb to know how to moderate. But I knew I didn't want to stray onto the thin ice of my grandmother's hardwood floor in that formal living room with the sallow ancestral portraits. Especially in front of the white-haired, rouged judges who pretended to like me during the compulsory exercises so that they could crucify me when it came to presentation.

I screwed up. I knocked cups over, scalding Mrs. Buckley, who barked like a seal, while dribbling tea on Mrs. Moody's silk, plumy scarf, which she got from—what do you know—Paris on a long-ago honeymoon with a non-Moody husband. My ancestors' eyes followed me everywhere, faintly amused, as I played the joker to my grandmother's queen. Mrs. Moody sniffed and pronounced me "coltish." Liking horses, I decided it was a compliment. The *coup de grâs* struck just as Mrs. Chambers made an astonishing six no-trump bid. Impressed enough to steal a look at her cards, yet unaccustomed to heels, even one-inch beginners, I tripped over a Venetian lamp cord and crashed into the floor with a platter of paté. It was a sitcom, *Little Miss Daisy*.

Without the laugh track.

I fled in humiliation, sticking my grandmother with the shattered pieces I left behind. All I heard as I bolted up the stairs was my grandmother, panic-stricken, shouting, "Play through, ladies! Play through!" I think Mrs. Buckley had started to blister.

I cleared my throat. Jay Leno told silent jokes on the TV, and the audience dutifully gyrated. Tit for tat. "No, we weren't close."

"Oh." Rakesh's hand hovered. My arm felt an absence, my body adrift.

"I *wish* we had been." I pressed all the pain in my life into that wish, looking at him with blurry eyes. My chin started to wobble.

"Yeah, I know." His hand recovered my arm, his eyes misted. My words, and eyes, prodded him like a laboratory animal that didn't know the experiment being played upon him. Poor Rakesh.

My chin broke. I started to sob. Rakesh folded me into his arms. He smelled of aftershave and ginger. I imagined him not washing his clothes since spring break, when he went home for his sister's Indian wedding. She had never met the groom before. How crazy, how possibly brilliant.

"I'm s-sorry," I sniffled, pulling away.

"It's okay."

I wanted to drown in those eyes, that skin. Sometimes a warm body is all that is needed. Especially when the warm body you really want is too busy studying for a gross anatomy final to come home for your grandmother's funeral.

"You never answered my question."

"What question?"

"Why are you still here?"

Good question. I had no good answer. Instead, I broke toward Rakesh and closed my eyes, in mute persuasion. I had hit bottom. What did I care if I slopped in the mud?

By pulling toward Rakesh, I pushed Andy away.

The wind from the teakettle started its mad wail.

Rakesh hesitated, then kissed me. It felt different, the things he did. Not better, but different. And because he felt different, I imagined that I was different. Just for one night. Grief is surely the best excuse.

The kettle started to shriek at us, and the couch springs played a broken symphony. We didn't care.

But Irene did. When I saw those trusting eyes widen behind her glasses as they absorbed our discarded clothes, our nearly naked bodies, I could swear I heard my grandmother yell, "Play through, ladies! Play through!"

Ghosts do talk, Mathieu. At the most perverse times.

"What are you thinking of?"

Mathieu is not one who believes in companionable silences.

"Oh, nothing," I reply, searching the false sky for inspiration. It is serenely flat, like the two-dimensional skies from pre-Renaissance paintings. Looking at it, one could believe she's in a storybook. "I was thinking about my grandmother."

"You mentioned that she recently died, yes?" He is concerned for me.

Mathieu and Rakesh align for a moment, like overlaid photos. "It's just that—"

"Go on," he encourages, rubbing my forearm.

I wipe at the corners of my eyes, astonished to find real tears. "She loved her tea parties, playing the hostess. We were very close. She always made a point of including me." I search my pocket for a tissue.

Mathieu gallantly produces a handkerchief, which makes me feel like a heroine in a nineteenth-century novel. I gingerly blow, but hesitate to hand it back all gunked up with snot. He motions for me to keep it, which I do, twisting the fabric in my hands.

I'm not sure why I do this. I know it's bad. Worse than playing with Rakesh, because I care for Mathieu and he for me. Perhaps Mathieu is more penetrating than my natural defenses can withstand. Or maybe I need to erase the past, devise a different ending. Who knows? Guilt is a many-layered soufflé I have no interest in dissecting.

I maintain the charade over our lunch, inventing a string of funny, and touching, anecdotes about my "Nana" culled from syndicated episodes of *The Waltons* I watched as a child, all of which affect Mathieu deeply. I can tell by his moistening eyes, which, at intervals, twist the knife in my gut because his grief is at the contagious stage where a sneeze of sadness from me could infect him with a melancholic typhoid. Yet I talk and talk, my mouth on cruise control, inventing other characters in my life—a manic-depressive aunt named Flo living in New York who appeared as Grizabella in an off off-Broadway rendition of *Cats* and still performs *Memory* at every family reunion; a medical ethics professor whom I assisted getting wasted and ruffling feathers at a sports bar after finals and begging me to "discipline" him when I dropped him off (okay, that one's regrettably true)—stabbing my ravioli from time to time, while Mathieu swallows his scallops with increasing wonder. It is quite the performance and runs flawlessly, as I land every note with the right degree of poetic or vulgar emphasis. When it comes to the curtain call, I have almost convinced myself. Mathieu is transfixed. I cannot say that I enjoy the improv. But I don't stop.

I guess I do it because I can.

We are there about an hour. When we leave, the tables outside are empty. There is no sign of the previous occupants, no legacy of their words, their glances, the time swallowed from their lives. Their presence here might have been a fiction.

But for some inky stains at the bottom of their teacups.

Oh, to read tea leaves on a day like this!

Chapter 12

I want a nap. My mood has dipped with our return to sightseeing, and I am sluggish and temperamental, like I've been squeezed too hard. It's not Mathieu. If anything, I feel more bound to him. I would like to drop our plans and duck under an obliging chestnut, drifting off to the sound of his heartbeat, awakening at its alarm, so that under the cover of darkness we might eat and drink and flirt some more. No, it's not my darling guide in this journey we've hazarded, and to whom I now press closer, which has me itching to flee this sidewalk lined with the dead façades of fashion playhouses. It's these extra people dogging about, held hostage by vanity, and numbed by expectation, who trigger this little tantrum. As anybody who feels the advantage of special insight, I look scornfully at the pretenders scurrying through the streets with quotas of sites to see, shopping to do, none of them content to rhapsodize this city with aimless exploration as we do. I have, in half a day's time, morphed from conformist tourist to wanderlust adventurer, and like any convert, am eager to shout my creed.

I sniff. "Why on earth would anyone want to go into these

places?" I ask as we pass another trendy clothing store.

"What do you mean?"

I motion derisively to the slick displays behind the glass. "It's all so much nonsense. To think how people waste their money just to satisfy their vanity."

Mathieu halts in front of a women's shoe boutique. "Not at all, Daisy. You misunderstand."

"Oh, really?" Squinting, I point with some triumph. "Three hundred euros for a pair of heels that might cripple my feet? That doesn't seem silly to you?"

He pauses to consider the red heels. "Definitely not practical, no. But to call them silly is rash on your part." Mathieu turns toward me. "You find art beautiful and engaging. Why should you not have the same attitude toward what you wrap yourself in? Fashion can be less about vanity than about creating an alluring aesthetic for the people around you. Have you ever worn such shoes before?"

"No. Besides bankrupting me, I have no use for them. Where would I wear them—to the lab?"

Mathieu smiles and leans against the glass. "Perhaps that is your problem. You do not resent the shoes so much as the lack of a proper destination?"

I laugh sharply. "No, really—it's the shoes."

"But do not think about the money. Just look at the shoes. They are lovely, no?"

I look. They are a conflation of red leather and suede, with a neat bow collecting the asymmetrical straps at the center, and a four-inch heel that could mortally wound a man. Very feminine. Very sexy. Foreign.

"Yeah, so they're not hideous," I admit. "But as something that costs the same amount of money that could feed an African family in a year, they don't look so hot. In fact, thought of like that, they look criminal."

"And you are inclined now toward such charity?"

Hmm. The bastard.

Mathieu starts to pull my hand.

"No, Mathieu. Really."

He pulls harder.

"They're not for me!"

But he is as obstinate as Napoleon at Waterloo.

He pulls open the glass door, and I stop resisting. Now I must saunter in, like three-hundred-euro shoes are something I have a casual sense of ownership about, and Parisian salesladies are not the most intimidating Martians on this alien French planet. This would be easier without my Keds on.

A colorless woman with tamed hair and costume earrings approaches with an unfocused smile. Thankfully, Mathieu takes the lead, as my talent for playacting withers like a meek flower dwarfed by a greater bloom's shade. The boutique, from walls to carpet, is as red as the reddest bordello, or Victoria's Secret.

They speak in French, and Mathieu points out the shoes in the window. She archly examines me, before asking, "And you are what size, my dear?"

It might be less humiliating to meet a French person who wasn't conversant in English. But their maddening competence persists like a bad habit they'd like to break, but can't.

"Uh, eight," I mumble. "That's American, I don't know how to translate that to European sizes."

The saleslady gives a perfunctory nod. "We are accustomed to such, as you say, translations."

She motions us to a red, armless thing that looks like an oversized ottoman before disappearing into the back. There is an oval mirror on the wall that is large enough for me to note my smallness. I look about as lost as you'd expect for someone who gets her shoes from Payless. I try to scorch Mathieu with my eyes, but he is examining a pair of silver sling-backs with a level of absorption American men would find disgraceful. The shoes, along with smart matching purses, are exhibited like museum pieces atop glowing display cases. But no museum, not even Graceland's, with its fat Elvis toilet of death, has ever made me want to flee like this one. It's like being suffocated by cherry blossoms.

The mannequin returns with a couple of boxes tucked under her arm. I curse myself for not removing my Keds. More humiliation to suffer. I slip them off, as well as my gray cotton socks, while she asks Mathieu something. Evidently, he is in charge here.

"Daisy, would you like a cappuccino?" Mathieu asks, beaming.

What the hell is he so happy about? The saleswoman's non-specific smile is back.

"Um, no thanks." Let's get this over with.

The saleslady hands me a pair of footsies. I wince at my unpainted, longish nails, and curl my toes into the plush red carpet. The saleslady liberates the high heels from their box and seizes my right ankle with the kind of command mothers have over their children's uncooperative feet. She wordlessly slips the shoe on and fastens the buckle on the strap before repeating the exercise with my left foot. She doesn't like being on her knees all day before people's stinky feet. I don't blame her, though I wish I could be certain it isn't *my* feet that offend her so.

I rise stiffly, dreading the inevitable teetering during my Miss America promenade.

Hushed, portentous tones: We are now entering the shoe portion of the evening, ladies and gentlemen. And oh dear, June, this is quite an unfortunate scene—the contestant from Ohio appears to be experiencing some difficulty in walking like a woman. Clucking tongue. *Yes, Hugh, a shocking lack of coordination. Very disappointing, I must say, especially for everyone back home in Dullsville who held out such high hopes. Her impassioned defense for research on inner ear hair cells completely won over our celebrity judges, but I'm afraid she may have lost any chance at the title with that fall. Her foot looks like it may be sprained, in fact.* Assenting rumble. *Indeed, June, it's starting to swell. What we have is a cankle on our hands here. Avert your eyes, ladies and gentlemen . . . .*

Yet in spite of the mortifying scenarios playing out in my head, I do not wobble. These shoes have splinters for heels, but I do not fall. Perhaps I've gained a measure of balance in Paris.

I take small steps over to the mirror, wondering if this is what it was like for Chinese women who had their feet bound. Hmm . . . probably worse. Those caricatured bird steps they were forced to perform, making perverted fetishists out of their men. Yes, perverted, for while it is a little laughable for a man to be granted the permission to suck on an indulgent woman's toes, it is sadistic for a husband to get off on his wife's crippling pain and perpetuate the practice for his generation. The little lotus, my ass. Is that really the most apt metaphor they could assign for the process of deformation, infection, gangrene, and permanent disability? I wince a little. My arches are starting to cramp. Maybe we are not so modern. Maybe we are bound by the same tired delusions that gender roles have prescribed for centuries. Maybe Mathieu secretly—

Shit. I look good in these things.

The mirror reveals a ray of track lighting licking the small buckle on my right shoe, where—*magnifique!*—it explodes like a dazzling sunburst. The suede is so rich that it murmurs at me, in French (but of course!), through velvet, rose petal lips. I adore that little bow, winking saucily up at me, and wiggle my toes in delight. Everything about these shoes elevates. I stand differently in them. My back arches, my breasts emerge. My legs, though concealed, are firmer, sexier. My pelvis feels tighter, like I could squeeze a lemon between my thighs. Heck, I could pin Mathieu against the wall and not lift a leg. I place my hands on my hips and preen like a beauty queen. It's a shameful display of vanity, but I cannot tear my eyes away from the four-inch wonderfucks on my feet. This must be why women get boob jobs. It's such a convincing illusion of transformation.

I see Mathieu and the saleswoman eyeing me in the mirror and wipe the blissful, self-satisfied smirk off my face. Tom Petty's "American Girl" dies on my mind's tongue. This isn't my *Pretty Woman* moment. I'm not really any taller. They are only shoes. And they cost as much as Andy's first car.

"How do you feel in them?" Mathieu asks, hand cupping his chin. Not how do they fit, but how do I *feel?* The metaphysical interpretation of a shoe's worth, as opposed to the less romantic, but more pressing "what will these things do to my pinky toe blister?" reading.

I shrug and plop down on the ottoman to yank them off. "It doesn't matter. They're out of the question."

The saleslady plucks them from my paws, her smug chin turtling into her neck, which is starting to slacken into waddle. I said something awhile back about not stereotyping the French, but what can I say: sometimes the shoe fits.

"Wait, please," Mathieu commands, and she stops.

I pause with one sock hanging off my foot. "What?"

"I would like to purchase this for you."

"It's out of the question, I said."

Mathieu sits down and turns to the saleslady. He says something, and she promptly withdraws. "Daisy, please. Stop what you are doing."

"Listen, Mathieu. It's sweet of you. Really. I appreciate the gesture. But I wouldn't feel comfortable with it."

"And why not?" Mathieu grimaces, but admits, "The money does not mean much to me, Daisy. If I want to do this for you, why should you object?"

I sit and stare out the window, watching a patchwork of profiles glide by. A little girl, not more than four, with ribbons on her hat walks with her mother and slows to peer in at a display. Her pretty, round face brightens as she points out something to her mom, who nods and pulls her past. The girl looks back wistfully before disappearing. I strain my neck to see what entranced her but cannot locate the prize. I picture Dorothy's ruby reds tucked between the Prada and Gucci. Cinderella's glass slippers residing on a silk pillow. They were supposed to be fur, but there was a mistranslation from French to English along the way. And luckily, as fur slippers seem a predictable, even trashy, extravagance. Glass slippers, on the other foot, impress me as being infinitely more exquisite in all their painful fragility. Walking—no, dancing—on glass cut from gossamer that persevered through the alchemy of unlikely love. This is the province of fairy tales. This is the stuff that makes little girls' hearts patter to the unworldly rhythms of imagination. And it is the stuff that sticks when little girls mature into rational beings. No matter how enlightened, or cynical, they regard themselves.

I am living a fairy tale. What right have I to refuse my prince?

I set about tying my laces. "All right, Mathieu, I will let you."

He brushes my cheeks with kisses until they are pink and pliant. I paw him away and laugh. "But."

"Yes."

"Only on the understanding that I do not have to wear them. That I have the right to peek in on them, rouse them from their tissue-paper slumber, and perhaps try them on in complete privacy when I feel daring. But no one else sees me in them. Not even you."

"I understand," he agrees, flushed with his small triumph.

There. "Oh, and if we end up getting in a fight, promise me that you won't resent me for the shoes. That you won't use them as an excuse to stop kissing me."

"It will take more than some silly shoes for me to want to do that."

The saleslady is forced to watch, and I am helpless to stop him, even as Mathieu bends me back on the ottoman and brushes the hair from my eyes with his hands. I permit the suffocation. Surely, there are worse ways to die than by Mathieu's lips. But I can see her over his shoulder, practicing her grateful smile at the counter, impatient for the feel of Mathieu's plastic in the manicured fingers that have lain to rest youthful diamond dreams.

For the first time in Paris, my happiness is not enough. I want the world to sing.

I push Mathieu off and gather myself. He looks wounded but follows me over to the counter, where he mutely produces his credit card. A tidy pile of red business cards rests on the marble countertop, and I palm one while the saleslady packs up the heels. The card reads *Michelle Valmont*. Mathieu raises an eyebrow at me, but I brush him off with a careless shrug. On a stool behind the counter I notice a paperback, half concealed, bearing a dated jacket photo. It is a formulaic romance title from the eighties. I smile inwardly. If it had been philosophy, or a political thriller, I may have lost hope for Michelle. But she reads for romance. Which means that somewhere behind that superficial, controlled exterior beats the heart of a girl who still desires.

I smile at Michelle before we leave, thanking her so profusely that she reacts with a flinching retreat. As we depart, I look back at her black form silhouetted against the scarlet backdrop. She gazes at the ottoman where Mathieu and I just sat, and lay, together, perhaps impressing the image of our youthful joy in one another upon her bloodless heart.

Perhaps reflecting that she needs to stop at the market after work to pick up some meat for dinner.

Chapter 13

Mathieu receives a call on his cell phone as we leave the St. Germain area. His jaw clenches as he checks the number, and he holds up a finger to me, begging off for a minute of privacy. I smile and turn away to look in the window of a hat boutique, while he makes for a nearby alleyway. I sense a barely restrained tension plaguing his voice from ten feet away, and, forgive me, desperately wish I knew French so I might eavesdrop. My paranoia returns, and I imagine Camille is on the line. She wants to rendezvous with him, and he'll finally throw me over for someone he deserves. I clutch my stylish sack in a sweaty palm as the Eliza Doolittle hats perform a carousel dance before me.

Mathieu returns with an apologetic smile, and I turn toward him lightly. "Even you could not convince me of the necessity of these."

He chuckles. "No, these are awful." Mathieu runs a hand through his hair, and my stomach rolls. "Listen, Daisy. I am sorry, but that was my father. He is traveling and needs me to perform an urgent errand for him at his apartment. Unfortunately, he is starting to become a little, um, funny? In his head?"

I nod compassionately, secretly relieved it was his senile father and not his ravishing, questionably lesbian friend. "But he is worked up, and I should probably honor his request."

"Of course. That's no problem at all," I say. I hesitate before suggesting, "Why not take me with you?" I throw my hands up in the air, the bag flying recklessly about. "It's not like I have anywhere else I need to be right now."

This presents him with a dilemma. It's evident from his expression that he doesn't want me to see his father's apartment, yet I also sense he doesn't want me to know he doesn't want me to see it. I must say, I suspected as much. And I'm fishing. But Mathieu's father piques my curiosity. I sense a darkness in Mathieu, introduced by his mother, but metastasized under his father's care.

Mathieu looks over my shoulder and mumbles weak protestations like, "Would not want to ask that of you," and, "It is rather far away," while eying a hoary, homeless man taking a whiz in the alley.

I ignore the grunting satisfaction of the pissing passerby. "Come on. It doesn't take long to get anywhere in Paris. That's what the metro is for."

After much hemming and hawing, he assents. "Okay. But it will be boring."

The whiskery man zips up and passes us. He regards me with florid interest, before spilling something under his breath.

"What did he say?" I ask Mathieu, once he's gone.

Discomfited, Mathieu replies, "He said that he can tell American women by the way they smell. Vanilla on their skin and in their . . . er, vaginas."

Dumbfounded, I stare at Mathieu. "He didn't say vagina, did he?"

"I think the proper translation would be—"

"Pussy."

"Uh . . ."

"Cunt."

"Yes."

Someone's been reading his Henry Miller.

I wait a beat, dying to bury my nose into my skin, but gather myself and laugh. "Come on, Mathieu. Let's go to your dad's. I think we're due for a little boredom."

Mathieu smiles stiffly, and we walk toward the nearest metro station, me swinging my bag with all the manufactured enthusiasm of a child sent on a scavenger hunt. I have a family secret to collect.

Somehow, on this least vanilla of days, I doubt it will be boring.

We get off the metro at the St. Paul stop, exiting onto the Rue de Rivoli, the central artery through the Marais *quartier*. Mathieu, blocking me, raised a wall of silence on the train as we barreled through dark tunnels and darker doubts. I would abandon this adventure but for a fatalistic sense that the damage has been done, and I might as well see what I can get from it. I'm quite the little mercenary.

We start up Rue Malcher and skirt a section of the district that is largely Jewish. There are small, ethnic shops everywhere with signs in two languages: French and Hebrew. I sidestep an Orthodox Jew exiting a falafel joint, and yet, a minute later, am startled to see two young men holding hands outside of a delicatessen. They are the second gay couple I have seen since leaving the metro. It is the first time since arriving in Paris that I've had a sense of separateness, of the potential for tribal entanglements. The French pride themselves on keeping a united front, of being cut from a fine, vintage mold, but lassoed living must present challenges, especially in this cramped city that likes to impose an evolved, if determinate, Gallic order. Then again, I'm looking with American eyes, accustomed to the more unaccommodating polarities of my own country, where most Christians believe homosexuality is a "choice," and where the majority of gays likely believe Evangelicals are Neanderthals. Yet even there, we all sleep under the luckier stars of our flag. Geography is destiny. Nobody understands this better than the Jews and Palestinians in the West Bank. Even the American in Paris feels the strain.

It takes something monumental to slip the knot.

I quicken my steps to keep up with Mathieu. "Of course, I keep forgetting that you're American too."

"Why would you say such a ridiculous thing?" he mutters, distracted.

There is a musical trio performing on the street corner ahead of us. Violin, cello, clarinet. They perform a Hungarian waltz that, like the pied piper, summons the rats, or in this case, tourists. A clutch of onlookers encircles the group, siphoning pedestrian traffic into the street. Sunlight finds the gold of bracelets dangling from a second-story window, as their owner tosses a coin to the street below. The people laugh and applaud. The violinist, wearing a head scarf, raises her bow and dips her head in acknowledgment, never losing the lilting beat.

I turn toward Mathieu. "I was just thinking of the headline in *Le Monde* after September 11: 'We are all Americans.' For a moment there, we belonged to the same nation."

He frowns and tries to speed up, though we've hit the snarl of bodies. "That was a sentimental gesture, Daisy. I was not an American. Nobody believed that then, and certainly not now."

Stung, I slow. "I was just trying to lighten your mood."

"I am light."

"So light you might float away?" I shout at his back.

Diverted, some of the people glance over at us, annoyed that we've strummed this minor chord.

He rubs the back of his neck and says over his shoulder, "I do not think we should go down this road."

I slow to a stop. "I'm not going to censor my conversation because you have issues with your mother."

Mathieu halts.

"My *mother*?" He backtracks to confront me. "You believe I have issues with your country because my mother went there?" Mathieu laughs and wildly scans the crowd behind me. "How optimistic of you, Daisy."

Sarcasm is the cruelest first cut. I could gasp from the pain, if I had the breath in my body.

"Among other things," I reply.

He wipes at his mouth. "These things you speak of."

"What about them?"

"Were they responsible for your leaving America?"

I look at him in confusion. "No. Why would—no."

"Maybe they should have been."

"Mathieu, if every American who had a problem with Bush left the country, only the wackos would be left, and that would be a problem for you, too."

"All right. So what are you doing to deserve to stay?"

My mouth opens, but only the music follows.

He shakes his head, gathering himself, before chucking me under the chin and producing a smile. "I am playing with you, Daisy."

I knock his hand away. "No, you're not."

The trio wraps it up, and the onlookers briefly applaud before dropping away like bombs. I can feel the wind of their movement lick my back. We remain stalled. We could wrap it up too, drop away . . . explode in different places.

"I am simply tired of Americans using the cover of that day. It cast a long shadow over your country, but that is no excuse to plunge parts of the world into darkness."

"I agree with you."

He stuffs his hands into his pockets and rocks back on his heels. "And American suffering is no more legitimate than the suffering of Iraqi citizens."

"Not at all."

"In fact, compared to the trauma inflicted on Iraq, you got off easy."

"Yes, *I* have."

"It was such a foolish, unthinking calculation." He places his shoe over the woman's dropped coin, which bounced out of the cello case and onto the sidewalk. The musicians, packing their instruments away, do not notice.

"It always appears so from a distance."

"Are you saying it was not foolish at the time?"

"I'm saying that nobody intended it to have the effect it did."

Mathieu's face grows red. "That is no excuse, Daisy."

I grab hold of his hand with both of mine. "No, it's not."

There are tears of anger in his eyes. But I am not so foolish as to think they are directed at me, or even my country. Or that he will let them fall.

One day is all it takes for some people to forget geography. But there are those they leave behind.

"Mathieu, you don't live in darkness anymore. You made your own light."

He shakes off my hand, and bends down to retrieve the euro, smoothly pocketing it.

When he looks up at me, his eyes are like lead. "I do not know what you mean, Daisy."

He turns and walks away.

I recall what it feels like to be alone, in this church called Paris.

"We are here."

Yes, I followed.

Mathieu opens a heavy wooden door with rusted hinges and ushers me toward a winding walkway that bisects the courtyard. He does not look at me. And I do not look at him, though I am so conscious of not looking at him not looking at me that he is like a phantom limb I cannot see but still cruelly feel. I wonder if this is the beginning of the end. I am equal parts terrified and relieved. I do not like that I followed; I do not like that he took my following for granted.

The courtyard is tranquil and idyllic, like every secret garden in Paris. Ivy loops around and through the crumbling stone walls, waning blooms bob from imperfect pots, while the shadowy possibility of Parisian cats beckons at every turn. Once again, the sound of water, leaping from the lion's mouth, attempts to soothe our pique as we venture deeper into this temporary asylum. An orange tabby, balanced on a windowsill, tracks us as we silently cross the cobblestone path. I feel nauseated and gray, the charm of the scene lost on me. With each step, I grow more aware that the physical magnetism Mathieu and I share, along with a wealth of good intention, may not save us from flaming out by the end of this golden, if fading, day. I am no longer merely adorable to Mathieu, and if part of me is proud, I also feel the loss of our childish delight in one another—the beautiful belief that we could shelter that spark of passion through all storms.

Mathieu suddenly sinks down on a lichen-covered stump and pulls me down beside him. Something catches in my throat at his touch, and I feel the warm weight of the stolen coin in my hand. I hesitate before allowing myself to look at him, but when I do, his eyes are drawn and sad, his face a collection of my doubts and miseries. What relief to find this reflection in the looking glass . . . and not one expressing scorn or anger. I let myself breathe. His hand finds my face, and I am solid again. I lean my cheek into his palm. We watch the flickering expressions, tender and doubting, erupt and pass over one another's faces, like the rapid shedding of masks, until we are all that remains. There is a hypnotic vigor to his eyes that wipes the slate clean. To look into this face and not take refuge in ego through playacting, or retreat into self-consciousness, is the most freeing sacrifice to be made. We simply give ourselves to one another. It is the most difficult experiment of my life to be this frank with another soul. To not blink. There is no final answer to arrive at, no conclusion to reach, or punch line to deliver—just the generous gift of more questions to be raised. Something stirs in my gut, and there is an unraveling of fear into perfect peace.

There is one thing to say at a moment like this.

"I didn't really like my grandmother so much."

"I sometimes wish I believed in God."

I rise and throw the coin into the bubbly water of the fountain. It makes a small splash and sinks to the bottom.

An odd kind of promise to make. But I sit back down, and we nod, like these pearly words were a vow and the coin toss the kiss that followed. It is the only pledge we can offer to one another. A promise to end all thought of promises. For our eyes are opened from this point on. We have traveled beyond words. The tree we rest on is as good as dead. The water behind us flows on and on and on and . . . .

Chapter 14

I am unprepared for his father's place. Nothing about the innocuous building suggests the kind of luxury to be tiptoed over inside. The staircase up to the fourth floor (third European, though I refuse to concede the logic) is in need of refinishing, the wood starting to show gaps. I know because I clung to the banister as we inched up the stairs. Mathieu had some apologizing to do. At every stair, and landing.

When Mathieu opens the door with his key, I gasp. The apartment is sumptuous. I wish I could do it justice, but I have no vocabulary for these opulent objects. French furniture is particularly tied to its history, and I have no method for discriminating between a Louis the Something-or-Other chaise and a Third Republic one. They all look like something you shouldn't sit on. If forced to make a stab, I would say that this place sings of the Belle Époque, with mismatched, eccentric bric-a-brac punctuating more elegant showpieces. There are elaborate moldings, Oriental carpets, crystal chandeliers, and gold-gilt mirrors stretching the length of walls. The ceilings are high and delicately bordered by gold-leaf vines, the fireplace mantel is a buxom slab of red marble, and the only sound to intrude upon the immaculate stillness is the uncollected murmurs of several clocks. Attractive ancestral portraits of ladies with taffy hair and gentlemen wearing riding outfits comingle with pretty landscapes in an aristocratic *joie de vivre*. An ivory tusk and African mask reside on a lowboy next to a maudlin Rococo figurine and a brandy snifter that sports some reddish residue. It is the only sign that someone could possibly live in this palace. There is no theme to tie a knot around everything except for a kind of dazzling, if dated, affluence.

Mathieu's father's apartment is an opera singer. She thinks a lot of herself, but the problem is, nobody much goes to see opera anymore.

"Geez," I blow out.

Mathieu is busy looking through a drawer. "Yeah."

"Does your dad actually *live* here?"

He does a quick sizing up of the place. "Of course."

"And did you live here when you were younger?"

"Yes. From fourteen to eighteen."

I nod and walk around, trailing my finger along the edges of furniture. There is no dust. He must have someone in to clean. Either she forgot the brandy snifter or she was having some fun. Good for her. This place could use it. I lower myself into a three-corner wooden chair, whose sided cushions depict birds imprisoned by flight. Sitting opposite a mirror, I rest my elbows gingerly on the chair's coiled, decorative arms. I cross my legs, then switch them, and meditate uneasily on my reflection, which is distorted in the waxy glass. If I had lived here during my adolescence, I would have lost my mind and become a recluse, or lost my mind and run away. Live in a museum long enough and you risk growing an unhealthy attachment to *things*, or alternatively, you may feel suffocated by the sensation that you are just another object and flee to preserve your humanity.

I think it likely, from the way he grimaces and sweats over the files in the lowboy, that Mathieu felt compelled to run. It makes me ache for him—for the boy in him.

"I have to use the bathroom."

"Down the hall and first on your right," he replies, barely looking up. He will not tell me the reason for his errand. And I will not press him for it.

The bathroom was an excuse. I slip down the hallway on a mild prowl, pausing to peer in at the beamed kitchen overlooking the courtyard. A curmudgeonly oven range capped by an enormous exhaust system throws out some attitude, while the granite countertop looks like you could bash someone's head in along its edge. An awesome collection of knives stands at razor-sharp attention next to an array of pill and vitamin bottles. Overall, the kitchen seems a threatening place. And that's without any French cooking bubbling menacingly on the stove. The one note of interest is the scheme of decorative wine racks floating above the cabinets, in which every pod is occupied, like slumbering space travelers fixed in suspended animation. I would love to check the dates on the bottles, some of which look musty, but don't want to overtly snoop. I give the kitchen up and come to a door on my right. The knob doesn't turn, so I continue down the hallway. The adjacent door opens, and I stop short.

My pupils dilate. The heavy, stiff curtains are drawn over the window opposite me. I open the door further, allowing the natural light from the hallway to diffuse into the dimmed space. This is not the bathroom, but a bedroom of sorts. Except there is no bed. Or any furnishings. The entire room, probably fifteen by fifteen, is packed with paintings leaning stiffly against the four walls. They are protected with yards of bubble wrap, so I cannot detect the quality of what's underneath. But I can make out what's hanging on the white walls. And it sucks my breath away.

There is certainly a Monet over there; some of his haystacks, I think. Very probably a Toulouse-Lautrec to the left. A Degas opposite that, with those scrawny dancers of his. That small one near the corner might be a Morisot, though I could be inferring because it shows a seated woman with a parasol, like the one in the Cleveland Museum that I adore. And something that looks remarkably like a blue-period Picasso hangs to my right.

And then there is the Matisse, near the window, its faceless woman with flowers waiting patiently for light.

Holyholyholyholy. My eyes are crazed, greedy. I feel like I've just happened across the tomb of King Tut. That I've cracked physics' Theory of Everything. That pure, eternal beauty has found a home inside Mathieu's father's apartment in this overly trendy section of Paris. That all the ostentatious stuff down the hall was a false perfume to throw me off a sublime scent. That this room, and not the cathedrals choking this city, is where God must live, or at least summer. I have strayed off the beaten path—no, I have soared, with borrowed wings, from any path. I cannot believe my height, yet my hawkish eye catalogues every detail, from the electric green brushstrokes of a fanning collar around Toulouse-Lautrec's cancan girl to the stark, heavy outlines of Picasso's robed woman, bent from age. I strain my neck across the paintings on the floor to look for things I would not bother with in the Orsay. Like the quality of the frames, which seem original to my museum-conditioned eye. Like signatures, some of which look as familiar as my own: Picasso's muscular dash, Monet's more delicate expression. Because I have the luxury to do so, *on my own*, making me feel, briefly, ecstatically, like I am the first to behold them. Because foundational to our definition of beauty is that we never expected to find it. I was going to take a pee. Instead, I glided into an art historian's wet dream.

I do not think, at the time, of how they got here. I do not stop to wonder at their incarceration in this improbable room.

I forget about Mathieu down the hall, and whether I should be here. When immersed in a dream, you don't stop to think whether you've been served an invitation. You don't examine causes or consequences. You just are.

I save the Matisse for last, the climax.

Such insatiable color!!! He earns this giddy enthusiasm, by God, so that I have some hope of conveying the intensity of caramelized color rupturing the cones inside these irises. The darkness cannot mute Matisse's bold hand; instead, *it* is the fluorescent light bulb that illuminates. The canvas is roughly three by four and invents a space unbothered by perspective, where a faceless woman backed by an ocher wall sits at a table so saturated by red, pulsating strokes that it looks alive, like blood spilling from oxygen-rich lungs. Balanced on the table are blue vases stuffed with flowers and bluer plates overflowing with tipsy lemons and a chance, plum apple: the banal stuff of still lives everywhere. Only, like Cezanne, a still life is never still with Matisse, and never banal. Everything rolls toward a beautiful transition, with lemons waddling like ducklings, an orgy of common flowers splaying, odd details disappearing and reemerging like lovers' legs. The lesser vases are filled with a suggestion of stems and petals, but the large vase to our left, where our eyes, liking big things, naturally curve, is ornamented with more exotic faire: something purpley and Eastern, maybe peonies or plum blossoms. The sort of crisp flower you'd expect to see on a gorgeous Japanese or Chinese calligraphy scroll to mark the start of spring and life's renewal. They stand stiffly, priggishly, marking their superiority to the spraying mess of ejaculate below.

And so it is here, at Matisse's feet, that I realize why I chose Dr. Choi for my mentor over a year ago. Why I didn't gravitate toward the sexier Parkinson's research in Rosenberg's lab and have my name attached to some important articles, nudging me further up the Alpine career path. It was so simple: I was beguiled by a pretty picture and wanted to linger awhile. There was a painter's precision, and unruliness, to the hair cells in those fluorescent microscopy photographs in Choi's darkened lab. The brilliantly dyed projections were so tightly arranged, like a Fibonacci sequence of petals in a flower, yet shaggy and playful at their ends. Recklessness and restraint. It was all there, inside my ears, making its own kind of music.

Matisse, of course, is jazz. All gorgeous, playful improv flirting above the elemental rhythms of a master technician. He makes me move.

"Did you find what you were looking for?"

I jump, and when I fall back down, it is really like that: a return to earth. Mathieu's earth, but still earth. He stands with his hands on the doorway.

"I'm sorry," I say, stepping back. "I really was trying to find the bathroom. The doorknob wouldn't turn."

"You must turn it to the left," he replies, lightly enough.

"Ah. The left."

Mathieu enters, and I squint to read him. He nears but passes me to jerk the curtain open. I blink rapidly in the light, my pupils constricting. Out there is the street, the people, the commerce: the workaday world of Paris bustling on. Mathieu clenches his jaw dangerously. I think I preferred the darkness.

"I am sorry, Mathieu. I suppose I should have closed the door. To be honest, it never occurred to me."

"I am not upset, Daisy." His eyes flit around the room like a wary animal's. "Yet I did not expect this. The fool."

"You *seem* upset."

"To the contrary, I thought I seemed in control."

"You do seem in control. Like the kind of vicious control a parent tries to muster when she's mad at her kid. I can tell you that, as the kid here, it's much scarier than yelling."

Mathieu chuckles, if not convincingly, and bends over the windowsill, peering into the dying sun. He maintains his position for a full minute: I know because I count the seconds. My eyes are still dancing, though, and it finally occurs to me to think of the money in these paintings. I suppose I always felt it. Maybe it was partly, if not consciously, responsible for my spasms of wonder upon entering the room. We are accustomed to assigning arbitrary values to objects that should defy such categorization. Paintings aren't home runs, purebred dogs, or real estate. Art ought to transcend the dogma of numbers, unperturbed by Adam Smith's invisible hand of supply and demand. How can something appreciate in value when its content has not changed? It was always this degree of beautiful, from the moment the last stroke of paint was applied to the canvas to the moment my eyes brushed its surface, a century later. It shouldn't matter to us if a Matisse fetches a hundred dollars or a hundred million dollars.

But it does. We can't help ourselves. And the market gets it roughly right. After all, Picasso is the all-time best-seller, the perennial record-smasher, that glittering name in lights on the auction house's marquee that makes fashionable people wet themselves, and would anyone argue that he was *the* genius of the twentieth century?

Well, me. I'll put my money, such as it is, on Matisse.

Mathieu turns and rests his backside against the window, crossing his arms over his chest. He has arrived at a decision on how to handle me.

"I would have liked to have saw the expression on your face."

Hmm. *Have saw.* A slip-up in Mathieu's perfect parade of past participles. Though it had to happen, I still imbue the moment with special significance. But I reply cheerily enough, "It was probably stupid. Stupidly stupefied."

"And what if I had told you they were all reproductions?"

I respond carefully. "I would not have believed you."

He nods. "Mmm." Mathieu motions me over, and I hoist myself onto the ledge next to him. "And why not?"

I shrug. "I don't know. You just feel it in your gut, I guess. Like you know a good melon." I giggle too stridently, the tension of the moment whistling out of me. He looks lost, and I nudge him in the ribs. "Come on, *When Harry Met Sally*? Billy Crystal? Meg Ryan?"

He shakes his head, and I groan, pained by his ignorance. Some things, like lifesaving pharmaceuticals and clean water, and Sally's diner orgasm, ought to transcend the confines of the nation state. Mathieu explains, "The only Billy Crystal film I have seen was something called *Mr. Saturday Night*."

"That's probably the only Billy Crystal movie I haven't seen."

"Yes. Well."

We lapse into silence. I want him to explain, but he resists. The paintings look at us, and we look back. My eyes will not abandon the Matisse; I'm afraid it might disappear. The sunlight has enriched and deepened the colors, cooling the blues, inflaming the reds. Parts of it look wet to the touch. I would like to touch it.

"So which is your favorite?" Mathieu asks.

That's easy. "The Matisse."

Mathieu nods, but I can tell he disagrees. "Why?"

"I don't know. I just felt it instantly, unlike the others. The colors ran right through me." I clear my throat. "Which is yours?"

"But of course the Picasso."

"And why?"

He reflects, staring at the austere, indigo canvas with an intensity I understand, if I don't share. "I like that mean look in the old lady's eye," he says. "It is an unsentimental portrait, yet manages compassion. She will not go quietly, he is saying."

"It makes me think of El Greco. That long, austere line . . . the unflinching sufferer." I shiver a little. "It is remarkable. But I cannot say that I would want it hanging over me at night. It would be a constant *memento mori*."

"You prefer Matisse's armchair prettiness to Picasso's piercing humanity?" he jests, probably thinking back on Mrs. Fanny from the Orsay.

"*You say tomato and I say to-mah-toe*," I sing. He rewards me with a smile. "Yes, and you won't shame me from my position, Mathieu. I'm twenty-three years old. There will be plenty of time for your existential angst and despair. But for now, please, humor me a little and allow me vases of flowers, and tides of color to wash away my cynicism." I squeeze his hand, and he responds in kind. "I will not believe that my desire for lightness over darkness speaks of any slightness of character, or that your liking such morbidity makes you deep. It simply makes you French."

He tousles my hair, relaxing into laughs. "I was not trying to be 'deep,' *mon petit chou*. Art is visceral, from the gut, as you say. Picasso will always speak to me—probably because he screams the loudest."

I bargain on the moment. "And your father? Which is his favorite?"

Mathieu licks his lips and turns back toward the window, driving his knuckles into the marble. "To have a favorite painting, you must have a heart"—he touches his hand to his chest—"that is hungry for art." He shakes his head and looks at me, his expression darkening. "My father is a glutton for many things, but fine art is not among them."

"Then what *is* all of this, Mathieu?"

"A longtime investment," he says, driving each syllable with his tongue as hammer. He turns toward me. "And that is all I can say, Daisy. Please forgive me. I would like to explain further." Mathieu takes my hands and places them around his neck. "But he is my father."

"Of course," I answer reflexively, grazing his mouth with my lips. I would like to probe deeper, but I have already traversed too far. It occurs to me that I am standing inside a room that is worth millions of dollars, if I am correct about the paintings' authenticity. It is a heady notion, but also slightly sinister. Suddenly, the idea surfaces that, for Mathieu, this is an *ugly* room; not ugly in the literal sense, of course, but a corrupting ugliness that spreads from some rotten place of contaminated feeling. His father may have poisoned it for him with . . . what? People who collect art don't usually do it for the money. They feed on the thrill of having something worth that much and vaguely hope it appreciates, but what they really are after is the prestige of the ownership, of symbolically belonging to a rare relic of beauty and sharing in its miraculous conception. The owner wants to trace the artist's immortality.

And so the collector becomes an art fanatic, and gets to "know" his artist, intimately. It's no longer about the money, but the fame. After all, there are much better ways to make one's fortune than purchasing risky paintings. So how did Mathieu's father accumulate, or hoard, a treasure trove that is being squandered in a vulnerable, neglected apartment that requires a curious cleaning lady to maintain it? Why would someone do such a thing without the passion driving him on? Who is this—

Hold on. Mathieu's tongue is in my mouth.

"What are you *doing*?" I ask, tearing away.

His mouth is a little desperate, and he clutches at the ribbon of material around my waist, kneading me closer to him. He is intent on releasing something, but I retreat. Does he want *me*, or am I just the useful vessel for acting out this Freudian nightmare? At my question, he stops kissing me and pulls back.

"I do not know," he says, voice breaking.

I look at him tenderly, sorry for it—the graceless questioning of this man's desire for me when it's all I have wanted—and there, across his shoulder, is Matisse's fresh, faceless figure, and past that is Picasso's decrepit woman, and beyond that is all hallway and emptiness and nonexistence. I abandon the paintings for Mathieu, for he is easily the most beautiful, and precious, and ephemeral, thing in a room webbed with still-life dreams. He, not quite a genius but devastating in his desire to be, pulls me, with the gravity of those downcast eyes, toward him like a planet powerless around its sun. I do not care about motivation, for it comes down to this: I could not celebrate any stroke of color more than the red covenant of those lips, and I could never form so perfect a poem as the one smudging itself in the verse of his eyes. He is boyish and lean and powerful and so goddamn stunning while he stands there second-guessing himself that I answer his doubt and that strange shame by locking onto his lips with the ferocity of a muse breathing inspiration into an artist desperate for resuscitation.

I love those lips. I love his kiss. I love him.

I love him.

We are clumsy and nervous getting started, and at times I have the overwhelming desire to laugh like a small child doing unchildish things. When he pulls me to the floor, I feel the thick Oriental carpet rub up against my naked back, and I smooth the surface of it with my free hand, thoughtlessly stroking the same pattern of paisley swirls, this time red, that taunted me in Cleveland. I laugh at this happy coincidence, loving paisley, and those mad little whirls of perpetual motion. Above me, Mathieu stops the wonderful things he was doing to move me with those increasingly assured hands to stare anxiously into my face.

"Is this all right?" he asks, shy and uncertain.

(Do not laugh during sex. Ever.)

I kiss him as my answer, fielding him closer. "You . . . are . . . always . . . talking."

He doubts me. "I was going to wait. I had it planned. We would continue our tour, building the sweet anticipation. Then, on the last day, with only touch left, we would finally do . . . this." Mathieu furrows his brow, made timid by this other, more strategically romantic self, who is adorable but rather tedious to me right now, since it isn't his hand running wild across my trembling, supplicant body. "I would have given everything to you, Daisy. Not just me, but Paris. It might have been perfect."

"It *is* perfect." I close my hands around his face. "I don't need Paris. And no stagey productions or plans for us—I'm so tired of thinking ahead of myself. I only want *you*. Now."

He abandons thought for me.

The soul drops back into this body and begins to sing. Muscles stretch fingers, nerves strike keys. Mathieu's mouth drags a bright weight down, down. From the broken capillaries of an earlobe into the dark bruise of tenderest pain. Lower still.

Lips form words, but sound is beyond.

I am fire, not air. Fire . . .

The room slackens and recedes. Mathieu's eyes are wetter than rain. My back curves, arms extend. I reach for him, wanting this destruction. Wanting our walls to shatter, all these colors to slather and run. He answers with a reckless drive. I lock my arms around him and bury my lips into his neck. Breathing his skin. Taking him in.

Mathieu.

That name the only language I could ever understand.

His body breaks like waves across my flame. Pressure tacks its tempest spot, and I surrender to the swell. Fingers ripping tension. Legs pressing need. If I cannot get inside of him, I commit to drown.

Please . . . please.

The final curtain tears. Darkness pours between us. My eyes roll with light. I fracture far and wide.

And walls that feared, die.

CHAPTER 15

Lovers, and readers, will become torpid and dull after sex. After all, the sharply drawn tension now lies like a sloppy noodle on the spoiled floor, and page. I know that I can't top first sex for gratifying voyeurism. Few can. It doesn't matter if it's not great: it's still new, and a thing of poignant mystery. After the first ten times, no matter the improvement in technique or the deeper connection forged, we're still trying to recapture that first-time revelatory experience. *His* hands on *my* naked thigh, *his* tongue on *my* . . . plum blossoms. There is no high like the first high. That first kiss, or climax, is often the climax *and* the resolution of a certain kind of movie, and we, the audience, drift out of the theater manipulated and sated, aglow with tender notions, not entertaining any end but the lovers' projected bliss. Too many affairs begin out of little more than a kind of fatal boredom. And so I linger by the Matisse, by Mathieu, worried, and thinking about the married couples I've tangled with in Paris. They might yet be our bookends.

But I want to believe that even they would read our story.

We rouse ourselves after a while, yawning like big cats after a satisfying kill. Time might have stood still, but now it clicks on, like a projector sluggishly firing, and I sink back into this animal body. There is my stomach growling, and Mathieu's too, and we laugh about this, our warring bellies, listening for the loudest battle cry. Mine wins, and I tell him that it must be an American thing, or at least a Midwestern thing, since we eat around six o'clock, when Dad gets home from work, and Mom takes a bubbling casserole out of the oven to place before his wearily smiling frame. Some artifact of 1950s living that endures because it's comforting to have routine. Even with a mom who works, I have rarely eaten past seven o'clock. Only Europeans are this laid-back, I tell Mathieu, a little disapprovingly, not falling under the spell of Monet's pillowy haystacks.

"Maybe Americans are just hungrier than we are."

"Fat, you mean."

"Morbidly obese," he teases, poking me in the squishy part of my belly, making me squeal and scramble away like any self-conscious girl, American or French.

He scrambles after me, and . . .

Some minutes, or an hour, later we dress. Now we're all buttons and business. It is time to eat. I want a steak, a Coke, and a bloomin' onion. Or at the very least some French fries.

And make that steak rare.

Mathieu insists that we walk along the quay first, that the restaurants are empty at this time of the evening, that nobody in his right mind—he's excepting Americans—eats at ten before seven. He wants me to see something.

The beauty of the evening and the hum in my heart are in such harmony that I readily agree.

It is the magic time of the evening, dusk, when the burnt sun at our backs slips past its horizon, and the Paris sky inflames to a purplish fever. The sky is larger in Paris, panoramic. There are no skyscrapers to choke its view, and like everything in Paris, I have no doubt that it was by design. You have to admire a city and its people for having such perfect consideration for one another. Ahead, rooted to its isle, is Notre Dame, her chameleon sandstone absorbing the last light of the evening and alchemizing it into this fiery façade that glows from within. Like an opal, she is Paris's fairest jewel.

Mathieu and I walk in silence, our hands joined, the Seine flowing languidly beside us. I marvel at the day's thread. I have experienced years that unspooled faster, and with less to show for them at the end. I haven't grown so much as enjoyed many life-times. Was it just last night that I called Andy, that schoolboy, with whom sex was as satisfying as a wet sneeze? This morning that I fantasized about a vigilant autonomy, a sacred aloneness? Now I belong to Mathieu, and he to me. I do not feel any kind of sacrifice at the giving. He has not stripped me of my independence but sharpened every particle of my being until I am downright aerodynamic—a woman made to fly—making more of this thing I call my *self* than I could have been leaning over my balcony, a Juliet without her Romeo.

With no great fanfare, the lights of Paris blink on.

"Ahh," I sigh, my heart thumping its admiration. Mathieu smiles. This is what he wanted: to flood my darkness with light. The bridge ahead, one of nineteen straddling the Seine in Paris, illuminates as a *bateaux mouche* tucks under, and the happy couples on board, drunk on life, clap their joy. A lone artist, desperate to finish his painting, fights against the darkness on the quay, squinting into the light above his easel, dabbing color onto the canvas while a thicker paintbrush remains slung behind his ear. He curses under his breath, disgusted with the night's claim. His painting of slaps and dashes is unremarkable, but his fierce commitment fills me with pleasure. I breathe in his turpentine as we pass. It is the pungent scent of someone following his bliss.

Musicians are out, filling the lovers and *flâneurs* with song, trading on their talent for the sporadic drop of a coin. It seems a hard existence, until you breathe in the languorous Paris night, the charm of the open-air concert hall in which they perform, and a deliberate choice to shun convention and embrace a life of unimpoverished poverty. Ahead, the ubiquitous accordion player stands, too stiff-lipped and dignified for parody, and squeezes the sound out of his instrument with the care of a surgeon massaging blood into his patient's heart. The notes are tremulous and sad, a quivering sob pulled from his fingers. Tears fill my eyes, for when the heart is full, it does not take much pressure to make it burst, splattering the contents in an emotional carnage. I wipe my eyes and scavenge for a euro from my sweater pocket to drop in his case, to repay our earlier debt. If only there were some way of letting him know it's not charity. I look at him, wanting the connection, but his eyes, including the paralyzed, droopy one, are closed in meditation. He hears the *plink* of my little tribute and nods gravely, maintaining his inward focus. I come to a realization: these people are not here for our money. This is prayer.

If I relaxed my eyes, blurring the electric lights into gas, it might be a hundred years earlier. This is why Americans come to Paris. It may wax and wane in our collective imagination, but its gravity is as reliable as the moon's upon the oceans' tides, its effect on us undimmed through the ages. It, like the Matisse, remains the same. It's we who change.

I look up at Mathieu to find him lost in thought. His remoteness pleases me. It feels good to ignore one another, to reclaim the quiet of solitude, if not its heavy sentence. I want to walk all night by his strong, silent side. I want to sail under dark bridges and whisper sweet nothings to the reflectionless water, as we push toward long horizons. I want to seize an instrument, any instrument, and pound out the fugue inside my heart. I want to swallow time and hold it pregnant within me. I want to dance on the graves of saints and sinners. I want to suck out all the marrow out of the marrow of life . . . and belch when I am full.

I want to live so deep that I cannot find sunlight.

Chapter 16

We eat with our hands. Like cavemen, or toddlers.

The restaurant is Ethiopian, and the setting this stuffed basement room in the Latin Quarter. We rub shoulders with strangers whose plummy faces, unaccustomed to feral, African spices, glisten with exertion. Heaping platters of colorful dishes are placed in front of our new friends, who initially look taken aback (so which one is the ox?), then tentative, then transported. I begin to understand the effect imaginatively prepared food and that elusive variable called *atmosphere* (which cannot be scooped from the troughs we call "buffets"—ironic French word origin notwithstanding—back home), can have on people. There is a fragile unity here that is temporal, but felt. We are sharing in something neither trivial nor profound. We are simply eating communally, and in so doing we perform a ritual that transcends time.

Intricate basketry and African masks adorn the restaurant, along with more modernist paintings that brook the divide between the continents. Some look like reinterpretations of Chagall, with floating people, and grinning skeletons, serenely rendered in primary colors, while others remind me of Hindu mandalas, or Aztec calendars, in their circular iconography. It is at moments like these when I marvel at the sameness of people across the globe, how the points of departure are really that: small diversions that exploit, and elaborate on, our commonality. The world is a sphere, without beginning or end, the divisions arbitrary, ghostly things. For the first time in Paris, in the belly of this humid restaurant, I have no sense of being a foreigner. The place has a comforting sense of inclusion, and movement.

It is American jazz, those throaty steppes of Stan Getz's sax, which buoys our conversations, and not the muscular, driving beat of Ethiopian drums. Paris has a raging hard-on for American music—particularly old-school jazz. My mom would approve. I will have to tell her when I get back. If I get back.

When it is our turn, I am so hungry that I do not hesitate. I grab a piece of *injera*, a crepe-type bread, and plow it through the red-peppered chicken stew, stuffing it into my mouth, where it sizzles on my tongue. I like how the food is served—all entrées to a single ceramic plate. No pretensions; what's mine is yours, *mon ami*. I take a big gulp of water, ignoring my sweating wine, and dab at my temples with a cloth napkin.

Mathieu grins. "Too much for you?"

"Are you kidding?" I scoff, throwing back another mouthful. "I grew up with a mother who challenged us to jalapeño pepper contests and made Indian curries that set our hair on fire." I cough. "This is nothing."

"I grew up in cafés and restaurants, the waiters my extended family, until I learned to take care of myself." Mathieu's hand pauses halfway to his mouth, and his eyes catch a sparkle from someone's glass. "Someday I will cook for you—real Provençal cooking, Daisy—and you will finally appreciate this cuisine that frightens you so."

"Frighten is too strong a word. I'm just skeptical of any nation that puts egg on pizza," I retort, smearing my bread through the meat and veggie mixture. "It makes me question everything."

He volunteers a healthy bite of his *injera*, with spiced lamb heaped on top. I hesitate, before gingerly taking it into my mouth. It is so tender it curls on my tongue. Closing my eyes, I treasure the subtle flavor. I would never eat lamb, or veal, at home. But I would never remove my shoe in a restaurant and slide my foot up to my sweetheart's crotch, either.

"Yummy. But it's not French." I laugh, wiggling my toes. He squirms, and I dig in harder.

But playtime is interrupted. The couple to my left, whose female elbow I could touch, is jawing at one another. They whisper in French, spewing their animosity across a delightful looking vegetarian dish, tainting the poor turnips with venomous spittle. I felt real generosity toward the pair only moments ago, when I saw the smiling waiter set the food down before them. I have always admired vegetarians in the same way I admire nuns or monks. I could never do it, but you have to respect their devotion and sacrifice. They seem like more empathetic creatures than the rest of us. Outside the crooked imagination of some reality-television creator, it is impossible to think of monks fighting with monks or nuns fighting with other nuns. And it would have been nearly as impossible for me to imagine the girl vegetarian reaching over and yanking out her partner's eyebrow stud with a twist of her fingers, if I hadn't just seen it with my own two eyes. She tosses the piece of silver into the turnips and heads for the stairs, unmoved by her boyfriend's moans, as he patches his eye with one hand while digging through the veggies for the stud. Jewelry claimed, but self-respect in tatters, he throws some money on the table for the half-finished food and follows his hot-blooded mate up the stairs. Maybe it was just too spicy for them.

Dumbfounded, I allow my foot to fall and lean in toward Mathieu, who takes the melodrama in stride, working methodically away at his lamb and glass of vintage Bordeaux. His imperturbation reminds me of my father, whose natural state is to exist as his own island.

"What were they fighting about?" I whisper. Everyone in our cozy, model United Nations anxiously eyes the scattered remains of the absent diners' food, like they might hold the penetrable secret of this failing country's civil war.

Mathieu, the equitable secretary-general, shrugs. "She thinks he has been cheating. He does not deny it to her satisfaction."

"Really? And so he admitted it just now?"

"No, not at all. He told her that she was being absurd." He licks his finger. "She did not appreciate this so much."

I sit up. "Who would? The bastard!" I gulp some wine, barely tasting it. Mathieu wants to laugh at me, of course. He is amused that I automatically take the woman's side. I'm sure he thinks it quite irrational. "Have they been together long?" I demand. "And he's already cheating on her . . . Jesus! Were they planning to marry?"

Mathieu holds up his hands in defense. "Have mercy, Daisy! I cannot know. I heard one minute's worth of conversation."

I nod, somewhat accepting of this.

He continues, "Why do you get mad at me? Does my being male make me complicit?"

I consider. "Maybe. You see, that could be us at some future dinner table."

"When?"

I am a little light-headed. The wine, I guess. I frown at my food and shove it away. "Any time, I suppose. Now. We have had sex, you see. So in the space of a single day, I've gone from being the lovely temptress to an old hag, jealously guarding her happiness." Placing my head in my hands, I groan, "And God, I've just realized that I am *such* a little tramp."

Mathieu motions for me to lean in. I do. He plants a sweet kiss that cools my mouth off. "Mmm, yes, sex changes everything—especially sex with slutty American college girls." He draws away, adding, "It makes everything tastier," before grabbing my knee to squeeze it.

"But for how long?" I ask, not entirely distracted. "Until people decide to get married, there is that tension. That paranoia about what the other person's doing, or thinking. If he's going to duck out on you. No one can ever achieve total relaxation in a relationship."

I think unhappily of Andy, acknowledging my suppressed suspicion that he simply found somebody, more available for Saturday night karaoke and the silly, sloppy sex that follows, to replace me. Perhaps I needed *him* less than his complete devotion.

Can it be a coincidence that I only started fantasizing about marriage once we were apart?

"You have a lot of faith in marriage, Daisy."

"Maybe I do."

"But why?"

"If my parents can last as long as they have, anyone can."

"And they are so happy?"

"No. But they're faithful," I reply, with some force.

"Faithful to what?" he asks.

"I don't know . . . an idea, I guess. A very American idea of what happiness should be. Nice house, two kids, members of several philanthropic organizations to lessen their class guilt." I squirm, feeling like I've betrayed them. "Don't get me wrong. They do love each other—in a way. It's just not passionate. I'm not sure if it ever was. It's more like they're caretakers of one another. Lifelong protectors against loneliness."

"You make it sound so romantic."

I swat Mathieu on his arm. "It's not romantic. But it's—I

don't know—" I shrug, embarrassed. "It's sweet, I guess. And a little brave. Or cowardly. I can't decide which."

Mathieu nods and sits back. "Then that settles it."

"Settles what?"

He snaps his fingers. "We are now married."

I laugh, pulling my plate back to break off some bread. "Cute."

He leans forward. "I am serious. If marriage is only an idea, then what stops me from having this idea and making good on it? If *I* say we are married, and you agree, then whose authority do we need?"

"Oh, I don't know . . . the state of France might have something to say about you marrying a no-account American *alien*, who doesn't have a green card, and more importantly, couldn't figure out for the life of her why the Bastille wasn't where it was supposed to be when she looked for it a week ago." My fluttering heart belies my light tone.

"You are talking about legalities. A social contract." Mathieu grabs my hand with the bread still pinched in it. "I am talking about a union of two people responsible only to each other. For this one night, we are married. In fact, we have been married for years now, yes?" His eye invents a new sparkle, and he summons the crooked smile that slays me. "As long as your parents, at least. And we have a history. A beautiful tapestry we have threaded together, over time, which cannot be unraveled."

He squeezes my hand, the bread drops. "Tell me again, Daisy—my memory is so poor lately—what was the name of our first pet? That little furball on Rue Lepic in Montmartre?"

The waiter sweeps away the memory of the unhappy couple to our right. Just like that, there is a fresh linen tablecloth sanitizing the table, and two new wineglasses waiting to be filled. Soon a new couple, with hope in their hearts, will sit down and drink. I look into Mathieu's face; he's waiting for me to play my role. A scratch tickles my throat. I do not acknowledge that this is our one crack at having a history because I can see the bittersweet knowledge of it reflected in his eyes. I swallow any regret and say, "I can't believe you don't remember, honey. Our Jack Russell was named Fonzie."

He slaps the table. "Yes, of course. You named him. I had wanted to call him Balzac."

"That would have been tragic. Poor little guy would have had to put up with nonneutered dogs thinking we were making fun of his ball-lessness."

Mathieu crinkles his forehead, and I giggle.

Smoothing my napkin across my lap, I continue, "Still, darling, would it have killed you to pick up little Fonzie's poop from time to time? I could never let you walk him because it embarrassed me to leave it lying there on the sidewalk." I shake my head in what I consider to be my best approximation of the scolding wife. "I will never understand, after living here for twelve years, why a French person cannot bend down to retrieve some dog waste. Something in the French backbone will not allow it."

"Twelve years?" He frowns, the static of confusion interfering with our picture of domestic happiness.

"When you take into account our half-years in New York, of course."

He coughs. "Of course. New York is lovely in the spring," he says, almost managing wistfulness. "All the trees . . . blooming like they do."

"How would you know, dear?" I ask, popping more bread. "We spend the autumns and winters in Greenwich Village."

"New York is lovely in the autumn. All those leaves . . . turning in Central Park."

"Mmm."

"The Christmas windows in Macy's."

"Mmm."

"Ice skating in front of Rockefeller Center."

"Mmm . . . yes." For someone who doesn't like America, he has an awfully Normal Rockwell vision of the place. Or maybe he's seen more Nora Ephron movies than he cares to admit.

"Taking the kids to the Met."

I cough. "Oh yes, the kids."

"Colette and Jean-Paul loved the Picassos there."

"Well—er, Colette?" I raise an eyebrow, and he nods. "I believe *Colette*, with her keen eye for color, was more enamored with Matisse's *Dance*."

"She gravitates toward the obvious choices," he laments, before smiling broadly. "Now Jean-Paul takes after me." Mathieu thumps his chest like a daddy gorilla, and I don't try to dampen my smile.

I pick at something on the table. "Yes, that's true. The boy will not shut up. Just the other day, Madame Pompadour told me that he stopped her outside the grocery store, when he saw her buying . . ." I look around, before whispering, "A frozen quiche . . . *from Italy.*"

I shake my head sadly. "The poor lady—afflicted with Meniere's disease because, as you know, scientific funding has been cut in France in favor of more triumphal arches—anyway, she just couldn't handle making a five-course meal anymore, what with the dizziness and ringing in her ears, but Jean-Paul stood there and berated her for not understanding the 'historical origins and cultural implications' of buying *locally* overfed goose livers for a good fifteen minutes. She said she wanted to faint, but she was afraid of offending such inspired self-righteousness."

Mathieu, chin resting on his hand, observes, "Such a fine boy."

I reach across the table and take his hand. "Yes, he is." I smile and squeeze his fingers. He brushes the inset of my wrist with a kiss.

Mathieu clears something from his throat and releases my hand. "I have to say, Daisy, that I am overjoyed we still make love so often."

"What? Twice a week?"

"More like six times by my count," he says, grinning wickedly. "And that is only because you insist on taking Saturdays off."

"Did I convert to Judaism at some point? Am I forgetting this?"

"No, Saturdays are the days you teach your art school program at the Orsay. It really wears you out, does it not?"

"Mmm, it does. Just last Saturday, I was doing a tour and little Philippe took out his Magic Marker and drew a moustache on an Ingres nude. I told him he has great instincts, but he needs to work on his form. Then I asked his father for a check." I sigh. "That's why I am so relieved to get back in the lab on weekdays. It's just me and my electron microscope."

He pouts at the microscope but brightens and strokes my knee. "I adore making love against your electron microscope, listening to you talk dirty about my ear cells."

I burst out laughing. "Yes, well, it's not always that comfortable, but I'm just so happy that after twenty-five years of marriage, you're still willing to take your chances and fuck me against a million-dollar machine. Some couples, you know, aren't so lucky. Some married couples, I am told in confidence, experience a total evaporation of their desire and passion for one another." I shudder dramatically. "I know it's impossible to believe such a thing."

Mathieu looks into my eyes. "I think you are more beautiful now than when we first met."

I swallow something in my throat. "I believe you. I have never wanted you more, *mon mari*."

He is touched by my remedial French. I am delighted to find him so easily touched. We are giddy with our playacting, but there is an undercurrent of poignant recollection as we sit and imagine things that will never become. I see Mathieu at fifty in the flickering candlelight, graying at the temples but undaunted by age (no cornered look in *his* eye), his jowls loosening, softening him, those marvelous lips thinning but still vibrant and warm as he presses them to my slackened skin, mapping the familiar terrain. He makes a fine fifty. Less strident, more measured, but still eager to jump into a debate with me and conquer imaginary worlds with all the weapons his words can devise.

Still eager to jump into a debate with someone, I correct myself. Some shadow woman who watches Truffaut films, nibbles brie, and is the final authority on Simone de Beauvoir. She is out there, even now, absorbing *The Razor's Edge* in a single sitting while lounging in a gorgeous black-lace *chemise*, her red, manicured nails smoothing the pages as Erik Satie's piano drips a ghoulish melancholia into her soul.

I cannot hate this woman. But God, I envy her so.

Two men come and sit at the adjoining table. One of them is a puffy-faced but commanding gentleman in a three-piece suit with blue tie. I blink at him, uncomprehending.

It's Al Gore.

He gives me an inscrutable look as he lays his napkin over his lap, and I could swear, really swear, that it is Gore, the same man destroyed by a butterfly ballot in Florida and labeled a psychopath by the media upon his impassioned objection to America's first preemptive war. His look makes me feel complicit, guilty. We lock eyes, and then he turns to face the wiry, stooped man across from him. He's got a face for listening. It zeroes in on you.

Mathieu smiles quizzically. "You have escaped me again," he murmurs, playing with my fingers.

Tearing my eyes away from the bizarre hallucination, I try to smile. "You will just have to keep coming after me."

His eyes are clear and wide. Like a bruised Paris sky.

"I always have."

Chapter 17

It has become freakishly cold out. Luckily, the alcohol is a slow
drip of warm solvent through my veins.

It being our twenty-fifth anniversary and all, we walk to the
place where the deal was sealed. My memory must be hazy—it's
gotta be the two, or three, or seven, glasses of wine fogging me
over—because I keep thinking he will take me back to Luxembourg Gardens, or to the Orsay: someplace whose meaning can
be met halfway by our infant selves and the derivative couple we
shadow. But no, we are walking, a bit slatternly, toward the Seine.
I am a little nervous that we took the plunge on a river cruise, unsure that my forty-eight-year-old, inebriated stomach can handle
a boat ride right now. I kind of want to lie down on the little
cobblestone pillows and explore the intoxicating idea that I might
be exhausted and/or stupid drunk.

"Wouldn't be prudent . . . at this juncture," I mumble,
hiccupping.

"What did you say?" Mathieu asks. His arm feels like pudding.

"I said the first George Bush was a real hero, a can-do kind of guy, a regular mutton chop of a presidential person when you consider what a raging fuckup little W is." I list to the side, and Mathieu steadies me.

"I had forgotten what a light drinker you are," he says, propping me up. "I like it when you drink. You are so honest. And loud."

"W . . . can you imagine the childlike brain that answers to that nickname?" I feel wonderfully chatty, ex*traor*dinarily intuitive, so I answer my own question. "No, of course *you* can't. Do French people even have nicknames, or does it corrupt the language?"

No reaction from the Frenchie on this.

"Anyway, little W needs to go back to presidential preschool, where he can take a shellacking from Papa Rove, his strict constructionist, no longer isolationist, thumb-up-your-ass-ist governess, before taking refuge in Karen Hughes' matronly bosom." I giggle. "I'd love to see Rove in pantaloons, wouldn't you? And definitely a bonnet. He has that nice, bland Midwestern face about him. It's so deceptively dull—not nearly Machiavellian enough. He looks like he should be the general manager at the South Des Moines Walmart. But put him in a bonnet, and it'd be precious—I could almost start to like the bastard—like he was a pudgy monkey playing dress-up, and not the puppet master of the free world."

Mathieu only gives me a look. I have to work harder.

"I can hear George and Babs scolding the little shit, can't you? *Georgie Porgie, you'll never be as bright as big brother, Jebbie, so take a spoonful of Texas sugar, let the inferiority complex go down, and maybe in fifty years, after a Republican amount of repression and resentment, it'll explode like an oil well to make a cowboy of you.*" *Hiccup.* "Too bad the rest of the country, and the world, has to endure a Freudian pissing match with his dad, but what're you going to do?" I absorb a small stumble over the undulating sidewalk. Weebles wobble, but they don't fall down. "Such a shame that Daddy didn't show him that arms are for hugging."

Mathieu loses his amusement and nods stiffly at some she-person supported by a cell phone. The instant we pass her, I step on a sheet of newspaper rolling like tumbleweed down the narrow Parisian street. The thing sticks to my shoe before I shake it off, and it goes tumb-a-ling, tumb-a-ling again. I shiver and look across my shoulder. "She was pretty, I think. And shaken to see you."

He gives me no lead. And so I take it. "Why is it that you only know pretty people, Mathieu? Where's that *boulangerie* you were talking about? I would like to see your fat, jolly, *old* friend about now. I'm a little bothered by this parade of beautiful women you attract, especially beautiful lesbian women. They have this weird side effect of making me feel for Georgie."

I teeter to the left, scraping my elbow against an historic French building and leaving behind a bit of personal history. I feel no pain, even as I watch the cut skin struggling to clot, my body's cavalry of platelets riding to the rescue without my over-sight. *Fibrinogen molecules unite! We've got a real situation at the intersection of humerus and radius. On the double, proteases!* If I am the God of my machine, I must not be omnipotent or omniscient, because I don't have control over any of it, and I don't know what the fuck's going on. But it runs pretty smoothly. The blood soon coagulates, forming a thick putty over the wound. All is saved. *Good work, soldiers: at ease.*

Fascinating mechanism, really, but my mind, like a triggered Venus flytrap, closes upon the red stuff itself, that salty porridge swimming through our veins and which drips warmly down my arm. The liters of blood that must have washed down this Paris alley. My DNA comingling with the genetic muck of Paris in an international cocktail. Rivers of blood and human waste have been absorbed by Parisian cobblestones, saturating the rocky surfaces before finding the Paris sewers (what a city: even its *sewers* rate tours), and flowing toward the open sea to find dilution of its memory. The Seine should be a sludgy bloodbath, but it's forgotten the revolutions, too, or is holding them a watery secret.

Oh, the city pays tribute to these acts of terror, is even rather boastful of them, like their monuments wink knowingly about a rakish, if lovable, past. Yet it's been whitewashed, gilded. Funny how removed we feel from the chaos that came before. It's only been a few generations since a bunch of raging, murderous thugs scurried like rats through the maze of Paris streets, slicing and dicing other rats at random, making heroes of brutes and victims of laypeople. Have we evolved so rapidly? Do we have less capacity for bloodlust now? No. We've simply promoted technology to do our dirty work.

It takes a monster, feral or groomed, to kill a man with his bare hands. The monster has the peculiar talent for looking into a victim's eyes and not recognizing that shared throb of humanity. He will always see the Other in place of a Brother. Today, it only requires a feeble imagination to commit the same atrocity, on a more spectacular, *shock and awe* level. The computer acts as an indifferent intermediary, the distance serves as buffer. Rarely do we have to confront "the whites of their eyes" anymore; rarely do we, as a nation, have to witness the consequences of war. Rarely has war been born so lightly. Little W—a man who is neither omnipotent, nor omniscient, but believes himself to be—has made us all small. I hope we grow into our shame.

For Americans love to point to our national origins as a sign of superior pedigree and character. After all, we threw some tea over a boat; the French revolutionaries cut people's heads off and staked them on poles. We invented a new form of democracy, largely on the strength of a few men's prescient ideas and iron will; they cut some more heads off. But now our nobility is slipping away. We've become the punch-drunk aggressors—gnashing our teeth in time to the heroic beat that swings flags and corruptible hearts, offering up our liberties like devotionals to a new god called fear—and the French are the wannabe diplomats whose sincerity would be more believable if there wasn't all that bloody history to dampen our confidence. Funny how things change. I think it was Jefferson who penned, "All tyranny needs to gain a foothold is for people of good conscience to remain silent." The French know something about that. But I, too, have been a mouse, my conscience a muffled squeak in a noisy world too littered with mice, all scratching out small, rodent existences in a bigger rat's house of ideas. When what we need are some trumpeting elephants.

Yes, it's funny the difference a day makes in one's level of out-rage. Practically unreal, some might say. Fair enough. But I was asleep. Now I am awake. My life is no longer a dream, or a night-mare. It is the pale moon of Paris *and* the silver guillotine.

And I felt something of its blade upon my neck as another of Mathieu's pretty ghosts brushed my shoulder, while a foreign (it could not be American) newspaper attached itself to my chance, gummy shoe. I looked down and saw a small Iraqi boy with no arms looking haunted and aged—like, it must be said, without a whiff of hyperbole, a concentration camp survivor—beneath my foot, which has no claim on its good fortune other than landing luckily upon this earth in some geopolitical realm that doesn't punish the riding of a bicycle around my yard with losing two limbs and, who knows, very probably a family. Because wasn't it *lucky*, in someone's (but not God's) twisted imagination, that this liberated boy pedaled while his five siblings sat in a house constructed of glass and wood and nails whose carnage quotient was regrettably (*so sorry, folks, didn't mean to!*) realized only after the errant bomb hit? After that tissue-paper flesh serving as the barrier between the rigid outside world and the multitudes of wondrous things—from inner ear hair cells to dizzying, first-love dreams, which were whirling like a rainfall of falling helicopter seeds within that softly mortal interior—was eviscerated.

There is a new moon tonight.

And so I think to wonder, for the first time, what my country's military industrial complex is up to in the middle of this moonless night, in a faraway country where the people are brown, the oil is black and bubbling, and the children's fear tastes metallic, like the blood congealing on my arm.

It's enough to make me think back to that restaurant mirage, and further, to that ballot in Florida. What a butterfly effect it predicated. Where have you gone, Al Gore? A nation returns its lonely eyes to you. We'll accept the stiffness of your spine, as long as it's connected to a conscience.

And hey, drunk people can use words like *incorrigible* (if not actually *say* it) and get misty-eyed about Jefferson and that pack of holy white men, and Al Gore, too. You can be shit-faced and homesick and have verbal diarrhea at the same time (again, see our friend Henry Miller). The personal becomes political, if you open your eyes. What else should I think about? That the soulful girl with scarlet fingernails looked at Mathieu with more longing than Bergman had for Bogart at the airport? Why would I want to think about *that*?

I want to believe in Mathieu, and America. I just wish they'd stop giving me reasons to suspect them of a lousy betrayal.

"That was not a lesbian," Mathieu finally says. He does not notice my elbow, which depresses me.

"Oh, so there are straight women in France?"

He pauses. "Yes, occasionally they are past lovers."

"No."

"Mmm." He takes my elbow reassuringly.

"As in a lover you've had recently?" I ask, not reassured.

"As in a lover I had before you. Not so recently, however. At least twenty-five years and ten days ago by my count."

"As recent as that?"

He grins. "It feels like an eternity ago, Daisy. A different lifetime."

We walk.

"She looked like Natalie Portman."

"Who?"

"Nothing."

My left elbow throbs. Paris has pricked me. Her pacifist persona is just that: studied, false. Beneath this perfect beauty beats the heart of a lioness straining against her chains. She would like to ravage the world again, eat us alive. Just give her the motivation and a vision.

She could be a real bitch if she wanted to.

We stand in front of a nondescript storefront. My eyes swim toward the lettering above the doorway. *Shakespeare & Co.* I feel less than reverential. I was not married on the street in front of a bookstore—Iraqi boys with no arms notwithstanding. My still-vigorous self-interest insists it didn't happen.

Mathieu looks at me expectantly.

"Really? Here?" I ask, pulling the corners of my mouth in.

"It is the perfect blending of the English-speaking world and the French." Mathieu smiles. "We invented a new nation here twenty-five years ago, Daisy." He circles around me, dragging his foot. "You and I. It is the only place in Paris that could mean something equal to the both of us."

I look again. The idea is nice. But behind me, over the quay, is Notre Dame, luminous and lasting. "I don't know, Mathieu. I could have sworn we ducked into Notre Dame and got hitched there."

"People do not duck into Notre Dame and get hitched. Especially non-Catholic people who do not believe in marriage as a holy sacrament. It is not Vegas, Daisy."

"Okay, okay. Settle down. I guess we got married here." I turn my back on Notre Dame, scuffing my foot on the ground. "Since you thought of it first."

He stands rigidly, hands jammed inside his pants pockets. As I watch him mope, it occurs to me that we are children fighting over a petty game of make-believe. And we both want to be the white knight. In reality, I am ferociously tipsy and more than a little upset about the Queen Amidala clone, and he is perturbed because I have casually, even heartlessly, drop-kicked his romantic idealism over onto the Right Bank, that more pragmatic realm of Paris of which we dare not speak.

We seem to be at an impasse. Someone's got to say it.

"We seem to be at an impasse."

He sighs noisily. "I thought you would be happy with this. It seemed . . . inspired, back in the restaurant."

I sigh noisily. We find a nearby bench. The sidewalk outside the shop is bustling, even at this hour. Two Muslim girls frown and bury their chins into their chests as a group of teenage boys give chase, nipping at their head scarves and laughing. Apparently, being a meathead is not an American invention. I have an urge to follow them, but they've curved the corner and disappeared. I turn to Mathieu. He is looking the other way.

"It's a lovely idea. I just think I've run out of romantic steam. It occurs to me that I have twenty-one hundred American dollars left, and that when it is gone, I am too."

He leans back into the bench, his arm thrown behind me. "I thought we would not entertain the idea of endings yet."

"I can't help it." *I time my orgasms to the precise, soulful crescendos of favored songs.* "I mean, I figure out what I'm going to TiVo in monthly increments. I do my Christmas shopping in the summer. It's in my nature to look ahead."

Mathieu narrows his eyes and looks again to the couple occupying the bench to our right. They nuzzle each other's necks, the girl shyly laughing. I can feel the wish in his silence. He already wants to change me, make me more like him, oblivious to anything but the moment. I tried it, I liked the novelty of it, but it looks a bit phony on me, like these shoes I awkwardly carry but may never wear. Before and after making love, I thought about my mother's words, and considered, in a disembodied way, our lack of a condom. I never would have had sex without a condom back home. The idea would have terrified me. I permitted it here because I wanted Mathieu more than I cared about the future. I *needed* Mathieu. Swimming in the current of those arms, I'd have taken the rough gamble of water over the life preserver and drowned happy. The thought shames me now. Especially since it's about thirteen days after the start of my period. Time is nauseatingly relevant and as pressing as a fist against my belly.

If we're not careful, the two of us could formulate a new and semipermanent Franco-American alliance that has my determined chin set within Mathieu's stubborn jawline. And which flexes both when it doesn't get its way.

Mathieu strums my hair, running his fingers down the length and back up again. It feels good, and I lean into him. The night is not so cold with his arm around me. I banish thoughts of a little Jean-Paul from my splintering head and remember where I am: my parents' bookstore, the one they both believe in. The site of my first Paris pilgrimage on that fleeting, rose-colored day. I left Shakespeare & Co. disenchanted, after coming across a copy of *The Razor's Edge* braced on the shelf like a silent accusation. Seeing it led me not to my father, whose disappointment I was accustomed to, but to Mathieu, that sphinxlike stranger on my first Paris train.

He had thought I could answer his riddle. But I didn't even know the question.

I realized, emerging from the doorway beside me, that I didn't know why I had come to this city that could only hold borrowed meaning, but that I knew, I *knew*, in a moment of perfect clarity, with the dust of old books and the fur of indolent cats-in-residence making my eyes tear, that it wasn't some quixotic quest for truth and understanding, but more like a break I could never have managed without the excuse Andy gifted to me. I had been walking my own razor's edge—juggling the roles of precocious student, perfectionist daughter, and determined girlfriend—all of my life, on a journey that swung me in circles. I wanted to fall off the blade and rest. Paris provided a good leaping-off point.

And Mathieu has soft arms.

Yet this doesn't feel like rest. Instead, I'm walking along a cleaner edge, a prescient path through Sandburg's "impalpable" mist, where I breathe the purer, if more mysterious, air of blind men. This edge might take me somewhere. Mathieu is with me, but his weight throws me, and he keeps trying to circle around me to pull ahead. I don't know how to manage the both of us. I don't know how to make the journey my own and ours. I don't know how to have a relationship yet, and particularly this relationship. For this isn't some ordered, algebraic world I've programmed myself into, where the equation is always solvable for x and y. Our world is a god-awful differential equation, stacked with so many layers of independent variables that we can barely find one another in the baffling mix. Even then, when you solve the damned thing, what do you get but some kind of laborious graph whose meaning no one (not even my Chinese TA) understands, that looks like it was scratched by tying a gigantic pen to the tail of a meandering cow who doesn't know his ass from a hole in the ground.

And yet I am in love with him (Mathieu, not the cow, though

both would be astonished, in their steady, wide-eyed fashion, to find me thinking of my love life in terms of mathematical paradigms), and bound to him for the duration of this crooked journey. There's the rub.

Mathieu pokes me in the ribs, and I jump half a foot into the air. He shakes his head, amused by my perpetual distractions, and directs my attention toward the bookstore. "Go buy me a Christmas present."

Surprised, I look at him. "Are you serious?"

"Yes, as you say, we might not have a Christmas together. So let us enjoy one now."

I love this man. He is not unbendable. I clasp his boyish, pliable form, and he looks pleased, if embarrassed, which moves me more than any grand romance he might invent. I stand and play with his hair, grazing his ear with my fingers, while he fixes me with those eyes, willing me toward something again. I turn to go but stop and spin around. "Wait, don't I rate a present too?"

"I thought I gave you your present earlier this afternoon." He shoots off a shit-eating, *American* grin at me and hangs his foot on his knee.

I swat him on the arm, as girls do when they like a boy, and he pulls me on his lap, as boys who fancy a girl must do. He kisses my neck and assures me that he will find me something later. Like I really care. He's right, of course. Making love to Mathieu under the Matisse sure beat my mom's homemade, beeswax candles that I got for Christmas last year. I kiss him on his cowlick and leave him behind to complete my mission.

Shakespeare & Co. is a shrine for people who try their worldly best to scorn shrines. It might be the secular humanist's style of worship to kneel at this rather shabby storefront and be filled with the grace of the written word, as penned by mere mortals. The bookstore is the ultimate beacon of egalitarianism, though the light it emits is low wattage, with scores of books presented in the same, haphazard manner—leaning against one another for support, some careworn. Each book's ultimate, intangible worth is to be determined by the reader, of course, and not by the unassuming people who mill about the place, and whom one supposes, by their vestments of unwashed T-shirts and jeans, must be the employees/tenants since they drowsily eye the collection plate.

If the whole of Paris enjoys a utopian reputation for struggling artists, its *café crème* and red wine the locally grown panaceas for what ails your inspiration, then this modest building, with its mossy appeal, must be the writer's inner sanctum, its primeval Shangri-La.

It is no wonder my father and Mathieu love it so. My dad, the bibliophile, wants to consume it all, while Mathieu, the writer-philosopher, wants to create the masterpiece worthy of its shelves.

There is a lot of pressure on little ol' Daisy, who has not felt confident in bookshops since *Professor* Lockhart took her to a *Walden's* and directed her toward *The Canterbury Tales*, forcing her to pronounce words like *sovereyn pestilence*, while she eyed the complete set of *Frog and Toad* stories, envisaging herself as the upbeat, eternally patient Frog and her father as the more grousy Toad explaining the Christ symbolism in the Prioress's tale. Mathieu, too, expects a bona fide home run, something dazzling and brilliantly discerning. For gifts say a lot about the giver. How I wish I could get by with a three hundred euro pair of red high heels! How easy that would be. Finding the perfect book to give Mathieu is like trying to find my mother that obscure jazz record she doesn't have, has somehow never heard of, and will love anyway. The last one I tried was a Duke Ellington collection of b-sides. She patted my head and said it was something my father might have given her. This seemed a bit harsh. And not entirely accurate since at least I got her the compact disc and not the 78 LP my dad would have triumphantly wrangled for a quarter at a garage sale.

There are the biggies up front. *Ulysses*. Purported to be the best novel ever written, though I couldn't stick to the first ten pages while simultaneously clinging to the notion that I was not half retarded. *A Moveable Feast*. Obviously Paris-centric, by Papa Hemingway's unsentimental, if still tender, hand. It wouldn't make much sense to buy it for Mathieu, who I am sure has read it, though nowhere near the Café de la Mairie bordering St. Sulpice, of course. Moving on . . . Henry James, you inscrutable prick. How could you have written both *Washington Square* and *The Golden Bowl*? How is a mind capable of such murky digressions and convolutions (she asks, digressing)? Wade into late James, and you might drown in the swirling vortices of his saltwater sentences. My finger traces the thin binding to my namesake's story. Nah. Too obvious. And I still can't forgive Ms. Miller for dying at the end. Though I begin to see why she had to.

There are the lesser titles in the main stacks, the great majority of which I have never heard of. A few stick out in sharp relief, like welcome friends in a room full of strangers: *A Room with a View*, *The English Patient*, *The God of Small Things*. Old friends. A few authors are more intimately known: Jane Austen's a beloved, spinsterish aunt who brings gossip and excellent advice; e.e. cummings is that shy, might-have-been boyfriend from college with the awful acne and scary talent; Patricia Cornwell is the embarrassing, experimental "friend" I took up with during a confusing phase and will never speak of again; and Jonathan Franzen is the hermetic, alcoholic uncle who shows up out of the blue to symbolically shit on your neat suburban lawn one day in order to demonstrate the constipated state of your soul, which might be annoyingly obvious were it not for the fact that he does it *so goddamn well*.

Some of them might find the company of the others suffocating (I can well imagine Franzen shriveling before Austen's glorious, surface directness). But they all mean something to me—oddly, maybe—for it is a distinctly lopsided relationship we keep. I can never return the favor of their friendship, yet I have held onto something dear and unintelligible from each, fingerprinting the cadence of their words, and the burden of their characters, onto some untouchable place in my heart, like a charcoal grave rubbing that smudges with time, but never entirely fades.

This is why it's nearly impossible to find the perfect book for someone. Movies, art, and music are universally shared experiences. Books are a sweetly solitary affair. The author can invent the characters and nudge them along an arc, but the reader is the most important character of all, the one who sees and judges everything: the architect of that supple third dimension. And the question is: what kind of world does Mathieu want to preside over? What will I be saying about myself and how I view him when—

Oops. I am not alone.

There's a puckish kitten with a pink nose and green eyes stretched out, at eye level, between Samuel Beckett's *First Love and Other Shorts* and (Sister) Wendy Beckett's *Joy Lasts: On the Spiritual in Art*. She yawns at me and demonstrates her pink, fuzzy belly.

"*Bonjour*, little friend," I coo. She mews in return and responds eagerly to my petting, running her whiskers through my fingers, the long nails gouging the book she sprawls across with a limpid entitlement that cats just naturally possess. No wonder the ancient Egyptians worshipped them as goddesses. They are nervy without showing us anything so humble as effort. "You're a funny little girl," I laugh, as she sits up and contemplates me with her head cocked to the side.

"She doesn't really belong here," an American voice says.

"Excuse me?" I don't feel so drunk anymore and can't understand why I would be hearing voices. Or seeing cats.

A girl's face peeks out from behind the kitten, and she chirps, "Hi. Sorry." She has a snub nose spotted with freckles and a do-rag covering a mess of hair.

I give an awkward wave. The kitten licks her nose with a sandpaper tongue.

"Yeah, this cat doesn't belong here. We already have a shop cat. This one just wandered in here this morning, and nobody had the heart to kick her out yet." She sighs and pets the kitten, which arches her back and lifts her tail. She's missing half of it, though the cat seems unconcerned of this fact, waving it about like a mast without its flag.

"She *seems* friendly," I say. I have always been a dog person. Cats I don't entirely trust.

"Yeah. They all are," she replies, like it's a common thing for homeless animals to seek refuge here, along with their human counterparts.

"What do you think will happen to her?" I ask, with a sense of foreboding. Little tiger kitty yawns again, revealing her sabertooth incisors, before resuming her washing.

The girl shrugs. "We can't take another one on. There's enough cat fur around here as it is, and George would never allow it. So I guess we'll have to throw her out before closing tonight, or someone will take her to a shelter."

The kitten stops licking herself. She mews and settles down on her books, resting her pert chin on Samuel Beckett's *Waiting for Godot*. She blinks, content to wait forever.

"What will happen to her at the shelter?"

Maybe the Parisians (being so enamored of their bureaucracy) have a system in place, some established protocol, with reams of absolutely necessary paperwork involved, whereby adorable, abandoned waif-animals are corralled into shelters and dispersed by government clerics into the rustic French countryside. There, they take up residence in charming barns, *chateaus*, and wineries, where they can live out their days with the cows, gentle people, and luscious grapes of the Bordeaux region, picking off a mouse here and there for sport, staring down sheep dogs with a superior detachment when queenliness is called for. This is why people love socialism, right? It takes care of everyone, from mighty cats to lowly humans.

"The same thing that happens back home. If she's not picked up after a couple days, she'll be killed."

Ugh. My faith, such as it was, in France's bleeding heart is officially dead. Someone wipe away the cobwebs, and stamp the death certificate.

A little American initiative is in order.

When Mathieu, lounging on his bench, sees me emerge from Shakespeare & Co. with a reconstructed box in my arms, he smiles his confusion. *Ah, she could not decide on just one. How sweet.* As he hears me baby-talk to the box, he drops his smile and looks wary. *Can she still be drunk?* As he sees the plucky feline head pop over the edge of the box, his eyes widen in alarm. *Has she gone completely insane?*

I smile sheepishly. I wish I had dimples like Camille's. They might be useful in these kinds of situations.

I approach him breathlessly and relay as rapidly as a child in a toy store, "I know I shouldn't have, but she would have died—no, been *murdered*, Mathieu—and I couldn't have that resting on my conscience, not when I've had the best day of my life. We couldn't send an animal to her grave on a night like this, could we, darling? And really, I know I was supposed to get you a book, but isn't receiving a living, breathing creation of God's—or random happenstance, rather—better than getting a book that you'd read in a couple nights and then ignore as it faded away on your bookshelf next to a hundred more? And if you're not a big cat person, that's okay, because I am a *huge* cat person—really—and I could always take her when I, you know . . . go home."

I appeal to him with my lapis blue eyes. "I know I'm changing our history here, Mathieu. But Fonzie was our first dog, that's all. We simply forgot, in our pre-Alzheimer's state, about our first kitty." I place one of the kitten's paws in Mathieu's limp hand, and do my best simulation of a cat's handshake. "I'm Beckett, Mathieu."

Mathieu slowly removes his hand. And looks at me. I smile. He glances around, his shoulders growing heavy with resignation. I feel the faintest exultation of a real wife. I am totally going to guilt him into this. And yes, a moment later, he clears his throat, and says softly, *"Enchantée*, Beckett. Let me show you to your new home." He reaches forward to take her paw again.

She promptly summons a guttural sound in her throat, somewhere between a *grrr* and a *yowl*, and starts to gnaw on his finger with a sense of limpid entitlement that cats just naturally possess. Mathieu extracts his punctured appendage and looks at me again.

I laugh nervously. "Silly Beckett." I reach for Mathieu's handkerchief from my jeans pocket, and thump the little carnivore on the head. "That's your Daddy, don't you know?"

Not two minutes later . . .

"Why call her Beckett? Why not Godot?"

"Who's Godot?"

"Well . . . hypothetically—"

"Yeah, no, exactly."

Ch**A**pter 18

After buying cat food, a dish, a rhinestone collar (she is a Parisian kitty), and a litter box from a twenty-four-hour supermarket, we hop aboard the metro. While retreating into daydreams (*Daisy Lockhart: Saving the World . . . One Cat at a Time*), Beckett accomplishes a slippery escape, taking up a haunched, dismissive stance behind a pungent, drunken man's legs, and only returning to us once a proper bribe—salmon, equally rank—is offered. Gashing a couple holes in the side of the box, I shut it and, daydreams contained, make for Mathieu's *quartier* in the fourteenth *arrondissement*.

I am surprised, after witnessing the sumptuousness of his father's place, and knowing that they still maintain a relationship, to find Mathieu living in near squalor in a tiny studio whose window is open on this cool October evening. Everything is in order, but there's not much to it: a bed, a bedside table, a bureau, a few abstract prints by artists I cannot place in my limited contemporary lexicon. For someone who supposedly loves to cook, the kitchen is little more than a galley, the refrigerator of the miniature, neglected kind. But there are the predictable mountain ranges of books that, overlying imagined fault lines, list heavily, with the occasional erosive boulder tumbling toward the valleys below. I see French and English titles on the crooked bindings. *Les Liasiones Dangeures*, meet *Dangerous Liaisons* two peaks over. Strangely enough, a copy of Camus' *The Fall* is in English, while Shakespeare's sonnets have been served up in a yeasty French.

There is a cleared path pointing to an ancient typewriter, chained, with padlock, to its desk. The legs of the chair have worn grooves into the hardwood floor. When I sit down, the chair squeals its complaint. I stand, flinching at the rebuke. A breeze enters and swirls around me. His walls are decorated with torn scraps of paper, French and English words slashed across their surfaces. Some are yellowing. They rustle in the wind. I hear their brittle whisper.

I am voiceless, and shy again here.

While Mathieu is in the bathroom, Beckett, in a frenzy of alpha-kitty payback, establishes the borders of her new territory, knocking an English paperback copy, as thick as my thigh, of Proust's *Remembrance of Things Past*, off its high pedestal. It glumps open to a random, tissue-thin page, where the words *prelude, obstacles,* and *volume* have been underlined in light pencil by, I presume, Mathieu's youthful, questioning hand.

So this is how he does it. Proust must be marginally more interesting than a French-English dictionary, though maybe as much effort. Mathieu had no need of travel, at least in the literal sense. He's acquired English the impossible way, through literary osmosis. I feel guilty for picturing him as some kind of French spy in Wichita, and maybe disappointed. Yet I still wonder at his total devotion to learning a language spoken by people he has so little use for.

I hear the toilet flush and hurriedly place Proust back atop a biography of someone named Derrida. When Mathieu emerges from the bathroom, I am trying to convince Beckett that climbing Mathieu's curtains is an overrated tourist jaunt from *Fodor's*, four years ago. But she does an awfully good impression of a vulture, roosting on her curtain rod, and starts to drift off, a sentry patrolling her castle turret with half an eye out for trouble. Mathieu wordlessly relocates some books and sets up her bowl and litter box in a cobwebbed corner of the room, while I try to swallow the guilt that is starting to blister the back of my throat.

He doesn't want us here. He has been violated, now that I've barged, with my cat, into his *chambre* before he even extended the offer. He feels wary, burdened, as asceticism seems a more worthy and familiar companion. Mathieu is a writer, an artist. And aren't they legendarily crotchety and foul-tempered? Can he afford my problems on top of those of his own invention? How many marriages did Hemingway attempt before he put a gun to his head? I search my head, desperate for anecdotes about happy writers and their equally sanguine lovers. Gertrude Stein and Alice Toklas were relatively happy, right? Does that count? Maybe it is just men who are the problem.

That's too easy, of course.

Edgy, I walk toward his desk again, creaking the floorboards, and notice something written on the paper kept by the carriage of the typewriter. I don't linger over it. Instead, I focus on the photographs pinned to the wall above his work space. One is of a hauntingly beautiful woman, turned slightly away, her face obscured by shadow. She must be Mathieu's mother. Unaware of the camera, she smiles to herself, and I can imagine the torment of this—how that resistant profile and private conversation must gall him into fits of remembrance for what he lost, or never quite had.

There are other girls on the wall who bear a striking resemblance to the same woman, and are likely his three sisters, though the pictures must be quite dated. One wears a flimsy, high school graduation gown—strange how traditions transplant themselves around the world—and is posing with a diploma, uncertain to be mock proud or the real thing. Another rests her head on the shoulder of some mystery person, who has been excised, the elusive smile of her mother's stretching the girl's heart-shaped face, widening the margins, while the third has her eyes squeezed shut and is cheerily—and boldly, considering her youth—giving the finger to the camera. They seem an aged progression of the same person, and I reflect upon which of the three I most identify with. I'd like to say the second sister, with her easy, liquid drowsiness, but it is the first, with that phony, perfunctory smile shrouding her insecurities. She is the overachiever of the bunch, and the worrier. I wonder what she thinks of her little brother. If she acts as a stern, substitute mother (*Mathieu, when are you going to get a* real *job?*), or if the years swimming between them were too daunting after the awful deed—her losing a mother at the time she needed one most, during the tumultuous time called puberty—was done. Now she may be only a memory on Mathieu's wall, a fading reminder of some alternative life, a longed-for collage. A place Mathieu can point to and say, *Things could have been different, if only . . . .*

His obsession with English was born the moment his mother stepped foot in America. His contempt, too.

We all have a trauma in our lives, somewhere to pin the blame when that elusive road of Robert Frost's seems more a brag than promise. Mine might have been Andy's breakup with me. It still could be.

There is a gap in the middle of the family photos, a lonely tack wearing a thin rim of white, in that provocative way tacks present themselves when their underlying photographs have been ripped away. I worry over the missing person, wondering where she has gone, why she was discarded. Is that where my picture would hang? On what day would he similarly sicken of me, or I of him? I absently finger the keys of the typewriter while I worry ahead, feeling their cool, contoured smoothness, and look downward. I have to smile. No computers for Mathieu then.

But broken butts, yes. The nicotine-stained papers, the open window. The room is choked by cigarettes. Why did I not notice until now?

"Do not look at that." Mathieu bounds across the room and rips out the paper from the carriage. Beckett cracks her eyes into slits.

"I wasn't looking at the paper." Seeing the fear in his eyes, I lick my lips. "I was looking at the ashtray."

Mathieu places the paper on a stack inside the desk's drawer and sinks down into his chair, rubbing his eyes. I frown at his weariness. Beckett allows those second eyelids to slip back over her eyes.

Mathieu looks at his hands. "I am sorry. I did not mean to sound so abrupt and defensive. But I never allow anyone to see what I have written."

"That's not what I'm upset about."

He rumples his hair and jabs a palm into the air. "Would you—do you want me to apologize for smoking, Daisy? Are you suddenly *ma maman*?"

"No. I just didn't realize that you were."

He looks up sharply.

"You lied, Mathieu. In the Orsay, you told me those cigarettes were your mother's. You acted like she was weak for wanting them."

"I acted like she was weak because she is. Was." Mathieu slumps in his chair. "The cigarettes just happened to belong to her."

"So why didn't you tell me that you smoked? Why haven't I seen you light up today?"

"I only smoke when I write."

"How precious." God forgive me. I want to be cruel.

"And sometimes, too, when I want to piss off uptight American tourists." His chair scrapes backward.

Mathieu slides a cigarette and a book of matches from behind his typewriter and strikes a match, though his hand shakes slightly. His cupped palm obscures his face. Relaxing, he moves deeper into his chair, the smoke blooming from his mouth.

"I'm allergic."

He flicks an ash on the desk and grimaces. "So am I. To cats." We look at each other.

"I guess we're screwed then."

He takes another drag and blows toward the water-stained ceiling. "Guess so."

I sit on Mathieu's bed and watch him. My head fills with smoke, and my eyes tear. A part of me wants to shove his face in that ashtray, and a part of me wants to—

No.

I rise. Discard my shirt, unhook my bra. Walk to him. Slide his lap between my legs. Stealing the cigarette from his hand, I gently kill it. He lets me.

He would let me do anything.

"You are still drunk," he says.

"Am I?"

"Aren't you?"

"I don't know. Sing to me, and see if I swoon."

"I do not sing."

"What a pity."

I trace my thumb across his lips, and they follow.

"Whose face used to be up there?"

"Justine."

"Who is Justine?"

"The girl we saw on the street."

"Why am I here, and she is not?"

His neck drops back, his jaw slackens. "I grew bored. She caught me with Camille, the sometimes lesbian, the night after my mother died. It seemed a good time to end things."

I nod. Force my mouth on his ashy lips. His elbow slips, striking the typewriter keys.

Click.

"Your father."

"What about him?"

"Why does he have those paintings?"

"He was an officer in Darnad's *Milice* during the Vichy days. Many of the paintings were 'prizes' awarded from their Nazi friends, scavenged from the Jews they rounded up. When you have a father as old as mine, these are his sort of youthful indiscretions." He shrugs and adjusts his elbow. "Others have been purloined from troubled collectors who cannot afford him as a creditor."

The chair slips back again, rubbing a new groove into the floor, and I wobble dangerously. He pulls me forward and seizes my lips.

Click.

I work for balance.

"Why haven't you done something about it?"

"I found out only recently, when his mind started to go, and he started flaunting them like . . . American rap stars with their bing."

"Bling."

"What I said is no less absurd," he murmurs, playing with my hair.

"Yes, well."

"I have had nothing to do with the man, or his money, for ten years. But my sisters wouldn't take his calls after our mother died. Me? I took pity, but only because he still seemed to love her, through some untenable crack in his character." He closes his eyes. "So *I* take his calls, and *I* become his Sancho Panza. His nurses at his new home, you see, are the always advancing windmills."

"What were you doing in his apartment today?"

"Removing his gun."

"What?"

"And his bullets."

"His gun."

"He believes it's his duty to fight, with mortal force, the traitors in the Resistance and round up the Jews for deportation. You can see why the man needs a gun. And bullets." He smiles. "They killed his Dulcinea."

"Where is it?"

He jerks his chin toward his bag.

"You're not going to give it to him, are you?"

He motions me closer and brushes my neck with his lips. "Not unless you think I should."

My spine bows, and I lean into him. We fall into a new kind of story.

Click. Click, click, clickclickclick . . .

But the dream is too impossible.

"How could you afford to buy me those shoes today?"

Flushed, he groans into my ear, "You made me."

"I did not."

"You made me love you."

"Sweet. But not good enough." I smile and draw back, placing my hands on his chest to restrain him. "You're destitute, Mathieu. And you like it. So why do you have a platinum credit card?"

"It is one my father gave me years ago. I never use it."

"Except when you want to impress girls."

"Except when I want to impress this girl."

"Good excuse," I say, curling my fingers around his neck.

He flinches and backs away.

Click.

"I do not like that word."

"Neither do I."

Our eyes sweep, search.

"Who is Andy?"

I laugh. "Tit for tat, right?"

He cups my breast. *"Oui."*

"He's my ex-boyfriend."

"Yes."

"And that's all."

"I see." The hand slips to his side.

Locking my arms under my breasts, I worry my lower lip.

"Why have you finally told me all of this, Mathieu?"

"Because I want you."

"How do you want me?"

"Just this. I want you like this. You have become a part of me. If I kept things from you, it was only because we owed each other nothing." He swallows and tries to smile. "Now I owe you."

My elbows slacken.

He holds up a finger. "But. I also owe you this: I am a writer, Daisy. I am a tour guide when I have to be, and a writer because I have no other choice. If I must do without to write, this is fine. It is better than fine. But nothing means more to me. Nothing."

Yes. Well.

He cuffs my wrists with his hands. "I tell you this so that you will trust me, Daisy. No more secrets, and no expectations. We will live freely." He squeezes, hard.

Feeling his heat, I glance up at the lonely thumbtack.

Nothing means more.

Untangling myself, I rise.

I walk to the open window. Leaning into the dark, frosty air above a deserted courtyard, I breathe deeply, the cool air impaling my bare breast. It will be winter soon. Somewhere, Andy breathes. Rakesh too. We cannot discard our histories in the course of a day. We cannot build new cities, either. The pages behind me flutter in the draft. I shudder and fancy myself falling forward, pitching this body with its barnacled heart into the swell below. I close my eyes. If only I could forget myself for the length of this breath, if only I could forget . . . .

If only I could be a girl again.

I close the window. It grinds with the effort, and Beckett bolts for safer corners.

I turn toward Mathieu, who looks at me gravely, that sickle-shaped scar on his cheek a shock of white. He looks like a stranger again. I do not know his name, the name he shares with his father. But it's not Quixote. And I'm no Dulcinea.

I grab my shirt from his floor and pull it on. Turning back toward the window, I catch my reflection in the dirty glass. I smooth the hair from my face, pulling a ponytail holder from my jeans pocket and pinioning it back. Mathieu was right. I rotate slightly and extract a wavy curl of my hair, so that it rests on my neck.

"You want to know something, Mathieu? You called it."

He blinks in quick succession.

"What do you think of your orphan girl?"

He says nothing.

Uncertain that I can trust his word on anything, I go over and look in that bag.

Jesus. Was not expecting *that*.

"Daisy."

I look at him, but he is like that marble of Rodin's, melting into its base.

His words on the wall warn me: *words are loaded pistols.*

"You don't fucking say."

I leave everything, including the orphaned cat, and my spent heart. I close the door, and it rattles against the doorjamb, like a dropped kiss.

I will flee to the Hotel California. Where people go when dreams die.

Chapter 19

I nstead, I ascend. To Montmartre, that is.

Unable to face a hotel room after envisioning a night of lying in Mathieu's arms, I do not truncate my perfect Parisian day yet. It may end sour, but it will be by my lemons, not the ones Mathieu has hurled at me. I storm the hill up to Montmartre, tears raining from my eyes, reaching for higher air. There is a hand squeezed around that heart I thought to leave behind. The Sacré Coeur awaits me at the top. She is gaudy and obvious next to Notre Dame, like someone advertising her virtue by taking a chastity oath and then flaunting her assets at the next kegger. Slippery metaphor, perhaps. But apt when viewing the three milky breasts topping the great roof of the church, through which Jesus' love pours to nourish the wicked and suffering.

I stand at the top of the stairs, chest heaving, mission completed. I haven't the foggiest idea of what to do with myself.

This is not the spot for me. The place is infested with lovers—the parasitic people—snuggled together on the steps leading up to the Sacré Coeur, bodies pressed against one another, for heat, at the curved balcony. I shiver uncontrollably, only wearing the sweater I thoughtlessly grabbed this morning, when Mathieu was but a Monet in my head, and I a girl pushing freedom. I wrap the sweater around me, but it does not feel as tight as Mathieu's arms and provides only a modicum of warmth, and no heat.

I turn my eyes outward, across the plain of city lights, a sparkling wonderland that ought to—on any other night and to any other person—bring pleasure. The view of Paris at night is stunning, of course: the Eiffel Tower glittering in the distance like a shattered diamond. But with no one here to share it, and the quiet laughs of others insulating me in my loneliness, the sight of all this untouchable beauty is like viewing a dearly departed in his open casket. The familiar, beloved form is there, but the magic has flown, and you wish you hadn't looked after all, because why would you want to remember that?

I briefly wonder which light is Mathieu's light, his small spark among the thousands of embers crackling into the night sky. I have no instinct for where his home sits, no feeling for it. He is lost to me. Shutting my eyes, I turn my back on the Sacred Heart and all her laborers of love and set about exploring the rest of Montmartre.

It is something to do, you see.

If Paris has multiple personalities, Montmartre might be the vivacious tart who can't hold her drink. Named for a martyred saint who lost his head, the former medieval village is where Picasso and his macho *compadres* roped modernity, and where his good friend Casegemas, snubbed by love, took his own life after firing upon, and missing, his lover. The man's legacy of misery bled the hypoxic hue into Picasso's Blue Period. Cheap rent, easy girls, and a surprising countryside transformed this bucolic hilltop into a refuge for artists, writers, and drunks of no discernible talent but for drinking themselves to death. Merry men, all. Who knows about their women. Not much is ever written about the women. Maybe a nod, if they're lucky, for shaking their asses, or being a mother. Casegemas's lover, Germaine, owes her fame to Casegemas, who owes it to Picasso. She's third-rate famous, at best.

Montmartre still evokes bohemian Paris, but, elbowing my way past the swarms in the narrow village streets, while protecting my wallet from the pickpockets that Rick has intimated are everywhere, I have the same feeling I often have in Paris: that crawling sensation of the "just-miss." If only it were a hundred, or fifty, or thirty, years ago, what I would have seen . . . then. If Paris isn't dead, she hibernates. Everything belongs to the past in this city—and God, what a past—but there is the musty smell of a desperately preserved reputation hanging in the air, like aged books being ravaged, one moth at a time. People peck at the ground to find the seeds of inspiration F. Scott Fitzgerald or Toulouse-Lautrec planted in the soil of their fecund talent, growing tangled roots that ran to the other side of the world. They could still persist, like the vineyard that has endured for centuries on this hilltop sanctuary, but there are too many garish weeds sprung up for me to even see what I am stepping on. One thing is for sure: Josephine Baker and her sly, sweet rose are nowhere to be seen.

Instead, the Frat Brigade from Duke tries to be heard back in Durham, hailing a bottle of "absinthe" that looks like green pee outside a packed café. Vendors ply me with limp paintings that would make Thomas Kinkade wretch and the infamous moustache of Salvador Dali—another renowned Montmartre dweller—droop. Leaflets for music and sex shows down in "Pig Alley" rain from the skies. There is an atmosphere of gluttonous consumerism here, if not for *things*, then for a bygone feeling. Carnival music, from a modern-day, patrolling minstrel group, no less, is the tongue-in-cheek soundtrack to my night. I am complicit in the rundown, riding my merry-go-round called Distraction. It's a circular ride, and you never really arrive anywhere. But it simulates the sensation that you've traveled far and seen lots of stuff.

I wonder what Mathieu might think of Montmartre today. We didn't make it here, though I can imagine his insistence that we stop at Rue Lepic, knowing that I would want to pay homage to Van Gogh's rundown apartment. He lived there with his brother, Theo, before the infamous ear chop and his best work, which, since his is a tragic tale, barely sold while he was alive. Supposedly, there is a spray of sunflowers nodding from the window on 54 Rue Lepic. Yes, Mathieu would have brought me to Van Gogh's street, so I could see the flowers whose blind faces track the spindling sun. Their mute devotion, mirroring Van Gogh's faith in Christ, charged him with an artistic and religious outpouring so fervent that he worked eighteen paintings of that simple, now iconic, vase of sunflowers. He wanted to get it right. I can understand the feeling, if not the motivation. Such obsession forces—with a fist— genius from talent and brings madness along with it, like a jealous, bruised lover who demands all the attention.

But admirers will trek toward this crappy apartment tonight, tomorrow, and for as long as there are sunflowers in this world— partly for the art, partly for the tormented soul that produced it—where the great man spent a year of his abridged, nineteenth- century life. They will stand vigil outside, just to catch a whiff of his perfume. Mathieu, meanwhile, would have brought me there—not for the flowers, which he'd find a touch overdone—but because this was the street we lived on in our alternate reality. The one with Fonzie, our aborted doggie.

Resigned to the frantic energy of this Montmartre, I sip warm beer in a loud bar populated by tourists and, I think, prostitutes, at the bottom of Rue Lepic, which I have stumbled down without allowing myself to look for sunflowers or the ghosts of Jack Russell terriers. But even here, a question dogs me: where does Mathieu go, if anywhere, to find his inspiration, or is it always with him, like an inflammation of the fingers?

Answer: who the fuck cares, Daisy. Right?

"Can I buy you another?"

Right.

It's one of the Dukies. How do I know? Because he looks like a cocky son of a bitch, and he sports a shirt that reads *Duke . . . it even sounds cool.* His mandatory baseball cap (Yanks) is backward, and his shorts boast a blue devil insignia. He reeks of cologne and opportunism.

I take a generous sip and set the glass down heavily on the bar. His smile is sure, and he's not bad-looking. He's got that sanitized, premed look about him. It's one I know well. "Sure," I allow. Why not?

"Oh, good, you speak English," he says, hopping up on the bar seat next to me. "I thought you were American."

"Oh, you too?"

He smiles uncertainly. "Well, yeah . . . can't you tell?"

I finish off the glass. "I was just kidding," I enunciate, staring at the emptied pint. I don't like beer either.

He titters and motions to the bartender. "Set up another for the lady here," he yells, pointing to my head.

So now I'm a lady. A lady whose pants he'd like to crawl into. He must be attracted to mopey, dejected types whose aura of rejection screams, "Challenge!" Or it went something like this: *Hey, man, see the sad sack of shit in the corner? Ten points, and a pint of Guinness, if you nail her.*

"What's your name?" he shouts, his bared teeth an advertisement for Crest Whitestrips.

"Dana," I yell back, jerking my head up and down like a yo-yo.

"Cool . . . like Dana Scully, right?"

"Yeah, but much less trouble."

He slaps his hand on the bar. "Man, I loved *The X-Files* back

in high school. They had some crazy stuff go down on that show."
He sticks out a tanned paw and says chummily, like he respects me
and shit, "I'm Matthew, by the way. But you can call me Matt."

Really. The name, pronounced in his faux humble way (covering for a New England, prep school background, I suspect), still
affects me. My heart skitters back to an unsteady rhythm, like this
seismic coincidence has been foretold by the great oracle of Delphi.
"Nice to meet you, Matthew," I say, more softly, allowing my hand
to remain in his.

His blue eyes widen, or maybe it's his pupils zeroing in on
their target. He pumps my hand, belying his innocent intentions
by allowing his finger to graze my wrist. Letting go, he hitches
himself up and bellows, "Hey, mate! A Guinness for me, please."

Our drinks come. Matthew turns to me and asks, "So what is
it you do back home, Dana?"

"I'm in the FBI."

"No way," he gasps, and I almost smile. Almost.

"No. I'm in a master's program in neuroscience at Case Western Reserve University in Cleveland." I take a swig of my beer,
stifling a yawn. "We do outstanding work on inner ear hair cells.
Really cutting-edge kind of stuff that would blow . . . your . . .
mind." I try to whistle. My lips must be numb, because I can't feel
a thing. *You know how to whistle, don't you, Steve? You just put your
lips together and . . . blow.*

Matthew frantically chews his gum. "That's awesome. Man,
it sounds like you're really on the fast track. Here I thought you
were still a lowly undergrad like me." He blinks too fast. It's unsettling. "You going for your PhD after that?"

My head tips back. There are mirrors on the ceiling. It is impossible to find myself in the swirling crowd. "Sure."

"Cool. You'll be tenured in no time, I bet." He gulps his beer,
and a little bit falls outside his mouth and rains down on the bar.

He quickly wipes it up with his napkin, which he had folded to the size of a postage stamp.

I make him nervous. I'd laugh, but I might throw up.

"I'm over here on a foreign exchange program from Duke," he explains, pointing helpfully to his shirt. "I'm history, pre-law."

Ah. I knew it was pre-Something. It's apparent he's not Something, in spite of the low lighting and fortuitous name. "What are your plans after conquering law school, Matthew?" I shout, playing the game.

"My dad has a firm in D.C. I might clerk there, and then, who knows?" He shrugs. "Run for Congress maybe, in ten years' time." He takes another drink, this one smoothly disappearing.

"Really?"

Maybe I haven't given him enough credit. The guy is still young and wears that obnoxious, entitled air of the filthy rich, but perhaps he feels the rub of good fortune on his conscience. Maybe he wants to give something back. Maybe Matthew will be Something Great someday.

"Yeah. I'm already head of the College Republicans at Duke. We've experienced a 23 percent boost in our enrollment since I became president," he boasts, smiling broadly. "Of course, that could be due to the war."

Maybe Matthew is pre-Neanderthal. He does have a large, sloped forehead, come to think of it, and a lantern jaw.

"Oh, man, you're not a Democrat, are you?" he asks, the back of his hand concealing a smile.

"God, no. That would be a fate worse than death."

"What?" he yells over some god-awful French pop song. Ah, Edith Piaf. The Sparrow has flown, apparently.

"THAT WOULD BE A FATE WORSE THAN DEATH."

"I'll say." He smirks. "Say, I gotta joke for you: how many Frenchmen does it take to screw in a lightbulb?"

"Oh, I know this—"

"None! They just surrender to the darkness." He snorts.

I laugh. "Ain't it the truth. Pussies."

He looks at me hungrily. The man is aroused by smugness. He probably has mood lighting and a jar of Vaseline set out for Ann Coulter's weekly appearance on *Hannity & Colmes*. So she has a neck like a Modigliani, without the humanity. Ad hominem attacks are the most potent aphrodisiac for people who live outside the reality-based universe.

"So would you describe yourself as an idealistic neoconservative out to spread freedom throughout the uncivilized world, or are you more of an old-school, let's-drain-the-bathtub, Grover Norquist type, or a what-would-Jesus-do, let's-protect-the-stem-cells, waitin'-for-the-Rapture kind of guy? Personally, Ronald Reagan is my hero, so I guess I'd be the middle one, with a token touch of the latter." Burping a little, I add, "Because God knows Reagan would be a mite suspicious about this whole Iraq thing!"

"Uh, I'm a little of all three, I guess. But mainly I want to lower taxes."

I smile brilliantly at him. "That's so refreshing to hear. It's not many people who can be that optimistic about their own self-interest."

It rolls off him like water. His eyes are fastened, like some fantastical missile detection system, to my cleavage, since I'm leaning in cozily. He must be desperate to gawk at the nubs. "Yeah, well, I try."

"So what's a freedom-loving American patriot doing in France?" I ask, relaxing my head on my hand to look more deeply into this young man's untroubled soul. There are no scars on these cheeks. They look laminated.

He shrugs and takes his cap off to run a hand through the gelled hair. "These things look good on your transcripts, and I want Georgetown." He lifts his drink. "And while Parisians might be a bunch of pacifist wusses, they can still party."

"I'll drink to that." We dutifully clink mugs.

"And why are you here?" he asks, wetting his lips.

"Ohhh . . . to get laid by a dirty, yellow Frenchman, I guess."

I think his jaw might unhinge. He starts to choke, before checking himself. "Wait, are you serious?"

I stare at him. He looks away and holds his beer for support.

At last, Matthew sweeps in, gaining courage at this unprecedented chance for the easy score, and whispers/shouts in my ear, "Would you settle for a filthy American who wants nothing more than to be with you tonight?" His hand, complete with class ring, grazes my thigh.

Nothing more.

I feel myself closing in on his earlobe. "That depends."

"On what?"

"On how long you can make me feel like I'm someone else."

His eyes flap their confusion. I help him out by laughing.

"And on if you have protection."

Now I'm speaking his language. Matthew grins and nuzzles my ear.

"You bet." He kisses my neck and pats his pocket. "Never leave home without it."

I barely fight the inclination to shove him away and bring my hand to my head. "Please," I beg. "Could we not talk quite so much?"

He smiles. This is all so easy. "I promise to be as quiet as a mouse, Dana."

We leave a minute later, his buddies giving him the old wink-wink nudge-nudge routine. There's an erotic museum down on the Boulevard de Clichy (I wince at that hard ch- sound charging from that clumsy, American mouth) he tells me is awesome *and* tastefully done. Wow, because I was worried it might not be tasteful. Nice attempt to walk the line between perv and gentleman, little man. Anyway, it works because I go with him.

I guess he considers this to be our foreplay.

Why do I go?

It's something to do, you see.

Ma vie en rose.

Chapter 20

There is nothing less erotic than looking down a green plaster vagina with a man who giggles like a little girl.

No, I don't have sex with the blue devil.

Although much in the museum is, dare I say, devilish and fun. The drawings and Indian sculpture are deliciously perverse. Two bodies twirling into one. Legs that laugh at beginnings. Boudoir coquettes, fannies round and raised like baboons' invitations. In the end, the unflappability of human lust is gently comical and poignant. I am an animal. Mathieu is an animal. The rest is just obstacles we invent to keep it interesting.

Matthew, or Mr. McGrabby, is a big obstacle. But he's not interesting, and I'm not a drunken sorority girl. So I tell him I have to use the restroom. He waits for me by a sculpture of a woman's leg slung outside a window. I make my escape by the more conventional front door.

I wouldn't feel too badly for him. He still has a war he has no intention of fighting in to turn him on and enough simulated vaginas engorging him to keep him randy and snickering through the night. Mine will not be overly missed.

I have learned a few things since Rakesh. And, somewhat infuriatingly, though I was with Andy for years, I could not cheat on Mathieu after this day. I may hate it, and chafe at the bit, but he owns me. Distance or distractions cannot dilute the claim. I can still feel the shock of his hand on my breast, fingerprinting me. I was the one to leave, yet I know he feels my pulling toward him, like a boomerang about to turn. Which is why I keep walking the other way.

I catch the metro back "home" to my pink hotel room, where I confront the fact that this is the life I have scratched out for myself in Paris. Here is the chick-lit confession: after watching a dubbed rerun of *Friends*, I looked up *mon petit chou* in my French-English dictionary, and in my bewilderment at what I found, cut my toe-nails, did *not* try on my shoes, ran to the market in the falling rain to buy the nearest thing to *Ben & Jerry's Fudge Brownie*, ate the whole pint, before packing myself in between the bedsheets and mulling masturbating. But I fell asleep before I could work up the necessary energy, or move beyond the green vagina in my thoughts.

As for Mathieu? He refused to show himself at all.

The day dawns gray and chilly, as it should. I awake, underslept and bewildered at my surroundings. I had dreamed that Mathieu and Andy were fighting over me . . . in a manner of speaking. Andy tried to goad Mathieu into a fight so he could pound on him, but all Mathieu would do was turn toward the viewless window (with Van Gogh's sunflowers sitting on the sill), and repeat, *"Words are loaded pistols"* in his soft, portentous way, Andy bobbing and weaving behind him in an impersonation of The Champ. Finally, tiring of their shared ineffectuality, I snatched the flowers from the vase and threw them out the window, before smashing the two of them over the head with the heavy urn, dropping them into a people puddle, *à la* The Three Stooges.

All that was left out was the canned laughter/cheering and a fat, black, sassy woman yelling, "You go, girrrl!"

Groaning as I get out of bed, I notice a dribble of brown ice cream on the sheets that has spilled from my demolished carton. It gives the embarrassing impression that I soiled myself overnight. Filled with high hopes for the day, I trudge to the shower.

Shivering in the anemic stream of water, I begin to experience a change of heart about the whole situation. *Maybe you overreacted,* the damp, hypothetical angel (looking like a jolly Grandpa Matisse) on my right shoulder purrs. *What is it, really, that Mathieu has done? So his father colluded with Nazis. Or, at the very least, sat by while Jews were sent to their deaths. Stole priceless pieces of art that the world should own. Surely you can't blame the son for the father's complicity in the biggest horror show of the last century, a genocide that felt as ancient and removed as the old black-and-white footage that chronicled it, until now.*

Of course you should, the equally hypothetical, if plainly indignant, devil (disguised as a head of Picasso/body of a bull thing) on my other shoulder hisses. *What's he doing about it now? Nothing. Take it from me: lying is all men are good for, Daisy, and he got you— good. He lied about Camille, he lied about his distaste for smoking, which, while not a big deal, somehow is, because it's in the minor details where true character lies low, like an outlaw. And, while not lying about Justine, he didn't come clean there either.*

And then there's that bag. Didn't see that coming, did you?

Zut alors! But you didn't come clean about Andy, sputters Matisse, more forcefully than I'd like for a Grandpa sort. *Not to mention* with *Andy. And you lied to Mathieu about your grief for your grandmother, and that ridiculous story about Aunt Flo. People lie, Daisy. Love? You two barely know each other. You're going to be on guard for a period of time. You want to project an illusion of lovability . . . a garden of flowers.* He clasps his hand to his chest and bows.

But she owned up to most of that stuff, Picasso interjects, waving a dismissive hoof. *He was a phony all along. While having the co-jones to convict you of lying to yourself about your religion. Hell, he's not even a real writer. More like one of the sycophants who trailed me my entire career.* He sniffs and puffs up his bull-chest. *They still yap at my heels.*

Jesus Christ, Matisse swears, rolling his eyes. *The ego on you: talk about bull crap. Camille was a charming girl, Daisy. Would you have been able to resist her while your heart was bathed in sorrow?*

Of course she would have, the Picasso/bull thing spats. *He is in control of the choices he makes in life. All that junk is just a convenient excuse to make him feel better about himself. Mathieu is a lout. And once a lout, always a lout. Trust me, I know.*

God, I hypothetically hate both of you. How about an offended silence all around?

Stepping out of the shower, I come clean with myself: his father's crimes, while revolting and deplorable, do not taint Mathieu. We all want to protect the people we love, and his crime, if any, is that he cannot give his father up while he's receding into obliviousness. And I can understand, if not condone, his sleeping with Camille. Hell, it's not like last night with Matthew couldn't have happened. One more pint, and I'd have lapped up my self-loathing with as much gusto as a coed in Cancun. And the smoking thing is neg-ligible, although I despise it and don't understand how he could continue to kill himself in the aftermath of his mother's death.

The bag. The bag is not unforgivable. Just . . . perverse.

No, what I can't forgive is the moment when he, with flagrant honesty, told me that *nothing* meant more to him than his writing. I cannot compete with characters inside his mind for his attentions. That probably makes me as big an egoist as he is, but I already languished in a relationship in which I played second fiddle to a man's relentless pursuit of his ambition.

It's not going to happen again.

"You could choose Case." I circled the empty pizza box in the middle of his room. "I promise I won't tell anyone that you settled," I added, cupping my hand around my mouth in an exaggerated whisper.

"It's *Harvard*, Daze."

"And I'm your *girl*friend, And-ee."

He mumbled something unintelligible and flipped through the Harvard class catalogue. His desk boasted an iMac, sporting the Harvard Medical School homepage. Harvard as the new porn.

"You'll still be my girlfriend. Now you can just be my girlfriend who comes to some kick-ass Red Sox games with me."

"Sure. With all of my copious free time. After all, I'm not in *med* school. Just a lowly neuroscience program at a second-tier university. I wonder if they'll even make me go to class, or if they'll just tweak my nose and tell me that I'm cute."

He whistled and flung the catalogue on his desk. "Sounds like *some*-bo-dy has an inferiority complex." Grabbing my hand, he pulled me onto his lap and tweaked my nose. I tried to bite his finger, but he had the reflexes of a jackrabbit. "You could have gone to med school too, you know."

"You're forgetting that I have no desire to be a doctor. Too many sick people."

"Too many people."

"You say toma—"

"—yeah, yeah."

I looked him directly in the eye. "Do *you* want to be a doctor?"

Andy lost his smirk and furrowed his brow. "That's a dumb question." He started fiddling with the computer mouse.

"Is it?"

He pushed me off his lap to put the catalogue on his shelf. "Yeah, it really is."

"I think you want people to think you want it. I think you're in love with the idea of being a doctor, the pulpy prestige of the thing." I added, more softly, "I think you want your parents to stop calling you 'the athletic one.'"

"I think you took too many psych courses in college. It's a pseudoscience, you know," he replied, looking for his iPod.

I could never stick Andy with anything sharp enough to make him really twitch. He was too goddamn happy. He ran on the fumes of a ridiculous energy. Especially then, with the shimmering bricks of Harvard beckoning like The Promised Land.

"I just wonder."

"What do you wonder?"

"Whether we'll make it."

He screwed up his face. "You're worrying over nothing. Absence makes the heart grow fonder."

"Absence makes the heart forget."

He tackled me onto his bed, smelling of sweat and the wet leather from his basketball. "I could never forget you. Even if I wanted to. You're too damn . . ."

"Too damn what?"

"Something," he mumbled.

We shrugged out of our clothes. The sex was more passionate

than usual. Nothing like the prospect of parting to make you want him to remember.

But he never glanced at that web of skin above my iliac crest. He'd stopped years before. It was just anatomy by then, something he'd be seeing a lot of in the weeks to come. Yet in the middle of our lovemaking, I saw his eyes lock onto the acceptance letter from Harvard, pinned to his cork bulletin board, next to the Red Sox pennant and a signed letter from Senator Voinovich.

I even thought I heard him give a small sigh.

I hear the Red Sox have a real shot at the World Series this year. Nice that old dogs should learn some new tricks—especially when bellied up to curveballs that come dangerously close to ripping off your balls.

The truth is that I will never be as attached to my work, or my microscope, as Mathieu is to his imagination. I wish it weren't so. I have been conditioned to view work as the end game. The American feminist call to arms was to seize the office and make it the new, liberated home, swapping that vacuum cleaner for some goddamn self-respect. So my mind responds, like Pavlov's dog, to the bellwether ideas of American success: Harvard, post-grad, assistant professor, associate professor, tenured professor. The Ladder Doctrine of American living. But my heart lies somewhere else. Or rather, many places, for it is a fickle, promiscuous organ— one moment responding to a Manet, the next to a Matisse, one minute to an Andy, the next to a Mathieu, loving them equally, if differently. Yesterday it attached itself to so many things that it split at the seams, drawn and quartered by its conflicting desires.

And I liked it.

I liked the rush of that sensory bombardment, the headiness that shoots your feet off the ground. Back in Cleveland, I existed. I was even content. Yesterday, in Paris, I thrived. It's the spiritual difference between prose and poetry. I'd like to be able to write something as majestic and clean as Emerson's *Self-Reliance*, but I want to live as successfully, and recklessly, as Whitman in *Song of Myself*. I, too, want to possess the origin of all poems.

Across the golden hours of yesterday's dreamscape, Mathieu and I were hedonists worshipping at the altar of Dionysus, and each other. If we stumbled at the end and let our chins graze the earth, it is only because nerves stretched to such great heights must also endure long falls. We touched the sun with waxen wings. How many can boast the same? Even Louis XIV, that fabled Sun King, ended badly, with a failed war, no living children, and a nasty attack of gangrene that finished him off in excruciating fashion. Yet we remember the outrageous high heels, the iron rule, and the palatial Versailles. I want to live, if not decadently, then splendidly, turning my back to the long shadow cast by the hands of clocks, certain that time will come to love, or at least ignore, me.

Today I will do the things I would not allow myself to do yesterday with Mathieu. I will don my jeans and Keds and order a *café crème* at the Café Flore, wondering, with a shadowy thrill, who sat in the chair I now occupy. I will poke my head in Sainte-Chapelle and admire the jubilant stained-glass windows, without anyone whispering over my shoulder that my reaction to them is fraudulent, or that they're a pretty fiction filtering a darker truth. I will go to the Musée Picasso and acknowledge that I only like about half of his stuff, and that some is downright mediocre. I will embrace my squeamishness and hold my nose when passing a *fromagerie*, trying my damnedest to quell my gag reflex while eyeing the hunks of moldy goat's milk that are supposed to make my knees quake with gratitude at their pungently ripe bouquets. I will shed my inferiority complex and wear my Americanism as casually as I do back home: that is, without being conscious of it.

I will finally conquer this city by not pretending that I must love the whole of her.

I am reaching for my sensible raincoat in the tiny closet when I notice a note wedged under my door. Fingers expressed, my hand remains caught as I stare, somewhat fearfully, at the small, white rectangle atop the tangled red roses on my carpet. My body hangs on a silver thread, the fleeting tenseness of the moment begging for Andrew Wyeth's sharp eyes and earnest hands. There is a pull to the raincoat, to my day's plans lining it, which my arm cannot abandon. And yet the envelope, with its clean white mystery, waits impatiently, its scrawled *Daisy* a promise of complications. It must be from Mathieu. I let it slip I was staying here over dinner, even telling him the room, twenty-three, because I believed the number to be portentous. Perhaps it is.

I open the note, of course—even if curveballs are most dangerous when you least expect them. This is how it reads:

I do not sleep. How do you sleep so fitfully? My ear presses against your door, but there is nothing. A nice trick, Daisy. I admire your composure. It is enough to make me question my existence. For how can I exist without finding myself reflected in your eyes? The night is long (Chagall's moon flown), the hallway silent, except for the occasional growl from the pipes.

You have shattered me, by the way. I guess one should say that first. You may gloat, for I write to you with broken hands. I tried to pet Beckett before, back home, with broken hands, and she hissed your name—your awful, cartoon name—and leapt away, scolding me as harshly as your eyes all those hours ago, when you swiped the room's walls of my color.

You act like I disappoint you, and I would like to rip you apart, you child. What do you know of disappointment? You have been spooned your own sense of importance all your life by two loving parents, and by an insulated nation that fetes its children almost as much as its flag, and you have become bloated and gassy from all this attention. What do you know of me? You have the American instinct for making rash judgments, which will prove fatal to any true growth of your character.

And yet . . . I feel your disappointment keenly, like you have dug around the open, raw sore at the bottom of my heart, hunting for some place still untouched by your radioactive hands. I cannot bear that superior look of yours, though I am desperate to rip this cheap door from its hinges, to see what you look like asleep (that was my right tonight), your changeling mouth finally at peace.

What do you dream of, fairy?

I despise Delacroix, and my mother. You have inserted yourself between them and me, blocking them in the shadow your scorn casts. A man's pride is all he has, Daisy. It stops me from knocking upon this door, though I appeal to your extrasensory knowledge of me like a dead man asking to be killed quickly. To think that a day ago, you were but a dream in my head. I invented you on that train, but now you have somehow become the puppeteer, pulling my strings until I am tied in—there! I heard your toilet flush. I have roused your bladder, at the least. It is all I can hope for tonight.

You do know me. Perhaps this is why I hate you a little.

Are you asleep yet, my love? Are you fading to black once more? Have I insinuated myself into the next dream, the delirious preface to our next story? Will you rise in the morning and think first of me? Or will I have become lost in an airy pocket of soft time, a distant memory? "I, too, had a Paris romance . . ." Let it not be that, Daisy. Anything but that.

I will not come for you tomorrow. The choice is yours. I will look for you all afternoon at our fountain in the Gardens. Just know this: I have been to America. But I will not go back. There is no writer's life for me there. It was bleached of poetry for me the moment—

You deserve to know this. So if you come, know that I am part of Paris, as permanent a residence as the Seine, if similarly in a state of flux.

And remember this too: Daisy Miller was ahead of her time, a real revolutionary.

A lifetime spent in Europe need not be a death sentence.

Mathieu

p.s. This is not said with vindictiveness, but might it occur to you that your father (the man said, by your lips, to have caressed the fuselages, spoken in strained tongues, worshipped Henry James, and languished in an unhappy marriage) might be secretly gay? It is something to consider.

Ka-pow.

I hurl the note to the floor and step on it, like it's a bug I could squash. I have always hated the epistolary postscript. They're flakey, self-indulgent. This one is particularly mean and spiteful. An act of revenge so transparent (with the phony qualifier at the beginning) that I can see his small, black heart languishing behind its pointed jab.

And yet, he called me his "love." He wants me with him. He will wait for me today. It is my choice, he whispers.

I pick up his note, smoothing the creases. His handwriting is more accomplished than my own; the hand that wrote this did not shake or hesitate. His fluidity, as always, impresses me. And it is comforting to have received a handwritten letter this time. Andy's e-mail was a poison dart, cowardly shot from afar, made more poisonous by its indifferent medium. Mathieu's letter, while vitriolic in parts, is softened by the psychology of its writer (look how he addends his name with that wispy flourish), his words radiating a luster that a computer, for all of its invention, cannot replicate. A part of me wants to tuck the letter in my bosom (*á la* Jane Austen) and start madly diagramming my own. *Mrs. Cogsworth, my quill and inkwell, please!*

Instead, I pluck *A Razor's Edge* from my nightstand, where it has patiently gathered the Parisian dust blown through an equally idle window on its jacket like a talcumy grit. I insert the note in between its leaves, which swallow it whole. I hesitate, before blowing the dust off the book's cover. Lying sideways on my bed, my raincoat forgotten, I crack the novel open. A clean, white space envelops me.

True love waits. Or it should.

I do not stop reading, except for some liquid nourishment and a crusty, two-day-old baguette. I do not look at a clock. The television is a dead zone, the bathroom no barrier to my dogged pursuit. Mathieu, outside the printed page, is not forgotten, but if I think of him—which is often enough, since he and Larry, the main character, are not unalike—it is more as a fixed point, the static company to our fountain's statuary, and not as a living, suffering person in need of my touch or rebuke. I have no excuse for my callousness except this: sometimes books are more authentic than real life. And sometimes the stubborn character clutches at our imaginations, dangling by the skin of his teeth, refusing to release us to real time. And rarely, but memorably, it is a journey— of the imagination, yes, which ought never be trivialized, in spite of our slavish devotion to empiricism—that we take within a single step. Perhaps I'm in denial, or this is easy escapism. I don't care. I have been seduced.

Larry Darrell, skeptic of the American Dream and seeker

of his own, spends a year "loafing" in Paris, reading some good books, before his soul finds what it needs in a monastery in India. Simple enough tale. But told with the cutting social instrument of an Edith Wharton—or yes, yes, Henry James—and the wider spiritual aspirations of a Herman Hesse. It is a strange concoction: from the snobbish sitting rooms of fashionable Parisian apartments to the great caves of India. Yet it works because there is a consistently searching central character whose serenity and honesty are not desecrated by the superficial trappings of his mercurial society, and whose ego, whittled away by a conscious humbling, does not inflate with the wisdom he later attains. God, I like Larry Darrell. I like him more than I can say.

Loafing. I am quickly converted: this is to be my new creed. And judging from Mathieu's apartment last night, he already has an amazing aptitude for it. Yes, I like him too, in spite of his father's name. Staring out my window at the darkening Paris sky, a rumble of thunder guttural in the distance, I welcome the idea of an incorruptible state of reverie and accidental existence. In spite of the squawkers back home who, noisily grinding the wheels and cogs of their redundant machines, might balk at the idea of such applied, permissive leisure, I believe it might be the loveliest idea I've yet to adopt. To just do nothing, or something, as the spirit moves me. To scrape by. To sacrifice comfort for self-determination. To lean toward the next experience, confident that it will support my weight. This could be enormous living.

The only part still muddy to me, as the rain descends in sheets and I spring the latch on my window, is whether I will do it on my own, or with Mathieu beside me. I lean out and look, not to the cars and people below, but to the sky for an answer. The only response I get for my trouble is the slap of the raindrops on my flushed face and the faintest smell of wet pavement warming my nose with its ozone crackle.

It is getting late. My stomach reminds me that while idleness is nice, it does not fill the belly or pay the fatty rent on Paris apartments. Otherwise, more people might have taken it up by now. This could be a glitch in the grand scheme. I will just have to figure a way to live without money . . .

"There is a flower within my heart,
Daisy! Daisy!"

What the hell?

"Planted one day by a glancing dart,
Planted by Daisy Bell!"

Oh . . . my . . . Lord.

"Whether she loves me or loves me not,
Sometimes it's hard to tell
Yet I am longing to share the lot
Of beautiful Daisy Bell!"

A smattering of people stop, even in the downpour, even without umbrellas, to stare at the soaked madman clutching a handful of defeated daisies, serenading me from the sidewalk of Rue des Écoles.

He does sing.

"Your middle name is not Bell by chance, is it?" he yells up, blinded by the torrential rain.

"No. Margaret," I call over the din.

He considers. "That will not work."

"I wouldn't think so."

"Ah, well." He shrugs. And starts up again. Ahem, the rousing chorus, if you please . . .

"Daisy, Daisy,
Give me your answer do!
I'm half crazy all for the love of you!
It won't be a stylish marriage,
I can't afford a carriage
But you'll look sweet upon the seat of a
Bicycle built for two . . ."

The handful of onlookers clap, lobbing glances over at him, then up at me, hungry for the put away, as he moves haltingly into the next verse. I know better than they: the tune and timing are a little off. For this song happens to be stamped on my heart. My mom used to sing it to me when I was a wee little thing, and my dad later on, when I wasn't so much. I think Mathieu must have cribbed it from the Internet because he is consulting his right hand for silent coaching while the daisies, pummeled by the rain, droop in his left. So he's left-handed, I think coolly, checking off one more thing I have learned about him. Figures. Wasn't Van Gogh left-handed too? All the crazy ones are.

But I am not so blasé as I would have myself believe. For yes (*oh, yes*), there seems to be a smile sweetening this sour face that, weakened, I cannot tether down. Every girl who has seen *Say Anything* dreams of this moment, certain at that naïve age that it is due her, knowing, in turn, that *she* will not leave her own John Cusack out in the cold, with sore arms and a broken heart. It must be said, however, that I, lacking the proper imagination, never entertained the notion that my mystical troubadour would be doing the actual singing. And while the channeled Peter Gabriel easily has the better voice and range, Mathieu's nothing-to-lose, balls-out, purely French interpretation of this little American ditty from the Gay Nineties obliterates the competition. Quite frankly, it is a tour-de-force performance.

He boomeranged to *me*.

They applaud as he finishes. I hold my appreciation. There is something I must acknowledge to Mathieu, but also to myself.

"Hey! Cyrano!"

"Oui, Roxane?" he asks, falling to one knee.

"I'm going to outlive you by two decades, I hope you know. A woman lives ten years longer than a man, and you're already five years closer to death than I." I clear my throat, buying time. "So it doesn't look good for you is what I'm saying. *If* we should stay together, that is. And did you also know that left-handed people die five years earlier—again, on average—than right-handers?"

He waves the daisies dismissively. "But of course we should: our candles burn at both ends. But ah, my foes, and oh, my friend, we give a lovely light." He shifts to the other knee. "Besides, Idowhot bayleethen aergees."

"What?"

"I do not believe in averages! I only believe in me and you."

Nice.

"But there's something else."

"O, speak again, bright angel!"

"I don't want any Jean-Pauls or Colettes."

Losing his Shakespeare, Mathieu blinks into the raindrops. "Never?"

I shake my head, hair plastered to my cheeks.

He absorbs this while the onlookers disperse like marbles into the subsiding rain, disappointed by the murky conclusion of this performance piece. Mathieu shrugs, rises, and shakes some of the rain from his hair. "Okay."

"Really?"

"Sure."

I swallow. It is impossible for him to get any wetter, so he waits patiently. Finally, my heart finding peace, I smile broadly

218

and shout down, "So what are you waiting for?"

He presses his hand to his heart.

I give him lead. While I start to close the window, Mathieu, in lieu of using the more conventional stairs, tucks the flowers in the waist of his pants and begins to scale the wall of the Hotel California like a fauvist Spiderman, his red shirt splattered like an inkblot against the white wall. He steps on the huge potted plant, and wraps himself around a drainpipe, inching his way upward. Defying gravity and the slippery conditions, he reaches the wet bars of the mini-balcony on the second floor (first European, though I refuse to concede the logic), hoisting himself upward. Shimmying up the balcony, he stands atop the bars and surveys his kingdom.

I gape at him, certain that he will fall, if not to his death, then to a twisted ankle, which may sprain the romance of our reunion. I am learning that Mathieu can't just seize a moment; he must catapult over it.

He smiles cockily up at me, the trigger for me closing my mouth and yelling, "Are you out of your fucking mind?"

The smile widens, his leather loafer finding traction on the wall. But he has no potted plant here, and the drainpipe hangs unconfidently from this section of the wall. Shifting his weight, he starts to slip. I, in turn, let loose a real girlish scream, flashing my hands to my face in horror. His left foot finds the bars and, wobbling dangerously, Mathieu eventually restores his balance. The daisies, however, are lost to the street. He smiles up at me again, but with a little more humility, the crazy loon.

I repeat my sensitive inquiry. "Are you out of your fucking mind?"

"What would you suggest I do? Knock on these peoples' window?" He jabs a finger at it and starts to waver again.

"Yes, absolutely, that is what I suggest you do."

"No thanks. They are probably American, and keep a gun."

"The only gun I have touched in the last ten years of my entirely American life was owned by a Frenchman," I reply, crossing my arms over my chest. "And I live in Ohio."

"Yes, well," he grumbles, spitting something out of his mouth. "Reach through your bars and give me a hand, will you? All I need is ten centimeters."

"No."

"No?"

"Not until you admit it."

"Daisy, give me a hand!"

"Should have thought this out a little more, eh?" I yawn, and extend my hands above my head.

He hangs his head and braces himself against the wall. "You want me to admit a technicality."

"No. I want you to shout it from the rooftops."

"It is not possible."

"That's not the can-do attitude I'd expect of a—"

"Shut up."

"That's more like it."

He shifts his feet again. His left loafer slips off his foot and slaps to the ground, crushing the daisies. "Oops."

He lifts his head and owns the thing: "I am an American! I am a half-breed American whose mother's name was Flora Jean! Her ancestors owned slaves! She spoke with a twang and called me her little 'Bonbon'! She was the most . . . She was the most . . ." He breaks off, shaking his head.

His mother's memorial service program was in that bag. Her picture, aged, but still lovely, on the front, with her name underneath: *Flora Goodwin. 1953-2004.* There was a striking similarity to Catherine Deneuve. If Ms. Deneuve had been from Billings, Alabama.

"She was the most beautiful thing I ever saw," he finishes.

Mathieu looks up. "Until I met you."

I swallow the knot in my throat and ask, "Now, was that so hard, Yank?"

I give him my hand.

He makes it to the top, to me.

The people down below close their mouths and move on.

"There are these things called stairs."

"I was in the mood to climb."

"Those aren't good shoes for climbing. You should have a pair of tennis shoes, with a good tread."

Mathieu shrugs.

We squeeze into the three square feet of my balcony, two soggy, prideful people unsure about how to proceed now that the great moment of reconciliation has arrived. He is probably a little miffed at me for, well, any number of things. And I am still unsettled about last night's revelations and the conflicted message I received this morning by his smug, desperate hand.

Cartoon name indeed.

We confront one another warily, like circling animals, sniffing out the intent of the other. But our bodies, forsaking pride, are ripe with betrayal, warming to the other's treason, arguing their plans in a language too slippery for words. I list toward him, and our waists touch. The stem of the small, lone daisy poking out of his pants quivers comically.

"You're soaked," I murmur, embarrassed.

"Yes."

"How long did you—"

"Six hours."

"Sorry."

"I would have waited more. But as your name pounded around in my head, I began to recall this song that I heard on an advertisement once. The words to the chorus came to me through the water." He looks at his hand, streaked with ink, and smiles. "I wandered into a nearby library and copied the lyrics."

"I liked it."

He searches my eyes. "Did you?"

I take his hand in my own. "I loved it."

"Daisy, about my mother—"

"I don't care."

I run my hand over his cool, wet face, which is starting to shiver, like his body has just snuck up on him. His teeth are chattering too, and he looks all vulnerable and defiant at the same time. There are raindrops on his lips I would like to kiss away. I trace the scar on his cheek, and ask, "How did you get this? I have wanted to know."

He reaches up to remove my hand, but stops, pressing it more firmly to his face. He closes his eyes and breathes deeply. "I was walking along Le Pont Neuf one morning with my mother when I was six," he says, eyes still closed. "This was just before she went back home. I was thinking how happy I was because she let me hold her hand that day."

He laughs quietly, not afraid to humble himself. I can see his eyes moving behind the membranes of his eyelids, like he's living a dream. "Such a little thing, but it meant something to me. Usually, she hated to be clung to, slowed down. That damn American speed. But this day she allowed it."

I confuse the pulse of his words with my heartbeat.

"I was not thinking about my clumsy feet, of where we were headed. I was not thinking of her promise of ice cream later, if I was good. I thought only about how soft her hand was in mine and how lucky I felt to have possession of it for the day."

His eyes blink open and beat into mine. "So, naturally, I stumbled over a rough place in the sidewalk and planted my face in the concrete. I had not been holding tightly enough, you see." He guides my hand from his face, the illusion of time travel shattering. "There were pieces of glass from a broken bottle some drunk had discarded. One of them cut me. I should have been sewn up, but my mom wanted to show me a new installation at the Pompidou, so we made do with disinfectant and a bandage from a nearby pharmacy."

He smiles. "She was never much of a mother. Yet I cannot say that I ever regretted her choice, or the day. And I am lucky enough to have this mark on my face to remember it by."

The tears roll down his cheeks, mixing with the rain, imperceptible but for the accompanying ratchet of his shoulders. I bring him close and usher him through the window. Inside, I remove the daisy and his wet clothes, drying him with a towel, like I would a child. I place him in between the bed's cool, crisp sheets, replenished just today, as I hid from the chambermaid, sitting on the toilet and doubting the shallow Isabel's devotion to the magnificent Larry. Mathieu becomes quiet and observant on my bed, watching me while I undress and set the damp clothes atop my suitcase. I still haven't unpacked.

Mathieu hitches himself up on an elbow and, with a dear, innocent look, asks, "Where are your scars, Daisy?"

I deflect him, shaking out my hair and bringing a towel to my head. "They are not so obvious maybe. But they're there."

"Will you tell me about them?"

"What do you want to know?" Flinging back my wet hair, I reveal my nakedness before his wandering eyes, made more luminous with emotion.

He gives a little shake of his head and leans back into his pillow. "Nothing, now. Just come to me."

I do as he asks. We make love sweetly, if not as hungrily as before, beneath a hotel painting of a country chateau. We are careful with one another, considerate. If yesterday felt like something being demolished, today is about constructing something lasting, something meaningful, between us. It is a more promising, if less ecstatic, opening, and I clasp my arms around the commitment, around the homecoming. Mathieu's homecoming, to me.

Afterward, he asks what I'm thinking about.

"Nothing, really."

"Come on, what is it?" he prods, trying to see my face as he spoons me.

I laugh. "My mind was wandering back to before. The rain and the song. The real Daisy Bell refused her suitor, you know."

He flips me on my back. "Is that true? I did not see another verse to the song."

I pat him lightly on the cheek. "Don't worry. She must have been a real gold digger. Totally immune to the charm of a bicycle built for two."

"And you?"

I think for a moment, as he eyes me cautiously. For a man dismissive of religion, he is superstitious, and doesn't like what I've told him. I caress his cheek. "Me? Isn't it obvious? I must call my parents."

"Why now?"

I surprise Mathieu by rolling over on him, pinning him to the bed. "Because they've got to know sometime that I'm not coming back."

His eyes widen with joy, and he canvases my body with kisses, lingering on the web of skin above the iliac crest, working his hand into the groove. Not worshipfully, but to discover.

I can live with that.

"The French flag is red, white, and blue too," I muse as he goes about his business. "I will simply have to invent new threads here. Become more French than . . . Victor Hugo . . . Edith Piaf . . . Gertrude Stein." Something tickles, and I suck in a breath.

"What are you blathering about?" Mathieu mumbles, from my belly.

I mean, why not? I sigh, working my fingers through his hair, committed to the insanity. No, not insanity. Evolution.

But when did I decide, and was it a decision freely made? My mind is now the treasonous one, not content to let things lie, even as my body tells the brain to shush, keen on enjoying its status as Mathieu's playground. Surely it wasn't the song. Or the scar. I am not that easily gotten. No, I made my decision before the first note left his mouth.

I remember back, to standing at the window. I remember wanting a sign. And it was then that it happened. My mind produced Mathieu at precisely the moment I needed him to appear. He made the decision easy for me. But it was still mine.

"This is the right thing to do."

"Mmm?" He is preoccupied with the far, shady corner of my neck.

"I said this is the right thing to do." I am calm, magnificent. My voice resonates with authority. I am prepared to loaf with Mathieu into the next century. Cleveland is a dark smudge, a malignancy caught and pulverized on the X-ray of my former life. I am in remission. Nay, I am cured. I feel powerful. This is an act of romantic rebellion. I cannot have my home and Mathieu. So I will adopt Paris, and make it my home with Mathieu. Already, I feel nearly a part of this magnanimous city. I cannot speak its squirrelly language, am uneasy about its customs, and have no friends or family here. But what do friends and family mean without Mathieu? He will be everything to me: teacher, lover, friend, and guide. The rest? Bonbons.

Mathieu pulls away. "Of course it is the right thing to do."

I nod, placated. Of course it is. Of course.

After all, I love him tremendously. When I am in his arms, nothing else matters.

Why is that not a comfort to me?

Chapter 21

D ad?"

"Daisy," he exhales.

"Sorry it's been a while." I have wound the phone cord around my fingers, and the tips are quite blue.

"What on earth were you thinking? Not calling or writing . . . your mother contacted the American embassy, I'll have you know. We've been frantic with worry."

I plop on my bed. "I never said I'd call."

"Some things, young lady, are assumed. We assumed you would have the courtesy to inform your parents if you were alive and well."

"I'm alive, and well," I quip, hoping he'll find this funny.

Or not. "When are you coming back?"

I stand and start to pace. "That's the thing, Dad—I'm not."

Silence. Then, "Explain."

"It's like this: I have fallen in love, Dad, and—"

"Oh, sweet Jesus."

Not a good sign that my father is appealing to Jesus.

Swallowing, I press on, "The man, Mathieu, has invited me to stay with him here in Paris. And I have agreed."

Silence.

"Uh, is Mom there?"

"No. She's with your grandfather. He's ill."

"What's wrong?"

"He had a stroke. Your mother has been heartsick. And your absence has made it that much more insufferable. So I want you to get on an airplane, young lady, and return to us. Today. I don't know what to do for her, you see . . ." My dad's voice wobbles but regains its gruffness as he says, "Quite frankly, this is the least you can do, Daisy, after putting us through so much."

I feel Mathieu behind me, though I try not to look. Shaking my head, I croak, "Don't bully me like this, Dad. My not being there was not responsible for his stroke, or Mom's sadness."

"This is unconscionable of you, Daisy! Have you no sense of responsibility to us anymore, or to yourself? Can you throw your life away on a no-account Frenchman whom you've just met and who likely has one thing on his mind? When he gets it, you *will* be discarded, Daisy. Have no doubt of that. Please tell me that you're not that naïve."

"He's already gotten that, Dad. And he still wants me to stay!"

"Well. Then you're a bigger fool than I ever imagined."

"I guess I am."

The silence is unbearable. I would prefer he call me a fool again.

"Andy called," he says, out of nowhere. "He sounded contrite about . . . everything. And very worried. We agreed that all of this is so unlike you. You were always a rock. It was Henry who could never be serious about anything." Voice cracking, he resumes, "So please, honey, when are you coming home? Your life is waiting for you here. And your mother needs you."

Pinching my eyes shut, I summon my voice. "Good-bye, Dad.

Tell Grandpa—and Mom—that I love them."

"Now list—"

I hang up, staring at the silent phone.

"It was bad, yes?"

Nodding, I turn toward Mathieu, who sits in a chair under the muted television. A car bomb killed twenty-three people in Baghdad today. There is a twisted carcass of a van smoking on the screen. I grimace. *Bad* is such a deficient word. I flip the TV off with the remote. "Yes, it was bad."

He gives me space. I could not bear any arms, not even those, around me right now. A father's anger and disappointment eviscerate any platitudes or comforting. I may melt into a puddle of self-reproach. No one else can slay me like this.

We have always gotten on well together, though we are not close (where is that girl out there who is close to her father, the lucky one who talks to him and feels listened to? I want to know so that I might admire and envy her). Although I find his absentminded professor shtick tiresome at times, I have always understood that it arises out of a desperate desire for security. He needs to establish himself as a certain type of person so he can cubbyhole his reactions to life's slings and arrows. *It is Sunday, and so I read the Arts & Leisure section of* The Times *in my leather chair while sipping my gourmet coffee ordered off the Internet.* This kind of self-awareness helps when: *I was not named the Winston Hollings Distinguished Professor of Literature, again, but I will grow the distinguished beard anyway, as an Oedipal statement on self-fulfilling prophecy.*

The man lives in a fortress, carefully shingled with his impenetrable theories and staked to the ground with the frail timber of dead men's dialogues. As long as he can talk *at* the regular people, avoiding too much *tête-á-tête*, and publish papers on the arcane subject matter that soothes with its crisp abstractions, he is content in his work. Though his students do not adore him, they respect his eccentricity and know not to bother him during office hours, lest he start to sputter and blink uncontrollably. I am the only one who doesn't mortify or restrain him. It is a great burden, and a gift.

Sensing in him a discomfort for social occasions, I tried to smooth the terrain by dominating events, feigning an extroversion I did not feel so he could watch and feel safe from the sidelines. In a lot of ways, it was I, as the oldest child, who was his protector. My mom, resentful of his demonstrable ability to live without her, stopped trying years ago, while my brother was a little embarrassed to claim such a milquetoast father. Henry tried out for football one year, rattling my father to the point of distraction. He told his son that if Henry—or Hank, as he now liked to be called—required an extracurricular activity for his transcript, the chess club would be far more fruitful and less likely to lead to "bodily grievance." Henry told him, with the bluntness that teenagers find intoxicating, that the possibility of "bodily grievance" (or "getting your ass kicked") was why guys did football and why the cheerleaders put out for them.

My mom, decked out in her "Hank's Mom!" jersey in 30 degree weather, whooped from the stands when Henry became the team's star wide receiver. My father, fussy in an overcoat and leather gloves, winced at every snap and looked as green as his tweed cap, a copy of his latest manuscript languishing on his lap as the other dads, macho men all, hurled insults at the refs, the other team's players, and even their own sons. My dad was unfailingly loyal, if bewildered. He could not convincingly ape the other men, yet wanted to show support for his son, which led him to mumble lines from a William Carlos Williams poem—about baseball, actually—under his breath at heart-stopping intervals of the game, when the only poetry called for was the sliding of the ball into my brother's quicksilver hands. The recitation of familiar words is known as prayer, of course, and just because my father's Bible was the great canon of American literature and poetry did not make him any less a believer in their ability to conjure miracles. The man could not recognize an I-formation if his life, or his son's life, depended on it, yet he came for every game. And I, more than my easily horrified brother, who lamented the absence of the mythical, "regular Dad," loved him for it.

Despite Mathieu's flippant comment about his sexuality, the truth about Stephen Lockhart is not that easy. It rarely is. The forging of human connections is simply too much effort anymore. If anything, he is asexual now, as cloistered as a monk, and equally impervious to the charms of male and female. Except for my charm. I can still seduce him when I want to. I could, anyway. The pain of his rebuff, and of our segue into some maudlin, father-daughter melodrama, has shriveled my hope and painted the night black. As foolish as it sounds, I feel like mourning my father: that baroque, if sensitive, man who never wanted kids, but somehow managed two more than his immortal hero.

But I am also mourning his loss of me. And that is a bitterer pill to swallow.

Suddenly, Paris feels like purgatory. And I am stuck in its Hotel California.

I could go back, just briefly, to sit by the bedside of my grand-father, a man I hardly know, in spite of his genetic proximity. Yet I understand that if I were to leave, it would be for good. The clock would sound midnight. The spell would be broken. Mathieu would be as real to me in America as Prince Charming. I am not fooling myself. Our tie is tenuous at best. There are too many voices humming in the wings.

And Andy? I do not allow myself to acknowledge his voice.

Mathieu skulks at the periphery of the room like an aimless soul. Or a man unsure of what his girlfriend thinks.

"Hey."

"Hey."

"I just don't know."

"This is difficult for you."

"It sucks."

He nods.

Standing, I start to pace. "Ugh! I'm equal parts mad at him and disgusted with myself. I mean, he treated me like a child, which I *hate*, demanding that I come home, like I've stayed out past my curfew." I sink to the bed. "And yet I acted like one too."

"How?"

I lean back and lay an arm over my eyes. "I should have called. I didn't mean for them to worry."

"You did not say you would call."

"Yeah, but he's right: they expected it."

"Maybe they should stop expecting things of you."

I pull my arm away and look at him, leaning against the wall, a somber look on his handsome face. "Maybe I should stop expecting them to be parents."

"Maybe so."

I laugh weakly. "I wish it were that easy."

"It could be."

"Says Sancho Panza."

He springs from the wall, fully loaded. "Not anymore. I phoned my father today and told him to stop calling. I only started having contact with him after my mother died. It was not so hard to stop again." Mathieu smiles thinly. "Unfortunately, in spite of his nurse's insistence to the contrary, he thought I was someone named Jacques trying to reclaim a painting. The Matisse. So it may be a conversation I have to revisit in the future."

I stand up and hug him. "Poor Jacques."

"Yes, poor Jacques."

Feeling his heartbeat through his chest, I say, "Maybe you should still take your dad's calls."

Pulling back, he asks, "Why?"

"He is your father." I cannot help but feel a twinge of pity for the old man, whirling through a vortex of time, unable to bolt himself to the present. He doesn't deserve my pity, but the very aged become the young—and almost innocent—again.

"He is a sick son-of-a-bitch." *A zeek zun-uv-a-beetch.*

I hide a smile and gently suggest, "A sick son-of-a-bitch with whom you share half your DNA."

The wound is so raw with Mathieu. He must be telling the truth about how long he's known. Or else, he is not one to forget, much less forgive. In which case, God help me.

"I share nothing with him. He gave that to me offhandedly, and so little else, that now it is only mine." Hugging me close, he argues, "No, sometimes you have to make the choice to cut people out of your life who are no longer good for you. It was a lesson I learned early, and I relapsed in a moment of weakness." Looking me in the eyes, he says, "Now I am strong again. And you will be too."

I nod and cling to him. Yet my mind shrieks at the comparison: *But* my *father is not some Goebbels wannabe! The poor guy just wants me to be there for my sick grandfather and frantic mother. He's a good man. He's my dad.*

Why is selfishness—the low-hanging fruit of freedom—so hard if it's supposed to make us happy?

"Let us get out of here," Mathieu pleads, holding me by my arms. "The night is still young."

"It feels old. Old and tired."

"It is you who feels old and tired. I have what you need to feel young again."

I must ask. "What's that?"

He smiles and bounces on his heels. "It is a surprise."

"What?" I moan, twisting away. "Just tell me so I can reject it and go to sleep."

He grabs my coat and key. "No. It will be better this way. Come on, lazy Daisy. It is Friday night, and you are in Paris." Flinging the door open, Mathieu hesitates before turning toward me. "But there is one question I need to ask you first."

"What? How does this French-American man have such surgical scorn for half of his heritage?"

"Not at all. My question is this: do you know how to roller skate, Daisy Margaret?"

"Skate?"

"Skate. Do you know how?"

I narrow my eyes. "Are you serious?"

"With equal parts French and American."

Shifting my weight, I recount my slim, fractious history on the subject. "My mom got me Rollerblades when I turned thirteen. Half of the scars on my body are because of those things." I shrug. "My mom's kind of a flake that way. She remembered that I liked purple, but forgot the pads."

"So you know how to skate?"

"Skate? Yes. Stop? Not so much."

Apparently, this is enough, for Mathieu hustles me through the door. "Trust me. You will not need to stop." He smiles and hikes his eyebrows up and down like a comic book villain. "Are you up for it, *Yank*, or do you still want to sleep the night away?"

And because I am also my mother's daughter, a woman so naturally competitive that she once started a half marathon and ran the whole thing because she felt it would be a "cop out" to stop, and because I am also the determinedly Plucky Heroine, I march out the door, fairly certain that this skating misadventure will not solve anything, and absolutely certain that I will fall.

But there is always the matter of maybe. And the curious question of how.

Spectacularly, as it turns out.

Chapter 22

The people are the surprise.

There are fathoms of skaters in a celebratory mood amassed near the Montparnasse Tower, that Rodney Dangerfield building in Paris only good for its lookout tower. There is a buzz in the air, an anticipatory glow, as electric as the nightsticks held by some of the revelers. Thousands of helmeted and padded skaters perform practice spins and rib good-naturedly with old friends and new. In a matter of minutes, I overhear five languages, from four continents, spoken. My tongue is a mite overcome, muted by the size of the crowd, and the nuttiness of my agreeing to be a part of it, when clearly I share nothing in common with these people. I don't even have a pair of skates on, so I am a dwarf among the giant people. It's funny what the new normal can be.

We have to buy skates from a man hocking them at a hugely inflated price. What are you going to do? This is street capitalism, and he knows his market. Mathieu fumbles with his wallet, but I check him.

"This is mine."

He opens his mouth to argue but is stopped by my expression. He nods and withdraws.

Skate Man grins repugnantly and makes a cutting remark to Mathieu in French, spittle spraying. I can only imagine what is said. I thought American guys were macho, but they have nothing on the French. After paying, I whisper to the guy, *"Vous devez avoir un pénis très petit,"* which, I think, means, "You must have a very small penis." (I have been very lonely at nights with my little dictionary and littler imagination.) But my pronunciation must be awful because he merely stares at me, my money hanging limply from his hand as I, not so cuttingly, saunter away.

Mathieu, understanding my peculiar dialect, laughs until his shoulders shake. He pulls me to an open gap on the curb where we remove our shoes and don the skates, which are as stiff as shackles. I use Mathieu's shoulder for leverage and perform a wobbly pirouette, rolling my eyes as he pretends to coach. Mathieu looks funny in skates. Andy could be an Adonis without even trying. I've never entertained Mathieu as the athletic type. In fact, France seems to shun exercise to a large extent. I have yet to see a gym, and unless they've installed a running track atop the Arc de Triomphe, joggers are few and far between. It must be all the sweating and awful workout clothes.

"Did you play any sports in high school?" I ask, circling him.

"Not in an organized way. But there were neighborhood football games."

"Football?" I blurt out. Then, "Oh—you mean soccer, of course."

"No, I mean football. You were thinking, I imagine, of that barbaric ritual known as American football."

My legs scissor like a drunk puppet's. "So what's the appeal there? With soccer?"

"It is a sport of strategy. Of patience, and slow failure." He wheels around quickly. Maypole removed, I sprawl to the pavement.

Mathieu smiles indulgently. "And sometimes, great surprise. It is not the American way of constant gratification. Football feels more like real life. It is long, arduous, and sometimes there are no winners or losers." He offers me his hand.

Ignoring it, I find my feet again. "Great. Sounds like fun." I practice my stopping, which is pretty straightforward when moving at one mile per hour.

"Who said anything about fun?"

There is a ripple of movement in the air. I hear a whistle sound, and a great, rousing cheer sweeps like an athletic wave through the crowd, which starts its tectonic shifting.

"But wait! I'm not ready!"

"Of course you are," Mathieu says, ignoring the charge of people. He skates backward and holds out his hands to me, as skaters swarm us like cicadas.

"But what about my shoes? Your shoes?" I yell, sucked into the great vacuum that a mob's momentum insists upon. There appears to be a hill ahead of us. A very frightening kind of downhill.

"Forget it. We do not need them."

Looking back at my Keds, their toes pointed neatly over the curb, laces tied, I am not so sure. I am abandoning an important part of myself back there. Those shoes have marked my steps for so long. God knows where these skates will lead me. Maybe I can return to pick them up laaaaatttteer—

"Aauugghh!" I scream, grabbing Mathieu's shirttail as we descend the first hill, which skis more like a mountain. "I can't stop!"

"You are not supposed to stop. Just let yourself go," he instructs, his voice the eye in my storm. "Or hold on to me."

He is right. Somehow, though chaotic, it works, and there are no major collisions or falls. The crowd is a single organism with many pulsing parts, all similarly programmed to achieve their end. Eventually, I gain the confidence to let go of Mathieu's shirt and, on flat ground again, even catch up to him, *swish-swishing* my legs to his constant rhythm. I look over at him and smile.

"I'm doing it," I yell, pleased.

"You are doing it," he agrees.

There are many tonalities to be plucked from the glittering lights of Paris, but the colors have dissolved tonight, the lights dragged long, like time-lapsed film. At intervals, I take note of something that won't be ignored, like the ornate Opera House or the tireless Louvre, streaming at the blurred corners of my vision. But on the whole, I fall into a state of Zen-like meditation. Mathieu and I coast wordlessly through the vacated city streets (*What did they do with the cars?* my baffled brain shouts above the Zen), which yawn so wide that they seem ordained for just this activity by some prescient nineteenth-century city planner. I pocket each foot forward, before discarding it as the next vibration ricochets up the vertical thrust of my legs, into my buttocks, and is killed by the package of vertebrae in my spine. The amplified friction of hundreds of nearby wheels kissing the pavement discourages talk and thought. I buzz like a small bee through the night air with my angry cluster, pulled by instinct alone. Does a bee think about destination? No, it reacts. And so I react. Continually. Reflexively. It is not until we hear a distant whistle and hit a wall of slowing skaters that we realize there is a break.

It feels strange to stop, once you get going.

We find another curb, and I hobble over in a post-runner's-high daze. My thighs are intractable and I sink to the ground in relief. I look at my wrist to check the time but my watch is curled on my nightstand, fast asleep. I have no idea of the time, or of how long we've been skating.

"Probably one and a half hours," Mathieu guesses.

"It feels like less."

"It always does."

"You've done this a lot?"

"A few times."

Just react.

"Ever with another girl?"

He looks at me, a line of sweat swathing the skin above his lips. "Not with one who meant anything to—"

"—because I do this all the time at home. Except in Cleveland we call it *How Long Does the Stupid White Girl Have Before She Gets Killed by A Crowd of Angry Motorists Wielding Tire Irons?*" I avoid his eyes, spinning my wheels. "Of course, the SUV drivers are usually the first to attack, followed by the mean grannies made late for *Wheel of Fortune*. And there's always a Hummer guy who tries to light some poor skater up with gasoline. Because, you know, he has so much of it to spare . . ."

Mathieu shakes his head and sighs.

"What?" I demand.

"Will you ever be able to forget about my past relationships?"

I give him a long, hard look. "Mathieu, I ran into two women yesterday, one of whom was a lesbian. Sorry, but I've never been part of such a diverse harem before."

He snorts.

"And God only knows who else is hiding in the shadows. But I don't doubt that I would be the ugly one." I cut him off with my hand. "Two women, one day, in a city the size of Paris. Please forgive me if I don't really like my odds."

"Daisy."

"So no, I won't forget. But I won't ask you about them. For self-preservation, if anything. I'm a bit of an ostrich yet."

Mathieu chews on this. "All right."

"That's all?"

He leans back on his palms. "I do not know, Daisy. You accuse me of holding back, of keeping secrets, when it is you who has not been frank."

He holds up a hand. "Let me finish. It took me a day—that is all, remember—to confess to you about my father, my mother, and my ex-girlfriend. But what do I know of you, for all my efforts? That you like Matisse more than Picasso. That your father has a strange hold over you. That you despise your dependency on—" He smiles sadly. "That you are always looking to wander, even while I hold your body close."

I blush and look down at my hands. "What else do you want to know?"

"Why you came to Paris? Who Andy is? Why you felt the need to run away from home?" Mathieu looks at me searchingly. "You are slippery, Daisy. You try to appear so straightforward, yet you push people away with your humor, your insecurities . . . your cowardly self-righteousness."

My neck snaps up. "Self-righteous? Are you serious?"

"You like to run. You will take any excuse," he says. "Tell me, did you leave my apartment last night because you were enraged by my lies—lies that meant nothing to our relationship, as far as I could see—or were you secretly relieved to have found a smooth escape from all the turbulence? Did I hurt *you*, or did I merely cut your pride, as you struggled to imagine yourself in a different fairy tale, without a worthless, poor writer who would never give up his worthless writing, not even for you?"

The whistle sounds again. The rest of the skaters rise and shove off. Mathieu and I remain seated. When the last of the lonesome skaters, loosely swerving backward, passes, I look at the retreating mass, feeling very much like a runt wolf abandoned by her pack and left to die.

We are near the Pére Lachaise Cemetery. The iron gates stretch forever. Jim Morrison, having broken on through to the other side, rests there in perfect silence.

"You and Sartre are right: hell is other people." I sigh, brushing my hands off.

Mathieu smiles, but it doesn't reach his eyes.

"If you must know, I haven't talked about Andy because I don't want to be judged. I feel a little bit protective of him. If you knew too much, you'd probably find a lot to scorn. Including me for loving him, once."

Mathieu pounces. "Do not shroud your motives. Andy was an excuse."

"Was he?" I demure, anger washing over me. Why must we fight about such nonsense? It makes me want to, well—damn him!—run. The skates are handy. I know I could beat Mathieu. The guy was built for grace, not speed.

"Yes, you wanted to get away. You hate these ridiculous classes of yours and the career you thought you wanted. You realized that life has more to offer than the crushing routine of your laboratory, that there is more mystery to be uncovered in the universe than you could ever hope to find under your microscope, and that you had rebelled from your free-thinking parents by becoming their opposite: a slave to science, when you have the soul of a poet."

"I thought you didn't believe in souls," I mutter, shrugging the skates off.

"I believe in your soul."

Maybe you wouldn't if . . .

I bite my lip and say, "You are wrong, Mathieu. I know you would like to be right. You have this picture of me in your head somehow. But you're wrong."

He nods, leaning back again. "Anything is possible."

"I didn't hate my life," I say, shaking my head. "You have this funny idea of scientists, Mathieu—like we're all programmed toward lives of logic and humorlessness. Like we're unfeeling robots or something. It's a cheap stereotype. The guy I work for? Dr. Choi? He is an incredible musician with this sweet soft spot for old musicals. I'm sure if he could spare some of the time he spends working to cure a debilitating disease, he'd compose an aria called 'Some Enchanted Utricle.' Oh, go ahead and laugh." I scoff at his bemusement. "But people find their inspiration in different places, and thank God for it. You should thank your lucky stars that these people care so deeply about this stuff. Otherwise, I would have died at birth because I was born with a hole in my heart, and you could have been sitting here with someone else, wondering, after pulling your eyes away from her assets, why you felt so dissatisfied with the level of her conversation."

"In spite of the pleasure I feel at your 'level,' Daisy, you still digress. You are not 'these people,' no matter how prettily you pretend. I have no problem with your professor's devotion. I am not against progress. But I am an advocate for authentic living. And I suspect that if you were to write an aria right now, it would be titled something like—oh, let me think—'Some Enchanted Evening'? It may be too obvious for you, but it rather captures the spirit of the thing, yes?" Mathieu grabs my fingers and kisses my palm.

He's wrong, again. Not *"Some* Enchanted Evening." *"This* Enchanted Evening."

I unscrew my shoulders and allow my head to loll backward. There is a smattering of stars blown across the sky, bright enough to pierce through the City of Light's guarded aura. Paris is not the entire universe after all. I wonder what The Big Dipper is called in French? *Le Gran Soup Spoon?* I look toward Mathieu, ready to say something, but he is also engaged with the night sky, his Adam's apple a tricky knot appealing to the heavens. I let it go.

There are nights, rare ones, in which you need the sky to put you in your place. I am so small. And yet, I am my everything. I cannot reconcile these two truths so easily.

I like to think that I could open my mouth on these nights and yawn it back inside, my belly ballooning to accommodate the undigested cosmos, holding it expectant inside of me, until it could be reborn. The Big Bang spewed it out there. But who lit the fuse? Science knows so much, yet understands so little. This is why people pull toward religion. The answers are so unsatisfying. Are we nanoquarks of God-matter, clashing with other quarks, equally infinitesimal and elusive, or are we chewed-up stardust trying to locate that lost radiance? Does it matter?

I am here. Mathieu is here. Dark matter dances all around us. We fight and are repelled. We make up, and there is attraction. And if I feel like a shape-shifter, a time traveler, sitting next to him (an unsettling thing—except to Einstein, maybe—when contemplating stars, because if you can't believe in your own robust shape and form, then how are you to interpret the universe and your place in it?), well then, so be it. I don't know where I stand with the universe, and I don't know where I stand when I'm with Mathieu. But still I embrace the company. And I like looking at the stars. They are not much bigger than I from here. And if they no longer burn, a legacy of light survives.

"You're right," I say, as the sequestered traffic spills noisily into our street. We pull our legs back and stand up, facing one another on the sidewalk, headlights bleaching our faces at intervals. "To some extent, anyway."

"About what?" His skates are still on, and with mine off, he towers over me. I tilt my head up, hating myself a little for appreciating his greater height. It's a movie heroine thing: it's been conditioned within me to demand the head tilt.

"I don't really like my schooling," I admit, looking past the sharp corner of his shoulder, toward the iron gates beyond. "But more to the point, I didn't really like Andy toward the end."

Mathieu guides my chin toward him. His eyes won't let me go this time.

"I cheated on him months ago. Never told him, of course. But when he broke up with me, I had the chance to play the victim and do something crazy." I shrug, but my chin trembles. "We're very alike, Mathieu. I, too, get bored, restless. Andy did me the great favor of giving me a reason to run. But then I tripped and fell into you. And I can't seem to get up again."

I look down and take his hands in mine. "Yet I know that the day will come when you or I will get bored, and run again."

He squeezes my hands and smiles. "It would be difficult to be bored by you, Daisy. You are too, too—"

Alarmed, I try to stop him. "Don't say any—"

"—too damn something," he finishes, his eyes flashing their surrender under the headlights.

"—more," I sigh.

"So what do you want to do?" Mathieu asks, tucking me closer, his voice low and resonant. If he were to say my name across an ocean, the pull of his voice would reach someplace deeper than sound to drag me toward him.

"Fuck it!" I laugh to the sky. "I want to do nothing. Absolutely nothing. With you."

We kiss. And the cars in the busy street honk their communion, and the stars sigh their pleasure. Mathieu and I don't make a sound. We have spun off the axis.

And so I do fall. Farther and farther. To some nameless place where imagination does not penetrate: beyond the stilted architecture of poetry, past the probing eyes of Hubble. These are still outward realms, after all. When what we desire is not to travel, but to find. To lock onto something, like a leech fastened to blood-rich prey. To feel the illusion of permanence in a kiss, a person, a moment, a God . . . even if we cannibalize ourselves in the process.

The gates of Pére Lachaise do not exist. They have retreated into the darkness. And Jim Morrison?

The Lizard King lives. And he can do anything.

The sun rises in Paris, and the grass is wet with dew. The sun rises in Paris, and the smell of baking bread hits you from nowhere and anywhere. The sun rises in Paris, and a statue in a park smiles over you like a guardian angel. The sun rises in Paris, and your lover's arm rises and falls on your blanketed chest. The sun rises in Paris, and your heart—that weak, shameless organ—aches with the tender beauty of it. The sun rises in Paris, and somewhere your grandfather may be dying. The sun rises in Paris, and you can taste the regret for the many mornings when you will not see the sun rising in Paris.

It is a new day.

Look at me I'm only seventeen
The many years between us
Have been broken
Look at me under the evergreen
Life is a mellow dream
Almost unspoken

By the way
You said you're here to stay
Let me love you 'til tomorrow
Then it will last a year and a day
Maybe we're here to forget

—Keren Ann

Chapter 23

I am, all modesty aside, a rather brilliant loafer. I wasn't sure if I could crack it, but it turns out to be a simple matter of cutting the noose called Time. My watch is a blind eye hibernating in my suitcase, along with Rick, my camera, and everything else. Once acquitted of the notion that I must do A by Time B, my body stirs only when our neighbor upstairs starts her ballet steps, my feet flexing in time with her indelicate *pliés* and *pirouettes* as Mathieu snores beside me, the late morning sun burning through the sheet over the window. Beckett, not immune to time's passing when food is indicated for, stares at me from her squat on my chest, while my belly, conditioned toward an idea of hunger before the feeling even made itself manifest, bears no complaint, now, to eating dinner when I would normally have thought about bed. The hours in between? They spend themselves in a new kind of education: reading without deadlines or exams, French lessons from Mathieu, learning that the best time to explore the Parc des Buttes-Chaumont on Paris's outskirts is during lightly raining days, when it is nearly deserted, and the mist hanging over the small canal transforms it into a Brigadoon emerging from its hundred-year slumber, just for you.

My favorite subject of study is Mathieu. How I measure our days together by the lengthening bother of curl on the back of his neck, which he vainly attempts to plaster down with the oil from his palm. How he types gustily—the noise ricocheting like weapon fire off the walls—with just his index fingers, and rebels when I suggest anything else might be more efficient. How he can't even shut up when asleep but carries on in conversational French, pieces of which I can now crack from time to time. Once he spoke of his mother. Once he talked about a fine roasted lamb. Another time he groaned my name, upon which I promptly had my way with him.

But it is in his rare quiet moments where I find the most to love. That sleepy-eyed smile when I thrust a disapproving Beckett into his face in the mornings. The wetting of his lips a half second before pouncing on a rhetorical point. How he closes his eyes when he listens to music, or to me, on those occasions when I'm particularly brilliant or maddening. And, most eloquently, the way those same eyes light up when I sneak up on him at a meeting place earlier agreed upon. He cannot disguise his glee. And so I find that I have not grown up after all, for I am still sixteen and loving a man loving me. I invent reasons to be away from him, and do not acknowledge the fear that cramps my heart on that beat before he sees me, when I despair of some hardening of that soft, pliable passion quickening in his eyes. Happily, it is always there.

The leaves have turned, so the Earth must be harnessed to motion. Autumn in Paris is a lot like autumn elsewhere, except there are fewer leaves on the ground. Paris is, of course, a conscientious guardian of her trees. Yet I miss the crunching leaves beneath my feet. I have to go out and buy many more sweaters (and another pair of shoes) than the two I brought, because it is getting cold and Mathieu's arms can only work so hard. Mathieu does not recoil at my buying them from a second-hand store. I think a part of him still believes that as goes my money, so go I. He doesn't yet trust that I am capable of sacrifice. He warns me that I will grow bored and hostile toward him for dragging me away from my "weekly trips to TGIF" and my "American fever for shopping malls and bad pornography." I ask him who the hell he thinks I am. His paranoia is silenced as he retreats from the solace of comfort stereotyping. I ask him, more tentatively, what the difference is between good porn and bad porn. He takes me to go see Bernardo Bertolucci's *Last Tango in Paris*, playing that night at one of the many art-house cinemas nearby. I tell him afterward, with a charley horse seizing my gut, that this is not porn; it's sex as human suffering. But maybe it worked, because we still had sex when we got home. Then again, we have sex every night. It just doesn't involve measurable amounts of butter or self-loathing.

We like to sit on the roof in the evenings, wrapped up in a blanket, a bottle of wine a silent third. It pains Mathieu to have to drink bad wine, but it would pain him more to go without. The medieval rooftops of Paris are a jagged topography, their scarred, rusted chimneys gasping for cleaner air. Close your eyes just so, at sunset, and behold an urban Cezanne: mercurial beauty disguised as permanence. We shamelessly peek into people's windows and invent lives to wrap around them, wanting them to be warm too. Mathieu's are character studies that can never clear loneliness; mine are bad nighttime stories parents might tell their kids, with fantastical *deus ex machinas* that surface when I've snarled the flimsy plots. We enjoy shaking our heads at one another. And we enjoy our lovely, aimless talks and lovelier aimless silences. You get a different feel for a city watching her (almost) sleep at night. I feel tender toward Paris now. She is not home, but she is something like it.

"Do you believe in God less now that your mother is dead?"

The question swoops through the thin, late October air and lands with a thud on Mathieu's head. We were having a lively discussion about book vending machines. Mathieu is adamant they could work. Just put in your three euros at the metro station, and out plops Goethe's *Faust*. And that's where we diverge. Maybe Goethe is wildly popular here. God, I hope so. But in Cleveland, it is more likely to plop a drippy mess like *The Purpose Driven Life*. Or, if it were a truly good dump: Ann Coulter (excuse the second reference to Ms. Coulter; I do hate her so, but she doesn't deserve the attention).

I love that Mathieu doesn't know who Ann Coulter is. That he thought Bill O'Reilly was an Irish soccer coach. He lives in a purer realm than I. We can't talk about a lot of the stuff that, viewed from a godly distance, has recently filled me with rage. And I, in turn, don't care a whit about the newspaper scandals that captivate the French, who have an inexplicable fondness for the government characters in their serialized dramas, like they're black sheep to be welcomed back into the fold after a public slogging. But they're not my family, and I didn't grow up with the clannish gossip of favored sons from the *Grandes Écoles* tickling my dinner conversation. I hail from a different place, where the cult of Big Celebrity was invented and refined. Bureaucrats don't qualify. Though, strangely, the pundits decrying them sometimes do.

Without those common points of reference, Mathieu and I are forced (what divine coercion!) to talk about books, art, and music. He has never read *Jane Eyre*. I am properly horrified. Yet I almost forgive him when I find his *The Carpenters* LP hiding out between his John Cage and Bob Dylan.

Somehow, though, it always comes back to God. Maybe because this is a more lucid, streamlined existence: a life unpoisoned by paperwork. Anesthetizing myself to the tug of intentions, I am saturated with thoughts and sensations. More obsessed with the origin of things than with their conclusions. I return to God because I envy Mathieu's clarity and desire some of that—if not its acrid flavor—for myself.

I kind of like getting him worked up, too.

Mathieu frowns. "How do you mean?"

"I just wonder. I know she left you long ago, but there's still got to be a sense of abandonment when the woman who gave you life—the only godlike figure available to us—is suddenly proved to be mortal. I can't imagine the sense of loss," I continue, my voice pinched at the thought of losing my own mother, who is very far away. "I just thought it might have swung you along the spectrum, if not from believer to nonbeliever, then from agnostic to atheist."

Mathieu scowls. "I think agnostics are the worst of the lot. Believe in *something*, for God's sake!"

I play with a ring on my finger and delicately clear my throat. "So what was the moment? Were you ten years old and God didn't answer a prayer? Fifteen and rebellious? Twenty and disaffected?"

Mathieu sets his wineglass down. "I was seven."

"Seven?"

Mathieu nods. "I had a teacher, *Mme.* Bellamont. Sweetest lady in the world. My mother told me she was going to be a nun, but she was too in love to go through with it. I liked her more when I heard that. And I was a little jealous of her husband. She had these amazing legs. They were not designed for a nun's habit. I was always looking up the long line of them, wondering what was concealed underneath those skirts." He smiles at me, but I wince at the idea of a sexualized seven-year-old.

He continues, more soberly. "She was the only good teacher I ever had. Most of my teachers terrified or bored me. But not her. I think she felt a little sorry for me . . . anyway, I was her pet."

He shakes his head and scoops up his wine. "Yet she died in a car accident the summer after—" He looks down. "She was to have her baby the following week."

"That's awful," I concede, after a small pause. "But people die all the time. It doesn't explain a seven-year-old abandoning God."

But your mother leaving the year before might.

"Of course it does, especially since church bored me to tears. My mother was homesick and took me most Sundays, trying to pretend that French Catholic bore some resemblance to American Southern Baptist. She never believed in it, but she, like so many of your country, sought that fool's gold of tradition and ritual. I was terribly impatient with it all. Even then, it seemed like prayer was a bargaining chip, a way of offering up some humility to cash in later for the ultimate prize."

His features are twisted with contempt. Mathieu is not indifferent toward religion, but actively hostile. The recognition unsettles me.

"I could accept *Mme.* Bellamont's death. But what was the point of the baby's life being started, if only to end so soon? I tried to imagine that fetus walking between my mother's pearly gates of heaven, but she kept falling over on little toothpick legs before I could get her there." He laughs harshly. "Then I imagined her being dragged around by the umbilical cord like a—"

"—okay, I get the picture."

Mathieu smiles wanly. "Sorry."

I nod but avert my eyes.

He adds, more evenly, "My point was this: what kind of afterlife could a fetus enjoy in heaven? None. So then heaven must be a fraud. What kind of personal God could be so perverse as to bring new life into the world, only to squash it before it could absorb its existence?"

What kind, indeed.

"Then why not believe in a more impersonal God? Like the

Deists. Or Buddhists."

"I like much in Buddhism," Mathieu acknowledges. "I like the idea of interconnectivity, of each of us being a jewel of many facets strung together in an endless array, infinity reflecting infinity. I appreciate the idea of karma, of being responsible for one's actions in life. And I admire the Buddhist's commitment to his cause."

"Then what?" I ask. "What stops you from considering it?"

"Truly? I would feel ridiculous."

"How so?"

Mathieu raises his palms to the air. "It is no accident that the vast majority of people in this world are born to their religion. It is the language of worship that feels most comfortable, and comforting, to us. Buddhism feels foreign, exotic. That which is foreign and exotic to us can never be completely comforting."

You don't say, I muse, watching a plane blink its steady path in the distant sky. "So you're ruling out the possibility of eternal enlightenment through the simple fact that you might feel ridiculous meditating on a yogi mat in the middle of Paris?"

"No, not entirely."

I laugh. "Then what?"

"I do not believe in their means."

"What? Transcendence? Enlightenment?"

"That is the goal. But to do that, one must forget desire. To lose your ego is to lose your identity. Which is the only thing that makes this life bearable. As a writer, I am my own God." Turning toward me, Mathieu says, "I would never sacrifice that, even for enlightenment."

"You are a terrible egomaniac."

"Yes, I am. But you should be happy of this. You may yet be immortalized."

I would not love Mathieu any other way. I love the spirit and the flesh of him. I would not sacrifice this world for the next, unless he could null the sacrifice by joining me. This world feels heavenly to me 60 percent of the time: the time I'm with Mathieu.

What do muses do with the other 40 percent of their time? Did Manet's Olympia let out a breath of relief, kick off her heels, and grow out of that flat canvas at nights? I will never know.

I point my toes toward the Eiffel Tower that night, and every night, on our rooftop magic carpet. It steadies me to witness its steely tip blinking atop that jumble of geometry, to sense its implacability even while I sleep. I have so little to orient myself here. When I am away from Mathieu, I might as well not exist. He is my entire salvation in a world devoid of familiar living.

This is, of course, what I was afraid of.

But *screw it*, I think, glowering at the replica of the Statue of Liberty on the Pont de Grenelle on a gray Monday afternoon. Autonomy is overvalued, anyway. So I had the freedom to be creatively unhappy before. Now one thing makes me unhappy: this empty, afternoon solitude in the most beautiful city in the world. I invent reasons to be away while he is writing because I don't want to be too needy, and yet while away, I need, need, need like a blind kitten rooting for the teat. Love carries us high only to knock us down. Or perhaps love gives us permission to make ourselves low. It is during this time of the day when I check for clocks: 3:23 . . . *is he missing me enough?* 4:14 . . . *should I take the long way back, in case he is finishing?* All of this should disgust me, but I'm too ripe with anticipation to care about self-respect.

Besides, he has it just as bad. This is our conversation, in bed, from two nights ago:

Mathieu: I cannot breathe sometimes when you are away. I will be working and things appear to be going well, and then I look up and notice that I am alone, and my breath will be sucked away.
Daisy: Good.

Mathieu (surprised): You want me to suffer?

Daisy: Of course.

Mathieu (frowning): I don't want you to suffer.

Daisy: Sure you do.

Pause.

Mathieu (finally): So?

Daisy: So what?

Mathieu: Do you suffer?

Daisy (kissing him on the forehead): More than you, silly. I never have to look up to notice that I'm alone.

Mathieu (puzzled): So why do you leave me?

Daisy: Because I love you. And I want you to keep on loving me.

Mathieu: I would not if you were here?

Daisy: Not as much. I would sense your distraction and feel that I was crowding you, until eventually you would feel like I was crowding you, and that would be a far worse world of suffering to me.

Mathieu: But I can't work anyway. You have ruined me as a writer. My mind is always elsewhere.

Daisy (a little triumphantly): I'm sorry.

Mathieu (perceptively): Liar.

He's starting to talk more like an American. He's even taken up contractions and tolerates my colloquialisms, though I have only been able to incorporate "that would puke a hound bitch from a gut wagon" (thank you, Grandma Lockhart, *Miss Parkersburg, West Virginia 1926*) once, on a novice trip to a meat market on Rue Cler. Mathieu stood in a state of incomprehension as I, weak-kneed, first encountered *boudin noir*, or blood sausage, a delicacy whose plasmatic origin is exactly as it sounds. While we still encounter cultural hiccups like that, the line is being redrawn in my direction little by little. I once surprised him with a bucket o' chicken from KFC, complete with mashed potatoes and something milky that aspired toward coleslaw. He feigned to choke it down, but then again, I didn't exactly force that third breast on him (he is a breast man, regrettably). Of course, afterward, I had to listen to him disparage the kindly Colonel Sanders for ten meandering minutes, accusing me of condoning the "Southern plantation mentality" through my complicit desire for delicious fried foods. But his heart wasn't in it, and before I could enlighten him that Sanders was born in Indiana, he broke off to lick his greasy fingers and grab a juicy leg (he is also, more happily, a leg man) from the bucket marked by the Colonel's folksy mug.

All in all, I'm loosening him up a little.

But he's still got that fierce disdain for America as an Idea, for America as the Great Homogenizer, I lament, arriving at my destination on the Champs Elysées, that shamelessly global boulevard in Paris where the Gap, Häagen Dazs, and Louis Vuitton comingle in a classless orgy of consumerism. I consider Mathieu's championing of the French way of life laudatory, as I am beginning to appreciate their insistence on fresh food and taking things slow, but would love to prove that he is capable of succumbing to those frothy experiences he righteously rants and rails against.

And so it is that, enjoying a scoop of chocolate chip cookie dough ice cream outside of a movie theater featuring a poster of Tom Cruise, sans smile, with gun, I hatch a wonderful plan. Not only will Mathieu learn to embrace America's fun side; he will have the pleasure of living in America—or in a stylized, Pop Art America—for an entire day. After all, if I am to go without gorditas and *The Daily Show* for the remainder of my days, he can put up with a smidge of retribution.

Not that I really see it like that, of course. I'm simply inviting him to the Happiest Place on Earth.

"Darling."

"Yes."

"My turn today."

"Hmm?"

"My turn, my turn."

"I'm listening," he says, eyebrow cocked.

I roll over, playfully pinning him. "My turn to play tour guide."

He smiles drowsily. "And where will you take me?"

"You won't like it."

"If it's with you," he murmurs, nuzzling my ear. The poor dear. There is no gentle way of breaking it.

"Disneyland. We are going to Disneyland Paris."

He loses his smile, and groans. Mathieu sloughs me off as easily as he might Beckett. Sitting up in bed, he places his head in his hands. "No, Daisy. It is not possible."

He says this in the same way people speak of peace in the Middle East. I run a hand up his neck, ruffling that hair which continues its backward progress. There has not been the time, or inclination, for haircuts, appointments, work: the clocking of real life. Our gears have seized at some graceful Nowhereland. I brace his head gently, but forcibly, making him look at me. "You can do it," I say. Stifling the urge to laugh, I declare, "I will see you through the whole of it, and I promise you this: we will escape unscathed."

His expression is that of a little boy who is told that he will have to go to summer school instead of baseball camp. A positive pout on those pensive lips that love to argue and kiss with equal fury and abandonment. It is the opposite of my reaction to the annual Disneyland pilgrimage, taken during the summer vacations spent with my grandparents. I was a different person in California. Nothing was expected. I was lazy, happy—afloat.

Never was the world more a blissful convergence than on the days when my mom and grandmother accompanied Henry and me to Anaheim's Disneyland. We arrived early and left late. I loved the faux nostalgia of strolling down Main Street, with its marble-tiled ice cream parlor, where you could find lollipops the size of your head and overpriced Mickey ears to be discarded the next day, when the magic ran out; I loved the sensory thrill of Thunder Mountain, where the wind whipped through my hair for a short pluck of time well earned by long lines and enforced cowboy music; I even loved "it's a small world" with its pretty promise of world harmony and that damnably catchy refrain that massaged my mind until I marched to its insistent metronome; and mostly, I loved my grandmother, a vigorous consumer of things and people, buying me a new doll with each visit—and not any old Minnie or Mickey—but exotic dolls from around the world, dressed in romantic costumes that bore no resemblance to cultural truth. They were prettier than anything real or, until then, imagined. I remember the French doll perfectly: she was a cancan dancer. I fingered the lace on her silk pantaloons, not understanding what they were all about, but knowing that they felt as soft as her name sounded: *Gigi*.

I know what Mathieu thinks. To him, Disneyland is like *The Matrix*: manufactured living for the slobbering masses. Walt Disney may as well have lobotomized me, before plugging me into a shared, commercial imagination, where Goofy did the thinking for all of us. *Gowsh, folks!* A warm wet dream. A fiction. A lie.

This is hard to argue. There is a reason you cannot see the outside world in Disney parks. They (a sinister word itself, especially when talking about giant corporations inclined toward soft mind control) want to induce a break from reality, a pleasure park for the

senses, where the gratification is born more from having expectations met than confounded. I'm sure Mathieu objects to all of
it: the corporate hegemony, the trite machinations spelled out in
singsong voices of enlarged, even grotesque, cartoon figures, adults
made equally grotesque by the aping of their children, the stock,
phony cheeriness of the workers, and the hard bottom line supporting it all. It is a French nightmare. One influential critic,
upon the park's opening outside Paris, described it as a "cultural
Chernobyl." I know this because I am a long subscriber to the
Mouse Savers Newsletter. There was some protestation by the en-
thusiastic—okay, rabid—ladies who followed this controversy that
the French didn't deserve "the Disney experience."

I'm inclined to agree. After all, not everything in life needs
to be examined from all angles, its intentions weighed and argued
until it becomes more abstraction than reality. We don't often get
a chance to touch upon the pleasures of childhood, and Disneyland may be the closest thing we have to a fountain of youth. Even
if it's bought and paid for by nervous stockholders swollen with
quarterly expectations.

"But Daisy, why would you want to?" Mathieu finally asks. "It
is like going to London, and having the chance to go to the Tate,
where the art is alive and magnificent and difficult, and instead
waiting in line with the herd at Madame Tussauds', so you can
have your picture taken with The Beatles."

"Ooh, can we do that when we go? I call Paul," I squeal, flip-
ping my hair behind my shoulders. "No, John . . . no, definitely
Paul. He's the cute one."

He throws up his hands, muttering something in French. He
probably called me a little artichoke, without its heart.

"Mathieu, you are being ridiculous."

"Am I?"

"Yes."

"Thank you for telling me this. There is nothing more absurd than someone who is ignorant of his own absurdity. It's what makes your Britney Spears so amusing." He looks at me evenly. "Perhaps it is you who is being absurd."

My Britney Spears? I throw on my shirt, neglecting my bra, and bark, "Is that right?"

"Yes. What is more ridiculous than an American, coming for the Parisian experience, who begs her French boyfriend to go to the most typically American, and bourgeois, tourist attraction in the whole of Europe?"

"I don't beg. If you won't go with me, I'll go by myself." I start with my pants but can't seem to work the zipper.

"Have fun." He waves me off, turning toward the infernal type-writer. "Give my apologies to Mickey Mouse and Michael Eisner."

The fucking teeth of the zipper are gnashed together, off their marks. I struggle, but it won't budge. *Merde!* I scream, jamming the thing for good.

Mathieu turns to stare at me before bursting into laughter. He springs at me, kissing my heated brow. "But you see," he says, lifting my chin and smiling into my eyes, "you are more French than you realize."

I cross my arms over my chest. "How American can *you* manage?"

He contemplates the set of my jaw and swallows something. "*On y va.*"

My shoulders slump. "I'm not French yet."

Mathieu zips up his own pants effortlessly. "*On y va!*" He turns toward the door. "Off we go."

ChApter 24

he Top Ten Things that Daisy doesn't miss about America:

1) Local TV news.

2) Fox News.

3) Walmart.

4) Christmas starting at Halloween.

5) Road rage.

6) Pickup trucks with

   a) Calvin pissing on a Chevy/Ford

   b) Dale Earnhardt devotionals

   c) *Sportsmen for Bush* stickers

   d) Jesus fish/Jesus fish eating Darwin thingy, or

   e) all of the above.

So pretty much all pickup trucks then.

7) The soul-sucking apathy.

8) Those awful local TV commercials wherein a car sales-man/carpet salesman/chimpanzee salesman shamelessly uses his children/spouse to vomit-inducing bad effect in order to hock some cars/carpet/chimpanzees.

9) Paris Hilton.

10) Living like I have something to prove.

The Top Ten Things that Daisy does, in fact, miss about America:

1) Being awakened by the Saturday Morning Lawn Brigade.

2) My crappy car.

3) Mama Santo's pizza in Little Italy.

4) My dog.

5) My parents.

6) My brother (hey, what the hell).

7) Walmart.

8) Smiling and nodding hello to people on walks and not having them look at me like I have *escargot* oozing from my ears.

9) Andy's obsession with the World Series, especially with the Red Sox and all.

10) Feeling comfortable in my own skin.

11) Oh, and Disneyland.

The sweet anticipation is the same. I feel it accelerating the RER to the park, which is about twenty miles outside Paris. Our car over-flows with electric Americans, snapping their gum and T-shirted up, and I smile good-naturedly at my equally toothy countrymen. Next to the world-weary Mathieu, they look like the friendliest souls in the world. The kids are excited and can't sit still, so they start a friendly game of "let's do crazy shit for as long as they let us get away with it" in the aisles. Their harried parents check the batteries in their video cameras and look distractedly at brochures for the main attractions, plotting their plans of attack and making adjustments to original allowances for discretionary spending. A sunburned boy, about five, who wears a Hulk T-shirt and whose name I have learned with the thoughtful aid of his mother's admonishment—"You're not a fire engine, Campbell!"—trips up to Mathieu and stares somberly into his face. It is remarkable how naked kids are. Watch Mathieu squirm with something akin to insecurity.

"Are you American or those other people?" Campbell finally asks, brown eyes crinkling with suspicion.

Mathieu's body bunches closer to the train window. He smiles uncertainly and says, "One of the others, I'm afraid."

Campbell nods dejectedly. "Thought so." He does a strange twisting thing, balancing briefly on his Nike tiptoes, and tumbles toward the other kids, forgetting us in the blink of a long-lashed eye.

Mathieu folds his arms over his chest and, looking peevish, ruminates on the nothing view.

I poke at him. "What? Are you bothered by that adorable little boy?"

He shrugs. "How do you think he knew?"

Laughing, I tease, "Maybe because you're the only one on the train who looks like he's bound for Auschwitz, not Disneyland."

Mathieu rolls his eyes at my hyperbole and leans on the window for support. I might be enjoying this a little too much.

"So why no kids if you think they are so adorable?"

Grrr . . . .

He gestures toward Campbell, who is now pretending to be a motorcycle. Or a Nascar driver. God knows. His mother, conquered, has her eyes closed and rests her head back on the seat, while his father booms into his cell phone, lamenting to someone called "Man" that vacations with kids are no kind of vacation at all. His dewy-eyed daughter, nonplussed by her father's desire to be rid of her, placidly sucks her thumb on his lap. Her Three Princesses shoe lights up as she kicks it rhythmically against the seat, and her pink T-shirt reads, in silver glitter, *I Know I'm Cute, So What's Your Excuse?*

"What was the question again?"

Mathieu has swiped my smirk. "I see. So you want to *be* the eternal child instead of having children of your own."

"Nope. You see the look on that mother's face over there? That horrible combination of exhaustion, worry, and resignation that warps her otherwise lovely face? Well, that's why I don't want kids. They're cute and everything, but a life with kids is no kind of life at all," I say, paraphrasing the words of the battle-scarred father over there. "Not if you prize personal space and sleeping in on Sundays."

"As I said, the eternal child."

"And you think your lifestyle right now would really support kids?" I retort, my dander up. He has a habit of cloaking loaded subjects in that light, irreverent tone. We had a balls-out fight about my using his typewriter the other day that started by his coyly announcing, "Andrè Gide almost knifed a man who once touched his typewriter." Real subtle stuff. "What, Mathieu, would they sleep cozily on the windowsills with Beckett? Crawl on their dimpled knees to the rooftop with us at night? Read a lispy Proust in lieu of Dr. Seuss?"

"You don't have to indulge children with material things, Daisy, to make them feel loved and secure. Kids are happy with very little," he says, very precisely, like a boy reciting his catechism. Or in a good imitation of what he thinks a father ought to sound like.

"Well then, our kids would be the happiest on the planet."

Mathieu's lips thin. "I knew you were not happy with the way we live."

"*I* am happy with it, Mathieu. That's not what we're talking about. We're talking about the bare necessities of raising a child. About having to get a real job. About me having to suffer the gauntlet of bureaucracy and apply for citizenship to get that job. About having the time, and not just the money, to devote to kids. About not being able to do things like this on a moment's notice." I tick the items off my air-list, sinking into my seat just as the train pulls into the station. "So if loving one's freedom means being a child, then I guess we both are hopeless babies."

Feeling guilty for abandoning his tour guide duties to live off my money, Mathieu starts sputtering about what having "a real job" means. While I, feeling like my father's hand just smacked the joy right out of me, float away . . . .

He wants me to recant on the children thing. I took him at his word that he was all right with my decision, when it is clear he senses an absence of female legitimacy within me. It is partly my fault for believing him before; he was wet and lusty, after all, which is never a good time to take a man at his word. Now I am lacking. If I were to become a bad mother, that would be one thing, and perhaps even anticipated. But to not feel the urge toward procreation—a radical form of womanly nihilism to many still, a generation after my mother insinuated herself into all-male bands—jars him out of his comfort zone. Mathieu requires a Mommy figure in his life more than the kids. And he needs the chance to prove to himself that he would do things differently, that he is not the sum total, or subtraction, of his parents' flaws, but a man with his own myth to sell. I wonder if it is a compulsion of most abandoned or neglected children to surround themselves with a family of their own someday, to fill one's life with noise and chaos, and plug up the terrifying void that came before. Mathieu is twenty-eight years old. That is a long time to endure in silence. It is no small wonder he never shuts up.

Yet I am twenty-three. I realize now how ridiculous my fantasies of marrying Andy were: no better, really, than the little princess playing dress-up in mom's ill-fitting clothes. I am not ready to fill that oversized role. Look at Campbell's mother, who is over forty. She likely waited until her thirties to get married, after finishing school and establishing herself in a career and achieving satisfaction on her own before the inevitable—well, anyway. My biological clock hasn't been wound yet, and may not exist. I forget to feed Beckett now and again because I *am* still a kid. And I'm fine with that. I thought he was too. Two dumb kids with nothing to lose, dancing a tango on the rooftops of Paris.

We are here. At the Happiest Place on Earth. Yet I feel like the most miserable creature on this Picasso-blue planet.

"—if my being a writer makes you embarrassed, or ashamed, then—"

"Shut up."

"Wha—"

"Just shut up."

He leans back as the rest of the travelers, happy and expectant cherubs with only minor clouds—those wispy, cirrus things—on their Nebraska blue horizons, spill noisily out of the car. They leave a gray vacuum in their wake. The car is deathly quiet, paused, while awaiting our decision. Stay, or go.

"I know what I said before." He sighs, overlooking my rudeness. "About it."

"I know what you said, too," I say, not apologizing. We stare at the worn seats before us. The threads are unraveling.

"It seems like such a small thing."

My missing period weighed like a stone in my gut.

"Not really. It seems huge."

"I meant for me. I did not know that I cared so," he explains, shaking his head.

Hearing the sincerity in his confession, I turn toward him more compassionately.

"I guess I am getting older."

And that's true. Five years divide us. When I look back to the person I was at eighteen, I see a grub. Everything was in place for me to grow, but that thing wasn't me yet. Who's to say how I may feel about Daisy at twenty-three when I am Daisy at twenty-eight? It's irrelevant. I can only act on my present convictions. Just as Mathieu is.

I can tell by the hitch in his voice that having kids does not fit into Mathieu's romantic idea of himself. Did Sartre have kids? Maybe bastard ones, if that. Mathieu knows that children are parasites, of the chubby-cheeked, lovable genus, yes, but still parasites. They survive by taking something from their parents. Call it life force, passion, or freedom. It all tastes delicious to the little darlings.

My mother only plays the piano when she has to, now.

Yet Mathieu is slowly positioning himself toward the beguiling siren of martyrdom that people must hear before embracing the idea of parenthood (it is impossible, I imagine, to embrace anything but the *idea* until the screaming, tyrannical babe is placed in your unprepared arms). Is it I—honest, at least, in my selfishness—who is the egoist here? Or is it Mathieu, naïvely believing he is capable of living two lives: that he will be a philosopher-poet in the mornings and a stay-at-home Daddy from noon until six? Maybe it is easier for men; perhaps, still, not as much is expected.

Is it lazy to pin the problem on gender, or am I wrong to believe that I would be the one to monitor every morsel of food that passed their impressionable mouths (when I wasn't feeling guilty for being away, due to my taking a crap job that no Frenchwoman, in spite of 10 percent unemployment, would possibly want) and that it would be me who couldn't sleep at night because one of them had a funny rash on her belly that might be Lyme's disease (if deer ticks were suddenly to infiltrate Paris like Hitler's army), and that it would fall on *moi*, in my broken French that makes *les mamans* smirk and avert their eyes, to make play dates and check out preschools, all while Mathieu got to be The Fun One when he wanted to be and

Absent (and so more fun by comparison) when something more fascinating than the subject of potty training came along.

Would we have time for our lovely, aimless talks then? Or would they, like us—and my poor mother before me—be plowed into a belly-up submission? I have no doubt that sacrifice is noble, if also self-serving, and necessary for the survival of the species. *The children are our future*, trilled Whitney Houston, astutely. And even Shakespeare's Benedick, abandoning his bright recalcitrance for dingy clichés, insisted, *The world must be peopled!*

But not by me.

I place my hand over my belly. *Please*, not me.

"Old and conventional," Mathieu says, cupping his chin in his hand.

"Downright bourgeois," I add, squeezing out a smile. "Watch out—pretty soon you'll be eating at Hippo's and shopping at La Samaritaine."

He smiles weakly back.

"And, God forbid, actually wanting to go to Disneyland."

The doors start to close on that opportunity. I grab Mathieu by the hand, hoist him up, and fling our conjoined body between the sliding partitions with the force of my determination that we have this day. We just make it, though the doors cough at us in protest, and open again.

"My coat!" He darts instinctively back inside.

"Mathieu!"

The doors are shutting. Mathieu snatches his coat and lunges toward me. But we had our chance, and the same doors that gave us lead before are less forgiving this time. Mathieu's face is surprised, then sheepish as he quickly abandons his hopeless clawing. He lays a sweaty palm on the glass and mouths something to me. The train starts to pull away toward its next destination, quite on its own authority.

"What?" I shout, placing my palm against the cool glass. I cannot feel his warmth, though there is the illusion that our hands are touching. A rising sense of panic floods me as the train hurtles down the tracks. I run beside it, not wanting to let go.

He repeats his message.

I can't help but smile.

He actually told me to have fun.

And, to my astonishment, I do.

It feels good to escape our prickly conversation and Paris, which for all her beauty, plays like a series of stereoscopic images just past my reach. It's gorgeous and dignified, but also a bit paralyzing. My television-suckled brain desires variation, even vulgarity. Disneyland Paris is so artificial that it flaunts its vulgarity on its taffy-colored chiffon sleeves. I let my guard down and allow myself to be lulled by her gauzy, vanilla-scented embrace.

Once I realize that Mathieu is gone and unlikely to return, especially since this is a good excuse for him to pretend that the idea was untenable (*but it wuz impozeeble, Day-zee!*), I shed the expectation of seeing him and the burden of convincing him of the park's charm, which is considerable. Smaller than Disneyland and more manageable by foot, I marvel at the remarkable symmetry it maintains with its sister parks, down to the Cowboy Cookout Barbecue in Frontier Land that serves racks of ribs and grilled corn on the cob. The people are eating it all up. It is a multicultural bonanza, but French is still the dominant language spoken and engagingly raised in sing-along here. A sizable contingent of Mathieu's countrymen does not share his horror of kitsch or sentimentality, and they reject his prejudices toward Chip and Dale, overpriced fish tacos, and perfectly choreographed parades.

I chat up an American group of senior citizens carousing around Western Europe on an Elderhostel tour while sitting on a bench and sipping a lemon slushy, and again in line for the Phantom Manor. I am happy to hear that many are nearly neighbors (*Cleveland? Why, I'm from Pittsburgh!*), conveniently ignoring the fact that this would mean nothing back in The States. Because it does mean something here. They are my countrymen and women, though many of them are fat and maybe a trifle dull (allusions to Sartre more likely to be met with nothingness than being). Probably half of them had the shortsightedness to vote for George W. Bush on an absentee ballot, but they are forthright and friendly and touch my heart with their direct, if still gentle, questioning (*You're not alone, dear? Does your daddy know you're seeing a Frenchman? Is he feeding you enough?*).

One of them, a lady named Ruth Ann, who has a lovely, if slightly tinted, permanent, volunteers to sit with me on a "Doom Buggy" as we curl our way through the not-so-phantasmagoric array of ghouls, goblins, and other animatronic concoctions. I try to imagine Mathieu seated next to me as the skinny, buffoonish ghost inserts himself into our reflected buggy image near the end of the ride, but the spirit seems a more hospitable and likely passenger. Ruth Ann actually yelps a little at the sight of him. We dissolve into giggles like a couple of schoolgirls, and she invites me to her home in Sarasota, if I'm ever down that way and in need of a place to stay. They do a killer dinner theater, apparently.

It's lame, but I cry a little when she hugs me good-bye. Her bosom gives slowly, like a quilted pillow, and she smells of Jean Naté and mint lozenges. I watch her walk carefully toward the restroom with her posse, those arthritic knees making her waddle slightly, but still owning the grace of a lady in control of her identity: American,

Jewish, Born in Brooklyn, Retired in Florida, Mother of Four, Grandmama to Eleven, Marvelous Millie-Loving, Purple-Haired, Kind Ruth Ann.

What could I say in return? One-time American, Now Nationless, Religiously Confused, Unemployed, Ex-Student, Modern Art-Loving, Unmaternal Lover of Mathieu. What does that say about me? Jesus, everyone and his gay brother loves modern art. The other stuff is so nebulously gray. Except for Mathieu, who moves deeper than all color.

So there's my identity for you. A bunch of nothingness, and a man who may no longer want me or my squandered ovaries. After all, he sacrificed his leather shoes readily enough the other night to do something he wanted to do. Why should he have gone back so impulsively to fetch his coat when cornered by something *I* wanted? To get away, I must assume. The subconscious is a brilliant strategist. Who knows? Maybe mine tipped me off that first day in Paris as I walked down the aisle of that other train and noticed a man so devoted to being alone that he could not afford to glance at any of the other passengers, even the striking foreigner biting her lip in feigned confusion, but burrowed deeper into his book with the monochromatic cover and impossibly Danish author. And maybe this same subconscious worked the numbers and devised a scheme—embarrassing, if ultimately successful—that would force him to confront her, and the Meaningful Book she clutched as a talisman to her intelligence. Maybe. Then again, I might just carry too much crap in my carry-on. What would Freud, or for that matter, Sartre, say? I should really start reading the latter. But whenever I pick up Mathieu's English copy of *Critique of Dialectical Reason*, I have this irrepressible urge to pluck my eyebrows, or something equally less excruciating.

To be honest (if that is possible while passing the Disneyland Paris version of the Becky Thatcher Showboat), I am beginning to wonder whether loafing really suits me. I know what I said before, about being brilliant at it, but I work hard at everything I do. It is the American Way to soak up new challenges, even when that means rejecting all challenges. But should I have to apply myself to something that ought to be effortless? Have I expanded my greedy hour from our little teahouse into a gluttonous bender that I cannot sustain? Did I embrace this unlikely style of living only to secure Mathieu? Are ponderous epiphanies allowed in Disneyland, or do I have to pay extra?

It is true that I have gained more understanding in the past two weeks than in any year, yet I am consumed by a terrible, animal restlessness I cannot shake. All of my energies seek Mathieu: when I can see him, for how long, and to what end. Every day I encounter sublimity. Yet it comes in flashes, like heat lightning that cannot be photographed, leaving me wanting, always wanting, in the blackness left behind.

I am jealous of a goddamn typewriter. I hate people who do not exist.

Even while dreaming, he slips away. The names of his characters—*Gerard, Jean,* and *Violet*—find his lips more often than my own lately. I guard his eyes some nights, watching for real and imagined betrayals with every twitch of that shuttered lens. I have become like Milton's Satan from *Paradise Lost*: expelled from this heaven of mine through my desperation to be the favorite, and the resentment of serving a higher power than my own. For Mathieu, in spite of his braying to the contrary, is writing, and in droves. His frantic, gunmetal typing is a shield I have no hope of piercing, and so I flee his apartment to escape the temptation to just ram on through, and be bounced.

For that strange madness—the artistic cycling of feeling into thought, and thought into feeling, which Mathieu describes as "an explosion of tongues"—is a beautiful thing to contemplate in the aftermath, when viewing a Pollock, or reading a Rimbaud poem. But viewed up close, in the act, it is frightening in its capacity for shutting out the world, and me within it. The channeled voices occupy him far more eloquently, and completely, than I could hope.

And now there is the politics of children gerrymandering us. How mundane for that to be the cause of our split. Not a clash of cultures, or egos, but a goddamn lifestyle choice. Yet it is a more impenetrable obstacle than his writing, for there is no compromise to be had. What other option is there but for me to eject myself from Mathieu's influence? Before I, like the fallen Lucifer, start corrupting his urge toward creation, which my better angel assures me is the most sanctified instinct we overgrown monkeys enjoy, but which my devilish side observes, not unjustly, as the last barrier between it and heavenly bliss?

How did this happen? At which instant did time, which I feigned to ignore, betray me?

I don't know, but Mathieu was right about my metamorphosis. What could be more French than thinking about Milton and Satan's fall while riding solo on a Mad Hatter's Teacup? I have succumbed to the circular bullshit. And I have petrified my day as a result. Turning the stubborn wheel before me, I start to spin, anxious for the torque to jettison these thoughts and feelings from my conscious mind, determined to become all feeling and action once more. The tiny stereocilia inside my ears, those precise instruments of orientation I abandoned, wildly respond, lighting up the vestibular sensors inside my cortex, which counsel me to stop the foolish spinning and come back to Earth. But I press on. Turning the wheel. Anxious for the next thing.

But I am not the god of this machine, and the ride stops. Dizzy and nauseated, I exit my teacup, a lone Alice following . . . what? A white rabbit? A grin without a cat? A dream?

Maybe it's time to wake up.

Disneyland is a day trip.

Chapter 25

Mathieu wants me to come to a dinner party with him. I am happy to go because it soothes me, somehow, to think of him with friends, to envision him looking more serene, relaxed, when of late he has been coiled like a rattlesnake threatening to strike. I hadn't thought of Mathieu with any friends outside his books. He's never mentioned anyone much, and besides, he has such high standards for things.

We haven't talked about Disneyland, the Matterhorn between us. As two hyper-reflective people, this probably doesn't bode well. To substitute, we have apparently decided to focus on sex. Big sex. Small sex. Loud sex. Soft sex. Sex that hurts, and sex that purrs. Sex as revolution, and sex as devolution. Sex, sex, sex. How much sex can one woman get?

Yesterday I craved Andy, that simpleton. Mathieu was exceptionally creative, yet I shrank from his artistry, desiring Andy's workmanlike hands, making their abbreviated rounds (boobs, butt, boobs, repeat). I strained to hear Andy's muffled climax— the Grunting Grizzly—in my ear. To see Andy's pleased smile afterward as he dropped off to sleep. I wanted Andy's innocence.

Which is not to say that I love Mathieu any less. Only that life is complicated, and I've been reading Anaïs Nin.

So this dinner party thing, while promising, also has me in stitches. And not the laughing kind.

"What should I wear?"

"Do we need to bring a gift?"

"What about food? Oh God, Mathieu, do we have to cook something?"

"Those fucking indefinite articles!"

"So they will speak French, right?"

"Of course they will speak French," he finally replies on the day of, rolling his eyes.

"But I won't understand a thing!" I wail, throwing myself down on his bed. Beckett opens her eyes. Perturbed by my histrionics, she looks balefully at me.

"You will understand more than you imagine," he says, sitting beside me. "The body is more expressive than words can possibly be."

"Maybe when flirting across a crowded room, but not when discussing the EU's battle over farm subsidies," I groan, flopping backward.

"I promise the subject will not come up."

Laughing, Mathieu pulls me toward him, kissing me in the suggestive way that inevitably segues into fun and games. The man is insatiable. Beckett leaps off the bed in anticipation, holding her nose aloft as she makes for the bathroom mat. The little minx cannot stand competition. Once resistant to Mathieu's charms, she, too, has been seduced.

Undistracted, I dodge his lips. "But something will, and I'll look like the fool."

Sighing, he pillows his head with his hands. "Your French is getting better."

"Yeah, I can talk like a preschooler now. *Moi likey Paris. It is*

raining. Do you have an umbrella?"

He smiles and, playing with my hair, says, "Maybe someone will bring up the weather."

"It's not funny."

"What can I say, Daisy?" He shrugs.

That you'll look after me. Protect me. Not because you're the man, but because I am dependent on you for my survival here.

"They will know that you are American. So they won't want to talk to you, anyway."

I elbow him in the ribs.

"Besides," he recovers, "it is a Friday night in Paris. What else do you have to do?"

This.

"Oh."

And this.

"Ah."

We swallow this silence like a last supper.

"I was right," he brags later, chewing on my shoulder. "Body language." Hitching himself on a shaky elbow, he counsels, "Do that, and they will not care that you are American."

What a gentleman.

The couple hosting the party knew Mathieu in college. He went for nearly a year. Evidently, a professor told him one day that he was aping Flaubert, and dismally, in his paper, so he quit. Not because of the criticism, which he now admits was just, but because Mathieu realized he didn't much like Flaubert.

The couple, Ivan and Gabrielle, had no such aversion to

Flaubert or securing their comfortable futures as a government administrator and a professor of French literature. They have a very smart, if modest, apartment in the sixth *arrondissement*, overlooking the Seine. Though the party was to start at eight o'clock, we arrive at 8:25 (I have started wearing my watch again), because to arrive any earlier would have been, in Mathieu's estimation, "shocking."

"Enchantés," I brightly repeat to my hosts, coloring to the exact shade of my new scarlet dress as we shrug out of coats. I still haven't risen above the self-consciousness that comes with speaking French and limit myself to this one word that, I suspect, betrays not so much sincerity as desperation.

Fluttering for traction on this slick foyer floor, I think, *Oh, Lord, why did I choose to wear red tonight?* I thought it was a bold choice when I saw it in the boutique—the light, sexy material and asymmetrical neckline showing off my shoulders to good effect— and snatched it up without glancing at the price. Besides, it went with my heels, those four-inch pedestals that are elevating enough for me to be knocked down from later. I wanted Mathieu to be proud. Only now, next to Gabrielle's chic black, I feel clownish and obvious. Like Joan Rivers at the Oscars.

Ivan and Gabrielle smile slightly, murmuring their greetings, and kiss me lightly on the cheeks before clasping Mathieu amid a flurry of rapid-fire French. It seems they haven't seen him for a while. He smiles ruefully and shrugs.

It's her. She won't let me go anywhere without tagging along.
Is that so? What a bore. Why don't you come without her, then?
(Helplessly) She withholds sex when I "misbehave."
What a little tease. These Americans with their sexual politics. I'm surprised she'll have sex with you at all.
It's not as often as I'd like. And pretty unimaginative when she does.
Americans are notoriously prudish, yes?
And gassy. She toots in her sleep.

*How typical. Americans with their hot air and cold pussies.
(General, smug laughter)*

Okay, to be fair, I think they might be discussing Justine because Mathieu looks defensive and Gabrielle concerned. Ivan places a hand on his wife's shoulder in a proprietary way that makes me cringe a little and ushers us into the living area. Another couple is ensconced on the leather couch, a partition of silence dividing them. The man looks at the ceiling and draws on a brown cigarette while his blonde partner stands to greet Mathieu and me. Meet Nicole and Luc, shrouded in matching, noncommittal black, cradling glasses of red wine. I grin strenuously, determined to build a bridge of understanding across my pearly whites. My pits are clammy and my mouth tacky and pasty. It seems I am a virgin again. A French dinner party virgin. Not sure what to expect, but still eager to please. Excited . . . but tense. And pretty damn convinced that it will hurt more than I'd planned. To top it off, I was a little too aggressive shaping my eyebrows this morning, so now I look like a Vulcan. I had an evangelical classmate in the first grade who shaved off her eyebrows, explaining, *The devil made me do it, Mommy!* Clever girl. All I can offer is, *The insecurity made me do it, folks!* Not that I, even, would confuse the French for "folks."

I sink into a leather sofa, which farts against the back of my sweaty legs, and hitch up my strapless bra, which is adorable, if elusive. The doorbell rings, and Mathieu abandons me to receive the final guest with Gabrielle. He is talking so enthusiastically in French as he leaves that I realize he's been suffering without his native tongue during the past weeks. *I really need to apply myself more to my French lessons.* Somehow I haven't—lately. Smiling vaguely about the room, I take a couple of deep breaths, trying to neutralize the acid pumping through my chest, and find my legs again.

Daisy, dear, your smiles don't convince. Look like you don't have a care in the world, and people will believe it.

I think my grandmother would have done well in France. I care too fucking much.

Ivan has gone to fetch Mathieu and me some wine. Luc holds his designer cigarette in a smoking place: his crotch. He raises an eyebrow at me and scratches his nuts in what can only be interpreted as a charming, come-hither gesture. Nicole, meanwhile, stares wistfully at Mathieu's back with her limpid brown eyes as he slips from her sight. When he's gone, she flashes her reproachful gaze in my direction before sinking her eyes behind the wineglass and backing into the loveseat, where Luc's serpent arm slithers around her.

Oh God, not again.

I accept Ivan's glass of wine, saying, *"Merci beaucoup."* Taking a big gulp, I cough. It is not wine, but a deadlier liqueur. I should have noted the smaller glasses, but there's the ticklish matter of Nicole's perfume to distract me. Not vanilla, but musky.

Mathieu returns, smiling warmly at me. I glance at Nicole, but she is buried in Luc's arm and staring impassively at the final guest to be welcomed.

It is an older man. Fifty-something, balding, and stuffed into an ice cream suit, coral scarf wrapped around his mottled neck. He presents himself as Henri, and as he kisses my hand (the first in France to do so, in spite of Chirac and Laura Bush), I can identify every hair follicle, each terrible in its specificity, wiring bravely out of his scalp, only to collapse over the scabs of his crown. Though it is cold outside, he sweats with the effort of walking and dabs at his glistening forehead, a slight wheeze whistling through his words. He might have been repulsive, or at least pitiable. But banish the thought, for he has a quick smile and easy manner that quickly puts me at ease. He speaks my language deliberately and beautifully, with a lilting grace that tells of time in England. I don't feel like I'm talking to a Frenchman at all.

"Daisy, then. What a charming name, my dear."

"*Merci.* Um, thanks."

"Named, perhaps, for your mother's favorite flower?"

I shake my head. *"Daisy Miller."*

He scratches his face while pondering this. "What a burden to place on a child," he finally sighs.

"Yes!" I laugh reflexively and with relief. "I mean, thank you."

He smiles and pats my hand. "But you are managing well, yes?" His eyes flash toward Mathieu, deep in conversation with Ivan, before swinging back around to me. "It is such a relief to see a lady who knows how to wear color."

I smile gratefully and whisper, "Thank you."

This gentleman could make an ice queen melt. I wonder if I still have Shoe Store Michelle's card . . . .

"I'm sorry, but what is your relationship to Ivan and Gabrielle?" I ask him.

The air is warm, and the quiet chatter of strangers' voices is the cushion I needed to lay down my defenses. Of course Nicole desires Mathieu. I feel sorry for her.

"I am Gabrielle's latest project." Henri winks at me.

"How do you mean?"

"My wife and I lived upstairs until a month ago." He rubs his wedding band, a gesture that looks habitual. "Now it is only I."

"Oh! I'm so sorry, Henri."

He chuckles. "Caroline lives, my dear. Just not with me."

"Oh."

Sometimes there is not much to say. And sometimes there is, but we just can't say it. *What happened?* I want to ask. *Was it someone else? Or did she just tire of hearing your voice after a while? When did love come to mean less than something new?*

"Yes," Henri continues, "but Gabrielle has decided that I am not to be a hermit. She extends the courtesy of an invitation nearly every night. Even when the other guests are all half my age." He smiles and sips his drink. "I must confess to never paying for a meal anymore."

The escalating voices prevent us from pursuing our conversation. Mathieu is arguing. I can tell by the bridge of his nose: it's puckered, like he smells something bitter. Usually his outrage is directed at me, so I'm curious to observe how it plays upon others. With his palm turned upward, he might be extending the opportunity for some education, or begging for a real argument. Ivan, taking a broader approach, waves his arms around, grasping for metaphorical straws from the thin air. Luc jumps in on Mathieu's side, yet it seems a halfhearted effort, that sad cigarette butt he's jabbing around a limp echo of his rhetorical prowess. Even Mathieu ignores him as he starts to his feet and begins to pace.

Fights are funny to watch when you can't understand what's going on. Like vaudeville, or opera.

Nicole says nothing. With her pale complexion setting off lips chiseled in with black liner, she looks like a geisha. Not so much docile, as empty. The *tabula rosa* of some males' fantasies.

"They are enjoying this, no?" I ask Henri.

He purses his lips and settles into the couch. "Men enjoy fighting, feeling anger. It is a method of cutting themselves loose from this"—his hand encompasses the stylish room—"and activating their primitive sides. Engaging with the real world."

"But what are they talking about?" I whisper. Ivan is now standing, though he has turned his back on Mathieu.

Ahem. Our setting: the legendary French *salon*. The players: all those brave enough to enter. The choice weapon: a rapier wit. The style: cutting, clever, and often cruel. Employed: only upon assurance of mortally wounding an adversary. Your manner: ironic, detached, and always effortless. Means of death: mortification. Attention: novices will not be granted a handicap. To note: laughing at your own jokes is not permitted. Smiling, too, is frowned upon, unless furnished in a malicious, deprecating manner. Men and women may do battle with one another. But when locking horns, it is recommended that the female jousters take their cleavage into consideration. After all, a timely lean-in can be as deadly as a wicked tongue-lashing.

Okay, that's the way it worked in *Ridicule*. Mathieu is sweating all of this too much. And nobody's looking at my cleavage. Not even the lascivious Lothario Luc.

"Mmm . . . let us see," Henri says, leaning in. "Mathieu believes that Zidane is the best football player ever to have graced the field, while Ivan argues for Shevchenko. Mathieu points to the team successes for Zidane, while Ivan counters by stressing Shevchenko's legendary standing as a striker. Mathieu suggests that Ivan is allowing his Ukrainian fealty to color his empirical critique of the situation. Ivan finds this laughable, since Zidane is French. Yes, Mathieu notes, but of *Algerian* origin. So it is not as much of a—how do you say, my dear?—of a jerking-the-knee response?"

I nod, a little sad. Sports. That's all. And nationhood. How common. Versailles is still a museum. And what does it say about Mathieu that he points to this Zidane guy's background (Algerian Muslim) as making him less French? What does it say for us?

No wonder Nicole is silent. What is there to say?

Mathieu throws up his hands and, glancing at me, pronounces, "I am bored with this argument. Let us move on."

Cued, Gabrielle emerges from the kitchen, looking impossibly composed for a woman about to serve a four-course meal, and informs us that dinner is ready. The men immediately break off their argument, forgetting their trumped-up outrage in favor of a surer kill. I rise. Mathieu finds me with his eyes and smiles. My smile must look more tentative because Henri takes my elbow and remarks, "You look pale, Daisy dear. Let us get you some food."

We make our way over to the elegant dining room table and

part ways. I can see the riverboats sparkling through the window as I take my place, and something sharp and melancholy stabs at me. Perhaps it is just hunger. I couldn't eat before, due to nerves. The little zucchini, olive, and tomato salad that Gabrielle has set down on the delicate, ivory tablecloth before me feels like a taunt, but I dutifully shovel it all into my mouth, even the olives, which I normally shun. Only when taking the last bite do I feel embarrassed. I am the first to be finished. Probably because I am the only one not talking. Mathieu sits to my right and Ivan to my left, at the head of the table. Nicole is across from me, with Luc sandwiched between her and Henri. Gabrielle reigns at the other end. Somehow, I feel all alone.

Novices get no handicaps.

I feel regret about being parted from Henri. He is the only one, including Mathieu, that traitor, to take note of me. I thought Ivan might try harder, being an immigrant himself, but he either doesn't know much English or is afraid that someone might think to link the two of us as outsiders. I find some solace in the thought that Henri would rescue me if he weren't already buried in conversation with Gabrielle, that fat, round head of his bobbing up and down from time to time with touching gravity. I continue to grip my fork, hitting the tines against my plate now and again to give the impression that I am manipulating some imaginary rabbit food. Never have I been so irritated by the French language, streaming without pause, or by the contrary French slowness, as my stomach curls around the paltry vegetables. I take a long sip of my wine, grimacing at the dryness. I want milk. My mom's lasagna. The plastic fruit centerpiece I got for her in middle school, which she holds onto, in spite of the stemless orbs and boomerang bananas. There are teeth marks in the red apple: a Lockhart family mystery, still unsolved. These butterfly orchids of Gabrielle's could be crushed by a firm sneeze.

I am the child who's been put at the grown-up table: bored, fidgety. My legs swing restlessly, and I jab Mathieu's leg with my shoe. Since they're pointy enough to kick a gnat in the ass, he finally pays me some notice.

"Sorry." I grin.

"Is everything all right?"

"Spectacular," I spit. *But nobody's talking about the weather.*

Mathieu blunts the sharpness of my look with a nod. "Good." And resumes his conversation with Luc and Nicole, who has reanimated herself and is leaning forward in a cleverly attentive manner that allows her V-neck bodice to ripple like a lulling wave. She wears a gray lace chemise against her skin.

Two points, Nicole. Three, if it had been black.

It is humiliating to be a child at this table. To know that I could be scoring points with these people if they would only speak my language. It's unfair of me, the lowest common denominator in the room, to expect everyone to sacrifice their natural eloquence for my native tongue, yet I do. I think noble thoughts about how I would do the same for them if the situation were reversed. After all, guests are treated like royalty back home, their security and comfort so attended to that they can feel manhandled at times. The expression "kill them with kindness" must have originated in America, where women like my grandmother wielded the title of hostess like a bludgeon. But in France, guests are outsiders to be tolerated until, through some implausible transformation, they prove themselves worthy of bother. This is perhaps a more genuine attitude to strike, if equally lethal. If it were left up to me, I would rather be suffocated by consideration than naked with neglect.

More than all of it, I hate being Mathieu's appendage, his arm candy. I dolled myself up merely to make him look good. Throbbing with potential, I am consumed by a hubristic overture to demonstrate my intelligence. Yet all I am capable of is this chiseled smile and a poke at my boyfriend for scraps of his attention.

Why is it that Colette should so often be (faintly) praised, by Mathieu and others, as France's greatest *woman* writer? God, I hate that.

I scoot back my chair, placing my napkin on the table. *"Pardonnez moi."*

To my surprise, everyone stops talking and looks at me attentively. Jesus, am I supposed to give a toast or something? *"J'ai besoin d'aller . . ."* I bite my lip, hard. In the white silence, only Frank Sinatra whirrs in the background, *"You'll never know . . . ."*

Shrugging, I smile brightly. "I need a potty break."

Moving into the hallway, I try to decide if I just said "potty." I must have substituted my preschool English for preschool French. Nonetheless, I have to laugh at the *faux pas*. I don't belong here. I am still the American on that train, bumbling for my footing. Mathieu and I were wrong: I haven't become more French. Yet I have changed. It has nothing to do with nationality. It's the yolk of experience that nourishes adaptation. I don't, in actuality, really *want* to belong here. The idea slows me as I tread through the long hallway. I have always wanted to belong.

I have always wanted to attach myself to something.

I find the bathroom easily enough. It's next to the macabre, and strangely comical, George Grosz reproduction in the hall. Ivan and Gabrielle have a thing for pre-Third Reich, Weimar Republic art. Grossly caricatured pieces advertising the worst in human nature, exposing the gristle, like cartoon figures to be unzipped and turned inside out. The kind of thing that should have teeth and human hair embedded within so that you can touch the Hobbesian depravity, and try not to recoil. It manages to feel dated (the Weimar look) and contemporary (everybody is for sale). It is admirable, evocative art that should have been hailed as a warning by the German people. Yet I must admit to heaving a sigh of relief when I turn on the bathroom light, revealing a pleasant seashell motif, complete with scented soaps. I don't think I could pee in front of that stuff. It seizes up my insides.

Noticing the streak of blood on my wad of toilet paper, I almost sob. My good Aunt Flow. How bizarre that the shedding of this blood—that monthly surrender of my body's evolutionary purpose—should fill me with such gratitude. Logically, it goes without saying that I, a woman with no talent for unselfish love, would come to love a child once it was a thing of flesh, and not merely this skeleton of an idea rattling after me over the last couple of weeks. Particularly Mathieu's child. And yet, as an idea, the phantom child has haunted me, infiltrating darker hours when I threw up daytime blockades. And why should that be? Isn't it true that if I *were* to have been pregnant, it would have bound me more to Mathieu, and Paris? Hadn't I already committed myself, anyway?

Well, hadn't I?

I turn on the sink, and the water falls over my hands. I allow the current to get as hot as I can stand, before turning it off.

This room is deathly quiet and has no windows; it's like being embalmed, with rosewater slowly filling my veins.

"Lay your head down, sweetie."

It was a November night in 1995. I had hopes of the first snow that night. Algebra test in the morning.

"Ten more pages? I'm not even tired, Mom."

I was, though. I shot up like a weed that year—three inches by my dad's count—and slumbered like a baby. My freshman year passed in the fog of a midsummer night's dream.

My mom smoothed my hair. Her hands were always warm. "I want to tell you about something. Something I think you should know."

I rolled my eyes, squirming under my flannel nightgown. "Thanks, but I got the pink pamphlet already, Mom."

"Not that."

Her eyes sobered me. They were scared. It is a terrible thing to see your parents show fear. I was old enough to know better, but I still wanted them to be invincible.

"It's about your birth, hon."

I became very still. "Okay."

I felt small and lacking under the faded blue sheet with the tiny white daisies. My room was stunted in its middle school incarnation, when I thought to own my name by displaying it everywhere. Only the books matched my new height, the Brontë sisters dislodging Sweet Valley High's chirpy duo with the sharper elbows of Heathcliff and Rochester, bulls shrouded beneath the sisters' creamy prose.

Looking up at the wedge of my mom's face, as she struggled to bring the words, I noticed lines on her skin that I had never seen before. I was horrified by a black, brittle hair infiltrating a mole on the jib of her chin. Her looks were starting to go. She was aging. *She will die someday. My mother will die.* I got a little mad at her about it. Childish, yes, but I was a child, and the anger steeled me against the hard rain of her words.

My mother touched my cheek. But her hand had turned clammy, and I turned on my side. She sighed. "I think you already know that we hadn't planned on having you. I was still in school, and your father and I hadn't made things permanent yet." She slipped off her engagement ring and rolled it like a Rosary bead between her fingers. A nervous habit, it always seemed like a game of chicken to me.

I nodded, pulling my legs up to my chest. They were furry. I hadn't met Andy yet. I never wore skirts or shorts. My breasts were still empty promises.

"So when I found out that I was pregnant, it was a big surprise. Shocking, actually. I mean, we had taken precautions, of course."

Embarrassed, I looked beyond her, to the *Beauty and the Beast* poster on my wall. How I wanted to be Belle at that moment. To be swirling the dance floor in a dress dreamed up by Wordsworth's daffodil maidens.

"I was supposed to tour the summer you were born. Your father and I were going to see how that went, as a kind of 'test' of our devotion." Yielding, she jerked the diamond back on her finger, where it swallowed up the wedding band. I never understood why the engagement ring should be the prettiest. I assumed it had something to do with God.

"So when I found out I was pregnant, I panicked a bit." She patted my shoulder. "I started exploring my options."

Options?

Her grip tightened. "Honey, I'm telling you this because I've always stressed how important honesty is to a relationship. I waited this long because I wanted to make sure that you were mature enough to handle it."

I nodded again, turning on my back and feeling vaguely heroic. Nightgown aside, I so wanted to be mature, to be worthy of Jane Eyre, nestled against my pillow.

"After a long and very painful deliberation on my part, during which I weighed all the pros and cons, I went to get an abortion."

I stopped in mid-nod. "Wait, what?"

"I had an abortion, Daisy."

I threw her a withering look. "Um, no you didn't, Mom."

"Yes. I did." She tensed, and I felt her fingers nip into the muscles of my shoulder. "Well, I thought I did. It was later decided that I was pregnant with twins, and that they only got one of . . . you."

One of *who*?

"You know, your grandmother was a twin. Her brother died young, though."

"What?"

"Of polio, I think—"

"Wait, *what*?" I threw back the sheet and shot up in bed. Jane succumbed to the floor.

"I understand that you're upset."

"You tried to *kill* me?"

She took my shoulder again, but I shook her off. "Now, Daisy, let's not be overly dramatic about it. After all, you weren't you yet. You were the size of a pea. You had no consciousness. You couldn't feel—"

"Why the *fuck* are you telling me this?"

"I don't think that—"

"No, no, no." I shook my head. "What did Dad say?"

She looked down.

The tears hung on this reply. *Please, God, don't let him. He didn't know.*

"He agreed that it was probably for the best. We were both so ambitious and unsettled, Daisy. We didn't know what we wanted yet."

I reached up to touch my face. But my lips were woolly. So I looked to the floor.

Reader, I married him.

Oh, Jane.

My mother grabbed my hand and cupped it under her chin. But I didn't want to be claimed, not now. And I didn't want to touch that mole, with its dirty black hair.

"Why isn't he here?"

"He didn't see the point in telling you. We were so h-happy, you know, afterward. We *are* so happy." She bowed her head and started crying. But I couldn't bring the tears. I wasn't quite real, after all.

And ghosts don't cry.

I looked down at her. Her hand fluttered against her lips as she struggled to gain her breath.

"I want you to leave now."

She sobbed like a baby. But I had matured. Sprouted my first thorn. My eyes were bone dry.

Somehow, in spite of my parents, I was all grown up.

I linger in the bathroom, washing my hands again in the med school way Andy demonstrated over the summer (was it just last summer?)—working under the nails, circling my wrists, the hot water provoking the blood below the parchment skin. Looking at myself in the mirror, I blanch at my overly made-up face, wondering where I begin underneath all the war paint. Mathieu had been excited by the new look, stirred up. He called me his Olympia. I smiled, uncertain.

I do look almost beautiful tonight, my sharp features and full mouth a natural canvas for the reds and blacks that have cowed the imperfections and heightened the drama. But I'm tired. Of trying too hard. Of believing it means anything. Of fooling myself. Scrubbing my face with pink soap, I think of my mother again, and what she confided to me a few years ago: *I fell in love with your father because he was the first person who didn't want to change me.* I was stunned to hear her speak of loving my father. I swam in those words, wrapped my limbs around them like a life preserver, until my parents' next silence crashed to drown me in doubt anew.

I recognized for the briefest of moments that I was not responsible for her slide into mediocrity, that I didn't have that much power over another person's life. She chose the life she thought she wanted, at the time. It didn't work out the way she planned, but it was still hers. There is nothing shameful in that.

I still don't know.

It's not that Mathieu thinks to change me. He just doesn't know what it will take for me to live here. He can't. This is home for Mathieu. I'll always be the tourist. The line will always be drawn closer to him. After all, evolution is stubbornly slow. Even a leap of faith is but one small step in a lifetime littered with footprints.

I wipe my hands.

Henri's affable face greets me when I finally open the door. Surprised, I blurt out, "Oh! Are you escaping too?"

He smiles easily, not offended. "No, not escaping." Chuckling, he explains, "I have the old man's bladder, I'm afraid."

"I'm sorry." I sigh, placing a hand to my head. "I'm not normally this rude. I guess I'm out of sorts tonight."

"Are you?"

I smile tentatively. "What do you mean?"

"It seems to me, my dear, that you know exactly what you're doing."

Our eyes meet and hold, until he laughs again and starts to turn away. But his eyes, absorbing the Grosz, stop him, and pin him to the wall behind me.

"How do you see it?" I ask him.

I feel humble before this contradictory man with the shrewd eyes and unassuming smile. He could be writing my story. I am amused at the idea, oddly solaced by the thought of being a character in his bulbous head, where whole libraries of stories must be gathering dust. Of having Henri invent me, and make my choices. *Daisy Lockhart.*

"It is quite powerful, I think," he says, considering the reproduction.

Smiling, he surmises, "One of Ivan's, I imagine." Henri shakes his head and continues, "But I do not like it."

Stifling a smile at his offense, I ask, "Why not?"

"To be great," he asserts, taking a rich breath and raising his hands, "a work of art must lift up the heart." Turning toward me, eyes clear and lucid, Henri sags a little. "This painting damages mine."

"Mine too," I whisper.

"I am tired of always looking backward. The French are too— well, we must move forward, yes, Daisy?"

"But how do I—how do we know which way is forward, and which way is just standing still?"

"You always know. Can't you feel the wind on your cheeks?" He smiles and touches me gently on mine.

"I thought I did."

Or maybe it's the illusory breeze you feel when spinning in one place for too long.

"So did my wife, I suppose."

I squeeze his hand.

"Ah, well." Pulling up, Henri nods at me. "If you will excuse me, my dear. It is certain that the others will be wondering by now."

Touched by this antiquated social consciousness, I return his nod and offer my apologies. I return to the dining table, which is just a collection of stylish things and naked people wearing more stylish clothes . . . by which I mean that I have nothing to prove. Mathieu smiles at me solicitously before touching my knee, but he feels far away.

I am alone in a crowd. That's all.

It's my story to write yet.

Chapter 26

We have collapsed in the living room after surrendering our stomachs to Gabrielle's all-fronts culinary assault. The fashionable clothes are rumpled now, the conversation sloppy, some belly laughs easier to come by, if punishing to our grotesquely dilated diaphragms. I did not mentally prepare myself for the brie, I groan silently, sinking back into the sofa, or I might have paced myself better with the *poulet á la provençale*. The cheese course was a dolorous surprise. Poached pears with sorbet slid down only with some effort. I have no idea why French women don't get fat. It could be all the fabulous shopping. More likely, it's that food is simply a joy to be sampled, and not a societal obsession.

The eyes around me have a bright torpor shining through them, and I imagine their owners as nautical comrades to my youthful Saturday mornings spent watching Popeye and Brutus, the alcoholic tide rising to flood their irises and slosh around. Mine may be filled with the same lubricant, though I cannot find the corresponding anchor to any real conversation. The same cannot be said for Henri, who, having drunk quite as much as the rest of us, still looks sober and dignified, perched on his leather chair, a wise prophet enlightening the rabble. Mathieu, lounging between Nicole and me, is smoking one of Luc's ass-cool cigarettes. He has been good about not smoking in front of me, until now. I very gingerly cough.

After a brief exchange with his wife, Ivan grabs the remote and turns on the flat-screen television, rifling through a substantial video/DVD collection on one of the bookshelves.

"What's he looking for?" I ask Mathieu, just to say something with this fat tongue.

Mathieu leans into my lap, smiling. I don't know if I've ever seen him so giddy. I wonder if these people are his real family, and if so, why he has never talked of them before. If he has clung to his friends the way I, even while renouncing them, have always clung to my parents, protecting them with his silence. If he worries over how to reconcile me into their hard knot of family, or if he is too busy enjoying their reunion to consider me at all.

"He wants us to see this panel show where Gabrielle was a guest," Mathieu explains. "The host was so stoned he kept confusing Foucault with Baudrillard."

"Stupid man," I snark, flashing a disinterested eye toward the television.

"Is there something both—"

"Wait a second. Stop!" I yell to Ivan, putting up my hand and grimacing at the screen. My eyes have found an anchor. "Please."

Everyone looks at me before swinging their eyes to the television.

That robed, gaunt figure. The perverted shaman. The unholy warrior. His mouth moves silently above the lectern while the half-lidded eyes remain hard and ruthless, like fixed tissue. The murderer disguised as diplomat. The piss-poor, A/V-club quality to the recording, to remind us that technology cannot trump will. He is as unintelligible to me as the people in this room, although the words, "Allah," "Bush," and "the American people" track solemnly by on CNN International's scroll. Like it matters what he says. Bin Laden has presence.

"And what effect this will have on the American election just four days away is anyone's guess, Richard," the attractive brunette split-screened with bin Laden says.

"Perhaps we are finally witnessing that October Surprise, Dalaja," Richard agrees. "But the question remains: is Osama bin Laden tipping his hand in this video? And if so, who does he want the American people to vote for, come Tuesday?"

I slump into the couch, staring not at the television, but at Ivan and Gabrielle's lovely Oriental carpet beneath my feet. Not paisley this time; more geometrical, modern. Hard as hell. I dig in my heels.

"What is it, Daisy?" Mathieu asks, placing his hand on my arm. Ivan stands with the video in his hand, looking uncertain for the first time this evening.

"I never voted, you know."

"You never . . ."

"Voted," I say, more strongly, my head snapping up like a hairpin trigger, just squeezed. "I never had the chance to vote. I should have gotten an absentee ballot, though it might have been too late." I swallow something. "I just didn't plan for it."

"Why are you worried about this now?" Mathieu presses, the little line in his forehead troubling itself over me again.

"Don't you see?" I ask him, and the room. "*Who does bin Laden want the American people to vote for?*" I shake my head, feeling faintly nauseated. This must be how soothsayers feel when burdened by a glimpse of the future. "This will be all there is for the next three days. Wolf and Candy on CNN, The Wingnuts on Fox, Bob and Betty on *Channel Four Eyewitness News*. Bin Laden wants Kerry to win, they'll argue. No, no, he wants Bush. Back and forth, back and forth, until they've made the sale."

Mathieu inches forward, his hand still resting on—no, restraining—my arm. "But you said it, Daisy. It's a deadlock. Which means Kerry will probably continue his slight push in the polls." Mathieu waves at the screen with derisiveness. "Who would consider what a lunatic wants him to do, anyway?"

I look at him with a queer mixture of pity and wonder. "I'll tell you who. The remaining 5 percent of the American populace who have their heads too far up their asses to make a decision on their own. Even now, they're looking at bin Laden on their TV screens and quaking, 'I'm scared. This cave man scares me.' And who do children turn to when scared? Their daddies. The goons who have cultivated that fear and worked it to such gross advantage."

I rise and walk toward the TV screen, their eyes tracking me. "I'll tell you who bin Laden wants to win the election: it's Bush, of course, his ultimate recruiting tool. The poster child for his propaganda war. And he is clever enough to know that the only people who haven't made up their goddamned minds by now are the same nervous Nellies he can sway by sinisterly invoking 'Allah' a few times and working his madman magic."

Everyone is silent. Kerry is shown on a tarmac saying something about "hunting down" the terrorists with a creepy mixture of Bush-like bravado and limp desperation. I jab at the television to shut it off. Nobody protests.

"Even if what you say is true," Mathieu continues, that quick tongue working over his lips, "what does it have to do with you anymore?"

I consider him very carefully before replying, "Mathieu, I am an American. It matters desperately to me who wins that election." I pause. "It should matter to you too."

Mathieu starts to his feet to regain control. He crosses the room and, with his fingers, unfurls my fists into hands again. "But there is nothing that *you* can do, Daisy."

I look into his bright, pleading eyes. "You know that's not true, Mathieu." I smile to soften my words. "But thank you, all the same."

"You are not serious."

"I am."

Neither of us blinks.

Henri clears his throat. "What is it that you are going to do, my dear?"

I turn to face them. "I have to go back. It's ridiculous. And as meaningful as spitting in the wind, I know. But it matters." Looking back at Mathieu, I add, "If I don't vote in this election, I should kill myself."

Everyone starts speaking English. Like a switch has been turned.

Gabrielle (with fiery conviction, something like Delacroix's *Liberty Leading the People*): "But of course you should go back! It is your civic obligation!"

Ivan (with an abundance of melancholy): "It is as you say, Daisy. Lost, I fear. The American people have sealed their fate."

Luc: "Did you hear that bin Laden is possessed of Kylie Minogue?"

Nicole: "Obsessed."

Henri (The Statesman): "You must do what you feel is right, of course."

Only Mathieu is silent. Standing there, shell-shocked, he is the lost, abandoned boy once more. He frowns at the floor.

I shiver, thinking that I would hate to be the floor. But there is this: I know—I know—he loves me now.

When his eyes rise to meet mine, they are furious with love.

"You are a coward then."

"No, Mathieu."

"All it took was an excuse for you to come here. And now

another for you to leave."

"No."

"You want to leave. You made your choice. Run, Daisy, run."

"I—"

"You choose your security over your passion, your pretty, deluded contentment over authentic living, your—"

"—now wait a minute, Mathieu—"

He pushes me away and starts to walk toward the door. "You choose that sickly wasteland of Bush's where—"

I trail after him. "But that's the thing, Mathieu—"

He trains his hand on the wall for support. His breaths are shallow as his forehead kisses the door. "Where the feeble-minded followers are convinced that God is guiding their bombs and that the Almighty Dollar is leading them toward an Earthly Paradise . . . . Where your beloved theory of evolution is under attack by a medieval lynch mob. burning books and building museums to false science. The same Neanderthals who are probably still certain . . . oh, yes, they are terrifying in their certainty that Copernicus was right—that the sun circles still around the Earth, and more specifically, America—and where my dying mother spent the last year of her shitty life suffering at the hands of an insurance system that does not so much as usher the dying to their deaths as fling them against the wall to hurry death along."

"Mathieu." His knuckles caress the wall.

"I cannot condone—"

"Mathieu."

He reaches for the doorknob. Escape. Shoving off the door, he spins around to face me, his distraught face inches away, and shouts, *"What?"*

"I voted for him."

"What?"

"I voted for him. Bush."

His eyes circle. "When?"

"In 2000."

Mathieu shifts his weight to his other knee, arms hanging at his sides. "You voted for George Bush in 2000."

I clasp my hands, remaining as stiff and straight as a soldier before the firing squad. "Yes."

"George W. Bush."

"The one and the same."

He searches the floor now for answers. Not finding any, he tries my face. "But *why?*"

I need support. Feeling for the adjacent wall, I back into it, positioning myself beside the contemptuous eyes of Otto Dix. I will try to explain. *The devil made me do it . . . .* But, "I have no good reason."

"Some bad ones, then?"

The others are watching, horrified. Even Henri looks like he's ingested something distasteful. I have managed to secure my audience, just in time for them to launch the tomatoes. I almost find it funny. You'd have thought I just confessed to murder.

But I don't really feel like laughing.

"I don't know, Mathieu. Maybe I bought into his fairy tale about compassionate conservatism. Maybe I thought Gore was a bit of a stiff who couldn't settle on an identity if his life depended on it. Maybe I wanted to shake up my holier-than-thou parents a little bit. Maybe I thought that wedge issues like school vouchers didn't sound that important at the time. Maybe I was nineteen years old and didn't know squat about any of it."

I look at him searchingly. "Or maybe I was in the voting booth and the urge just came over me." I pause to take a breath. "It's dumber than dumb, but I guess I did it because I could."

"Mersault," Mathieu mumbles.

"What?"

"Nothing."

"But anyway," I say, shrugging off the wall, "this is why I have to go back. Because I have a sticky sense of culpability about it. Because the world will grind on, even as I pretend it's of no consequence to me. Because"—I pause and beseech him with my eyes—"because as histrionic as this sounds in an age of cynicism, I cannot abandon my country during its moment of crisis the way your father abandoned his."

His eyes flicker to my face, then down again. I have no pulse on him.

Finally, he says, "I was wrong about that painting."

"What?"

"You look nothing like the Orphan Girl. You look like my mother." He smiles brokenly. "But only from the back."

Tears fill my eyes. "Mathieu—"

"You will not come back then?"

"Do you want me to?"

His gaze settles on my face in a calculating manner. "I don't know."

I nod, my throat constricting. "Okay."

I turn toward Gabrielle and the others. "Thank you for inviting me tonight."

She nods while the others desist. Henri's hand remains on his breast, in lamentation. He never would have written this for me.

"Look after him, please," I say. Then, turning back, I walk past Mathieu. Our shoulders—mine naked, his concealed—brushing like two strangers in a train station choked with weary travelers. I have purchased my freedom through confession. Only it doesn't really work that way, does it? Other people matter. They all may feel differently about me now.

Definitely Mathieu.

So does the priest toward the confessor, I imagine. That's human. Maybe I *would* like Picasso's art more if he had been a better person.

And me? How do I feel?

Like the mother *and* the child. Reborn.

Chapter 27

Hail Mary, full of grace.
It's not just confession. There's atonement, too.

Notre Dame is spectral tonight, floating like a candle on her Seine. There is a vapor in the air—a Gothic, Brontë mist—drugging my sight, softening the stone of the cathedral until it's a luminous, lacey latticework woven around a flank and ribs of whalebone. While her rose window glows like a milky spiderweb spun by the moonlight. One hand on her façade, however, reminds me of her solidity. For Paris, the quintessential feminine city, has at her heart this molten stone to brace her against the furies. In a City of Light, she is the eternal flame. It was here, where I stand, in the square before the cathedral, that the last snaggle of Nazi snipers shot at de Gaulle's parade of liberation. There, within its famed sandstone, where Napoleon was crowned emperor. Here, at her lovely ankles, is point zero, the origin of all measured distance in France.

She is unflappable, timeless, this heart of Paris.

She is also closed.

I cannot believe the door's resistance. I absolutely trusted that church doors never closed. Isn't the church there to succor the suffering when the state turns its back, to offer a benediction and hope to the sinner during her crisis of faith, to provide sanctuary from such worldly, corrupting depravities that are most bountiful at this witching hour of night, when Freud's id wants to reign with such primitive and tyrannical authority? After all, what good are Quasimodo's fierce, protective arms—or God's, for that matter— if I cannot tunnel into their loving center?

I can't help but take it personally as I sink to the earth, my costume skirt flaring around my knees.

But then, out of the dying fall . . .

The sound of Paris. If music be the food of love, fill me again, for here is that guitar vibrato of Django's Gypsy offspring rubbing against my cheek to entice and seduce me again. And there is the young, black Esmeralda, with folds of peasant skirt in her hands, cutting elegiac circles around the square, waltzing the wind. Admirers stop to stare and throw coins in the guitarist's case. Oh, she is good, this lithe girl with the downcast eyes, playing upon our inscribed idea of this place, cleverly insinuating herself into our nostalgia with each flick of heel and toe traded upon the ancient cobblestone.

And yet, there is no ironical detachment to be impugned here— no sense of going through the exacting motions of expectation's hard choreography. Paris, she proclaims with an eloquent turn of her slim wrist, is proud of her history, even of her derivativeness. Hugo wrote his novel, in part, to shine a light back on medieval Paris, to stab at this dusty fossil that was a crumbling, forgotten edifice until it bled freely, to demonstrate that the old Paris, though brutal and capricious, had a purity and authenticity about it that his contemporary Parisians had sterilized to the point of infertility. Hugo believed that Paris was the ceiling of civilization, but that it had yet to reach its roof.

He grew its glory higher.

And so does our Gypsy girl with her Egyptian bangles and Mona Lisa smile. She, too, plays Paris as Rhapsody. She, too, understands that all paths lead here. The travelers around me nod to the music. They have heard the call.

And so it is, while straining my neck, as a skyscraper enthusiast might back home, toward the ghoulish gargoyles above, that I am struck again by the dichotomy of old and new, and how Europe is on one side and America on the other. How like infants we are, slogged by growing pains, next to the old Continent. How, at times, it seems we have no history of our own, or that our history is so fresh it remains a raw wound, like a canker in our mouths whose flesh we can't help but chew on from time to time, out of thoughtlessness or thorny temptation. Those Gettysburg reenactors who meet with such solemn reverence every year, the Confederate faction pining for a beloved "lost cause"—if not that one in particular, then a simulacrum—before retreating to their middle-class homes that chummily border their black, middle-class brethren. The Dadaist museumification of absurdist reliquaries: Roswell, the largest ball of twine, Graceland; like if you make people pay for it, there might be something worth seeing. Our obsession with anniversaries, as if the elapsing of time were something to be charged at and taken down by a nation of linebackers. How we embrace caricatures of ourselves—with unlikely names like *American Gothic*—without being sure where the truth ends and irony begins. That notorious tendency to view things in black and white—the shortsighted filter of the fundamentalist—which makes things simple and convenient, except when the refracted light contains the muddier truth. How we have the kind of unthinking arrogance of the hulking teenager on the block— the cocky jock flexing his guns—who knows that one fatal step on the basketball court could cripple his future. Yet he leaps for the dunk anyway, confident in his immortality because enough people have told him how great he is that he has no reason to doubt himself, no backup system in place.

No contingency plan.

Youth is a marvelous thing. But goddamn if the blinders don't have to come off.

Not that Europe is a piece of humble pie. But that's someone else's story to tell. I don't have the proper perspective after three weeks to indict a whole continent, or even France, for her panoply of failings. I am an American missing my country, unsure if when I go home I will find it again.

But knowing I must go.

A storm of roller skaters thunders across the bridge in front of me. Friday night in Paris. I look at them longingly over the several minutes it takes for them to pass, photographing their flight in my mind, the way people do when they're ready to say good-bye. I rise in their wake, abandoning the performers who have given me pause and comfort, happy that they were here for me, yet thankful that good-byes are not required. As I depart, the jangly riffs of a new song play off my back. I smile. That's the comforting thing about Paris: she can endure just fine without me.

I find myself at the bridge and fold my torso over its beveled edge.

"Promise me you won't jump."

Mathieu.

"H-how did you know I was here?" Seeing him, my convictions dive into the water below.

"I am God."

I roll my eyes and pick my feet off the ground. One of the heels clatters off.

Mathieu claims it and hops up on the bridge. Smiling thinly, he explains, "I was on my way to Notre Dame. I thought you might have come to beg for mercy."

I shake my head, scowling.

"You are very predictable, Daisy." Mathieu's smile doesn't convince his eyes, which are blacker than the inky water. "It was either here or that other favored cathedral of yours, the Orsay. And it is closed."

"So was she," I say, shooting my thumb over my shoulder.

He eyes the cathedral. "She is more beautiful from afar, anyway."

I sigh, easing myself down, and stretch my neck to look behind me. "I don't know. I think I wanted thick walls around me tonight."

"To support or hide you?"

I don't bother answering.

He sets my red heel down, toe pointed neatly over the water, and wipes at the corners of his mouth. Our eyes see every part of the world but each other. Strange that we should be uncertain again. But now the anxiety surfaces not from knowing too little, but realizing too much.

Unbalanced, I turn to face him. "I don't really feel the need to ask for forgiveness, you know." Gulping back yet another sob, it hits me that I have been like a desert enjoying, and suffering, through a rainy season. A monsoon of tears. "At least, not from you."

"You think that's why I came?" he asks, frowning.

"You looked like my father when I did something to disappoint him. You made me ashamed of myself. I didn't like it."

"*I* made you ashamed of yourself?"

I snatch my shoe from his stone throne. Slipping it on, I start to walk again. Toward where, I don't know. Mathieu tails me, always a pace behind. I can feel his eyes watching me. We chase the distance of Île de la Cité in the silence and cold, my crushed toes and hyperextended insoles screaming their consternation at my bedrock belief that I can outrun my problems.

Finally, we arrive at Le Pont Neuf, that "new bridge" which is so famously old. Lovers and drunks drape themselves like mollusks across its bow. None of them looks at us, and I, too late, remember Mathieu's scar. Hoping that he will not think the destination deliberate, I trip down the adjacent stairs, still intent on protecting him in a flimsy way from what he is daily confronted with. There is a stingy card of quay below the bridge, and I halt next to a banged-up dinghy thudding hollowly against the riverbank. The two of us—a hot atom hurling through this particle accelerator called Paris—shiver in the shadows and fog. Mathieu turns so that his chin is held level to the water, which ripples in anticipation.

The moment is pregnant with mystery and possibility. I take a deep breath . . . and blow out. I'm not equal to it right now. My grandmother—or was it Socrates?—once said that when your feet hurt, you hurt all over. Mine throb.

"So do they all hate me, then?" I ask, wrapping myself in a hug.

"Who?"

"You know, your mortified friends."

"I think they were puzzled at first." Staring at the ground, Mathieu rubs his jaw.

"And then?"

"Henri told me that if I didn't go after you, he would." He looks up at me and smiles.

I return the smile. "I think I'm a little in love with Henri."

He nods. "It is a good thing I came, then."

"Listen, Mathieu," I say, taking a tentative step closer to him, "the whole Bush thing was four years ago. I feel bad about it, yes. But I didn't order the bombs to drop. So let's not go down that slippery path of endless abstraction. In fact, I started regretting my vote not five minutes later. It became a different world about that fast, and there's not a chance in hell I would have voted for the guy once the rules changed."

"You think this is why I am upset?"

I stop my advance. "Isn't it?"

Mathieu bends down to pick up a stone. He judges the heft of it in his hand, like the old man playing *pétanque* on that sun-drenched afternoon, all our days ago. He rises and hurls it across the dark film of water. *Onetwothree*, it's quickly swallowed. He sighs and finds me again. "Daisy, I am not thrilled that you helped elect a buffoon to the highest office in your land. But that was four years ago. I have no claim on your past. It is your future, our future, that distresses me."

I grow still. The water laps behind me. "I might come back."

He shakes his head and looks away. "I might not be waiting for you."

Stung, I ask, "Will Nicole become the new face on the wall?"

"No." He hesitates before meeting my eyes. "But there will likely be another."

I turn toward the river, and step into the dingy, which whimpers under my weight. A small French flag that's seen too many revolutions rises from the stern. I sit down. The air under the bridge is loamy with mildew, dead leaves. It is the sort of stink that rises to the roof of your mouth and stews. I drift in place, the boat struggling to float away, while the dock line maintains a toothy grip.

"I see. I'm replaceable."

"We are all replaceable, Daisy. In death, and in life."

I look up sharply. "Your mother was replaceable?"

Mathieu grimaces. "Sure."

"Is that why you went to see her as she was dying? To tell her that she was replaceable?"

His hands find his hair as he retreats into the shadows.

"You did go see her, didn't you?"

"I have said as much."

"You have actually said very little about it."

"I have said enough, Daisy!" The explosion of his voice

reverberates under the bridge. A stranger with an overcoat approaches, meets my eyes, and hurries away.

I look down, pressing my lips together. The boat groans. Running my hand along the starboard side, I feel the crevices of a small plaque. Of course. Everything in Paris comes with a plaque. I squint to make out the lettering: *Caneton 505: 1954.*

Nineteen fifty-four. Old for a boat.

But young for a mother.

I tighten my grip on the boat's side. "Wait. Your mother was born in 1954, right?" *Flora Goodwin: 1954-2004.*

"So?" his voice, much quieter now, answers.

"So she would have been only twenty-two when she had you then." Numbers never lie.

"What is your point, Daisy?"

He must be the black shape flattened against the armpit of the bridge, and so I speak toward that. "You told me she had your sister at twenty-two."

The shape becomes as still as the stone supporting it.

It all becomes clear, even in the darkness. "Your sisters are half sisters, and younger than you. You have met them maybe a few times in your life. You probably even hated them a little." A small motorboat cruises by, bright, then loud, like lightning begging the thunder. Mathieu is briefly illuminated in the fury, and his eyes drill a child's fear. The boat passes, and he fades to black, while the waves rock my cradle and strain the line. "But not as much as you hated your mother for choosing them over you. For wanting more kids when she already had one she left behind."

"Please, Daisy. You sound so melodramatic."

I recall my knee dive in Cleveland, that strange prayer which spun a stranger story: *I don't know how to be alone.* I wasn't *meant* to be alone. I was meant to be twice as powerful, twice as loved. I have searched most of my life for that missing half, that fated Gemini, the ghost in my ear. When, really, I was lucky to even be alive.

Mathieu has been searching, too. But what he found never made him feel lucky. "The truth is often ridiculous, Mathieu," I say. "But never melodramatic."

His face emerges from the darkness. His cheeks look wet, but it could be the gloaming kiss of moonlight reflecting off the water. The story spills from him as he approaches. "My mother became pregnant with me when she was still performing. She never knew who the father was. When the man who came to be my father fell in love with her, she told him it was his. He believed her, until he saw me. Then he knew. I suppose a father always knows. But he loved her too much to let on. And so he accepted me, let her think he believed her. When she told him she was returning to America, that she had come to hate France, and him, he fought for custody to exact his revenge and make her stay. He never thought she would just fold and leave in the middle of the night."

Mathieu closes his eyes, swaying slightly. "I dreamed that night she left me in the Louvre. And every painting, down each endless hallway I chased, was Delacroix's *Orphan Girl*."

Mathieu opens his eyes and silently climbs into the boat with me. Shedding his coat, he wraps it around my shoulders and takes the bow. The boat is so small and neat, our knees almost touch. I can smell his scent on the coat and tuck it tightly around me.

"My father was stuck with me. Though he was successful in ignoring me for most of my life, I knew he hated me. It was only when I became old enough to be useful to him that he started to bother with me again."

I touch his knee. "What do you mean, useful?"

His head falls into his palms. "He enlisted me to help him with the paintings. Always minor things, like assisting him with his correspondence, keeping abreast of the market, setting up quiet auctions. I was desperate for the fool to like me, to pay attention to me. When it began to dawn on me what he was doing, what he had done, he told me that he would take a paternity test and disown me, if ever I told anyone." He rubs his brow across his arm, and I lay my hand upon his crown.

"He was the only family I knew. And yet he hated me, for reminding him of her."

"What did you do?"

He sits back and looks at me wearily. "Any family is better than none. So I shut up and did as I was told. Even when I left, at eighteen, and severed all ties with him, I never gave him up to the authorities. He was my only connection to her."

I bury deeper into his coat, my brow wrinkling. "What do you mean? I thought you saw her every couple of years."

"The only occasion when I saw my mother after she left was her funeral. She looked" —he grimaces—"quite different."

My mouth falls open, but I cannot speak. He stares past my shoulder as laughter rains down like shimmering coins from up above.

"She only wanted to see me once she knew she was dying. During the last year, she plied me with letters, including my sisters' photographs, sent American tourists to support me, and repeatedly phoned. I stopped answering after a while."

I press my cheek to my palm. "But Mathieu, why?"

"It was too late to take responsibility for what she did." Mathieu finds my eyes. "Given enough time, love flips to hate. I, too, wanted revenge, you see."

My eyes do not spare him, even as my heart splits in two. "And you were proud to take responsibility for that?"

He smiles, briefly. "Not proud, no. Yet I wouldn't change anything, Daisy. It was on my way home from the airport that I met you."

I shake my head a little, checking my tears. "That is a sorry kind of fate."

He laughs harshly and covers his face with his hands. "You and fate. Why, Daisy, do you insist on believing in fairy tales?"

Because there must be a reason why I was born, why I snuck through. That hole in my heart was put there to be filled.

After a long silence, I clear my throat. "What are we to do?"

He peels his hands away. "This is not for me to decide."

"I still love you."

He smiles sadly. "Yes."

"We could just push ourselves off, sail away." I imagine us shaking Paris off like a stiff corset, chasing the flat and free horizon.

"Just say the word," he replies. Removing a sign from under his legs, he adds, "This boat is ours."

I cannot read the French but understand this part: €200, and the phone number scrawled underneath. What do you know? It's cheaper than the bloody shoes.

A wind sweeps under the bridge, stirring the dead leaves, our hair, and the shaggy flag behind me. It flares, reaches out, and brushes my neck with its loose threads. Turning around, I pluck its mast from the stern, rolling it between my palms as I consider his offer. The French tricolor: *Liberté, Égalité, et Fraternité.* Red, white, and blue.

And yet, I cannot help but miss our stars.

The shoes I will give to Irene. Everything else I will keep.

I place the flag across my lap and clasp my hands over its faded colors. Looking tenderly at him, I shake my head slightly. "I'm no good here, Mathieu."

He takes my knee with his hand, in reassurance. "It only takes time, my love."

I touch his hand as gently as I know how. "I'm no good with *you*, Mathieu."

He blinks once, and falls silent, before taking possession of his hand again.

We sit like that for several minutes, rocking in our boat. I want to say more, to explain, but I resist. If I talk, he will talk. I am as weak as an infant and too capable of being swayed.

I don't remember who is the first to fall, but we find each other on our knees. I bury my face in his neck. His mouth finds my hair. We remain like so for minutes, or lifetimes. We don't want to let go. We understand what letting go means.

A modestly sized *bateaux mouche* slices under the bridge like a scalpel cutting through a womb, so terribly close that, if I squint into its klieg lights, I can make out the couples eating on the other side of the glass. A large man with a crew cut catches sight of our embrace and gives Mathieu a bawdy thumbs-up. I laugh, or sob, and pull away, cupping Mathieu's cheek in my hand.

"I just remembered something."

"What did you remember?" he asks, softly.

"My first day here, in my own *bateaux mouche*. They told us that legend of the kiss."

"Which legend?"

"The one about kissing under Le Pont Neuf. How you make a wish at the same time as you kiss your lover, without telling each other what the wish is? Then, within that same year, your wish will come true."

"You're thinking about Pont-Marie, and I don't believe—"

"—so anyway, I think it's a great idea." Looking into those bright, skeptical eyes, I do my best to smile, and ask, "Don't you, Mathieu?"

He *must* believe. There will be hope.

Mathieu sighs. Then nods in something like defeat.

I'll never forget this: his head, dipping from the shadows into a finger of moonlight, tilts to the side, while his lips (those lips, the very ones which have convinced me, without intent, to chase the god in Art) separate with a slight *puh*. Then his breath and mine, hot mixing with cold.

The Paris fever.

We kiss.

He is gone from the boat before my lips can taste his absence.

I look up at him, from my knees, alone again.

"You're in the stern, *mon petit chou*."

His eyes flash his meaning, while his hand holds the umbilical of the dock line.

I scramble to the seat, brushing my knees off. "I couldn't possibly. Where would I go?"

He smiles down at me. "As far as you want. Toward the stars. Make your own fate, Daisy."

I try to swallow my fear, appealing to him with my eyes. "But I have no supplementary oxygen."

He laughs silently, reaches in the boat, and removes the battered sign. "Merry Christmas, my love. And happy birthday, too."

I feel so heavy in this boat. Not buoyant at all. The night, and its shadows, can only hide me for so long. The people above us? The lovers and drunks, riding this old bridge into the sunrise? They cannot see us yet.

It doesn't mean we are not here.

I grab an oar, shivering again.

I remember Mathieu talking about Nietzsche's interpretation of eternal return up on our rooftop one night. How he theorized time to be cyclical, conscripting us to repeat our lives over and over again, much like they believe in the Eastern religions. How terrifying that would be for most people to think about experiencing the shame, suffering, and, most excruciatingly, the bleached banality of their lives on and on, *ad infinitum*. Camus' Sisyphus sliding down from the mountain to enlist our help. But, alternatively, how it could serve (and here Mathieu leapt to his feet with bracing conviction) as the ultimate affirmation of life for someone who might actually *wish* for such a crazy thing. His eyes blazed a trail across the sky, and I smiled. I knew he wished for it. I wasn't so sure, at the time.

I have lived many lifetimes. And in each one, I will be walking that razor's edge. My life with Mathieu was a cosmic blink of the eye.

But I will continue to point my feet toward the Eiffel Tower every night. Its steely tip will flicker like a flame through my dreams.

I will always wish for my watch to stop on Paris.

Tightening my grip, I smile up at Mathieu.

"Cut me free, darling."

Epilogue: The Gift

MoMA Nabs a "Missing" Matisse
by Elise Klayko
September 9, 2005

The recent acquisition of *The Plum Blossoms* by the Museum of Modern Art ends a decades-long search for a lost masterwork by one of the twentieth century's most preeminent artists, Henri Matisse. Purchased from an unidentified, presumably European seller, the 1948 painting will be displayed on the walls of America's most visited art museum within a week, according to Alex Stephenson, the Modern's chief curator of painting and sculpture.

"It is an exceptional find," Stephenson said in a phone interview yesterday. "Rarely have I come across a painting in such pristine condition. Or one this beautiful."

A lustrous and captivating interior from Matisse's final series of paintings before his death in 1954, its location had been a mystery to art scholars since 1970, when the painting was loaned for exhibition to the Grand Palais in Paris. *The Plum Blossoms* was purchased later that year by an anonymous collector. . . .

"About the Author"

Sarah Hina hails from Athens, Ohio. A former medical student and lab rat, Sarah now writes in between mothering two kids, watching films with her husband, and escaping into the outdoors with her camera and dog. *Plum Blossoms in Paris* is her debut novel. Visit Sarah online at http://sarahhina.com. Book clubs with ten or more members are invited to schedule her attendance, via Skype or speakerphone, at one of their meetings. Write to Sarah.Hina@gmail.com for all requests.

IN STEREO
WHERE
AVAILABLE

BECKY ANDERSON

Phoebe Kassner didn't set out to be a 29-year-old virgin, but that's how it's worked out. And, having just been dumped by her boyfriend, she doesn't see that situation changing anytime soon.

Meanwhile, her twin sister Madison—aspiring actress, small-time model, and queen of the short attention span—has just been eliminated on the first round of Singing Sensation.

Things aren't looking so great for either of them. But when Phoebe receives a surprise voice mail from some guy named Jerry, victim of a fake phone number written on a cocktail napkin, she takes pity on him and calls, setting in motion a serendipitous love story neither of them ever saw coming.

And suddenly Madison's got a romance of her own going, as one of twelve women competing for two men on a ruthless, over-the-top reality show. As Phoebe falls in love with the jilted high school English teacher who never intended to call her in the first place, Madison's falling in love, too—after a fashion—clawing and fighting her way through a tide of adorable blondes. Could it get any crazier?

Stay tuned . . .

ISBN# 978-193383620-1
Trade Paperback / Fiction
US $15.95 / CDN $19.95
Available Now

DARK SECRETS

⟡ OF THE ⟡

OLD OAK TREE

DOLORES J. WILSON

Following the end of her fifteen-year marriage to a high-powered attorney, Evie Carson returns to her small, Georgia hometown to open a fashion boutique. From the protective covering of her father to the tarnished shield of her husband, Evie has always lived behind the armor of a man. But she sees this move as her first step toward the peaceful, happy life she wants.

Trying to recapture a few moments of her youth, Evie climbs to the ruins of her childhood tree house. While hidden by the massive branches of the old oak tree, Evie is stunned into deadly silence as she watches Jake—a mentally challenged community member—enter the clearing below her with a nude, lifeless body over his shoulder. Hovering above the macabre scene, Evie is forced to look on as a grave is dug. When the body is rolled into the hole, Evie realizes the dead woman is her childhood friend whom she hasn't seen in years.

The authorities are sure once Jake is arrested, the town's nightmare will be over. But when he turns up dead and Evie's home becomes the center of bizarre events, Evie and an investigating state trooper fear she may be the next victim. Wondering if she can trust him, or anyone, Evie alone must face the *Dark Secrets of the Old Oak Tree.*

ISBN# 978-160542106-3
Hardcover / Suspense
US $24.95 / CDN $27.95
Available Now
w w w . d o l o r e s j w i l s o n . c o m

TRACI E. HALL
Boadicea's Legacy

Ela Montahue is a talented sorceress with the ability to heal, but distressed over a complicated ancestral legacy. Long ago, a mystical woman known as Boadicea, the famed queen of the Iceni tribe, issued a difficult decree.

As her descendant, Ela must wed for love, not practicality, or she will forfeit her supernatural power. In medieval England this is not a socially acceptable order to follow. For her family's sake, she should marry Lord Thomas de Havel, a vile landholder with a cruel streak and a desire to see slavery reinstated—a man with good connections to King John's court. This arrangement would put the Montehues in a safe position in the new regime. The stakes are high—her dignity, her pride, and possibly her life in childbirth.

When Ela refuses this repulsive marital transaction, Thomas de Havel abducts her and wages battle against her father in retaliation. Only Osbert Edyvean, a knight with the highest creed—honor, faith, and logic—can save her and preserve her gift. A businessman for the Earl of Norfolk, Osbert has been paid to find Boadicea's spear. Rather than bring back this obscure artifact, he rescues Ela, intending to take her to the earl and obtain his parcel of land.

Wary of the supernatural aura surrounding this woman, the admirable knight fights his overwhelming passion for a beautiful lady he wants to protect . . . and *love*. This is Boadicea's true legacy.

ISBN# 978-160542078-3

Paranormal Romance

US $7.95 / CDN $8.95

Available Now

w w w . t r a c i e h a l l . c o m

EMERALD EMBRACE

SHANNON DRAKE

Devastated over the premature death of her dearest friend, Mary, Lady Martise St. James ventures to foreboding Castle Creeghan in the Scottish Highlands to dispel rumors surrounding the young woman's demise and retrieve a lost emerald. Beneath the stones of this aging mansion lurks a family crypt filled with sinister secrets. Locked within this threatening vault is the answer to the most dangerous question, and the promise of the most horrifying death.

Amid jaded suspicion, underlying threats, and the dreaded approach of All Hallow's Eve in 1865, Martise encounters a witch's coven and meets Lord Bruce Creeghan, the love of her friend's life. Mysterious, yet passionate, Mary's husband elicits a deep desire and a profound fear in the core of her soul. He knows . . . something. And it's up to Martise to reveal what he hides from her prying intrusion.

Lord Creeghan wards off the invasion of his private fortress, yet he cannot resist his magnetic attraction to the beautiful sleuth. As strong as the inevitable pull toward the catacomb beneath their bed, an overwhelming obsession propels them into disheveled sheets of unquenchable hunger and lust. While savoring an affair that cannot be denied, Martise must discover whether her lover is a ruthless murderer or a guardian angel.

ISBN# 978-160542082-0
Mass Market Paperback / Historical Romance
US $7.95 / CDN $8.95

AVAILABLE NOW
www.theoriginalheathergraham.com

WILLIAM JABLONSKY

Ernst's world is one of endless admirers, including foreign dignitaries and heads of state. Hailed as a marvel of late nineteenth-century automation, he is the crowning achievement of his master, Karl Gruber. A world-famous builder of automated clocks, Gruber has reached the pinnacle of his art in Ernst—a man constructed entirely of clockwork.

Educated and raised in the Gruber household to be a gentle, caring soul, Ernst begins to discover a profound love for his master's daughter, Giselle. Just as their relationship becomes intimate, however, tragedy strikes and the family falls apart. Ernst's serene and happy existence is shattered and changed forever.

Abandoned, knowing no other life but the one he has led, Ernst allows himself to wind down in a kind of suicide.

Over one hundred years later, he awakens in a strange new land, the world he's known long gone. Along with his mentor and guide, a well-meaning if slightly unstable homeless man, Ernst attempts to piece together the events that brought him to his new home—and to let go of the century-old tragedy that still haunts him.

ISBN# 978-160542099-8
Mass Market Paperback / Steampunk
US $14.95 / CDN $17.95
SEPTEMBER 2010

THE ROAD THROUGH WONDERLAND
SURVIVING John Holmes
Dawn Schiller

The Road Through Wonderland is Dawn Schiller's chilling account of the childhood that molded her so perfectly to fall for the seduction of "the king of porn," John Holmes, and the bizarre twist of fate that brought them together. With painstaking honesty, Dawn uncovers the truth of her relationship with John, her father figure-turned-forbidden lover who hid her away from his porn movie world and welcomed her into his family along with his wife.

Within these pages, Dawn reveals the perilous road John led her down—from drugs and addiction to beatings, arrests, forced prostitution, and being sold to the drug underworld. Surviving the horrific Wonderland murders, this young innocent entered protective custody, ran from the FBI, endured a heart-wrenching escape from John, and ultimately turned him in to the police.

This is the true story of one of the most infamous of public figures and a young girl's struggle to survive unthinkable abuse. Readers will be left shaken but clutching to real hope at the end of this dark journey on *The Road Through Wonderland*.

Also check out the movie *Wonderland* (Lions Gate Entertainment, 2003) for a look into the past of Dawn Schiller and the Wonderland Murders.

ISBN# 978-160542083-7
Trade Paperback / Autobiography
US $19.95 / CDN $22.95
AUGUST 2010
www.dawn-schiller.com

MEDALLION
P R E S S

Want to know what's going on with
your favorite author or what new releases
are coming from Medallion Press?

Now you can receive breaking news,
updates, and more from Medallion Press
straight to your cell phone, e-mail, instant messenger,
or Facebook!

Sign up now at www.twitter.com/MedallionPress to
stay on top of all the happenings in and
around Medallion Press.

For more information
about other great titles from
Medallion Press, visit

m e d a l l i o n p r e s s . c o m

MEDALLION

P R E S S

Be in the know on the latest
Medallion Press news by becoming a
Medallion Press Insider!

<u>As an Insider you'll receive:</u>

• Our FREE expanded monthly newsletter, giving
you more insight into Medallion Press

• Advanced press releases and breaking news

• Greater access to all your favorite Medallion
authors

Joining is easy. Just visit our Web site at
<u>www.medallionpress.com</u> and click on the
Medallion Press Insider tab.